BAD DOG

Duncan White graduated with a Degree in English in 1984. The author has worked as a civil servant, merchant sea man, bank clerk and secondary school English teacher. Duncan has also performed some standup comedy. The author is widowed with two children, a boy and a girl.

BAD DOG

Duncan White

BAD DOG

Duncan White [signature]

Olympia Publishers
London

www.olympiapublishers.com
OLYMPIA PAPERBACK EDITION

Copyright © Duncan White 2011

The right of Duncan White to be identified as author of
this work has been asserted in accordance with sections 77 and 78 of the
Copyright, Designs and Patents Act 1988.

All Rights Reserved

No reproduction, copy or transmission of this publication
may be made without written permission.
No paragraph of this publication may be reproduced,
copied or transmitted save with the written permission of the publisher, or in
accordance with the provisions
of the Copyright Act 1956 (as amended).

Any person who commits any unauthorised act in relation to
this publication may be liable to criminal
prosecution and civil claims for damage.

A CIP catalogue record for this title is
available from the British Library.

ISBN: 978-1-84897-172-1

This is a work of fiction.
Names, characters, places and incidents originate from the writer's
imagination. Any resemblance to actual persons, living or dead, is purely
coincidental.

First Published in 2011

Olympia Publishers
60 Cannon Street
London
EC4N 6NP

Printed in Great Britain

To my late wife Sally

Acknowledgements

This novel is inspired by *Nova Express* by William Burroughs, and there are references to Burroughs throughout. *Fear and Loathing in Las Vegas* also proved a particular source of inspiration. I also need to mention the brilliant crime writers Dashiel Hammet and Raymond Chandler. I also found Edward Burman's *The Assassins* an invaluable research tool.

I would like to thank all the wonderful musicians whose song titles make up the names of the chapters. Special thanks to Dave and Nigel for your encouragement. And not forgetting my wonderful daughter, Daisy, whose proof reading skills spotted many a blunder.

Nothing is true, everything is permitted.

Hassan I Sabbah

Part 1

The Detective

Chapter 1

Nice 'N' Sleazy

'An Angel came from outside, had no halo, had no father, with a coat of many colours.'
The Stranglers

Second coldest February of the century-feeling cold to the bones, five or six jumpers, fuel bills too high, can't afford to keep warm. All the newspapers are filled with stories of old aged pensioners dying of hypothermia. At least there are no flies.

Children of the sixties, the love generation, hooked on smack, on the game. You can get it at school, first bag free from your friendly neighbourhood dealer. 'It's good stuff this smack, dead easy to give up if you don't like it.' That's the word on the streets, and who wants to know what the posters say? On the poster down the road someone's changed heroin to Thatcher, so it now reads, 'Thatcher really screws you up.' Liverpool is called 'Smack City.' It's also the home of the Militant Tendency, that's how to subdue the rebels turn them into junkies – good politics.

What the fuck. In Southampton the dream of the sixties has come to a shabby, sordid end. The ghost of the *Titanic* is never far away, imbuing everything with a desperate sense of rushing headlong to oblivion, it's cold enough for icebergs in the fucking Solent. Walking down the pub, need a few beers, got to climb away from normality, keep drunk; don't let it get to you. Walk in, stagger into a mindless wreck after a handout. 'Lend us ten bob mate.' Forget it. The last thing I need is to be hassled by another casualty on his way to the bogs, or Jack up City, or is that Jack off?

Where did it all go wrong? Armageddon just around the corner. 'Yes America you can turn Great Britain into a missile base.' Sold out by the Whore of Babylon, cruise missiles, Trident and smack. Copies of 'The Plain Truth,' neo-fascist Christian propaganda given away on the street corner, and rammed down our throats. 'You may be a mindless junky, but God loves you. God loves America.'

Fester and the vomits are playing tonight, three hours hard fast-moving rock, offering no solution, just a release. Party, forget about the Grim Reaper knocking at the door. Have a beer, have a joint, and try to forget about the nightmare in the toilets, he's already forgotten about you. Next thing you know the three hours are up and it's throwing out time. 'Finish your drinks! Move! Get out! Yeah? Well fuck you too! Haven't you got homes to go to?'

I was easy, no hassle, drink up the beer and go, but Clay, my drinking partner was having none of it. The beers had taken their toll, and Clay was doing his famous dog impression. I had seen it many times before, but always enjoyed watching someone making a complete drunken idiot of themselves. Clay was on all fours, and howling like a wolf. The barmaid decided we were the rowdy element and moved in brandishing a mop. Clay reacted instantly, jumping to his feet, a thin wisp of spittle trailing from his jaw, slobbering horribly, 'Hey baby, you're my moon-goddess, we can make it tonight.' 'Piss off creep,' and then in come the heavies. Clay goes flying out of the door and lands in a twisted crumpled heap, still howling.

Get up, walk off, don't give the buggers a chance, already police are hanging around outside, like vultures over a decaying corpse. Drunks are easy meat, keep up the quota of ten arrests a night easy. And if there's not enough drunks, pick up a junky or a prostitute, there are always plenty of those.

Where to now? Clay is totally wired, a savage insane fury burning in his eyes, he looks like Adam holding the forbidden fruit. Holding his loins, a perverse look of lust working its way across his face. Image of the long man echoing, the formation of a lusty power. The only way to relieve it is a trip to the red light district before it's too late. Clay howled once more and ran off into the night, clutching his groin, leaving a dark indelible stain etched into my consciousness. By now I was starting to feel the cold a lot more. I had to get in soon as the beer had taken effect. I needed sleep, total oblivion, head still rings; Clay's twisted grin tormenting me every time I closed my eyes; Fester and the vomits playing in my brain, better turn the noise down, no more complaints from the neighbours.

I woke up in a morgue, the glass of water by the side of my bed had frozen overnight. The gas had run out, and I had no more fifty pences. The sun was unreasonably bright, poking tiny searchlights through the torn curtains, sending razor sharp needles of pain into my forehead. A lark was singing cheerily, this seemed to make matters one hell of a lot worse. The sound set my teeth on edge, and I was convinced that the whole of the outside world was laughing at my pitiful state. Not just people and animals, but plants and inanimate objects as well. It was one of those hangovers where the pain rolls around in your head as you move. I pulled back the covers and got out of bed. I was still dressed, I hadn't even taken my coat off. I flapped my arms, and beat my sides trying to keep warm. There was no time for a shave, I was late for work. No toothpaste, so I'd need to pick some mints or something up on the way in. I quickly combed my hair, then I was outside. With the sun shining it was actually warmer outside than it was indoors. It was a surprisingly pleasant morning, and the crisp cold air seemed to have an anaesthetic effect, taking the edge off the headache. Even so, I still wished that I had remembered to wear my dark glasses, as I was half blinded by the early morning glare.

I was half an hour late for work. I opened the office door and immediately made straight for the radiator, and started to soak up the warmth. I looked up, I was all alone. This meant my partner was late too. More importantly it meant that I would be able to have a go at him for being late, and not the other way round. Maybe it was not going to be too bad a day after all. When I had warmed up sufficiently I took off my coat and began to open the mail. It consisted of two letters of complaint from dissatisfied customers and a phone bill for fifty quid. This meant it wouldn't be long before we were cut off. I left the post on the desk and made myself a cup of tea. This and a 'Disque Bleu' made up my breakfast.

Half an hour later my partner turned up. I showed him the phone bill and he pulled half a bottle of calvados out of his jacket pocket. No solutions just a release. Hair of the dog? Don't mind if I do, anything to get rid of this sodding headache. Any work? Did we have a case? No. All we had were letters of complaint, and bills, bills, and more bills.

I was sick of being a private detective, it wasn't at all what I thought it would be. I was sorely disillusioned. The dream life of the super sleuth was falling apart at the seams. It had denigrated into a life of excessive bills, all unpaid, and morbid drunkenness. The only work about was sordid divorce cases, where the clients were seedy and untrustworthy. I had always believed that being a private detective meant a life of fast women and fast cars. This was about as far from the truth as was possible. The dream life had collapsed into one long tirade of drunken failure. In fact the only successful case we'd had was a local businessman's floozy wife. She was having it off with the office junior. My camera never lies. As soon as the client saw it he welshed on the deal, accused us of engineering it all. We got the blame, so we got no money, not even expenses. Mention legal action and you come face to face with a bunch of high-powered business lawyers. Easier to get blood out of a stone. In ancient times they executed the messenger that brought bad news. Now they put them on the dole. The debts were piling up, the rent was weeks overdue. Even the milkman had stopped delivering, apart from the odd bottle of skimmed milk that he couldn't sell, just to remind us he's there, the creep. I've always found skimmed milk foul, watery and tasteless. So does the cat, refuses to touch any we put down for it.

My partner was in a particularly vile mood. He had a face like dead cod, devoid of all colour. A bleak Arctic wilderness save for the eyes, two tiny red points pulsating like lumps of rancid liver. He leaned under the desk, then spat into the bin, cleared his nostrils with one loud squelch, then spat again. 'So nothing.' he growled, 'No work, no money, I can't even sign on. He pinched the last residues of snot from his nose then wiped his fingers on the desk. He looked me right in the eye and with icy coldness said, 'I hate you... I've been thinking this over for some time now, and I really truly deeply hate you. I loathe you with an intensity you can't even imagine. You're to blame for everything. Why I had to listen to you I just don't know. If I'd stayed where I was, like my girlfriend wanted me to I'd be quids in. But no, I had to listen to you. I sold my house and joined this 'guaranteed gold-mine' of yours. Well that was two years ago, and here I am, no money, no girlfriend, and just your ugly mug to stare at.'

I grinned back at my partner, I was used to his little outbursts by now. They were getting regular. I referred to them as his 'mid-week specials.' My partner was never very good at accepting responsibility for his own decisions. He was always looking for someone else to blame, and I told him. He knew what he was getting into when he joined, I had lost just as much money as him, and I wasn't complaining. My partner didn't like what he was hearing. His face had started to regain some of its jaundiced colour, which was parchment pasty with bright red cheeks and forehead, like something used to living underground that had been left out in the sun by a sadist. There was something different about today's outburst though. His nose had taken on a faint bluish tint, and a vein was pumping wildly in his left temple. He stood up clenching his fists and gritting his teeth. I really thought he had lost it this time.

'Disque Bleu?' I asked amiably thrusting the packet under his nose. This threw him momentarily, he opened his mouth, but no sound came out. I prodded him aggressively with the packet. 'Go on.... Disque Bleu... Disque Bleu.' He sat back down heavily, and weakly went to take one of the proffered cigarettes. Then the phone started ringing. Quick to seize the advantage I picked the phone up, whipping the packet away before my partner had a chance to get hold of one. 'Hello, Solent Investigation?' Silence, I looked over at my partner. Apart from his throbbing temple, he seemed frozen in time. I counted fourteen pulses before anyone said anything, I was about to hang up. I'd had this sort of shit before, sad twats with nothing better to do except waste other people's time. I used to scream a tirade of abuse at them, but now I was too tired even for that.

'Hello, are you still there?' It was a man's voice, thin nasal and slightly Brummie. It was very quiet, and I had to listen hard to each word. I was very aware of my partner's emphysemic breathing.

'Yes I'm still here. This is Solent Investigation. How can we help?'

'I need someone to investigate a... a... a.' For a minute I thought it was the git from the office upstairs, making a prank call, taking the piss out of my stutter. It wouldn't be the first time. Then the person on the other end of the phone took a deep breath. 'I'm sorry, I want you to investigate a murder.'

'A murder?'

'Yes, a murder.'

For a moment I couldn't say anything, my mouth went dry, and I almost fell off my chair. I couldn't believe it, a real case, at long last, not some sleazy divorce but a murder. Real Raymond Chandler territory. The word murder kept echoing around my head. I felt dizzy a strange quivering sensation in my stomach. Murder, murder, murder. I let the word reverberate round the cortex, drinking in the sound. Great. Why couldn't people get murdered more often? I felt so happy, it was amazing how something wonderful like a murder could chase away the shadows of despair. I didn't ask for any more details, just managing to blurt out. 'We'll take it.'

There was a pause, then the voice continued, 'I don't want to talk over the phone, we'll have to meet somewhere.'

'What about The Carpenter's Arms, I'm easy to spot, I'll be wearing a pink carnation.'

'I'll be there tomorrow lunchtime about twelve. Don't be late.' Before I had the chance to ask him anything else he hung up.

I turned back to my partner, 'O ye of little faith. That was it, a proper case. A murder.'

My partner stared back unblinking. 'Murder, murder. Help murder somebody call the police,' he sneered. 'You must think I'm bloody stupid, all of a sudden the phone rings and we've got a murder case.' I couldn't believe it, the first proper case, and my partner calls me a liar, sod's law. It wasn't easy convincing him. In the end I had to offer to take him down the pub. He had to acknowledge that I couldn't afford to get him drunk unless I had a lot of money coming in. He leapt to his feet, smiled and regained his humanity, it was a miraculous transformation, like something out of The Bible. 'Take up thy calvados and walk.' He was out of the door in a matter of seconds. I had to run to catch up with him, and we left the building together, pausing only to flick the V sign at the milkman who was just finishing his morning round. We got to the pub just as it opened, and by the time we were thrown out all our differences were forgotten. For once we actually parted on good terms.

Chapter 2

Waiting For The Man

'He's never early, he's always late.'
The Velvet Underground

Heroes die young. I'm no hero, sod that. However, there I was plunged into the plot of a classic film noir. Solitary private detective on the trail of a murderer. And probably a twisted psychotic to boot, or even worse a professional hitman. I'd never had to investigate anything approaching a murder before. The nearest I had got had been a pair of stolen shoes, which I never recovered. After I got over the initial burst of enthusiasm, fired up by copious shots of calvados I had to admit the whole idea scared me shitless. A murderer has got nothing to lose, having murdered once, he can afford to murder over and over again to cover up his trail. Mother of sweating God! The notion of being shot away by some mad psychotic bent on self-preservation was not at all comforting. Dead men tell no tales. Even so, I wasn't dead yet, and I had every intention of staying alive. Fight fire with fire. My adversary would be armed, so would I.

Within ten minutes of arriving home drunk I'd come to the conclusion that I needed a gun. Just as well not to tell my partner though, it would just give him something else to worry about. I didn't know exactly where to get a gun, but Southampton like most cities has its own dark underbelly, and the underbelly had its denizens. One particular individual sprang to mind, I didn't even know his name. All I knew about him was he'd sold my partner a bent video, I can still hear his sales-patter. 'Don't let all those doom merchants put you off, Betamax is the technology of the future. I guarantee it.' I also knew what pub he used to drink at, The Madhouse, one that I was familiar with. Just because someone sells stolen Betamax doesn't necessarily mean they can lay their hands on a gun, but it was all I had.

Even though it was only seven 'o clock, the pub was packed out when I got there, but my man was nowhere to be seen. I had to get a drink without being hit on by the usual crowd of spongers, scroungers and wasters that hang around the bar, Society's detritus. Clay was there as usual, and was incredibly drunk; he must have been drinking steadily since lunchtime. Today must be giro day, (not necessarily his.) He was waxing lyrical about one of his favourite topics of conversation, the great penis in the sky. Unfortunately he caught my eye just as the previous unfortunate ducked away into the bogs. I was hearing for the fifth or sixth time how 'The Long Man' was a gateway to the real world, as opposed to this imaginary world which apparently this one was, when my contact walked in. He didn't walk over to the bar but wandered around like he was looking for someone. I gave Clay a quid to buy himself a drink and wandered over. 'Hi Man,' I smiled cheerily, 'Remember me?' He turned around, but it was obvious he didn't recognise me.

'Sorry no. Should I?'

'Yeah, you sold my mate a bent video.' This was way too direct, he turned away towards the bar.

'I don't know what you mean mate, I don't sell bent gear.' This wasn't going at all well, I grabbed him by the arm and pulled him back.

'Take a good look, I made you a cup of coffee for Christ sake's. Look, you sold him a Betamax with a copy of *Zombie Flesh Eaters*. Short ugly little bloke, looks like 'Herr Flick,' gone wrong. You know, 'Herr Flick' from *Allo Allo*. He leant forward and studied me a bit closer, frowned and scratched his head. A vague look of recognition flashed across his face.

'Yeah, that's right I remember now, it's... it's... it's...'

'Just call me Zippy.'

'You taking the piss?'

'Look, it's a long story, would you like a beer?'

'O Yeah, thanks. I'm skint at the moment, I was looking for someone to scrounge off.'

Two minutes later we were sitting down upstairs, squeezed onto a tiny table pushed out at the back where no-one could see. If a fire was to break out there was no way we were going to get out alive. I had to own up and tell him I'd forgotten his name. 'Dodge, call me Dodge, everyone does. I don't like flashing my own name around.' He took a long sip of beer before continuing. 'Well Zippy, what do you want? Betamax aren't that easy to come by right at this moment.' He had a mild scouse accent, not one of the whiney annoying ones, but a nice deep resonant scouse twang. I lit a Disque Bleu and looked back at him. This was the first opportunity I'd had to really study him. He was about six foot six with short ginger hair. It was neatly combed, and he was clean shaven. He was wearing a beige jumper and a pair of faded blue jeans. Looking around at the assorted low life, he looked as out of place as me. His eyes gave him away, they were dark brown, already slightly bloodshot, and just out of focus. A bath and a shave were all that separated him from the rest of the regulars. There had to be someone in this rat hole who could lay their hands on a gun, hopefully Dodge would know who they were. He wasn't giving anything away though.

'I need a gun.' He almost shot out of his seat, and put his finger to his lips.

'Shhh! Not so loud, you never know who's listening. What do you want one of those things for? Is it to shoot that moondog twat at the bar?'

'What Clay? No, it's not come to that... yet. No seriously, I'm not planning on shooting anyone, I just need some protection.' Dodge looked around before speaking. He lowered his voice and leaned forward conspiratorially.

'I don't sell things like that myself' but I know a couple of blokes who might be able to help you out. What sort of gun are you looking for?'

'Something small, easy to fit in my pocket.'

'Well, I think the going rate for pistols is about a ton. Ammunition is separate though.'

'How much is that?'

'About a quid a bullet, depending on what sort of gun it is. How much ammunition do you want?'

'About fifty rounds.'

'Fifty rounds, and you're not planning on shooting anyone. That should be a ton and a half or thereabouts.'

'So you'll do it then?'

'Yes if you give me my cut of twenty quid on top of that. And there's one other thing.'

'What?'

'Why do they call you Zippy? Are you some real fan of kids' telly or something?' I was hoping to avoid this territory, it brought back ugly memories of childhood bullying.

'I'm not a fan, anything but. You're right though it's from Zippy off of *Rainbow*.'

'Is it because you're yellow and furry?' I decided to ignore that example of scouse humour.

'When I was twelve and my voice started to break I sounded just like him, some git pointed it out and the name stuck. I know it's a bloody stupid nickname now, but in my line of business it helps not letting people know your real name. I doubt your mum christened you Dodge. Still I suppose it's better than being called 'Ginghah,' or 'Wanker.' Dodge gave me a sideways look, then deciding not to pursue the matter, poured the rest of his pint down his throat and passed me the empty glass.

'I'll have another.' I got up and walked over to the bar. I ordered another two pints, and got collared into buying another one for Clay. He decided to come over and join us. For once Clay's spiritual revelations didn't bother me, they helped take my mind off things. I arranged to meet Dodge at the office the following evening. Hopefully by then I would have enough money to pay for the damn thing.

Thursday lunchtime at the Carpenter's Arms. My partner and I were sitting at the bar talking to the landlord. We were bathed, well dressed and sober, well at least I was, everything private detectives should be. We were about to meet a million dollars. We were dressed in identical, blue pinstripe suits with carnation buttonholes. My partner was more soberly dressed with white shirt, black socks and blue tie. I was more flamboyant though, bright red tie, white shirt, bottle green socks and a yellow handkerchief to finish it all off. I felt as if I ought to be going to a wedding, and that's what I told the landlord, he didn't need to know our business. He wasn't really that bothered, preferring to talk about his favourite subject, the weather, that and how normal the punks who frequented his establishment were. As if, they weren't normal even by punk standards; the King's Road punk beloved of postcards spends a lot of time and effort cultivating their look, not the Carpenter's Arms punks who get their mohicans done and then leave it until it goes all lank, floppy and unwashed like a geriatric's erection. Still they stayed true to punk traditions by refusing to use their real names, insisting on being called after secure mental institutions. Anyway the landlord quite fancied himself as a bit of an amateur meteorologist, after jabbering on about occluded fronts, he told us that they'd picked a good day for it; it should stay nice all day, but would start raining in the evening. I wasn't paying too much attention to what he was saying. I looked around the pub, two punks, (Broadmoor and Rampton,) a couple of archaeologists and a few other assorted regulars. None of them looked as if they could afford to hire a pair of private detectives. I felt semi-relaxed, I was on familiar turf, we'd been there for half an hour, since twelve, and still had an hour and a half to go before lunchtime was officially over. I'd developed a nervous habit of looking over my shoulder every time the door opened, and so had my partner. I felt more like a fugitive on the run than a private detective waiting to meet a client.

Half an hour later our contact arrived, right on the stroke of one. He was a tall thin man in his mid-thirties, with grey hair, blue eyes and a neatly clipped moustache. He was wearing a dark grey suit and carrying a leather attaché case. He looked around, saw us, and marched purposefully over. I gently kicked my partner to get his attention. 'Solent Investigation?' It was the same nasal voice I had heard over the phone.

'That's us,' I said standing up and smiling. I offered him my right hand. It was like shaking hands with a piece of damp lettuce.

'My name's Green. I'm a lawyer. I believe we spoke on the phone yesterday.'

'That's right, about a murder inquiry.'

'Due to the delicate nature of this particular matter, my client wishes to remain anonymous. Therefore all business will be transacted by myself.' I was about to give him the customary reassurances about confidentiality, and the need for discretion and so forth when my partner butted in.

'As long as he delivers the dosh we don't give a fuck.' Now fortified by his third pint, and three tequila slammers he was beginning to take an interest in the conversation. There was an awkward silence, my partner, full of beery confidence, leered at Green who looked back horrified. Then quite unexpectedly my partner let out a huge belch whose echoes reverberated around the room. If I didn't act soon he would blow the whole deal. For a brief moment I toyed with the idea of twatting him one, and continuing negotiations over his unconscious mass, but that wouldn't have been the professional private detective's approach. Leaning forward I 'accidentally' caught my partner's fourth pint with my sleeve, knocking it all over him. It was like pouring petrol over a fire, he leapt up screaming, fists clenched, 'Shitting Jesus! You did that on purpose, you bastard.' I apologised profusely, and offered him the beer towel. He eyed me suspiciously, he wasn't at all convinced, but he went off to the toilets muttering profanities to himself.

I turned back to Green, he was looking decidedly unimpressed. I smiled, trying to look reassuring, 'I'm sorry about that, my partner does get rather high-spirited at times, but he knows what he's doing, he's a good man, and a great detective.' Green's expression did not change.

'Look,' he said, 'I want you to understand this quite clearly. I had extremely strong reservations when my client told me he wanted to use you. I have always used a completely different agency, who are extremely professional. I told my client about your reputation, but he was adamant we use you. I think my stance has been vindicated by this display.' I was about to open my mouth to protest when Green slammed his attaché case down on the bar. 'Anyway, to business, I believe your charges are £200 per day plus expenses.' I nodded dumbly. 'I have been authorised to pay you £1000 in advance.' He handed me a pen, 'If you could just sign the receipt.' He handed over a wad of cash and a brown manila envelope. 'All the information you require is in there, so is my card. If you need anything phone me. I'll call you Monday morning to check on your progress.' He snapped his case shut, and walked out without even buying a drink. The whole transaction took less than a minute. The landlord leant over and told me he didn't want any drug dealing going on in the pub. I couldn't tell if he was taking the piss or not.

I was in my second heaven, sitting in the office with a freshly brewed cup of Earl Grey, counting the money. Everything was going right for a change. I hadn't even thought of asking for as much as that, but there was a caveat though. This cash cow would dry up if we couldn't come up with results. My partner poured himself another cup of tea and gestured towards the envelope with a digestive biscuit. 'Open it then.' I sliced through the seal with a letter opener. Out fell Green's business card, a piece of typewritten paper and two photographs. My partner studied the photographs whilst I picked up the paper. 'Christ he's an ugly fucker,' whistled my partner.

'Well according to this,' I said waving the paper, 'He's the victim, Stephen Stephens. His mutilated body was found in his flat somewhere in The Jungle. We've got to give Green the name of the murderer.' My partner looked a bit concerned, the tramlines on his brow were more pronounced than usual.

'It doesn't add up,' said my partner. 'The Jungle's not exactly a nice area, and someone's just put a grand down payment to find the killer. Got to be something dodgy. Also, where do we start, I'm looking forward to spending some of that money, I don't want it to dry up too soon.' It was not often my partner asked me for advice, and I relished pontificating on the Raymond Chandler approach to detective work.

'We've got two choices. Either we can go to the police, and see what they're willing to tell us, or we go to the scene of the crime to find some hidden clue. Phillip Marlowe always went to the scene of the crime, but he always got there before the police. This guy was killed over a week ago. The trail's bound to be pretty cold now.' My partner nodded in agreement.

'So it's the police then. You had better go, I'm too pissed, and the police always give me the creeps. You can go after you've been to the bank.' It was settled then, I gave my partner £200, put £200 aside for myself, and put the rest inside a paying in book. Then I set off for the police station via the bank.

The police station was a nightmare. There were two coppers on the desk, Tweedledee and Tweedledum, a nice one and a nasty one. With the logic that seems to typify the police, they were using the same techniques they usually applied to interrogation, for community relations. The nice one, Tweedledee was talking to a small boy about a stolen bicycle. This left me with Tweedledum. 'Solent Investigation? Never heard of them.' He growled menacingly. His looks matched his manner. He was an ugly son of a bitch, about five six, and thirteen stone. He had a big black moustache which took over most of his face. His teeth were broken like his nose, and yellow like the rest of him. He had pale watery eyes. He held a small pencil behind his ear which was as badly chewed as his nails. There was a permanent sneer on his face, and everything he said had the same jaundiced quality as the rest of him. I tried to sound as pleasant as possible when I pointed out that we were a registered detective agency. There then followed half an hour of filling in forms, deciding who I was, and who I represented and so forth. It then took about an hour for all the information to be processed. Eventually the powers that be decided I could be given the same bulletin they had given to the papers. I would have been better off going to the library. I signed for a few sheets of paper, stuffed them into my jacket pocket and rushed out of the door. I was late for my appointment with Dodge.

I ran out of the police station frantically waving for a taxi, but just like policemen there's never one around when you want one. The nearest place was the train station. I quickly glanced left and right then shot across the road. There was a screech of brakes, and an angry shout, but I'd made it across to the other side. I flicked the V sign in the general direction of where the shout had come from and continued running. It was a short run to the taxi rank, but when I got there I was completely knackered. The taxi driver was sunning himself on the bonnet of the car. I was so out of breath I couldn't speak, so I tried gesturing, pointing to the taxi, vainly trying to communicate the fact that I wanted a ride. He leapt up suddenly, a determined look on his face, and started giving me the Heimlich manoeuvre.

After I'd thrown up I was able to tell the driver my destination. He seemed so pleased with himself for saving my life, that I didn't want to shatter his illusions. Lighting up a Disque Bleu I made a silent vow to pack in smoking. I was already half an hour late, but the driver shot through the traffic in a couple of minutes. I gave him a five pound tip for saving my life and ran into the office block, only to run smack into Dodge who was on his way out. He gave a loud groan as my head collided with his chest, then he toppled over and fell down the back stairs which lead to the basement. I followed closely after. We fell about fifteen feet. Dodge pulled my foot out of his mouth. He was holding his nose, blood was pouring out all over the floor. He was muttering furiously, 'You fucking stupid idiot. What do you think you're playing at?'

'I'm sorry man, I thought I'd miss you,' I said offering him my handkerchief.

'I wish you bloody well had.' I put my hand out to pick him up. I didn't feel too bad, Dodge had cushioned the fall.

'Look man,' I said, 'you'd better come upstairs to the office and clean yourself up.' By now my handkerchief had turned scarlet. Dodge kept it firmly in place. At the top of the stairs leading to the basement he paused to retrieve a small black briefcase. He followed me up the next flight leading to the office, leaving a trail of blood in his wake. I let us in and went to the sink to get a bowl of water. I also poured two glasses of calvados. Dodge accepted his glass eagerly, and downed it in one, before sticking his head in the bowl, which turned red. I knocked back my glass and poured a couple of refills. Dodge was whining like an old woman.

'Got a mirror?' he wailed, 'I want to see what I look like.'

'There's one over there by the door.' He got up, walked over to the mirror and looked at his reflection.

'Jesus Christ, I look fucking terrible!'

'Well you can hardly blame the fall for that.'

'It's not funny. I'm supposed to be meeting a bird in half an hour, and look at me; I've got a black eye, I'm covered in blood and my nose is in a right state.' I gingerly touched the tiny scratch just above my left eye.

'Look on the bright side. At least it's not broken. I'm injured too, and you don't hear me complaining.' I slapped him on the back. 'To business, it's no use crying over spilt milk, or should I say blood. Have you got it?'

'What?'

'The gun.'

'Oh yeah, that. I don't think you need one, you're lethal enough on your own.'

'Still I think I'd rather have it.'

'Ok den, here it is the Browning high powerL9A1 9mm automatic, it's what the SAS use, the clip holds 13 rounds.'

'Really, what the SAS use.'

'Yeah straight up.'

What the SAS used I liked the sound of that, I like to think I would have made a good SAS commando had I not been overweight, unfit and completely unsuited to military service. So we did the deal. I gave him £170 and he gave me the goods, I cocked it and put it in my pocket with the safety on. Dodge finished his glass of calvados, put the money into his jacket pocket, and staggered out of the office, muttering to himself.

Chapter 3

Femme Fatale

'She's just a little tease'.
The Velvet Underground

The next morning I was slouched at my desk trying to work out what to do next, when my partner spoke from across his cup of espresso. 'You know I've been doing a bit of homework myself. This Stephens guy was well known around town as a bit of a salesman, and not just a bit of ooky gear either. He was into the big stuff, smack.' When he said 'smack,' my partner pulled a really peculiar expression, like something out of 1930's vaudeville. He waited a couple of minutes, but because I didn't respond he continued. 'Where there's a smack dealer, there's loads of junkies just around the corner. Junkies like to keep an eye on one another, keeping tabs on the supply. All we've got to do is find one and I'm sure we'll be able to persuade him to help us.' I thought it over, it didn't really make a lot of sense to me. Junkies aren't exactly public spirited, I can't see them climbing over each other to point out a murderer, but my partner was convinced. Eventually I asked him why a junky would want to help us. 'Because of money that's why,' enthused my partner. They all want money, 'cause they all want smack. That Yank you know, doesn't he chase the dragon?' He was talking about someone I knew from a while back, a young American student called The Cheat. He used to be a real laugh when I first met him, we used to have some really good times, before he got into smack. I told my partner I didn't want to see him, it stirred up too many painful memories, you can only get ripped off so many times before you tell them to fuck off, but my partner was having none of it. 'If we get over there now he'll still be in bed, we can catch him unawares.' He swallowed the remains of his espresso, wiped his mouth and got up. 'Drink up Zippy, we've got an appointment with The Cheat.'

When we got to The Cheat's house, I kept my thumb pressed on the doorbell for three minutes, but there was no reply. I pulled a rusty old set of skeleton keys out of my pocket, and in no time at all we were in. The door was really stiff, and it soon became obvious why. Southampton was once the city of four or five free newspapers, and they were all there piled up on the floor. The hundred and one adverts wrapped around two or three in depth stories about lost cats and scratched cars. A couple were showcasing the local talent, teenage girls dressed in bikinis. They think it's the road to fame and fortune, but it's just the first step on the ladder to sleazy backstreet porn. The whole place stank, it was almost physical, a dank wall pushing us back making me gag. there was stale washing up, filthy laundry and a broken shithouse with a brown stain creeping out from under the door. I didn't want to investigate any further, so we made our way upstairs, to The Cheat's bedroom.

We walked in without knocking, only to be greeted by a scene of animal depravity. On a soiled mattress in the corner, huddled beneath a dirty blanket shaking violently lay The Cheat. The floor was festooned with all manner of disgusting shit, old chip papers, empty beer cans, spent prophylactics, a dirty hypodermic and broken bottles. The stench was marginally preferable to that which we had left downstairs. We crunched our way towards him; he turned over to face us, nose running, eyes bloodshot, looking like he had a bad dose of the flu, but it was junk sickness. I smiled down at him. 'Hi, we did try knocking but there was no reply, knew you wouldn't mind.'
'Got a cigarette man?' I threw him a crumpled Disque Bleu, it was the last one in the packet, and was a bit the worse for wear. I often wished they sold Disque Bleu in hardpacks like other cigarettes. I pulled out a can of Crucial Bru.
'Fancy a beer?' I opened one for myself, my partner had already started drinking his.
'Haven't you got anything stronger?'
'Sorry, this is all there is, take it or leave it.' He took it, and started taking tiny sips, all the while eying us with his tiny black piggy eyes, trying to work out what we wanted. I squatted down next to him smiling, and continued drinking, letting him simmer. It was my partner who broke the silence, giving the Cheat a filthy look; he lit up a cigarette and said in a cold monotone.
'We're here on business actually.'
'What sort of business?' Even though The Cheat knew he wasn't getting something for nothing, and was waiting for one of us to make a move, he still couldn't disguise the fear in his voice.
'What do you know about Stephen Stephens,' my partner continued in the same monotone. The Cheat turned white and looked down at the ground.
'I don't know who you mean.' My partner got very angry very quickly,

and slapped him hard across the face.

'Bullshit. Stephen Stephens, aka SS aka Gestapo. He was a fucking smack dealer. Of course you knew him.' I needed to step in before things got out of hand. I pulled a £20 note out of my pocket and as my partner was playing the part of Tweedledum I took on the role of Tweedledee.

'Relax,' I soothed, 'There's no need for things to get out of hand. Everything's cool, we're not the pigs or anything, all we're doing is protecting a few interests that's all. This won't go any further than us three.' I caressed the £20 note, held it close to The Cheat's face. 'You could get sorted with this, take away the shakes.' My partner grabbed The Cheat by the throat.

'Look, you're not dealing with your fucking junky mates now. We're fucking serious. Tell us what we need to know and I let go of your throat.'

There is something particularly repulsive about junkies, not just a revulsion with the physical state. The real horror is in the eyes. I could see it in The Cheat's face, some twisted demon masquerading as a human being. Even though he was in obvious pain he still managed to smile. For once someone wanted something from him, and not the other way round. We were as hungry for information as he was for smack. One junky can always recognise another. There's no honour amongst junkies though, and the creepy little shit was starting to get to me. I hit him as hard as I could. He opened his mouth as if to say something, then went flying across the room. My partner gave me a look of complete astonishment. I was as surprised as he was, I didn't make a habit of hitting people, but something had taken over. I could hear the blood pounding in my ears, everything had turned red. I wanted payback for all the bollocks he'd forced me to endure in the past, I needed recompense. I leapt over to where The Cheat was lying, grabbed his shirt and pulled him up hard against the wall. I put my face right up close to his and hissed menacingly, 'Who knew Gestapo?' The Cheat was panic-stricken by my sudden transformation. His eyes were bulging, his lower lip was trembling. A thin trickle of blood was working its way down his jaw, issuing from his left nostril. He started jabbering.

'He knew lots of people man, he was a main dealer.'

'Who was the candyman?'

'I can't tell you that, they'll kill me.'

'No, if 'they' find out, 'they' may kill you. They'll definitely kill you if we put the word out you're a grass, remember you owe us.' I meant it too, there was something in his eyes that brought out some hideous sadistic fury. It was not a feeling I enjoyed. The Cheat was broken, he looked down at the floor.

'Slashface was the main dealer, but don't let anyone know I told you... Can I have my twenty quid now?' My partner patted me on the shoulder.

'Give him the money, and let's go,' he said quietly. I dropped the £20 note on the floor and turned to go. I couldn't bear to look at the snivelling little wreck. The worst of it was I could see myself in his eyes. It was like looking into some hideously distorted fairground mirror, the demon smiled back, I just had to get out. When we were halfway down the stairs The Cheat started up, calling us every name under the sun. We kept walking, because I knew that if I went back up the stairs and started hitting, I wouldn't be able to stop.

Slashface was an ex-junky, if there was such a thing, a particularly nasty piece of work. He got his name from the razor blade he kept hidden in the trilby he always wore. People thought it was just an affectation, but it was far more than that, if anyone crossed him they would get a taste of it. On more than one occasion people would come screaming out of the Cambridge Arms, clutching their faces. I wouldn't be seen dead in such a place, it was where you went if you couldn't get served in the madhouse. Even I had some standards, but my partner often went there for the odd early evening pint, before things got too heavy. I think he got a kick out of the sheer bedlam of it all. It did mean that my partner was the obvious choice to try to make contact.

This left me in the office sorting out the accounts. Once I'd paid what we owed there was precious little left. We needed to be able to tell Green something when he phoned on Monday or we would be stuffed. I was looking at some brochures for fast cars, not because I was particularly into fast cars, but because I could foresee some point in the future when I would have to get out of situations quickly. I knew absolutely nothing about cars though, being more concerned in the aesthetics than anything else, the aesthetics were all I understood anyway. I had just poured myself a cup of Earl Grey and lit up a Disque Bleu when there was a knock on the door. 'Come in,' I replied straightening my tie.

She was blonde with deep blue eyes, full lips, and hardly any make up. She was wearing a lilac dress cut just above the knee, which clung to every contour of her body. She was one of the most beautiful women I had ever seen. My mouth went dry, my jaw dropped open and my face started to prickle, I opened my mouth to say something, but no sound came. I quickly took a slurp of tea, and managed to splurt something out, about how I could help, or some such nonsense. I must have looked like a total buffoon. I have always felt ill at ease when dealing with beautiful women, and she was no exception. With a voice like a soft summer breeze rustling through a corn field, she told me she had been sent by the job centre; we had advertised for a secretary. For a minute my mind went blank, and I panicked inwardly whilst trying to appear nonchalant. Then relief flooded through me as I remembered. My partner had placed the advertisement when we had first set up shop. So full of naïve enthusiasm we thought that not only could we live comfortably from the business, we could afford to employ someone else. It wasn't long before the harsh reality had soon set in, and we had decided to withdraw it, but had never got round to it. With typical civil service efficiency they had only just got round to sending someone for the job, but what a someone, I could easily forgive them for the delay. The prospect of employing her was really exciting. Now we were working, we could probably afford it. I gestured to the chair in front of the desk and asked her to sit down. Suddenly panicking once more as I remembered I had never interviewed anyone for a job before, I was going to look a total prat.

She smiled and sat down, crossing her legs, her stockings were lilac as well, and I could just make out the tops as she sat down. I suddenly realised that I was staring at her legs, and felt like a complete pervert. I quickly looked away, and stared down at the ashtray, stubbing out the dog end. I moved way too quickly, and upset the ashtray all over my trousers. She gave a tiny giggle, and I started to redden once more. Grinning nervously I brushed down my trousers and decided to press on as best I could. I said some sort of bullshit about how we'd already had lots of interest in the job, what with the nature of the business. She thought it was just general office work, so I told her what we did, trying to sound impressive. I fixed her with my best Humphrey Bogart stare, but probably just looked constipated. She looked back, a little concerned. I tried to continue without sounding too stupid. I told her that we spent a lot of time out of the office, that we more or less needed someone to run the office, and she would pretty much have free reign. At this she looked interested, seems she was pretty fed up with being stuck in a typing pool, wanted something with a little more responsibility. I couldn't help feeling that I was the one being interviewed, not vice versa. I desperately tried to think of what to do next and almost visibly sighed with relief when I asked her what qualifications she had. She handed over some certificates, which, with the exception of a few 'O' levels meant absolutely nothing to me. I tried to look as if I knew what I was doing, made a few reassuring noises then handed them back to her. Then asked if she had any questions. Straight away she asked what the starting salary was, once again my mind went blank. For the life of me I couldn't think what the going rate was for this sort of job. I suddenly blurted out, 'One hundred and ten basic.'

'One hundred and ten?'

'Basic, before overtime, bonuses and stuff.' I tried smiling reassuringly, but probably looked dyspeptic.

'And where will I work...? Here? There's not a lot of room.'

'No, there's not is there?' I shuffled uncomfortably in my chair. We'll probably spend most of our time in the side office, give you a free reign.' I was starting to repeat myself, I really didn't want to look any stupider.

'Can I see it then?' A thousand Benny Hill gags ran through my head, I almost fell off my chair.

'See what?' I croaked.

'The side office.'

'Oh yes of course,' I tittered nervously getting up. Then I stopped dead in my tracks, remembering the state of the side office. It was like a wino's dustbin, beer cans, empty tequila and calvados bottles, and an ungodly reek. My partner said that he had once seen a rat in there. I sat down quickly, No, you can't, it's been condemned, asbestos.'

'Asbestos.' She visibly recoiled with alarm. I would have been better off telling the truth.

'It's alright, they're getting rid of it, vacuum bags the works, it'll be all gone by Monday. And anyway, you'll be out here, I'll be the one working in there. Me and my partner.'

'Your partner?'

'Yes, but don't worry, he's very much a junior partner, I make all the real decisions. Still, as a matter of courtesy I'll have to discuss it with him first, but the job should be yours, if you still want it.' I really hoped it didn't sound like I was begging. She sat musing it over quietly to herself.

'Well, I'm not happy about the asbestos, but if you say it will be gone.'

'It will, it will,' I enthused like a pathetic cocker spaniel.

'O.K. I'm still interested, but I'm going to have to know soon. And I want to sign a proper contract and everything, before I hand my notice in at the bank.'

'I'll phone you Monday.' Then came a delightful first for me, a beautiful woman giving me their phone number, and for once it wasn't Shirley Nick. Out of force of habit, I quickly checked it wasn't, then I noticed her name for the first time. 'Veryanne, that's an unusual name.'

'Yes it is. Isn't it? What's yours?'

'Just call me...' I swallowed, hesitated, then bit the bullet. 'Zippy.' She looked even more shocked than Dodge had been. 'It's a long story,' I murmured apologetically.

'You'll have to tell me about it sometime,' she smiled, 'Look forward to hearing from you Monday. Ciao.' Then with one fluid graceful movement, and a final wiggle of her hips she was out of the door. I waited until she was out of earshot then let rip with a huge fart that I'd been bottling up ever since she walked in.

Five minutes later my partner burst into the office like an exploding zit, all yellow and splattery. I was polishing my glasses on my tie when he started jabbering lustfully, 'You should have seen the bit of stuff I clocked on the way up… What's that fucking smell? It's you isn't it? Lay off those fucking pasties, I'll open a window.' For once he had a point, it really reeked, but it wasn't the pasties that were to blame, it was a chicken vindaloo. My partner was sweating heavily, and his face was red with exertion, or was it arousal? I couldn't tell. He was pacing up and down, prosaically describing Veryanne. I let him continue until he had run out of steam. Then I told him her name, and his mood turned ugly. There was some name calling, and in the end I had to come clean and tell him what really happened, but not before I was ready. He needed no persuasion to employ Veryanne, and I could see that she would be yet another point of conflict between my partner and myself. After he had settled down, fortified by a couple of shots of tequila I reminded him of the state of the back office. I was expecting a huge row about tidying it up, but he just accepted things passively. I suppose it was not all that surprising considering what was at stake. Eventually my partner told me what he had found out; Slashface was going to make a deal at a party on Saturday night. He didn't know much else, save that it would be somewhere in The Jungle. That meant going on a pub crawl and keeping our ears open, just like any Friday night.

Chapter 4

Floating Anarchy

'Alpha, Beta, Gamma, Hubba Dubba.'
Gong

Blood will have blood, and smack will have smack, and more smack, can never get enough of the vile stuff. It's here today, special offer. Can't get hold of dope, but there are three different varieties of smack on the streets. Forget unemployment, forget eating and drinking, and breathing, but you can't forget smack, it won't let you. 1980s culture, digital watches, home computers, a programmable lifestyle, and a programmable society, if there is such a thing as society, Thatcher was supposed to have killed it off. Visions of mindless junky zombies all going through the same routine, in perfect synchronicity. All with the look of death in their eyes. Everyone's dead before they even come out of the womb. Paranoid Schizophrenia is the norm today, there's no peace of mind, no real demand for it. Everyone would rather have plenty of freely negotiable western currency, a pair of Levis, and smell like Armani. 'The end is nigh,' shrieks the fanatic outside the bank in Portswood, 'Repent, Repent.' I quite believe it, but I want to have something to repent when I meet my maker, which might be a whole lot sooner than nigh the way things were going.

It was half past eleven when I finally woke up. I started to take an appraisal, I was in a bed, really good. I was in my bed, even better, and the bed was clean, no shit, piss or vomit – brilliant. All the rest was detail, I lay back and waited for the memories to come creeping back. They slunk back in fragments, isolated images of drunken depravity, staggering, vomiting, wild lurching and jabbering, all disconnected, no sense of whole, nothing remotely holistic. That would come later. I sneaked my hand out from under the covers and turned the gas fire on. Then I lay there waiting for the room to warm up, thinking of all the pubs I would have to stay out of for a while. I pulled back the curtains, it was raining again, really pissing it down. Looking out gave a distinct sense of déjà-vu, a half-remembered dream, the beginning of a new day.

After about ten minutes, once the room had warmed up, I got out of bed, and made my way downstairs. There lying on the doormat was a large brown envelope. I opened it up, and out popped a heavily censored version of the coroner's report on Stephen's death. I got it courtesy of the lawyer we kept on a retainer, prudently that was the bill I always made sure got paid. I put the report down on the side and put the kettle on. I took a couple of paracetamol and made a pot of tea, only to find out that we'd run out of milk. Fortunately I had some whitener, but it wasn't the same.

Stephen's report made gruesome reading, He had been hacked up into thirteen pieces, but what was even more disturbing was that they had only recovered twelve of the pieces. The piece that was missing was the 'lower abdomen.' There was a sudden whoosh as a piece of long forgotten trivia forced itself into my frontal lobes. Clay, amongst his insane rantings about moon-goddesses and the great penis in the sky had mentioned something about a similar dismemberment. It was something to do with the Egyptian gods. I couldn't remember what exactly, but it was something that I would have to put on hold until I saw Clay again. I had no idea of knowing when that would be. I hadn't seen him since the Dodge episode, and he had a tendency to disappear for long periods of time. Owing to the fact that he didn't pay rent he could be anywhere in town moving from squad to squat, just a day away from the next eviction notice. I would have to put the word out amongst his cronies, some of the middle-aged flotsam and jetsam of the love generation.

I couldn't do anything about it now, and I had plenty to do anyway. There were two likely parties on that night. It meant that my partner and I would have to split up, cover a party each. This was a bit risky, as neither of us would have any back up, but it couldn't be helped.

I couldn't be bothered to do any cooking, so I decided to eat out. This meant a pint and a pasty at The Carpenter's. I arrived there drenched, totally soaked through. When I put my hand in my pocket I found that I was totally skint. Fortunately I was able to persuade the landlord to let me cash a cheque, but at one point I thought I would have to go down on my knees and beg. After that I had to nod politely and make agreeable noises when he reminded me of how he had predicted this weather last Thursday, kept going on about 'sunspots, and their long term effect upon the weather.' The pasty went down very slowly and so did the first pint. By the time I started on the second my headache had started to go. After the third I began to find the landlord's conversation interesting. That was the signal, time to call it a day. Go back home and get some sleep before the party, recharge the batteries. I used the pay-phone in the pub to call my partner. I arranged to meet up with him later that night, then went straight home.

My partner was looking rough; he hadn't shaved since the meeting with Green. He was wearing a baggy old jumper, oily jeans, and an ancient pair of pumps with a hole in them. I wasn't looking much better, dirty blue denim jacket, tatty yellow and green T shirt, faded burgundy cords and an old pair of Doctor Martens. We needed to look the part, blend in with the rest of the wasters cruising through Saturday night. We arranged to meet in The Carpenter's the following day. We made our goodbyes, I bought two cans of lager and set off into the night. First dark alley I came to, I checked the pistol, better to be safe than sorry

At first it was a distant hum, getting louder, then an indeterminate noise, then a very obvious noise steadily increasing in volume. I had no problems finding the party, the house almost looked like it was jumping up and down like in an old Tex Avery cartoon. The front door had been kicked off the hinges, I just walked straight in. All of my senses were hit at once; 'Floating Anarchy' by Gong was blasting out at full volume along with a constant hubbub of voices as people screamed at each other, desperately trying to be heard over the music. What a collection of people as well, I recognised a few faces from the pub, but there were a hell of a lot more I didn't recognise. I'd heard a rumour in The Carpenter's that afternoon that the wilder element of the convoy were in town, brooding away somewhere, trying to figure out what to do about Stonehenge. They were all here, all manner of strange hairy freaks were leaping around the room, some were drug addled, benign, smiling senilely at the world, cavorting about. Something very hairy of indeterminate age dancing with a slightly less hairy tatterdemalion of indeterminate gender. And the children, packs of young boys aged between six and ten running around the house scrounging alcohol, cigarettes and drugs. Not all the adults smiled stupidly, others stomped around with raging eyes looking for trouble. The stench was overpowering, a faint smell of patchouli, trying desperately to mask the smell of long unwashed hippy, fag smoke, dope smoke, vomit and dog. The hippies had brought their big smelly dogs that were slobbering around, pissing and shitting all over the place. So much for all my preparations, I wouldn't have looked more out of place if I had been wearing a dinner suit.

I opened one of the cans of lager and walked into the hallway, I looked from side to side, trying to catch a glimpse of Slashface. It took me ten minutes to get as far as the bottom of the stairs. The place was packed solid; I was reminded of an old engraving of The Black Hole Of Calcutta. I knew just how a sardine felt. A small dark-haired boy of about seven looked up at me, 'Gizza Blim. Gizza Blim. I got tobacco and Rizla. Gizza Blim.' I looked away, desperate not to make eye contact. He suddenly yelled, 'Wanker,' punched me in the bollocks then slipped away. My legs gave way, and I fell back against the wall. I stayed there for a few minutes, nursing my injured gonads, and finishing the first can of beer.

Having recovered slightly I went to check out the upstairs. It was nice to see that some people were still prepared to queue up to go to the bog, even though others were shitting and pissing all over the floor. The upstairs had been turned into some sort of crusty knocking shop, that offered attraction only to the really desperate, or truly demented and drug addled. I caught sight of the small boy at the far side of the landing. He smiled back to me and waved, 'Hey meester,' he called in a mock Mexican accent, 'You want to fuck my seester, she's only eight.' Even Slashface wouldn't hang around a place like that, drug deal or no, I turned around and went back downstairs, I still had to check out the kitchen.

I had just started on my second can when a huge shape reached up from the shadows and snatched it out of my hands. A huge gargantuan hominid of prehistoric proportions, with 'Fuk Yoo' tattooed on his forehead. Without saying a word he started pouring the contents down his throat, snarling and gurgling, staring at me menacingly. I stared back, totally gobsmacked, nobody had ever done anything like that to me before. He took my silence as weakness, and continued his menacing. Throwing the empty can over his shoulder he growled in a broad Glaswegian accent, 'And you give me two quid you bastard.' It seemed like the sensible thing to do, I felt my hand going automatically into my pocket. This was a seriously frightening individual, I needed to get rid of him. Instead of finding two quid, I found the L9A1, and wrapped my finger round the trigger, this changed everything. I felt an immense feeling of relief, and a newfound confidence that only a gun can bring. I looked balefully back at him.
'Sorry mate, I'm skint. I was pointing the Browning right at his testicles. I was looking forward to blowing them off, I wondered how much blood there would be. I stared deep into his red eyes. He appeared puzzled, people didn't normally behave that way, I didn't hit him when he snatched the drink, why put up a struggle now? Then the fury started to creep back, he opened his mouth displaying rows of rotting teeth, with their own unique form of halitosis. He growled, and my finger tightened on the trigger, 'Any

minute now,' I thought.

'That fucking hit me you fucking bastard!' Up from the bowls of the party pounded another huge malevolent atavistic nightmare, clutching the empty can of lager in its right hand. It brought the can down heavily on the Glaswegian's right temple, blood spurted out and hit me in the face. The Glaswegian spun around to face his new adversary, finding himself off-balance, he went tumbling downstairs. He went flying into my newfound ally. I pressed myself up against the wall, just in time. The room shuddered as they landed heavily on the floor, and remained motionless. This was as good a time as any to make a move, I stepped over their prostrate bodies and made my way towards the kitchen. The second my foot touched the floor I was flattened against the wall by a wave of crusties desperately trying to get a glimpse of the action. By now they had both recovered enough to carry on fighting, the Glaswegian was slightly quicker getting to his feet. There was a stomach-churning thud as he smashed his opponent's head against the wall. I had seen enough, the last thing I wanted was to get caught up in all this random violence. I slowly inched my way towards the kitchen.

Eerily, the kitchen was deserted, except for a small figure sitting reading a pornographic magazine, there was a large bowl of punch that seemed untouched. It was an oasis of calm in a sea of brutality. The rest of the party seemed a long way away. After all the trouble on the stairs, I was in desperate need of a drink. I examined the punch suspiciously, there were no obvious signs of contamination, broken glass, fag ends, or obvious bodily fluids. I washed an empty pint class under the tap and poured myself a pint. It was a queer orangey brown, when I sipped it; it had a strong taste of scrumpy with a distinct after taste of gin. It wasn't at all bad, and I poured myself another pint. It still struck me as very strange that the punch was more or less untouched, I would have thought, considering the guests it would all have disappeared in a matter of seconds. However, there was no point in looking a gift horse in the mouth, and it was soothing my badly tattered nerves.

'Oh wow! It's you!' I looked up, and for a brief moment thought I saw a huge cobra staring at me. I shook my head, and to my relief found myself looking back at Clay who was smiling benignly, the magazine lowered, but not forgotten. I passed Clay a cigarette, which he accepted eagerly. 'Oh wow! A Frenchie.' I had never smoked anything other than Disque Bleu, yet Clay always reacted with surprise whenever I gave him a cigarette. We sat chatting idly for the next ten minutes or so. I told Clay about the juicier aspects of our last case. Clay paid particular attention when I told him about the video evidence, and was bereft when I told him we no longer had a copy. He wanted to talk about the girls in the magazine he'd been reading. He spoke as if he knew them all intimately, showing me a picture of a blonde pulling back the lips of her vagina, he told me her name was Angie, and she was a deeply spiritual person, a real moon-goddess. He told me he thought that another one of the girls was at the party. I thought it unlikely, the magazine was called 'Young Ravers,' not 'Hideously malformed crusty 'women' caked in unmentionable filth.' That sort of title didn't exactly trip off the tongue, but it summed up what was going on upstairs.

I suddenly remembered what I had to ask Clay about, but I had other things to worry about. There was a weird fluttering sensation at the back of my throat, and everything looked a bit sparkly. I had forgotten how to tie my shoelaces up. I didn't want to get found out, what if there was a test or something? I would look really stupid in front of a whole bunch of crusties. I decided to press on regardless, and hope Clay hadn't realised I couldn't do my shoes up. I asked him about The Egyptian gods. He paused for a second then grinned demonically, and I was aware of the huge cobra once again. This was only fleeting, and Clay quickly transformed back into his canine self. I never realised how much Clay looked like Huckleberry Hound, when he wasn't doing cobra impressions.

'This is the story of Osiris,' intoned Clay in grandiose tones. 'Set, right, Osiris's brother was really bummed out with him. He got hold of Osiris right, and cut him up into thirteen pieces, and scattered them all over the world. Then Isis right, Osiris's wife got a bit freaked out by it all, and she went looking for him. She could only find twelve of the pieces, the bit that she couldn't find was his dong.' He paused for a moment as if mulling the word 'dong over to himself. He had done a really good dog job on himself. At times he was the spitting image of Scooby Doo, and at other times he was his barely hominid usual self. He still hadn't sussed that I couldn't tie up my shoelaces though. Clay rolled his eyes as if unable to focus, he scratched his tousled sandy mop, which had really started growing recently. He was grinning insanely, he got up and pointed his finger out like a conductor's baton. 'And the story goes,' he continued, 'That woe betide anyone who finds it, because the same thing will happen to them.' He sat down pleased with himself, smiling with the demeanour of someone who has just made a world shattering statement.

My stomach started twisting, cold sweat started pouring down my back.

Without any warning at all, a long orange arc of puke came pouring out of my mouth, barely missing Clay. That wiped the smile off his face. He leaped to his feet, grabbed me by the shoulders, and dragged me out into the garden. The cool night air had an incredibly powerful healing effect. I retched once more then belched, and the nausea disappeared, just as suddenly as it had begun. Clay appeared concerned, 'Hey man, Are you alright?' I wiped my mouth and got to my feet, taking in deep gulps of air.

'Yeah thanks, I feel fine, I don't know what came over me. I've never been like that before.'

'It's the acid.'

'The what?'

'The acid in the punch.'

'No, it's not that, I never get an acid stomach, I always make a point of drinking a pint of milk before I go out.' Clay started chuckling, quietly at first, but getting louder and more hysterical by the second.

'No,' he chortled, 'Not that sort of acid. The acid I'm talking about is LSD.'

'LSD?'

'LSD.'

I didn't like the sound of that. I'd never taken LSD before. In fact all I knew about LSD was something I'd heard at school. Someone took LSD and thought they were an orange. Everyone agreed on that point, but they were equally divided on what happened next. One body of thought has the protagonist curled up in a corner whining piteously, 'Please don't peel me.' The other version is that he gets hold of a knife and peels himself; that was the version I preferred. Standing in the kitchen with a head full of acid surrounded by a bunch of violent swamp people and talking to a dog I wished there could be a third scenario, one where he gets the knife and cuts everyone else up.

So far so good, I didn't feel the least orange-like, the LSD probably wasn't affecting me like the rest. I must have some built in tolerance to it. Some sort of tough guy gene. All I had to do was stop Clay turning into a dog, then I could go home and hide all the shoelaces, safe and dry. I took control of the situation masterfully. 'Clay, stop turning into a dog, it's getting a bit predictable now.'

'Yeah right, Sirius. I'm a Pisces, born in the year of the dog. That makes me a water dog… Sirius… Keeper Of The Gates Of Hades.' This was a side to Clay I had never seen before, he usually spoke a load of bollocks, but not tonight. Tonight was pure gold, first all the stuff about Osiris, and now this. I tried smiling cognitively, reassuring Clay, letting him know I understood. 'I am from Sirius,' he intoned. 'I am from another planet.' And I was the one witnessing it all; out of all the people on Earth the dog people had chosen me with whom to make contact. It was a proud moment. I would be Earth's cosmic ambassador. It wouldn't be long before we would be whooshing off into space. Spacemen didn't use shoelaces. 'Where will you be when the spacemen land?' chanted Clay. I smiled back beatifically.

The serenity was shattered by an ear-splitting roar. There silhouetted in the doorway stood Glaswegian's bane, clutching the same beer can. 'Jock said this belonged to you,' he said throwing the can at me, he reached into his jacket and pulled out a Bowie knife. I stepped back, feeling in my pockets for something to throw. This was a third LSD scenario, you don't feel like an orange, but someone still wants to peel you. Once again my fingers felt the cool comfort of an illegal firearm, and I wasn't afraid any more. I was going to blow this big bastard's head off. As I pulled the Browning out, the trigger caught on my sleeve. There was a surprisingly loud boom, and a bullet drilled itself into the ceiling, bringing a large lump of plaster down on my opponent's head.

Everything came sharply into focus. It was time to make a run for it. Pausing only to brush the large pieces of plaster off I made a beeline for the door. At the foot of the stairs I went flying into the Glaswegian, who looked like he was nursing a broken noise. I was going so fast I knocked him down, and kept going, hoping to escape without any serious injury. He'd recognised me, and I was followed by a stream of incoherent threats and menaces. I ran out of the front door, not stopping until I reached the middle of the road. I felt like a rat fleeing a sinking ship. That house was evil, I turned round expecting it to be dragged down into the pits of hell like at the end of 'Poltergeist.' The house was rocking in classic Tex Avery style, and did not look like it was going to be dragged anywhere. The Glaswegian appeared, framed in the door, which split into three, each with its own Glaswegian. I pointed the Browning, but which Glaswegian was the real one? All three stood irresolute, looking uncertainly at the gun. I was sweating heavily. There was a thunderous squeal of brakes and a huge American car came roaring down the road towards us.

Chapter 5

Tricky Dicky

'I'm doing very well.'
Ian Dury

A huge red Oldsmobile Toranado came cruising majestically down the road; it was so big it almost took up both sides of the street. There wasn't a lot of room left for me. Death, I was sure of it. The Glaswegians were still eyeing me malevolently, and now I was going to get run down. After all this, just another road accident, just another statistic. It was all some disgusting conspiracy between the driver and the Glaswegians. And probably my partner, and Green, in fact every bastard I had ever known. And I wasn't being paranoid. As I felt the car draw closer I threw myself against the pavement. The Toranado pulled up next to me, cutting off the Glaswegians. A scrawny unshaven face with a front gold tooth smiled down benignly at me. With a flood of relief I recognised the proprietor of the local sex shop, Bazzer The Book, a man who was never without a camera. Sounding like Sid James trying to appear posh he asked, 'Spot of bother old chap?' I jumped up and yanked the passenger door open. I would have got into a car driven by Satan himself. 'Drive!' I screamed.

Bazzer slammed his foot down hard on the accelerator, and the Toranado roared into life. I looked back at the house, a giant cobra was rising above the house staring malevolently down. Spacecraft from Sirius' third planet were hovering just above its head. An old Ford Transit limped off the pavement and started in pursuit. I was in a state of suppressed panic, certain we were both going to die. I could plainly see the dog insignia of the flying saucers as they swooped over the car. I quickly checked my genitalia to be on the safe side. 'I see 'em,' yelled Bazzer. For a second I thought he was talking about my testicles, but I realised he was talking about the spacemen. We hit the roundabout at seventy five. 'Front wheel drive,' murmured Bazzer. 'It helps grip the corners.' I grunted mutely in reply, I had momentarily lost the power of speech. 'That disciple's still with us,' continued Bazzer, 'This'll get shot of him.' As we flew past The Polygon Hotel, Bazzer executed a couple of quick handbrake turns and within seconds we were tearing up Bedford Place, heading towards the ice rink. I was impressed, not only had Bazzer thrown off the van, but he'd managed to give the spacemen the slip too. I sank back into the seat and lit up a Disque Bleu, passing one to Bazzer.

Bazzer took a deep pull on his cigarette, and asked me what all the bother was about. For the first time that evening since leaving The Carpenters I relaxed. I knew Bazzer very well, not because I spent a lot of time in porn shops, but because he was a long standing regular at The Carpenters. When I told him about the LSD he guffawed loudly. It was like being locked up in a cell with Sid James at his most lecherous who was slowly going mad. After what seemed hours he reached under the dashboard, pulled out a small brown bottle, and handed it over. 'This should sort you out,' he burred. I asked him what it was. 'Don't worry about that, just stick it under your nose, and take a great big sniff.' I needed something to get rid of this hideous mental condition, I did as I was instructed. The contents of the bottle smelt vaguely chemical, but completely unfamiliar. At first nothing happened. I was just about to take another sniff when I felt my heart beating faster and faster, pumping the blood straight to my head. My head was pounding, the only noise I could hear was my own heartbeat. Then my head started to swell up, soon it was the same size and texture of an enormous pumpkin. I thought my head was going to explode all over the inside of the car, then very slowly the swelling stopped, and gradually my head started to deflate.. It was only then I realised I'd been holding my breath. I lay back and drew in huge lungfuls of air, trying to regain focus. My hearing came back, Bazzer was laughing like a drain.

'Jesus Christ, what the hell was that stuff? Are you trying to kill me?' Bazzer was laughing so much the tears were rolling down his cheeks. At least someone was enjoying themselves. I wasn't, the spacemen had come back, and were swooping down at the car. I dived under the seat and checked my gonads.

'It's amyl nitrate,' he chuckled. 'The sausage jockeys use them. It dilates the arse 'ole.' I couldn't believe this, maybe Bazzer was preparing me for some homo-erotic piece of debauchery. There was no way I was getting bummed I couldn't handle that.

'Why did you give it to me, you sadistic bastard?'

'It's a powerful heart stimulant, I thought it might help clear the system, just a theory. Well anyway here we are. Chez moi.' The car stopped, and Bazzer pulled up outside his flat. 'You'd better stay with me, until you straighten out. You're not fit to be out on the streets.' I got out of the car and staggered over to the front door. I felt dreadful.

Barrett the evil nocturnal parrot had called on me during the night. My night time tormentor had swooped down, using my open mouth as a lavatory. This alone did not satisfy his bloodlust, with his long beak he had drilled holes onto my forehead. I was no stranger to the ravages of Barrett, but this time he had been particularly brutal. I tried opening my eyes, but it was way too bright. The light peppered tiny splinters of pain through the holes in my forehead. I lay back down again and tried to compose myself, trying desperately to remember what had happened. The only things I could remember that were real, were the emotions. Fear, horror, panic, disgust, they were all real enough, apart from that it was hard to distinguish between fact and hallucination. I was convinced that I had spent most of the previous night being chased by ancient Egyptians, determined to rid me of my testicles helped by Scooby-Doo. That couldn't be right.

I decided to risk facing the outside world once more. I peered through a tiny slit in the blankets, letting my eyes become accustomed to the light. Then I had to try to get them to focus, which wasn't at all easy. I was in an unfamiliar front room, leather three piece suite and thick electric carpet. It was like the set from some really tacky porn film. Then I realised where I was, the next moment the door flew open and in burst Bazzer sounding horribly cheerful. He was whistling discordantly, carrying a chipped china mug brimming over with milky tea. He bounded over to the sofa and thrust it towards me, and spilling about half of it over my chest in the process. I screamed in agony, only to be subjected to the Sid James chuckle once more. 'That'll teach you,' he chuckled. 'Learn how to tie your shoe laces yet?' I panicked, things were starting to come true.

'How do you know about that?' I pleaded.

'You takin' the piss? I had to stay up for two hours teaching you how to do it when I should have been bastard spotting. You were bloody useless, I could have taught a two year old quicker.' I was confused, I didn't really know what was happening. Was bastard spotting anything like train spotting but less geeky?

'Bastard spotting?'

'Yeah, spot the bastard before they spot you.' I stared back blankly, either Bazzer wasn't making sense, or the effect of the acid was permanent. 'I'll explain,' Bazzer continued. 'Yesterday I got a phone call, from a mate in London. Seems last time I was down there I ruffled a few feathers, so they've sent a bastard to beat me up. Still, my mate tipped me off, the bastard they've sent plays the referee in '*Sloppy Mud Slut Wrestlers 14.*' All my dirty mud wrestling stock's been mislabelled, I've been going through them all, I wish it was the ref from '*Sloppy Mud Slut Wrestlers 12*,' he's just a little guy.'

'So have you seen it yet?'

'Not yet, but I'm only half way through the stock, still, that's what you get for helping people.' I sipped what was left of the tea, it helped wash away the parrot guano, but it wasn't doing anything for my hangover, so I asked if he had any painkillers. Without a word he bounded off. Within seconds he was back, triumphantly clutching a packet of junior aspirin. I couldn't believe it. When I asked what he was doing with them he looked genuinely hurt. He hung his head dejectedly, 'They're orange flavour.'

'Alright. How many do I need?'

'Let's see,' said Bazzer reading the packet. 'Do not give to children under two years old.' Hur, hur, it doesn't say anything about mental age.' I couldn't take this, my head was splitting, I begged him to get to the adult dose. 'Doesn't give one. It says, 'Children over thirteen, four tablets.'

'Give me four tablets then.'

'Can't do that, there's only three left.' I took the last three tablets and swallowed them down, hoping that despite all indications to the contrary that they would actually do something. I had to ask Bazzer what day it was, I honestly couldn't remember, all I knew was that it was the weekend. When Bazzer told me it was Sunday I was worried. I knew there was something I had to do, but I couldn't remember what. Then very horribly it dawned on me. It was half past eleven, and I was supposed to meet my partner in The Carpenter's at twelve. After that we had to clean up the office, get it ready for Veryanne. That didn't make the hangover any better.

The journey to The Carpenter's was at a more sedate pace than the previous night's jaunt. I got washed and dressed as quickly as possible. We got there at about half past twelve. My partner was nowhere to be seen. The landlord said he was probably waiting for the rain to pass, and it would be over in about half an hour. I ordered a pint for myself and one for Bazzer. It was quarter past one when my partner finally turned up. In the intervening period Bazzer had knocked back five pints, and was starting on his sixth. I never realised he could drink that much, I had only just started on my second, but my headache was just starting to subside. My partner walked over smiling, for some reason everybody else seemed in a really good mood that day. Even the landlord was whistling.

I took my foul temper out on my partner, gave him a rollicking for being late. Nothing fazed him, he grinned back merrily. 'Well that's bloody rich, I come in here with a result, and you chew me out. Buy me a pint you miserable sod.'

'I could do with another,' said Bazzer putting his empty glass down on the bar. All in all it was turning into a pretty expensive lunchtime. But my partner had not been lying when he said that he'd got a result. It turns out he was able to follow Slashface without being noticed. Slashface made the deal and went home quickly. He was currently sitting on two grand's worth of smack. My partner told me it was my call now, he'd done the tail, got the information, it was down to me to decide what to do with it.

My partner wanted to know what had happened to me, he could see I was looking even rougher than usual. All chances of me drawing a veil over the night's proceedings were shattered by Bazzer's insistence on telling all the gory details, much to my partner's amusement. He didn't tell everything though, and I kept my conversation with Clay a secret. It was bad enough looking a total prat without looking insane as well. No, I would keep Clay's information close to my chest. I wiped the grin off my partner's face when I told him about the state of the office. My partner loathed physical work, but lechery had got the better of him. I thought I was eager to see Veryanne start work until I saw the look of excitement in his eyes at the sound of her name. Groaning, he finished his pint. Then we set off for the office, stopping off at the Happy Shopper to buy some cleaning materials.

'One chop suey with sweet and sour pork, one beef chow mein with egg fried rice, Five pounds and seventy five pence please.' My partner handed six pounds to the grinning Chinaman. He gave back the change grinning the same grin, the same grin he'd greeted us with when we walked into the shop, the same grin he wore when we took the orders down. Never saying anything that didn't need to be said. Place your orders, pay up then go. Once my partner tried to engage him in conversation, but every enquiry was greeted with one word replies coupled with a broad grin. Every now and then the silence was punctuated by frantic shouting in Cantonese to his fellow countrymen behind the screen, who unlike Victorian children, were never seen, but always heard. The crashing of pots and pans, and the wild cries of an indecipherable tongue.

I wasn't particularly interested in conversation anyway. Having just spent the last three hours tidying up the office I was completely knackered. I collapsed onto one of the uncomfortable plastic chairs and picked up a copy of, 'The News Of The World.' This said a lot about what sort of customers The Chinaman thought frequented his establishment. It made perfect sense why he didn't want to get into conversation. I wouldn't want to either. Yet another rock star had been involved in some cocaine fuelled sex orgy with a couple of media whores. Its only redeeming feature was that there was no mention of AIDS, unlike every other sex scandal. It read it all before, the only thing that had changed were the names. It was with a deep sense of relief that I heard The Chinaman calling out our orders.

My partner's flat was in an even worse state than mine. I cracked open a beer and sank down into an armchair whilst my partner ran to get plates and some cutlery. It took him about ten minutes to get everything together, and by the time he came through I had completely seized up. I gazed helplessly at the plate, I didn't feel at all hungry even though I hadn't eaten a thing all day. Every mouthful was a struggle. Even the most delicious food imaginable would have been hard going. This was not the finest oriental cuisine Southampton had to offer. My partner was tucking into his with obvious relish, and had finished before I was even half way through mine. I ate a tiny bit more then gave him the rest to finish off. When he had finished he took the plates through and returned with a six pack of Castlemaine. I took mine gratefully sinking back into the armchair, I was about done in. Fortunately I didn't live far from my partner's. My partner was far from done in, and eager to continue the conversation. 'So you're all set for tomorrow? You'll sort out Slashface, and I'll deal with Veryanne.' I almost choked on the beer.

'What?' I spluttered.

'We've already discussed this. I got the lead, you've got to do the next bit.' I didn't remember agreeing to anything like that, but I was far too tired to argue. 'You look fucked,' my partner continued. 'I'd get home if I were you, you've got a big day ahead of you tomorrow. Get a good night's sleep.' Before I knew it I was out of the door, still clutching the freshly opened can of Castlemaine. As I staggered off down the road my partner called after me. 'Make sure you let Slashface know we're onto him! Put the frighteners on him!'

I didn't wake up until ten. When I checked the alarm clock I panicked before realising that I didn't have to go into the office today. My partner was doing all of that. I could afford to lie back and relax for a while, not that there would be much relaxing. I had to go and 'put the frighteners,' on Slashface, not an easy task; it was like trying to intimidate King Kong. I pulled the last cigarette from the packet beside the bed. I lit it up, and lay back contemplating the ceiling, trying to formulate some sort of plan. I still had the residues of the previous day's hangover, but the hideous feeling of all over exhaustion had gone. I went into the bathroom and began pouring myself a bath. While it was running I got a couple of paracetamol from the medicine cabinet, shaved and brushed my teeth. I sat down in the hot bath. Hot baths are one of the best cure-alls known to man, they seem to clean both the inside as well as the outside, taking away the physical and mental pain.

It wasn't until I was sitting in front of the fire watching *Play School,* that I started thinking about the day's itinerary. This was the really big test, if I could deal with a brute like Slashface, then I was in the same league as Phillip Marlowe. The price of failure was high, no re-sits. Fail this one and they would be fishing me out of The Test, while my partner wined and dined the pretty young secretary, sometimes there's no justice.

I had all day to get myself killed, so I decided to have a long relaxing breakfast. It took about an hour, in that time I had consumed half a pint of orange juice, a pint of Earl Grey, three shredded wheat, two rashers of smoked bacon, two eggs, one large tomato and three slices of toast with butter and marmalade. I piled the washing up in the sink then went back upstairs to get dressed. Freshly pressed white shirt, with grey slacks and matching jacket, finished off with shiny black brogues, a purple waistcoat, bright red socks and a thin blue tie. I checked my pistol, then set off to pay Slashface a call.

I walked for about a quarter of an hour in the pouring rain, I felt like a condemned man on the way to the gallows. It took me about five minutes to pluck up the courage to press the doorbell. There was no reply, I took out my set of skeleton keys and let myself in. This wasn't The Cheat's door, and I was on my own. The stink hit me like a solid wall, it was ten times more repulsive than that which had greeted us at The Cheat's. The pistol was in my hand and my heart was in my mouth as I slowly edged towards the front room, where the stink was coming from. Inside there was a battered old black and white television, a couple of broken wooden chairs and Slashface.

I ran back into the hallway, just making it to the bog in time. I pulled up the lid and lost my breakfast down the pan. I flushed the toilet and split open a fresh packet of cigarettes. I lit one up, then went back to see Slashface, or what was left of him. There was blood all over the carpet, and the various components that had once made up Slashface were strewn all over the floor. I could count twelve, and didn't like to think of the whereabouts of the thirteenth. It wasn't a pretty sight, but it was a chance to uncover some evidence before the police started poking around. The blood had coagulated and the air was thick with flies, which suggested that Slashface had been killed some time previously. I made my way over to Slashface's torso, took a deep breath, and put my hand into his jacket pocket. There was a small black leather-bound notebook, I popped it into my back pocket. I was just about to leave when I spotted something glinting in his right hand. I prised the fingers apart, and my heart sunk when I found a small ivory phallus. Clay's words were rushing back to haunt me less than 48 hours since he'd spoken them. I put it in my jacket pocket. This done I was desperate to leave, but first I had to make sure I hadn't left any fingerprints or other incriminating evidence such as Disque Bleu dog ends. I wiped all the surfaces I'd touched, took a quick shufti outside, then legged it.

I was breathing heavily, trying to get the filthy stench out of my lungs. I took my trilby off and let the rain run down my face. As soon as I got home, I ran another bath, and didn't get out until every inch of my body had been scrubbed clean. After bathing I took my clothes and piled them into the empty bath. There was a deep red blood stain on my shirt. I took a bottle of surgical spirit and poured it all over, then lit a match and set fire to the whole lot. I sat there watching it burn, making sure nothing was left. Then I washed the ashes down the plug hole and opened a window. I put on a clean red T-shirt, blue jeans and stripy jumper then set off to the off-licence for a bottle of tequila. On the way back I stopped off at a public phone box.

'Emergency, which service do you require?'
'Police.'
'Police, can I help you?'
'Donald Paulson is at 140 St. Mary's Lane.'
'What?'
'140 St. Mary's Lane. His name is Donald Paulson, it's important that you remember that.'
'Why?'
'The coroner will want to know.' I hung up the phone and went home to get drunk.

Chapter 6

Ever Fallen In Love With Someone You Shouldn't Have Fallen In Love With?

'Doo doo doo doo.'
The Buzzcocks

What was I doing here? How did it all come to this? All I wanted was a quiet life, with a reasonable income, and perhaps a little bit of romance and adventure thrown in, but not this. I was now the proud owner of Osiris' knob with all the karmic baggage that comes with it. I was lying on my bed staring at the ceiling with the empty bottle of tequila lying next to me. But I wasn't drunk, I'd been trying to get drunk all night, but I couldn't. I felt like I had walked into one of Clay's perverse fantasies, and now I was being forced to live it out. And there was only one ending, with me being ripped apart my some supernatural Egyptian fury. A savage echo of a brutal past.

Every time I closed my eyes all I could see was Slashface's mutilated remains. The pistol was loaded and within easy reach, but what good was a pistol against furies and ghosts? I didn't know what to do, what sort of protection I needed. There was no point asking Clay for his advice, all his stories were given with a weary mystical fatalism, there were no get-out clauses in Clay's universe. Ever since I went to that horrible party and swallowed that evil drug, everything had gone wrong. I'd never even heard of Osiris until a few days ago, and now... Shit.

What if I ran? Post the phallus to my partner, and leg it, leave Southampton. Hope the furies will forget about me as they tear my partner apart. I might even be able to claim on the life insurance. But there was no guarantee the furies would forget about me, and where could I run to? Was anywhere safe? Would anyone risk giving me sanctuary? Who would believe my story? It was insane, the whole bloody affair, and the more I thought about it, the more I began to doubt my own sanity. I kept my eyes closed trying to will away consciousness, but every dream turned into a dark chthonic nightmare, featuring Clay, Osiris, dog people, crusties, and a shit load of snakes.

I got up at half past six and poured myself another bath. I may not have been able to get drunk, but I had a hangover right enough. I got into the bath and fixed myself a couple of paracetamol, and sat there trying to work something out. Then it hit me, it might not be Osiris' knob, it could be some ghastly hoax, by some sicko. Like the way people carry out copy-cat crimes. In fact that was more likely, thinking about it in the cold light of day. That didn't mean that I wasn't on some sicko's death list, but sickos are flesh and blood, they can be stopped by bullets. I was thinking of souping up the ammunition anyway; I'd found some old mercury thermometers when I was tidying up the office. I wanted to be able to blow a hole the size of a house in anyone who came after me. I'd carry out some modifications before I left the house.

That gave me something positive to do but I was still no further from the truth. The sense of impending doom had gone, but I still didn't know whether I was dealing with the supernatural or not. I really needed some advice, I needed to know whether or not the phallus was genuine. I didn't have to think for long, there were a load of archaeologists digging holes around the six dials roundabout, and they all drank in The Carpenter's at lunchtime, surely one of them would know how I could get this thing dated.

It was just an ordinary walk to work, just like any other day but it wasn't. I spent the last three hours drilling holes in bullets, filling them up with mercury then sealing them off with a soldering iron. I was twitchy and paranoid, hung over and still semi hallucinogenic. I couldn't escape hideous images, I'd glimpsed all kinds of weird shit in the past couple of hours. I'd studied the ivory phallus, but I couldn't get my head around it, it always looked different. Sometimes it was covered in writing, weird scratchy hieroglyphics, other times there was nothing there. I didn't know what was true anymore, what was real and what hallucinatory. I didn't recognise myself when I looked in the mirror, but the face looking back was scrawny, unshaven, (I couldn't hold a razor,) with black sunken eye sockets. I shuffled along the road, wary of every shadow until I got to the six dials roundabout.

He was standing up to his waist in a thin narrow trench, holding a trowel in one hand and examining a piece of pottery. Tall, suntanned, balding, with short cropped hair, sharp intelligent face and heavy black glasses. I waved a cheery smile of recognition, he scowled immediately.

'What do you fucking want? Looking for a game of pool are we?' With a hideous sinking horror I remembered why I hadn't seen Victor for a while, his pool table. His brand new pool table that he'd just had installed in his garage. His garage that was made up with its own bar. His own little private shebeen. A special club house for honoured guests, like fellow sportsman triumphantly drinking to victory at The Carpenter's.

That is how it had been, for once The Carpenter's cricket team, the one both Victor and I played for, had won a match. Towards the end of the evening Victor had been boasting about his new pool table, so it was only natural that the team should go back there after closing time. The landlord's pasties had not been sitting too well with his guest real ale, well not in my stomach anyway. No sooner had Victor lifted the cover off his most treasured acquisition than I had sprayed it with a melange of pasty and 'Old Traditional.' I was hideously drunk and can remember little else of the whole evening, but Victor and I hadn't talked since. In my twisted state I had completely forgotten about it.

So here I was staring down pathetically at a man who wanted to punch me on the nose. I tried to sound apologetic, bereft, but my voice came out like a cold grey whisper. 'You look like fucking shit.' He growled. 'What the hell have you been up to?' My mouth was too dry, I couldn't speak. I fumbled around in my pocket for a cough sweet, and the ivory phallus fell out. 'What are you doing with that you sick fucker?' He stared at me with thinly veiled disgust as I bent down to retrieve the phallus. Things weren't going at all well. I swallowed hard. 'Look Victor mate, I'm really sorry about your pool table, and all the bad language, and the blasphemy, and for what I said about your wife, and what I did to your dog, and for what I left behind in the pot plant. But I'm in a real deep pile of shit right now, and I really need your help. This isn't how it looks.' Victor's expression hadn't changed at all. 'Anyway, the good news is that we're being paid for a big case, and can afford consultants.'

Five minutes later we were sitting in a draughty old shed, Victor's site office, sipping cups of PG Tips. I just opened up, it all came out; the party, the acid, Osiris, his knob and Slashface. I couldn't really go down any further in Victor's estimations, he already thought I was insane, any further revelations couldn't do any harm. He looked at me with an expression I recognised. Once when Clay was ranting on about the Long Man, I had caught sight of myself in the mirror. It was the same expression.

I didn't get to the office until gone half past ten. I spent quite a long time with Victor and ate all his hob nobs. He agreed to carbon date the phallus, but it would cost, enough to cover the cost of resurfacing a pool table for starters. Also I had to go back there later on to drop the phallus off. He didn't want it lying around with all the shards and pieces of antiquity. In his opinion it came from Anne Summers, and he didn't want his fellow archaeologists finding it.

I almost took a double take when I walked through the door. This wasn't our office. All the stray pieces of paper had been filed away, and there was a faint smell of honeysuckle in the air. My partner was sprawled back in a leather armchair drinking a café latte and reading the paper. He peered over the top, muttering something imperiously about me being late. I was in no mood for my partner's scathing wit, I walked over and snatched the cup from his grasp. 'Not bad, a little too milky for my tastes though. You didn't make this, your coffee's lousy.' Looking round I could see the brand new coffee maker bubbling away. It wasn't the only thing though, everything was brand new, including the leather sofa my partner was spread out on. It wasn't just new, it was trendy, the latest concept in interior office design. I felt sick, it was ghastly, I couldn't imagine how much it had all cost, or where my partner had got the money from. 'We can't afford all this… this… trendy shit. I can't believe it. How did you manage to change it all? I've only been gone a day.'

My partner jumped up pugnaciously, 'We can't afford not to. Good business is all about creating the right impression. Don't worry about the cost, it's all on interest free credit, with nothing to pay for a year.' My partner stopped, and stared at me. 'Jesus, what happened to you? You look like shit.' Without pausing for an answer he continued. 'That Veryanne's a wonder, helped me organise it all. We're very lucky you know, she was able to start straight away, said she was sick to death of the typing pool. She'll be back in a minute, she's just popped out to get some soft furnishings.' Soft furnishings! I couldn't believe it, Phillip Marlowe never needed soft furnishings. I was close to tears, I wasn't ready for such a massive piece of culture shock.

Veryanne swept into the office like a cool spring breeze. I looked up, and was reminded of how awkward I had felt when we first met, she was even more beautiful than I had remembered. Her arms were filled with huge oversized carrier bags overflowing with cushions and cuddly toys. She draped her arms around my partner's neck. 'Pardy, be an angel and go bring the rest up…Oh, and can you pay the taxi driver too.' Like an overenthusiastic spaniel my partner shot up and ran out of the office. Then Veryanne fixed me with her beautiful blue eyes.

I smiled back, trying to appear detached, professional, trying to keep the inner spaniel under control. 'Hello again,' I wheezed, 'I'm sorry I'm not looking my best right now, but I'm working the streets, keeping my ear to the ground. I'm sure my partner has told you all the relevant details.'

'He told me you were sick.' She paused, and studied me further. 'Are you sure you're not sick? You look really terrible. Why don't you go home and have a lie down?' I was starting to get sick of people telling me how bad I was looking. I coughed, clearing my throat. I assured her I was fine, but could do with a coffee all the same. She went over to the coffee machine and came back with two fresh café lattes just as my partner came puffing up the stairs with the rest of the soft furnishings, beaming widely.

All three of us sat down at reception. I felt distinctly out of place. Veryanne looked like she had just stepped off the cover of Vogue magazine. My partner was also kitted out in the latest fashions, he looked like he had just opened an account with 'Next.' There was a waft of expensive aftershave, and he had just had his hair cut. In contrast I was dressed in my oldest jeans and jumper. They were clean when I put them on, but I had spent half an hour squatting in a ditch with Victor examining Saxon strata. They were both smiling conspiratorially, I felt like a real gooseberry. Defensively I fixed my partner between the eyes, 'Pardy?' I said.

Veryanne laughed, and her laugh was like soft music, lightening the heart, and brightening the office. 'That's just my little nick-name, I just couldn't get his name right, then I remembered how you always called him your partner. Pardy just seemed so right.' That seemed fair enough, my partner's name was nigh on unpronounceable. Hell I couldn't even spell his name right. I needed to steer things back on task, so I told Veryanne that I had important aspects of the case to discuss with my partner, in the side office. As we turned to go Veryanne leant across and kissed my partner on the cheek. 'Thanks for the beautiful meal last night,' she whispered.

I felt like hitting my partner, and as soon as the door was shut I launched into a tirade of abuse. He sat back passively, it didn't matter what I said, all's fair in love and war, and my partner was definitely winning. Anything I said just sounded like sour grapes. When I had finished ranting my partner, quite calmly asked me how I had got on with Slashface. 'Don't you read the papers?' I replied. 'I was the one that found him.'

'I have read today's paper. Frank Bough had been a right randy bastard, but I don't see what that's got to do with Slashface.' Of course, I wasn't thinking, the papers had printed very few details about the murders. They wouldn't even release Slashface's name for at least a week.

'Look, we're in deep shit. Have you heard of Osiris?'

'Isn't he that Greek millionaire?' I corrected my partner, and told him all about finding Slashface, the ivory phallus and Clay's take on Egyptian mythology. My partner sat stony faced until I had finished, then collapsed into fits of laughter. 'Is that the best you can do? I saw that dildo in your pocket when you first came in. Couldn't pluck up the courage to give it to her eh? Not what we would call a romantic gesture is it? This is all acid talk. Go home and take some vitamin C. Have a lie down. Get over it. You carry on talking like this and you'll end up just like that freak Clay you hang around with or worse...like Braindeath.' He didn't need to say any more. Braindeath was the ultimate acid casualty, some sad nonentity shuffling around Southampton with a battered up old cassette player under his arm, desperately trying to sell it. I decided to cut my losses and go home.

I didn't tell my partner about the diary. After all the crap he'd given me over the ivory phallus I didn't feel like giving out any unnecessary information. I was sitting alone in the front room at home, leafing through it. It was hot stuff, lots of names and addresses, all connected to the drugs trade. The sort of thing the local drugs squad would give their eye teeth for. The correct thing to do would be to take it to the police. Then again I didn't give a sod about morals. Tweedledum and Tweedledee could fuck off. I had plans for the diary, lucrative plans. These plans involved our client. The only reason I could think for anyone being concerned about the deaths of smack dealers was if they were involved in the dirty business themselves. Green was representing some pretty dodgy people, and I was sure they would pay handsomely for Slashface's diary. Before I had left the office I got Veryanne to phone up Green and arrange a meeting.

Chapter 7

Killer Born Man

'Zoom zoom give me room, for I was born in the baby boom.' Screaming
Blue Messiahs

I poured myself a glass of Wild Turkey, and rolled myself a big doobie. In a way my partner had been right. I couldn't let things carry on the way they were. It was all too passive, too much like a victim. I needed to turn things on their head, go out and cause a bit of mayhem. Challenge the buggers on their own turf. Reefer madness, and what better way to go mad than behind the wheel of a car. Not one of the flash cars that I had been reading about, but my own car, a battered seven year old Vauxhall Viva. It did have superb road holding and a top speed of about ninety-five, it would have to do.

Drunk driving is a pretty stupid thing to do at any time, but you're much less likely to get caught if you go out on to the road during rush hour. At this time there are so many useless drivers on the road that the police are not going to go out of their way looking for drunks, unless you do it around Christmas and New Year. Pissed out of my head I was still a better driver than a lot of sober commuters, I was a darn sight crazier too. I took a large toke on the joint and gunned the car up The Avenue heading North.

The road was chock-a-block heading out of town, but there was hardly anything on the other side of the road. It seemed a shame to waste all that beautiful space. I threw the roach out of the window, opened a can of Castlemaine and lurched out. By weaving about over the road I was able to avoid most of the oncoming traffic. I did have one close call though. In order to avoid a blue Ford Escort I had to shoot up onto the pavement. I still smile when I think of the shocked expression of the face of the woman driving. It would give her something interesting to talk to her husband about when he got in from work, instead of the usual rubbish. I gave a cheery wave to the two children in the back as I shot over the roundabout.

I decided to burn through Chandler's Ford, cut through the middle of Hiltingbury, rich bastard's territory, put the shits up them. If anyone needed the icy hand of fear it was those creeps. I threw the empty can of beer out of the window and hit an oncoming Porsche. Transferred anxiety was a wonderful thing, my sense of impending doom had gone. My fate was no longer the plaything of the furies, it was a crazy mixture of swerves and nerve shattering skids. Scaring the shit out of the general public had a soothing effect on the nerves. I ran a red light narrowly missing an old age pensioner. I hadn't felt this good for ages.

When I got to Winchester I decided to stop off at the cinema. *Crocodile Dundee*, was playing. I sat through it three times, and eventually had to be thrown out by one of the ushers. On the way home I was stopped by the police and breathalysed. By then I had sobered up enough to pass. The policeman apologised for taking up my time and wished me a safe journey home. I thanked him, and drove off like I was taking my driving test.

I slept in, it was the best night's sleep I'd had in ages, a brisk walk into work with no blurred edges. Nothing lurking in the shadows. I took lots of deep breaths, eagerly looking forward to what the day had to offer. I got to work about half past ten. Both Veryanne and my partner were sitting on the front desk, and both were done up to the nines. I could understand it, Veryanne always looked wonderful, but for my partner to be groomed up two days in a row was really unusual, it must be serious. 'Where the hell have you been?' he yelled the second I strode into the office. 'I've been trying to get hold of you all morning? We've got to be at Green's in half an hour.' This wasn't anything to get upset about, I had told Veryanne to set up the meeting the day before. This was expected. I glanced over to Veryanne who gave me a sly sideways smile.

Initially I had thought that Veryanne had thrown her lot in with my partner, but this didn't appear to be the case at all. She seemed to be following her own agenda. I had another quick flash of paranoia, not the all-encompassing new life experience paranoia that comes with LSD, but the sharply focused survivalist type that I was familiar with. The more I thought about it the more suspicious I became. Was it just a coincidence Veryanne turning up in answer to a long forgotten advertisement the moment we land our first big case? I wouldn't bother raising my suspicions with my partner, he was a lost cause.

'And you're shitting yourself because you've spent the last two days shopping and mooning about the office. Don't worry, Green's not going to drop us. I know enough to keep him happy.' My partner opened his mouth as if to say something but I gestured for silence. 'It's all right I won't say anything about Egyptian gods and penises.' My partner sat back down, my newfound confidence was taking him off guard. It was all in complete contrast to the day before. Knowing things weren't all cut and dried with Veryanne helped as well. I decided to press home my advantage. 'Half an hour's plenty. Let's have a snifter first. Make it a meeting to remember.' My partner tried to splutter protestations, but I wasn't taking no for an answer. I polished the glasses, and he went to get the calvados.

We arrived at Green's ten minutes late. The receptionist told us as much. We walked in two very different looking figures. My partner was dressed in all the latest fashions, thin tie, white suit, black patent leather shoes and one of those repulsive wide striped shirts that were the height of fashion at the time. I was wearing an old green and yellow striped jumper with a hole in the sleeve and the only pair of clean trousers I could find; a faded pair of flared blue jeans, some ghastly remnant of the sixties given to me as a joke. In keeping with the joke I was wearing odd socks, one red and one orange, and a mauve cravat completed the washed-out sixties look. My old pair of trainers had a hole in them. By way of contrast I was feeling relaxed and at ease, my partner was nervous and jumpy, and his nails were bitten down to the quick.

The receptionist asked us to go through. We sat down in two large comfortable chairs at one end of a large desk. At the other end were two similar chairs. Green was sitting in one; the other contained someone who looked strangely familiar. The office was immense, covered in mahogany panelling, bereft of all other decoration, save a small picture of the Queen, hanging just above Green's head. Green gave a sickly smile as we entered, he looked uncomfortable something wasn't quite right. He gestured to the other figure sitting next to him, 'Gentlemen, may I introduce you to your client, Mr. Moraccan.'

I stared intently at him, he was a huge overpowering figure about six foot two weighing about twenty five stone. He looked slightly Mediterranean in appearance. He was wearing a wide lapelled blue pinstripe suit, with what looked like a solid gold Rolex watch, diamond tie pin, the works. Every aspect of his dress seemed to ooze opulence and wealth. He leant forward and opened a box of 'Romeo Y Julietta,' Havana cigars, and took the equivalent of a Cuban peasant's weekly wages between his bloodless lips. He bit the end off and spat it over his shoulder into the waste paper bin, it was an excellent shot, a skill that must have been nurtured with years of practice. He then pulled what appeared to be a diamond encrusted gold lighter from his pocket, lit the cigar with one deft movement then quickly put the lighter back in his pocket. He took one long drag, then grinning back through the haze of blue smoke said, 'Just call me Block.' He had a heavily accented Italian American voice, for a second I thought Marlon Brando had walked in the room. He sat there confident and in control, Green was sweating nervously, and kept mopping his forehead with a handkerchief. Something was not at all right.

The whole scenario was way too theatrical, 'Block Moraccan,' was a walking stereotype, but a stereotype of a bygone age, a head Mafioso from the 1930s. he didn't pull it off though, you should use a match to light a cigar, not a lighter, that way the taste isn't contaminated by petrol fumes, Ernest Hemingway never used a lighter. The whole thing was an obvious set up. When I looked at him again, I knew where I had seen him before, it was on *The Bill*. This was a jobbing actor Green had hired in order to deceive us. I looked over to my partner but he had been completely sucked in, and was speaking in his most obsequious tone. 'Pleased to meet you Mr. uh Block,' he smiled.

Block Moraccan's tone changed, 'Good, good, now I want to know what you two creeps have come up with and fast' he yelled, spraying spittle into my partner's face. My partner looked shocked, horrified and frightened all at the same time. He looked over for reassurance, but I just gazed back blankly. I was enjoying the recent turn of events, I wanted to see how things panned out.

'Well, um, there was another murder, a couple of days ago. We think they were connected,' stuttered my partner apologetically. Block stood up, towering over my partner, looking down on him like a huge bull elephant surveying a frightened rabbit.

'Of course dey was connected. It don't take no Sherlock Holmes to work dat one out. So do ya know anything useful? Where's da book?' My partner started stuttering again, looking back over for help, but I was staring disconnectedly at the ceiling. I wondered how much Green was paying Block, because he was really getting his money's worth, it was the best impression of Marlon Brando I had ever seen. I couldn't believe how my partner was swallowing it all, he wasn't anywhere near as shrewd as he made out.

'I don't know nothing about no book,' he pleaded.

I decided to put an end to the whole charade. 'Suppose there was a book

I said, containing the names and addresses of all of Slashface's associates. This book could cause all sorts of hardship were it to fall into the wrong hands. Its safe return would be worth something. The question is, how much?' Block was about to say something but Green quickly stepped in.

'I have been authorised to pay £5000 for its safe return.' I handed the book over and Green gave me a cheque. Our business completed we shook hands and went our separate ways. I told Green we would be in contact within the next couple of days.

Later that evening I sat cradling a pint and finishing off a pasty in The Carpenter's turning things over in my mind. When I left my partner he was getting ready to take Veryanne out for yet another meal, Ever since we had left Green's he had been in an intolerably good mood. He was so joyously happy and enthusiastic I didn't have the heart to tell him it was all a load of bollocks. Let him live in his fool's paradise a little longer, it would be interesting to see his face when it all came crashing down.

I was wondering what possible motive Green could have had in staging such an elaborate ploy. Why hadn't he kept the contact just between ourselves? I may have thought that he was representing a smack dealer, but I still couldn't have insisted on a face to face with anyone other than Green. And if he was representing a smack dealer then surely he would know what they look like, and sent someone believable to play the part. Block Moraccan was a weird creature out of cabaret, a hundred clichés sewn together with extreme overacting. So if he didn't represent smack dealers then who? Maybe the pigs? But the pigs would know what smack dealers were like. Block Moraccan was created by someone who didn't have a clue about how smack dealers behaved, but had seen too many 1930s gangster movies. How had he known about the book? I would have to do something about Green, but I didn't know what yet.

I was thinking this all over when Victor came in disrupting my machinations. He scowled, came straight over and sat down. 'Get them in then, I'll have a pint of best. And I'll have a pasty, and when you've done that I'll tell you what you want to know.' I did as he asked, and got myself another pint. One good thing was whatever the twisted reason, business was doing well, and I didn't have to worry about how much things cost. 'There's also the question of my pool table,' he said pouring a load of brown sauce all over his pasty, way too much for my tastes. I told him straight, how we had just received a large cheque and were waiting for it to clear. Fortunately I still had the bankbooks in my pocket and was able to show him the receipt.

I promised him a cheque today or cash in a week, reluctantly he agreed to wait. I had to wait too, until he had finished his pasty and I had bought him a second pint.

Victor could tell I was on tenterhooks, and deliberately took his time telling me, lots of unnecessary pauses and blind alleys, but eventually he gave me a ball park figure. The phallus was somewhere between one and two thousand years old. That was a relief, at the very most it could have dated from the Roman Empire, around about the time of Christ. The Romans and Greeks recorded everything, no mention of Osiris as anything other than a myth. Victor told me that a more specific dating would take a lot longer, and that it most probably dated from sometime during the Dark Ages.

He had to admit that I did have something though, it wasn't just an old dildo from Anne Summers, it was something else entirely. I didn't like the sound of that. It would have been so much more reassuring had he been right. This was still unresolved, alright it wasn't Osiris's cock, but wasn't the Dark Ages supposed to be a time of witchcraft, Morgan Le Fay et al? I stayed until closing time, managed to persuade Victor to get another round in before we switched to ouzo. I went home rat-arsed, and had another night of disturbing dreams.

Chapter 8

What Do I Get?

'I mean to stress, I need a caress. What do I get?'
The Buzzcocks

I was having a brilliant dream. It was the middle of the afternoon and I was having my mid-afternoon siesta. A couple of hours kip after work helped set me up for the night ahead, it also helped throw off some of the lunchtime's excesses. Things were really starting to hot up. Veryanne had agreed to leave Eyeore, The Pink Panther and President Nixon, and come up to my bedroom. The minute we entered the room she slipped off her dress and got onto the bed. She licked her lips and leant forward to kiss me, then some git started up a steam hammer. The walls started collapsing. I desperately tried to grab hold of Veryanne, but she had already started to fade, leaving me with a throbbing erection, and the steam hammer. 'BANG, BANG, BANG. I opened my eyes and stared at the ceiling, I knew I had lost the struggle. The bastard with the steam hammer was still tormenting me though. 'BANG, BANG, BANG.'

'Wake up, Wake up, Wake up Zippy, it's beer time.' Someone was hammering at the front door and screaming through the letter box. Whoever it was, it wasn't Wee Willie Winkie and that was for sure. I staggered out of bed and threw on my dressing gown. As I approached the front door the banging became louder and more desperate. I pulled the front door open and was faced with an enormous figure clad from head to toe in motorcycle leathers, with a case of beer under his arm. He thrust the case into my arms then brushed past me into the house. I was still half asleep; I took the beer without protest and dumbly followed him into the house. He walked into the centre of the lounge and pulled his helmet off, leaving me face to face with Dodge. He was grinning widely, and seemed to have grown since our last meeting. He ran forward and gave me a huge hug, knocking the wind out of me, and causing me to drop the beer on my foot.

'Having a hand job were you?' I looked down to see the erection peeking through the flaps in my dressing gown. It was just as well it was

Dodge; I could have easily exposed myself to Jehovah's witnesses. Then again so what, sexually harass the Godsquad on your own doorstep, it should stop them pestering decent law abiding heathens like myself. Before I could reply Dodge cracked open a can of beer. 'It'll be alright if I crash here for a bit? I need to keep a low profile. It won't be long, I'm off to Weston-Super-Mare to become a whelk fisherman in a few days' time.' He said the phrase 'whelk fisherman' with a solemnity that meant it had to be treated seriously, almost with reverence.

It was all too much for me to take in, I went back to my bedroom to get changed, leaving Dodge in the lounge. I pondered his arrival as I got changed. All thoughts of a quiet couple of days and nights had gone out of the window. Dodge had a reputation for hard drinking, and his travelling accessories showed today would not be any different from usual. I was a bit confused about why he needed to stay with me, and all that stuff about whelk fishermen. I went into the bathroom, mixed a glass of Andrews and brushed my teeth. Then I went back into the lounge to see what Dodge's plans were.

When I got back Dodge was sitting in the armchair, (my armchair,) watching the news. There had been another kidnapping in Beirut, already there were two empty cans lying on the floor. Without looking up he said, 'It's really good of you putting me up like this, I've got to keep a low profile, be careful who I associate with. I'm giving The Madhouse a wide berth.' I was intrigued, Dodge was usually all mouth and trousers, I didn't think he knew the meaning of low profile. Something had spooked him.
'What's wrong with The Madhouse?' I inquired.
'The place is crawling with pigs. Everyone's either getting busted or threatened with God knows what. Those that can are getting out. There's only the hard core left, those that can't get served anywhere else. Everything's turned to shit since the murders.'
'What murders?'
'You mean you haven't heard. Two smack dealers have been chopped up and some maniac's shot up one of the convoy's parties. Everything has suddenly turned very nasty. You did the right thing getting a gun. I'm thinking of getting one too. I've had to stop everything. Not that I ever did that much anyway. I'm just a little guy; I sell the odd bit of dope here, a tiny bit of bent gear there. I do it mainly to help people out. I don't make a lot myself. People can afford the things they need, and they don't have to deal with anyone heavy when they want a smoke.'

I had never realised what a saint Dodge was before. He put his empty can down and opened a fourth. I quickly got one myself. Dodge's generous gift of a case of beer was becoming less generous by the second. 'No, I'm going to be off in a few days' time. Been in contact with an old mate from the Mersey ferries. You know…' He launched into a brief crack throated rendition of *Ferry Across The Mersey*, then continued, 'He's a share fisherman now. They go out three days on, three days off, dredging up whelks. Everyone shares what they catch. I'm going to do some of that.' He stopped and stared me in the eye, 'Not everyone can handle it though.' Then he stared off into space wistfully, becoming more animated as he remembered something. 'Talking of dope have you got any? It's just in the panic to get away, I left my stash with Taffy the pillhead, and I haven't a clue when I'll be getting that back.' I passed Dodge the stashbox, and he proceeded to roll himself a spliff. He took a deep toke and sighed. 'This is really good shit. Where the fuck did you get this?'

'It's that last lot I got off you.' Dodge was puffing away, the spliff was almost half way through. 'Hey Humph! Go easy on that, there's not a lot left. That's got to last all night.' Dodge looked surprised, he passed the spliff over along with the stashbox.

'Look,' he drawled, 'If I had sold anything like that I would have known about it. You've got a really big lump, it'll last for ages.'

I looked in the box, he was right. There was a huge lump of resin I had never seen before. I picked it up and examined it closely. It was a pale golden brown, and very moist, very fresh. I gave it a sniff, it smelled really strong. When I took a toke it nearly blew my head off. I was up high for a moment before feeling a bit paranoid. How had the dope got there? Maybe I had picked it up at the party when I was tripped out. All sorts of bits and pieces were coming back in nerve shattering flashes. I wasn't going to be clear of that evening for some time.

I had been staring into space for some time before I became aware of Dodge pacing up and down in the room, looking out of the window. 'How long you been living around here?' he puffed. 'How well do you know your neighbours? There's a lot of really freaky looking bastards out there.'

'That's normal.' I answered, 'Everything's fine.'

'You have still got the gun haven't you? You weren't just buying it for somebody else?' I had been looking forward to an opportunity to talk about the gun, particularly about the modifications I had made, so I told him all about it. 'Jesus Christ. Do you know what you're doing? Sooner you than me,' he replied despondently. I asked him what he meant. 'Let me get this right. You drilled into the bullets whilst you were still strung out by the acid, and you expect them to work the way you want them to. Take my advice, throw them away. Only use the ones you've not modified. Otherwise you're more likely to blow your hand off.'

I wasn't having that, admittedly I was quite disturbed when I carried out the modifications, but I was certain I had done a good job. I wanted to show him. I went over to the chest of drawers and took the pistol out. I pointed it at Sue Lawley's flickering image. Let her have it, the cow. There was a tremendous explosion with a tiny splash as the mercury blasted out. Parts of burning television flew all over the room which filled with acrid smoke. The kick was no way near as bad as had been the last time at the party. I put the gun away and stamped out the smouldering wreckage.

'BANG, BANG, BANG.' Again there was another lot of loud knocking on the door. It was real déjà vu time, maybe I was just fated to have noisy visitors that day. I opened the door to come face to face with the landlord. A squint-eyed vicious old bastard who came breathing down your neck if you were a second behind with the rent. 'What the hell is going on in here?' he yelled, 'I thought the bloody world was coming to an end.' His face was deep red, he was really angry. I decided that attack was probably the best form of defence, so I screamed back at him.

'You want to get your wiring checked out. You nearly killed my mate.' Dodge, quick to react to the situation, started rolling his eyes and groaning. This stopped the old git right in his tracks. I decided to press home the advantage. 'You want to pray he doesn't take you to court. There's been a lot in the press recently about negligent landlords.' At this his manner changed completely, he became a pitiful pleading wreck, promising to replace the telly and get the wiring checked out. Before he left us I thought he was going to burst into tears.

Dodge decided to accompany me to The Carpenter's that evening. We got there early, and as Dodge was staying with me, and smoking my dope, I sent him to get the pasties in, and the first round. I saw him chatting away to someone unfamiliar. As soon as the landlord had heard what was happening at the Madhouse he decided to become more vigilant, ensure none of the wrong crowd made it into his pub. He hadn't been doing a very good job though. There were lots of Madhouse denizens in there that night. It was like Dodge had said, almost everyone had gone, there was only the hard core left. A beaming Dodge came over with the provisions. 'We've been invited to a party.' I didn't like the sound of that. All I could think about was the last party I went to. I couldn't handle anything like that again for a long time. Dodge tried reassuring me. 'Look it'll be really nice and relaxed. It's just some students from the University. There's a load of them share a big house down Cranbury. One of the girls is celebrating her 21st birthday. That bloke I was talking to he's one of them. I do a little bit of business with him. It's going to be a nice quiet do, invitation only.'

We stayed in the pub until closing time, then we went back to the flat for a smoke. That way it would be easier to back out of going anywhere else, once I was already home. Once I had had a couple of smokes I felt invigorated. Dodge was feeling it too. We set off to the party like men on a mission. Dodge had been right about the party, it was a nice quiet party in a clean, tidy student house. It wasn't a poor student house either, and about ten times better than the rathole I had squatted in when I was a student.

I wasn't prepared for how old I would feel. Everyone looked so young. I was only twenty-four but I felt centuries older than these bright young undergraduates. Dodge and I were easily the oldest there. That was until we walked into the lounge and came face to face with Bazzer. He was easily ten years older than us if not twenty. I couldn't believe how he had managed to gain admission. 'Not everybody wants to be reminded where they know you from. Not in front of their girlfriends at least,' he said by way of explanation.

I sat back, opened a can of beer and allowed myself to relax. I needed to take some time out, get away from myself. I had allowed the case to take over my life, and I needed to kick my heels and forget about things for a while. It was a nice house. There were three rooms downstairs, the upstairs was out of bounds except for access to the lavatory, and a queue had already started to form. There weren't a lot of others in the lounge. A couple snogging in the corner and a few brave souls dancing to a Madonna record. There was a political argument going on in the kitchen, and a smoke going on in the other smaller reception room. That's where the three of us headed.

Everyone was talking a load of bollocks, pure student drivel. I could tell by the way they spoke to us, that they thought they were smarter than us. They particularly seemed to look down their noses at Bazzer. I almost felt sorry for him, but he cheerfully continued, telling one filthy anecdote after another, oblivious of their snootiness. I couldn't let it go on, something had to be done, challenge them on their own ground. There was a group of English students who insisted on going on at great length about Keats. I only knew one thing about Keats, the sort of snippet of information you get told at the height of some bizarre drinking ritual. 'Keats was a total wanker. 'Ode to a Grecian Urn' is a Nineteenth Century wank mag. Bazzer's no different.' I suddenly blurted out. The whole room went silent, no-one knew how to respond. So I moved on to safe ground, Raymond Chandler. Or more correctly, how the spirit of Raymond Chandler was being kept alive in myself. None of them had heard of Chandler, which was good in so far as it allowed me to act all superior, but bad in that they didn't even know who Humphrey Bogart was, let alone Phillip Marlowe. One of them asked me what sort of detective I thought I was. I took a deep breath, ready to go over the whole genre when Dodge chipped in with 'Frank Cannon.' At this my momentary cool was blown as everyone dissolved into laughter.

The atmosphere became a lot more relaxed, all the barriers were broken down. I found myself talking to one of the girls. She was about nineteen, five foot six and very chubby. Dark hair, blue eyes with thick glasses. Her face was still spotty but not as plump as I would have expected. She had a tiny moustache, and was wearing way too much makeup. She was wearing a red T-shirt about two sizes too small which made her tits look enormous. She had a beaten up old pair of pumps and a pair of old jeans with a tear in the knee. Bazzer chuckled in my ear, 'I reckon you're in there, you should be shagging that no bother.' I told Bazzer that she wasn't exactly the girl of my dreams. 'Don't worry about that,' leered Bazzer, 'A shag's a shag. Take it home, do it, then get shot of it in the morning.'

This wasn't very politically correct advice, but what was I to expect from the proprietor of the local dirty book shop. I decided to take his advice though. What he was saying was true. I hadn't had sex for a very long time. I couldn't afford to pick and choose, I didn't know how long I would have to wait for an opportunity like this to come round again. Recently I had spent too much time thinking about sex when I should be working. Having a secretary like Veryanne didn't help matters. Dodge had an expression for it, called it, 'getting rid of your dirty waters.' I slid over to her and moved in close. In a few minutes we were kissing, and she had agreed to go home with me. As we left Dodge gave me the thumbs up, and Bazzer made an obscene gesture.

The second we walked through the front door she stuck her tongue down my throat, knocking me off guard and reminding me of the onion bahjis she was eating. I wasn't quite ready for all this just yet, I pushed her away from me. Muttering something about making a cup of tea and rolling a spliff, I set off towards the kitchen.

Five minutes later we were sitting down on the sofa together, drinking Earl Grey and smoking. Feeling the acrid smoke filling my lungs, I began to feel a minor re-kindling of desire. A little voice told me to stay strong, to hang on in there, there was no going back now. I passed her the spliff, she took a quick couple of tokes then put it out. She stuck her tongue in my mouth again. I stuck my hand up the back of her T-shirt and started to undo her bra. With one simple movement I slipped off both her bra and T-shirt.

One of her nipples was half an inch bigger than the other, with a long brown hair growing out of it. I tried ignoring it, and concentrated on the other one. She began breathing heavily and started pulling my shirt up whilst chewing passionately on my lower lip. I got another reminder of onion bahjis, but decided to press on regardless, undoing the zip on her jeans. Very soon we were lying naked on the bed together. She was looking disappointed I was as flat as a pancake. She kissed me again, and put my hand between her legs. It was like a pound of raw liver, despite her youth she'd obviously been round the block a couple of times.

I needed to move things on and quickly. I closed my eyes and tried to move away from the immediate situation, try to think of as many erotic thoughts as possible. I took a durex from the side of the bed and asked her to put it on for me. I closed my eyes imagining Veryanne, then I was stiff enough. I climbed on top of her and started pumping away as if my life depended on it. I was thinking about something Bazzer had said, about having sex with fat girls. 'It's easy,' he said, 'Just give them one thrust and you can ride the waves all the way there.' It wasn't true, it was bloody hard work, my back was feeling sore, and I was in danger of going soft again. I pushed my face in the pillow and started fantasising once more. I got my second wind, and started pumping faster and faster, while she started moaning loudly, and making noises like a small dog. With an overpowering sense of relief I ejaculated. I rolled back and closed my eyes. I pulled the condom off, threw it on the floor then sank into welcome oblivion.

Chapter 9

Trouble

'You bitch, you bitch you're trying to put me down, and there's another piece of Aztec gold ripped out of my toothless mouth.'
Flik Spatula

I was drowning in a pool of stagnant water, sinking deeper and deeper. I opened my mouth to scream but nothing came out. Then it hit me, a savage pain in the guts, and the bitter realisation that I was going to puke. I sat up, bolt upright, I had about fifteen seconds before I was going to vomit. I threw myself at the door, and was out onto the landing when the first spasm hit me. As I opened the bathroom door my mouth started filling up with the foul acidic wastes of the night before. I just managed to lift up the toilet seat in time as the first torrent of puke went cascading out of my mouth. I sank down over the pan, my whole body convulsed with spasmodic heaving. One was so violent that it set something off downstairs. If I didn't act soon I was going to shit myself. I dragged myself to my feet arching a long orange streak of vomit into the bath, and got my arse on to the seat as hot shit erupted from my anus. For the next five minutes I sat with my head between my knees, alternately crapping and puking.

When it was all over I surveyed the damage. It wasn't too bad, the only real spillage occurred when I leant over to puke up in the bath. I wiped my backside, flushed the toilet and ran the bath taps. I then got on my hands and knees and started wiping up with toilet tissue. I only paused once to have a second, less violent bout of vomiting. I needed to put an end to this. I got up and made my way to the kitchen. The stink coming from the bedroom was appalling, and for once it wasn't all mine. I could hear noises coming from there, but I wasn't ready to deal with the fallout of the previous night's fornications. I continued on my way to the kitchen, put the kettle on, then put a couple of alka-seltzer in a glass and ran it under the tap.

As I watched the tablets dissolve I thought about the previous night's nightmarish revellings. The noises from the bedroom were getting louder so I thought I had better make two cups of tea. As I was pouring the water over the teabags I heard footsteps. I began to brace myself for what would undoubtedly be a rather unpleasant scene. As the footsteps drew level with the kitchen they suddenly burst into a run, followed by the front door slamming shut. I could hear her running away down the street.

The initial sense of relief soon turned into a sense of feeling aggrieved. I had been prepared to deal with the repercussions of bedding what Bazzer had described as a 'right dog.' Yet this same 'dog' had legged it rather than be reminded of the fact that she had slept with me. If that was the way she reacted then what possible chance had I got with Veryanne? Sex was supposed to be a beautiful joining together of two souls, but this was a totally soulless experience, more akin to throwing a brick down Deptford High Street on a rainy day than anything else. I knocked back the alka-seltzer, and then took a cup of tea to the bathroom with me. I ran myself a bath as I took my second shit of the day. I was really loose, if I didn't get hold of some arret soon I wouldn't be able to sit down.

The water had gone cold when I woke up shivering. I got out and towelled myself down, but I needed the toilet again before I could get to some heat. There was only one dry towel left, and I tried to warm myself up by rubbing vigorously. Memory is a cruel thing, well it is with me. At first nothing, just a general sense of unease, then instead of coming back gradually, in parts that are easy to digest, the whole lot comes flooding back in one go. I got dressed quickly in front of the fire, putting on what was at hand. The way I was feeling, I could have been decked out in an expensive Saville Row suit with matching silk shirt, and still looked like a sack of shit.

I stopped off at the chemists on the way to work, got some arret, some more alka-seltzer and a couple of cans of fizzy orange with added vitamin C; it never hurts to put a little something back in. There was nobody in at the office. I took my medicine, and tore open one of the cans. There was an old copy of The Beano in one of the drawers. I sat back contemplating Dennis The Menace, envying him his simple existence and wishing I had a dog like Gnasher. I alternately sipped fizzy orange and alka seltzer and let out a loud belch. I was starting to feel human again, I only needed another cup of tea and I would be there.

When the phone rang I nearly jumped out of my skin. It was my partner hideously cheerful. He told me that Veryanne wouldn't be in because he had given her the day off. When I asked him when he had decided to do that, he told me he had said it over breakfast. As a passing bon mot he told me he was off to talk to an Egyptologist at the university. I couldn't believe it. That was the icing on the cake, the shortarsed little git. I felt hollow, like a blighted potato, all shrunken inside. What really pissed me off was that after initially putting my Egyptian revelations down to LSD psychosis, now he was taking them seriously.

I spent the rest of the morning going through the books, trying to take my mind off what was happening. At one o'clock I set off to The Carpenter's for my lunchtime pasty. It was a beautiful day, but an inky black mist swam around my feet, and I wished it would suck me up. Some vast impenetrable dark lay ahead of me; from now on things would only get worse. I had been dealt a bum hand, and could only wait to see how things panned out.

Dodge and Bazzer were both sitting at the bar, and from the state of things they must have been there since it opened. They shouted something incoherently as I walked in. I bought myself a pint and went over to join them. They wanted the all sordid details of the sorry affair. When they found out that she had run off, they both collapsed into hysterics, 'You must be the worst shag in the world,' sneered Bazzer. 'If you're really that bad I could probably get you a job making specialist videos for the truly sick.' Bad as things were I didn't think that I had sunk so low that I was prepared to fornicate with animals, just to make Bazzer and his associates rich.

Dodge was far more sympathetic, he slammed his fist on the bar, screaming to the landlord, 'Give this man a fucking drink. Such bravery must not go unrecognised.' A couple of tequilas later things didn't seem quite so bad. I allowed myself to be seduced by Bazzer and Dodge's anecdotes. I had heard most of Bazzer's, but Dodge's tales of rum, sodomy and the lash on the Mersey ferries made my hair stand on end. One good thing was that I knew my partner would never take Veryanne into a boozer like The Carpenter's. Despite his obvious desire to show her off, even he knew she was way too classy for a joint like that. It was just as well because I knew I couldn't bear to see them together the way I was feeling. Bazzer's stories got bawdier, Dodge's laugh became filthier, and I got totally pissed. When we were thrown out I decided to give myself the rest of the day off, I staggered home and went back to bed.

I called at Victor's about seven. I was fresh out of leads, my partner was out glory seeking with a bona fide Egyptologist. All I had were Clay's insane rantings. So I decided to follow up on the only piece of hard evidence we had; the phallus. I realised Victor hadn't had much time, and I was probably grasping at straws, but I desperately needed something. I couldn't believe how quickly the power struggle between my partner and me had flip-flopped. It was just the other day that I had seen him humiliated in front of Block Moraccan, and now he was back on top again. I had to admit, the creepy little shit was resilient if nothing else.

When I rang the doorbell there was no reply, I tried the door, and it was unlocked. Something was wrong, Victor was fastidious about security, it was one of his idiosyncratic ways, of which there were many. I reached into my pocket for the Browning, but I'd left it back at the flat. I didn't have time to go back, I gingerly crept inside, hugging the walls and making a fist. I had got about half way down the hall when there was a terrific crash, and Victor came lurching out of the kitchen. He was groaning, and clutching his side, where a dark red stain was getting bigger and bigger. He stretched his other hand out to me imploringly, gasped and fell flat on his face. Standing behind him, one hand clutching the phallus, the other clutching a bloody kitchen knife stood The Cheat.

This wasn't The Cheat I'd intimidated a few days previously. This was a totally different character. No longer cowering, he stood tall, proud, malevolent and dangerous. His expression was utterly demonic, and his eyes looked feral like a jackal's. A thin trickle of cold sweat tingled down the back of my spine. I wanted to turn tail and run, but if I did that he would stab me in the back before I could reach the door. He suddenly lunged at me with the knife, I swerved to avoid it, smashing myself back against the wall. A tremendous rage suddenly possessed me, the fear vanished, and I wanted to kill. A foul acrid taste filled my mouth and I spat into The Cheat's face. Catching him off guard I smashed him hard on the nose. He staggered back, dropping the phallus, but maintaining his grip upon the knife, a look of extreme astonishment on his face. He lifted the knife high above his head and charged at me. I moved to one side and I hit him hard on the temple. He went down. I kicked him hard in the stomach, and kept kicking until long after he had stopped moving. I pulled the knife from between his fingers, even unconscious he kept an icy grip, and went over to Victor.

There was a lot of blood, but Victor was still breathing. I ran into the kitchen, grabbed some tea towels and tied them over the wound. He let out a long groan, 'I wish I'd never met you, you bastard.' He was in a really bad way, he must have been delirious talking like that. I told him to 'hang in there,' then went into the lounge and dialled 999.

'That's a pile of shit and you know it. Now why don't you tell us what really happened.' I was staring into the bleak, unforgiving countenance of Tweedledum. He pulled back his arm, slapped me in the face, and I fell onto the floor. We were three hours into the interrogation, and were going around in circles. I had been given a real good kicking, by Tweedledum and his band of merry woodentops. Not that you would know it to look at me. A few weeks ago I had read an article in a magazine from one of the Sunday papers. It was about G. Gordon Liddy, the fall guy in the Watergate scandal. He was running a training camp, teaching surveillance, counter intelligence, and interrogation. One of the lessons taught you how to have a pregnant woman writhing in agony without leaving any visible marks, or harming the foetus in any way. It was a valuable skill to have, the minute I read it I made myself a promise. As soon as the company could afford it, I would treat myself to that course. I had never been on it, but I would lay odds of ten to one that Tweedledum had.

As I was getting myself to my feet, the cell door opened, and in walked Tweedledee, carrying two cups of tea. Tweedledum left the room. 'Sorry we've not got any Earl Grey, I'm quite partial to a spot of that myself, but I've made it nice and strong without any sugar.' I gratefully took the cup, thankful that I was spared the attentions of Tweedledum for the time being. 'You still a bit pissed are you? You had a right skinful this afternoon by all accounts. I've just got back from The Carpenter's, you're quite well known there. I understand you were on the tequila slammers. They can do terrible things to a man's sense of reality.' He paused and took a deep breath before continuing. 'Here's what really happened. 'You went home and continued drinking, and the more you drank the angrier you became. You went to Victor's to settle a few scores. Throwing up over his pool table…yes we know about that, just wasn't enough. So you went round there, stabbed him, then beat the shit out of some poor passing junky who was unlucky enough to be a witness.'

I went through the events one more time, but it was clear he didn't believe me. The major flaw in my story was The Cheat. He was well known to the police, and they knew him for the snivelling little coward he was. My description of him was laughable, completely unrecognisable from what they knew. I pleaded with them to talk to Victor, he would vouch for me, after all I had saved his life. Unfortunately Victor was undergoing surgery, and wouldn't be able to vouch for anyone for some time. I then told him to go back to The Carpenter's and talk to the landlord. He had seen me drunk loads of times, and knew I wasn't violent. This seemed to do more harm than good, admitting to my excessive alcohol consumption. Eventually I had to stonewall, I refused to say another word until I made my phone call. To my surprise they agreed. I didn't know who to call, of my 'friends,' Bazzer and Dodge would be too pissed by now to be of any use. Clay would have been even worse, and wasn't on the phone in any event. My partner would relish having me out of the way. Left with no other choice I phoned Green.

Chapter 10

Wolfpack

'Howling the pack in formation attack, in formation.'
Syd Barrett

At the stroke of midnight, Green burst into the room, arms laden with legal stationary. Tweedledum following meekly behind. 'I insist on being alone with my client,' barked Green, 'Leave us alone!' Compliantly Tweedledum turned away and closed the door behind him. I told Green everything, about saving Victor, fighting The Cheat, and about Tweedledum's overzealous interviewing techniques. I kept quiet about my reason for seeing Victor, he didn't need to know about the phallus just yet. He told me not to say another word to anyone until he got back.

Ten minutes later I was outside breathing in the cool, fresh, free air. I don't know what Green said to them, but it certainly did the trick. Green drove me to his office, saying there were other things he wanted to discuss with me. Things that needed to be said somewhere private, somewhere secure. That suited me, because there were things I wanted to discuss with Green, particularly the Block Moraccan episode.

Green's office seemed different after dark. The mahogany panelling was grander, more gothic. With the wind storming and blowing we could have been in some castle in Transylvania, not a rather pedestrian solicitor's office in the heart of the city. Green walked over to a drinks cabinet, and came back with a bottle of absinthe and two glasses. 'I'm going to start off by talking about your case,' he said pouring two glasses. 'The prosecution alleges you went round wanting to settle a few scores. Things got heated, you stabbed your friend and then beat up a witness. You then showed remorse for your actions and dialled 999. The knife has your fingerprints on it. The only people who can back up your version of events are both in intensive care. Both could die of the injuries inflicted.' He finished his glass and poured himself another. In your favour you did dial 999. Of the two Victor seems to be in a better condition. If what you say is right, he should be able to verify your story in a couple of days.'

I finished my glass and poured myself another. Green seemed deep in thought. He was staring at the ceiling as if trying to find the right words. 'But we both know you didn't come back here just to talk about your case.' At long last, an opportunity to get into the case, find out what was going on, because I didn't know. It was like one of those pictures you look at that have two images, the vase and the two faces, the rabbit and the duck. At first it looked simple, gangland killing, turf war for the smack trade. That's what the police thought it was, and my partner thought so too. The Block Moraccan encounter tried to re-enforce that view. On the other hand there was all the stuff about Egyptian gods that turned out not to be Egyptian gods, but something else. I had seen The Cheat, and nothing I knew could have transformed him like that. Even tanked up on angel dust he couldn't have appeared so imposing. Yet if it wasn't the case, then why did Green want the book? That book would only be useful to a dealer or a pig, or at a long shot a journalist. A journalist wouldn't pay £5000 for it though. I decided to break the ice, play my weakest card first. I told him how I had seen through Block Moraccan.

'I thought you would,' he sighed. 'Still, it wasn't really meant to fool you. As long as your partner believed it that's the main thing. Anyway, you really should be grateful to him, he's taken the bait, the bait that was intended for you.' I asked him what he meant. 'That pretty young secretary of yours. You don't think a girl like that would really want to work for a couple of cowboys like you two do you?' I almost choked on the absinthe. I had the same sinking feeling in my stomach that happened when my partner phoned me that morning, and I felt my face burning. I wanted to thump Green. I asked him straight if she was a plant working for him all along, secretly reporting back to him.

He looked troubled, and poured himself another glass. 'No she's not working for me. To tell you the truth I'm not exactly sure who she works for. Only that it's not the same bunch I work for.' He took another sip of absinthe. When he continued his voice was deeper and more resonant. 'Not who *you* work for.' He poured us both another glass. 'Ten years ago I was offered a large sum of money to lobby against cryogenics, you know, freezing dead bodies so they can be woken up in the future when the technology exists to cure them. So lobby I did, quite successfully, but you can only lobby so far. You can stop public money going towards it, but you can't stop private individuals investing in it. Evil old rich men who fear the day of judgement, and try to use their vast wealth to buy immortality. All this time, I never met my clients, we spoke by phone, and the only address I had was a post box in Switzerland. This was all to change.' Green was trembling slightly he finished another glass, looked furtively around as if we were being spied on, then leaned forward and continued in whispers.

'It was a night quite like this one. I had been working late on a case when one of them just stepped out of woodwork. I swear I never saw him come in. One minute nothing, the next second he was there. There was a knife at my throat, and I was paralysed with fear. He told me to remember that they could do that at any time. Then their demands became more insistent. They wanted me to do all I could to stop research. Object to all planning permission, exhaust every legal avenue to thwart the spectre of cryogenics.' He took another gulp and mopped his forehead. 'Not everything I did was legal. I paid people to cause damage, and the funny thing was, it started to become something more than a job. It wasn't long before I hated cryogenics just as much as they did. Even now, just thinking about it makes me want to lash out.'

This was all very interesting but it wasn't really answering the questions I wanted answering. I didn't give a shit about cryogenics and I told him as much. 'You will,' he replied. 'You'll end up hating them as much as me, or even more. The people I work for are incredibly secret. They take secrecy to a whole different level. I tried to find out about them, but there's nothing, no paper trail, nothing. They move like shadows in the night. All I know about them is what they let me know. They want you, and there's nothing you can do about it. Soon you'll be just like me.' I asked him what he meant, I'd not made any Faustian pledge, I had just taken on a client. It was a purely business arrangement. 'It doesn't work like that, they don't offer deals, they pressgang you. You're already aboard ship, you don't know it yet. I can see it in your eyes. Felt any sudden unexpected rages recently? Seen the red mist? That's them.'

I told him all about the phallus and about how I exploded with an unknown fury when I fought The Cheat. He looked concerned, asked me to describe The Cheat's transformation. When I had finished he looked pale and withdrawn, even more deeply troubled than before. It was a long time before he started talking again. 'As your lawyer I would advise you to stay in town, and fulfil your conditions of bail to the letter, but as your friend I advise you to get the hell out of town quickly. It's not safe here, you need to go to somewhere secure. Don't ask me any questions, because I can't tell you anymore. The people I work for are concerned for your safety. There's something dark out there, it knows about you now, and it wants to kill you. It's already tried once, the next time will be harder. You have to go. I can't tell you where, follow your instincts. They won't let you down. I can't tell you any more, you'll have to find the rest out for yourself.' With that he went over to the coat rack and handed me my coat.

I decided to stop off at the General Hospital, to see how Victor and The Cheat were doing. I got there at about four in the morning. After wandering aimlessly around a maze of corridors, a very nice security guard took me to the intensive care unit. I told him he was in the wrong job, he would have been better off working in something like customer relations. Joy of joys, Victor had regained consciousness. He was only allowed visits from members of the family, so I told them I was his brother. This should be good, I had taken a lot of shit off Victor recently, and now he would have to take it all back. I had saved his life, I was a hero for Christ's sake.

'I wondered when you'd turn up you fucking bastard.' Victor was back to his old pugnacious self, sitting up in bed swearing, and blaming the rest of the world for his problems. Even so, this was not the reaction I was expecting. Perhaps he was a bit delirious, maybe it was the drugs he was on. 'I nearly got killed because of you, you ugly shit. Why didn't you tell me how heavy this shit was?' I was bloody sick of Victor's selective memory. It wasn't the first time he'd conveniently forgotten stuff. I grabbed him by the throat and hissed in his ear.

'If I hadn't turned up when I did, you'd be lying in the mortuary right now. You knew what you were getting into at the time. You chose to treat it as bullshit. Well the bullshit ain't so funny now.' I put my face up close to his. 'Look, I'm facing a murder rap because of you. You just make sure you tell the pigs what happened or I'll cut you into thirteen pieces.'

Suddenly a hand came down heavily on my right shoulder. I turned round to come face to face with a huge muscular staff nurse. 'What the hell are you doing to my patient?' he snarled. I tried to explain, let him know that Victor and I were old friends, just larking about. I asked Victor to back me up, but Victor was pretending to be unconscious. The staff nurse grabbed my neck and held me in a head lock. I tried to struggle free but he was far too strong. 'Like to pick on sick men do you? Try me for size.' He frogmarched me out of the ward, all the way through the hospital towards the main entrance. I was aware of people pointing and giggling; it felt like a fucking freak show. I tried to reach him with my left arm, but he pushed my right arm up high and shouted in my ear. 'Listen fat boy, and listen good.

This is my ward. I'm in charge here. If I see you in here again I'll tear your balls off.'

With that he threw me out of the front door. I felt like a character from a Warner Brother's cartoon as I was catapulted out of the door and into the taxi rank. I landed heavily on my coccyx. I yelped involuntarily as the sharp pain shot up my spine. I rolled onto my side panting heavily as the sharp pain slowly turned into a dull ache. I suddenly became aware of laughter. I looked up, it was as if the whole of the hospital, doctors, nurses, porters, miscellaneous health care workers and patients were staring out of the windows. Most were laughing, some were jeering and making the wanker sign. The staff nurse stood in the doorway, arms folded, looking very pleased with himself. I tried to stand up, but my legs had turned to jelly. I crawled away to the car park, hiding behind a wall. I wished that I had let The Cheat kill Victor. I had learnt my lesson. It was the last time I would save anyone's life. It just leads to public humiliation.

I stayed there shaking for about five minutes before my old friend the security guard came along. He helped me to my feet and walked with me until we were off the hospital grounds. We sat on a wall and shared a spliff. He told me what a bastard he thought the staff nurse was. I told him the only reason he had beaten me was because he had got the drop on me, next time would be different. My friend had some useful information too, about The Cheat. It turned out he was in a really bad way, fractured skull, broken ribs, and a broken arm. He was in a coma, his chances were bleak, they couldn't see him lasting through the night. Things weren't too bad then, that little shit had had it coming for a long time, I would be pleased to see the back of him. Victor may be an argumentative git, but even he wouldn't let me go down for attempted murder. I thanked my new found friend, and staggered off home.

I slept badly. I could hear the dawn chorus when I finally settled down in bed. I ached all over, I'd never known such a violent night. All I had were paracetamol, but I needed morphine. I drifted in and out of consciousness and woke with the stench of liquid shit in my throat. I lurched into the bathroom and puked up a load of blood. I wiped myself with tissue and staggered into the lounge. Dodge was asleep on the sofa. 'Where's my fucking gun? The bastards have got it in for me.' Dodge awoke with a start wild eyed and frightened. I'd obviously disturbed some paranoid dream. 'Where's my fucking gun? The bastards are coming through the windows. Dodge jumped up muttering 'Shit, shit.' It made me feel good to see him like that. I wasn't the only twisted, confused git around.

I retrieved my gun and slipped it in my dressing gown pocket. Green's little speech had really hit home. From now on I wasn't going anywhere without it. I went into the kitchen and put the kettle on. When I got back Dodge was sitting up fully dressed rubbing his eyes. 'Jesus,' he said. 'What happened to you?' I told him all about the previous night's battles, but left out the conversation with Green. At the end of it all he started laughing. 'That's bloody typical that is. I'm supposed to be lying low and you get involved in two punch-ups in one evening. I thought you were the quiet type. Still if what you say is true you should be alright. Looks like your mate will vouch for you. You never know, you might even get a medal.'

I couldn't see that happening. I told him to get packed, he was going to go to Weston-Super mare a little bit earlier than planned, and I was going with him. I just had to go into work first. Dodge agreed that getting out of town was a good move. If things went well with the police then there was no harm done. If however Victor decided to stitch me up because he still bore a grudge about his pool table, then I would be away. Join the whelk fishermen and skip off away to sea. He didn't see why it had to be so soon. I didn't want to sound like Clay, so I wasn't able to protest too much when he suggested a smoke before I went into work.

I arrived at work feeling a lot more mellower than I had felt for days. Despite spending almost half an hour brushing my teeth I still had the foul acrid taste in my mouth that had been there when I woke up, the same foul taste I tasted when I fought The Cheat. My partner and Veryanne were sitting next to each other in reception. My partner was his usual vitriolic self. He knew all about my escapades. Green had been on the phone to him that morning as far as he was concerned the case was all wrapped up. Green had told him to submit the final invoice and to expect a decent bonus. We had proved The Cheat was the sick bastard going round cutting up smack dealers. He and Veryanne were just going out to celebrate. They would have asked me, but didn't think I would be in today, and they had already booked up the table. There were other things they needed to discuss as well. Things that didn't concern me. I should have been upset. A couple of days ago I would have been devastated, but blind terror changes a lot of things, and the urge to flee was overpowering.

My partner shot me a triumphalist glance as he strode out of the door with Veryanne on his arm. She smiled back at me and I looked deep into her eyes. There was something there that sent a chill down my spine. I looked down, and made as if to check the invoice my partner had just made up, but deep down I was quivering. I waited until they had gone then I hung up my coat and poured myself a glass of calvados. So this was how it went. As far as my partner was concerned the whole thing was over, but for me it was just beginning.

I was rooting around in the petty cash when someone walked into the office. I looked up and came face to face with The Cheat. He looked fit and healthy, more like he had just spent a month on a health farm, not a night in intensive care with a fractured skull. He was not alone either. He had brought two of his junky mates with him. They were standing either side of him. The one on the left looked completely out of it, but the one on the right was a different story altogether. He was lean and dirty with wild staring eyes. He was holding a well-honed sheath knife, and looked like he was having problems adjusting to his chemical imbalance.

'Surprised to see me?' jeered The Cheat. I didn't say anything. It had gone beyond words. I was sure the security guard was telling me the truth last night. Yet The Cheat was standing in front of me, large as life, feral and psychotic, when by all rights he should be gracing a mortuary slab. Green was right, I should have got out of town last night. I reached for my gun, but it was in my coat pocket, hanging on the door, and The Cheat and his junky mates were in the way. The Cheat smiled malevolently displaying a row of rotten teeth. The stench was overpowering, and it was familiar. The same foul stink that had been haunting me since our last meeting.

I gripped the calvados bottle tightly and stepped back. The Cheat lit a cigarette, and the dangerous-looking junky stepped forwards. 'I want his bollocks Billy,' snarled The Cheat, and the junky nodded grimly. I wasn't going to lie down and die, if they wanted to kill me they were going to have a fight on their hands. Billy advanced slowly, holding the knife in front of him, he had a cocky grin on his face, he was used to frightening people. After everything that had happened, I didn't frighten easily. I held the bottle with both hands and swung it like a club, it landed heavily on his forehead and shattered, showering Billy with broken glass and calvados. What a waste I thought, I should have finished the bottle sooner. Without thinking I smashed the broken neck of the bottle into his face and twisted. There was a sickening crunching sound, and he let out a shriek that made my blood run cold. His face erupted into a mass of red, and part of it fell on the floor with a slurping sound.

I felt sick, the other junky stopped smiling, and seemed to come out of his trance, but The Cheat roared with laughter. It was the most chilling sound I had ever heard, and it seemed to come straight from the bowels of hell. The Cheat casually walked over to Billy, and tenderly picked him up. Then a disgusting transformation came over his face. He opened his mouth, but the rotting teeth had gone, replaced with shining rows of razor-sharp teeth, like a barracuda. Then he started feeding on what was left of Billy's face. Billy's screams grew more frantic, his body convulsed desperately. Then abruptly he went still. The only noise was the squishing of flesh on teeth, and my sharp breathing.

'Go on then,' rasped The Cheat in between mouthfuls. 'You finish him off, or you'll be next.' The other junky looked terrified, uncertain of what to do next. He glanced at the door, then back at The Cheat, then finally at me. His face set, became grim and determined. I could tell, he didn't want The Cheat coming after him, so he was going after me. He picked up Billy's knife, swallowed, then started towards me.

What was left of the bottle seemed woefully inadequate. Most of the glass was either scattered all over the floor or embedded in Billy's face. Things were different now though, The Cheat was occupied, and there was a clear path to my coat, and the Browning. I jumped over the scattered desk and lunged at my coat. The junky thought I was making a beeline for the door and slashed the knife at my chest. Had I been going for the door it would have been fatal, but it still gashed a line along my ribs. It felt like I was being caressed with a red hot poker. I fell down in a heap, but just managed to grab my trenchcoat which fell down on top of me. For a minute I couldn't see anything, and I panicked, desperately trying to get the coat off my face. I felt a foot crunch heavily in my groin, and for a second thought I was going to puke. I looked up, and the junky was standing over me, clutching the knife in both hands, like a ceremonial dagger. 'This is it,' I thought, 'What a disgusting way to die.' Then I felt the pistol through my coat.

There was no time to get the gun out, I could feel the trigger. There was a huge explosion as the Browning went off. The junky stood silently above me, a huge hole in his chest. For a moment he stood there staring horrified, then he slumped back dead. I clutched the coat to my chest, it was starting to burn. I pulled myself to my feet and patted out the flames. I felt some vindication, after all the ribbing Dodge had given me about my modifications, this bullet had done exactly what I had intended it to do.

It hadn't fazed The Cheat though, he lazily looked up from his meal and grinned. 'Well done,' he sneered. 'You can kill junkies. How will you do against me?' With that he stood up, stuck his fingers deep into his face then ripped it off. Thick black hairs started sprouting all over him, as foul black ichor and gobbets of flesh splattered on the floor. I was reminded of the scene from *A Company Of Wolves*, where everyone started turning into werewolves. For a second I thought that The Cheat should have gone into film-making, but only for a second. I was faced with a creature of indescribable horror, like a huge black malevolent spider. I staggered back, still clutching the smouldering trenchcoat. 'You're mine,' it hissed. 'And I'm going to suck your soul.'

That did it, I was out of there. Green was right, I wasn't ready for this yet, I needed to get somewhere more secure. As I ran down the stairs sobbing with panic I could hear The Cheat screaming. 'There's no point in running, I will find you anywhere you go.' Well fuck you, that wisdom cuts both ways. I was running down the road like an Olympic sprinter, oblivious to the incredible pain, one overriding desire to flee. With any luck, my partner would go back to the office. The Cheat hated him more than he hated me. But I doubted that would happen, my partner's fate was different. I was doomed to be pursued by what The Cheat had become, whilst he was fated to shag the secretary. I leaped over the barriers of the duel carriageway, there was a screech of brakes as a silver Jaguar flew around the bend knocking me to the pavement. The door opened and a tall gaunt man got out. I remember seeing a row of perfect teeth smiling down at me, then everything went black.

Chapter 11

Hassan I Sabbah

'Guide us o though genie of the smoke.'
Hawkwind

I was awake, and the sudden realisation made me sit up. I sat blinking in the twilight, I couldn't remember falling asleep. I was sitting on a cold flagstone; two tiny slits of light came in through a tiny iron grate in the ceiling. I could hardly make anything out in the murky gloom. The only sound was the slow dripping of water somewhere outside the cell, and an owl hooting in the distance. Every now and then I could hear Al-waqif and Al-akhDar in the other cell groaning. I lay back down, I was still exhausted. I had a pounding headache, I needed some more sleep. I tried to make myself comfortable on the cold stone. Just as I was closing my eyes to go to sleep, I suddenly became aware of two piercing black eyes staring out at me from the darkness. For the first time I realised I wasn't the cell's only occupant.

My heart started pounding, and instinctively I went for my weapon, but it was gone. My mouth went dry, and I could feel myself starting to sweat. I peered back, trying to see a face. I could just make out the outline of another figure, sitting staring back. 'Hello,' I ventured, trying to hide the nervous quiver in my voice.

'So you're awake then?' The voice was soft, calm and resonant. The first soothing sound I had heard since I arrived. 'Do you know where you are?' The tone was comforting, reassuring, but it demanded an answer.

'Yes, I know where I am. Everyone's heard of this place, but despite all I have heard, I never thought it would be this foul.'

'Is that not also something you have heard?' The question was intriguing, almost philosophical, but very matter of fact. I was speaking to someone extremely enigmatic, the silences spoke as majestically as the words themselves. Soft spoken words with hidden steel. I may be about to die, but at least I was locked up with a civilised man, not some dribbling monster.

Before I knew it, I had told him everything, the whole sorry tale. A tale of stealing, murder and betrayal. Yet despite being incarcerated with no chance of escape, all I could think of was revenge. I had to admit that despite the treachery, there was no injustice in my story. I at least deserved to be locked up, unlike so many of the others held in the dungeons of Cairo.

Then in soft soothing tone without a hint of bitterness my companion told me his story. His name was Hassan. He once held a position of prestige at the Seljuk Court, but he, too, had been betrayed and had to flee for his life. He had then wandered, to Azerbaijan, Mayyafariqin and Damascus, before sailing to Cairo. Here he thought he could find work, but the reach of his enemy Nizam Al-Mulk was long. He had been arrested and thrown into the dungeons accused of plotting against the caliph's Commander-in-Chief, Badr al-Jamali. He had never hidden his distaste for Al-Jamali, but had never taken part in any plots against him. However, his support for Al-Jamali's rival Nizar was enough to condemn him.

His nobility made my tale seem even shabbier by comparison. I was a common horse thief, a brigand and a bandit. There were four of us, along with Al-waqif, Al-akhDar and myself there was our betrayer Al-arba-ayn. Together we terrorised the main roads out of Cairo. We had been robbing with impunity for twelve years, that was largely thanks to me, and my caution. We always avoided traps, and left our crimes long before the caliph's guards could catch us, even if it meant leaving plunder behind. It was Al-arba-ayn who got greedy on the last robbery, would not leave with the rest of us, laughing that he would come back rich and show us for the fools we were. It was Al-arba-ayn who got caught and betrayed our hide-out to save his own skin. Even then I could feel the heat closing in. I begged the others to leave, but Al-waqif could not believe Al-arba-ayn would betray us, and Al-akhDar always did what Al-waqif said. I wished that I had obeyed my instincts and ran leaving the others to their fate.

'Why did you not obey your instincts and run? You had always obeyed your instincts before, why not this time?' Since Hassan had finished his story, we had lapsed into a long period of contemplation. It made me jump; it was almost as if he had been reading my thoughts.
'What makes you ask that?'
'Forgive me, it's just that you appear to be a man concerned with procedure. Yet for once you deviated from procedure. It wasn't out of a sense of loyalty to your friends.'
'No, it wasn't loyalty,' there was something in his manner that ensured

I remain candid.'

'So, if not loyalty then what?' I was unable to answer, because truly I did not know. My companion continued. 'It's just that I, too, am a creature of procedure. I have found that my failure to follow procedure resulted in me being here.' He paused, and it was some time before he continued. 'I do not believe in accidents, I believe that somehow we were destined to be confined together.'

'But for what purpose? For surely we are both doomed to die.' Again my companion fell silent, as if trying to discern the reason behind our meeting. For if there was a reason he seemed more suited to discern any meaning. I was at a loss, for me, the universe seemed a series of random events, I was unable to see any reason behind it all.

After a while Hassan continued. 'Tell me, what sort of fate do you expect in the afterlife?' I had to admit that it was something I had not thought about. Even here in the condemned cell all I could think of was revenge. However, if what the holy men said was true, I was not destined for an eternity of pleasure. I had lead a dreadful life and was destined for a life of suffering. My morbid thoughts were interrupted by Hassan. 'Were you sentenced by Al-Jamali's deputy Al-afaaa?' I had to admit that I had. There was something about him that had unnerved me. I would never forget his wild staring eyes as he condemned me. It was almost as if he was condemning my soul as well as my body. 'Curious,' replied Hassan. 'Most find him to be an almost saintly man.' I wasn't quite sure what he meant by that, and I didn't have time to ask him because he lapsed into another one of his long silences.

It was a long time before he continued. 'When I was a young man I swore an oath with two others. With Nizam al-Mulk and Omar Khayyam, we swore that whoever became powerful would divide that power equally amongst all three. Al-Mulk broke that oath and betrayed me, if Omar Khayyam ever stops studying the stars and writing poetry he will need to watch his back. It is of no matter, because I will be revenged on Al-Mulk, Bu-Tahir will kill him, although he does not know it yet. No, what intrigues me most is our meeting. Tell me, if I were to free you from these cells would you do as I command?'

It wasn't a difficult question to answer, faced with certain death, but I wasn't sure it was meant to be taken seriously. I had never heard of anyone escaping from the dungeons before. Hassan appeared to have supporters outside, but he would need an army of thousands to rescue us. I couldn't see it happening, and had already resigned myself to my fate. Even so, there didn't seem to be any harm in swearing an oath of allegiance on the condition of my release, and that of my companions. Al-waqif and Al-akhDar were both useful people to have around, and moreover they were the only two people I knew I could trust in this stinking city. I didn't know exactly what Hassan had in mind, but I was sure it would involve great risk, and I wanted someone to watch my back. I told Hassan all of this and waited for his response.

It was dawn before he gave me his answer. In the crepuscular gloom I was able to make out his features, and to my surprise he was only in his mid to late twenties. I was sure that I had been talking to a venerable sage, not someone scarcely older than myself. He must have seen the astonishment on my face but chose not to comment on this. In the grey light of dawn he appeared to be deliberating with someone, although he and I were the cell's only occupants. 'You do realise,' he intoned, 'That this will be an oath you cannot break. And if you choose to involve your friends, then they, too, will be bound by your oath. Do you wish to continue, or to take your chances with the jailor?'

As far as I was concerned I had no choice, but I was a bit bemused by his choice of words. He had not said what would happen if I chose to break the oath, but that oath breaking was something I would not be able to do, like walking on water or flying. 'Alright then,' I said, 'If we ever get out of here alive I swear allegiance.'

Hassan's demeanour became even more sombre. He produced a copy of The Koran and insisted I swear allegiance upon that. As I did so he began muttering to himself, I could not make out any of it. He was not speaking in Arabic. As he spoke I felt the atmosphere changing. This was no longer a dungeon hidden deep within the bowels of the Earth; it was somewhere that had the attention of the whole universe. And I knew he spoke the truth. I was not just swearing an oath, but developing a compulsion.

No sooner had the oath been made then he vanished. I don't know who was the more astonished, me or the jailor. He almost dropped the breakfast tray when he found me alone in my cell. I could feel my heart pounding when he turned the key in the lock. The sweat started pouring down my forehead when he walked into the cell with two burley henchmen. I was in for the interrogation of a lifetime. Nobody had ever escaped from the dungeons of Cairo before. The jailor was determined that they wouldn't start on his watch. He would find Hassan if he had to roast me over hot coals.

I put my hands over my eyes, the jailor told his two henchmen to grab hold of me then he fell silent. I heard a couple of muffled grunts followed by dull thuds of bodies hitting the floor then silence. When I opened my eyes I was alone, save for the three corpses of the jailor and his men. They had all had their throats slit. Quick to recognise an advantage I grabbed hold of the keys then ran to free Al-waqif and Al-akhDar.

At first we were lost, disorientated, unaware of the right way to go, then I spotted Hassan beckoning from the end of a long gloomy corridor. I ran after him and the others followed. When we got to the end of the corridor we found two more guards with their throats slit, and Hassan far in the distance beckoning once more. Things continued this way until we made our way out of the prison and into the relative safety and anonymity of the busy streets.

We stood there incredulous, swallowing in the sweet air of freedom. Marvelling in the mouth-watering scents of spicy foods mingled with the beautiful scent of burning incense coming from the restaurants. After the stink of the filth of the dungeons the smell of the market place was the most beautiful scent on Earth. It was at this point that both Al-waqif and Al-akhDar wanted to run from the city, and catch a fishing boat to Aleppo. But far off in the distance Hassan was still beckoning, and I knew we had to follow. The others followed me. They both owed me the debt of freedom. As far as they were concerned, I had freed them, they knew nothing of Hassan. So they followed me through the streets of Cairo.

After about half an hour we arrived at a small gate. Hassan darted inside and beckoned me to follow. We burst through the door and slammed the door behind us, still wary of pursuit. As we sat back against the walls panting breathlessly we realised we were in a beautiful garden. In the centre of which was a huge table piled with an enormous feast. A distinguished old man was sitting at the table. He looked up at us and smiled, 'Welcome,' he said.

Chapter 12

Fire In Cairo

'The heat disappears and the mirage fades away.'
The Cure

It was an extremely exquisite meal, doubly so after the slop we had been fed in the dungeons. For a while we ate in silence, for we were ravenous. Our host ate little and remained agreeably taciturn throughout the meal. He said little save yes and no, and would not be drawn into conversation, smiling benignly when we asked a question. We were too relieved to be overly concerned about him, he seemed like a kindly old man watching over his wayward sons. We ate our full, and when we had finished he lead us to our chambers. We said our goodnights and went to bed.

My room was simple with plain white walls and no furniture save for the bed, a small table, a prayer mat, a jug for washing and a copy of the Koran. Compared to where I had been living it was a palace. I collapsed onto the bed wondering what the next day would bring, and had the best night's sleep since longer than I could remember.

There then followed a life of extreme asceticism. There were no more banquets, the meals were simple and plain, but still a thousand times better than the dungeon slop. We went to prayers five times daily, studied the Koran and discussed what we had read with the old man who first greeted us. Although he remained taciturn in all other matters, when it came to the Koran and its meanings he would talk for hours and hours. It was then that our true nature began to show itself. Of the three of us Al-akhDar took to his studies with most enthusiasm, his father was very devout, and had memorised the first five surahs. He would ask the holy man questions on intricate aspects of law. I was held by my oath, and listened attentively when discussing general issues, but switched off when Al-akhDar started asking questions. Al-waqif was by far the worst student. He was barely literate, and struggled with the simplest of concepts. He thought with his hands, and let others do the thinking for him. He spent these times squirming uncomfortably and looking out of the window.

Al-waqif wanted desperately to leave, go back onto the roads and start pillaging once more. I could not leave for I had made a promise. Al-akhDar desperately wanted to stay. His brief sojourn in the dungeons had terrified him. He had seen the errors of his ways and was seeking redemption. Al-waqif reluctantly agreed to stay, he couldn't do a lot of thinking without either of us, and staying was the easiest thing to do. We placated him by vowing that, once we had performed our task we would be revenged on Al-arba-ayn.

Days became weeks, weeks became months, Al-waqif became more agitated, and Al-akhDar became more devout. I became anxious, the longer it went on the more I longed to be out doing something, something that didn't involve reading the Koran. At the beginning I found I had more in common with Al-akhDar, but now I was sympathising with Al-waqif.

One day the old gentleman, (we never did find out his name) asked us to go into a room we had never been in before. This was a room unlike any of the others. The rest of the house was austere, no decoration, bare paving slabs, functional, but not comfortable furniture. This room had thick luxurious carpet, the walls were hung with colourful tapestries and paintings. The air was heavy with the scent of jasmine. The table was decorated with lapis lazuli and mother of pearl. Two jugs of sweetened rosewater sat on the table. The chairs were well padded and so large that even Al-waqif could lie out comfortably. There sitting smiling at the table, arms outstretched in welcome, sat Hassan.

After some initial chat about his travels he sat us all down and poured each of us a glass of rosewater. When we were all quiet he began; there was a sense of eagerness in the air. 'Tell me,' he asked, 'Who sits on the left-hand side of God?' Al-akhDar replied that whilst Michael sat on the right hand side of God, Lucifer had sat to his left. Lucifer rebelled against God and fell from grace becoming Satan. Hassan listened attentively as Al-akhDar recited the fall of the angels. He was half way through the story of Cain and Abel when Hassan interrupted him. 'Forgive me, but you cannot have heard me properly. I didn't ask who sat on the left-hand side of God, I asked who sits on the left hand side of God.'

At this even Al-akhDar fell silent. All of us knew who sat on the left hand side of God, but none of us knew who currently occupied the position. 'There was a vacancy, many believe there still is a vacancy, or that there will always be a vacancy, that the left side of God will always be empty. I know that there is no longer a vacancy. The position is occupied.' Hassan's words were almost hypnotic, and I found myself drifting off. Al-akhDar was similarly affected, but Al-waqif was still squirming uncomfortably in his seat.

'I don't see what any of this has got to do with us,' he groaned, 'I don't care who sits on what side of God, I leave that sort of thing to you.' At this Hassan suddenly flared up, his quiet friendly demeanour disappeared to be replaced by a raging tiger.

'It became your business the moment you stepped into this house,' he bellowed. 'Now do not interrupt me again.' Even Al-waqif was shaken by that. He seemed to shrink into his chair. After that there were no more interruptions.

'Lucifer was the lightbringer, the brightest thing in creation. When he fell, he fell into darkness, but he is not naturally a creature of darkness, and there lies the perversity. In light there lies corruption, but the new Lord of Light is Michael, most pure of all the angels, and he sits on the right hand side of God. Here lies the balance, if on one side there is light and the angel most full of love then what must dwell in God's shadow? Darkness and the most savage and ruthless angel, Gabriel the angel of death. Gabriel was always a dark angel, when Lucifer and his brothers rebelled, the dark angels stayed loyal.

The struggle between left and right had changed, both sides were loyal, but both wanted greater prestige than the other. The conflict so far as Heaven is concerned is purely political, although down here it is anything but. Gabriel feels aggrieved, Michael's the blue eyed boy, the one with the upper hand. Ever since the prophet Yeshua and the Christian's Book of Revelations, Michael feels he has Armageddon all mapped out. Gabriel has his part to play, but it is a part written by Michael. He feels truly aggrieved, doesn't agree with Michael's methods, and wants to try something else. That's where we come in.'

He paused as if waiting for us to ask what was expected of us. Al-waqif was still too intimidated to make a sound. I was used to Hassan's silences, and kept my counsel. Hasan would tell us all in his own time. Asking questions only delayed things. And so it was Al-akhDar who asked what we had to do. To my surprise Hassan answered directly. We were all creatures of darkness, our only hope of salvation lay through Gabriel. If we were to employ his methods we would escape the burning pit, and dwell in the shadow of God.

Gabriel's prime concern was with Death. Everything must die, and he had the powers to ensure that was so. He reminded us of our judge Al-afaaa, and all of us remembered his cold gaze with a shiver. He was an abomination, we heard. He was one who had dealt with Satan himself, and had immense power including immortality. Our task was to show Satan's gift for the sham it was, expose the nonsense of immortality at the end of an assassin's dagger, and take the power of life and death back for its rightful owner Gabriel. Our instruction completed Hassan got up and left.

For a while we sat in silence. Then without speaking all three of us got up and walked into the garden. When we got outside it had already turned dark. We felt excited, after many months of waiting we finally knew what we had to do. It wasn't the first time that we had been paid to kill someone, but it was the first time we could feel good about it. And it was only one task, not a lifetime of service, complete it and we could go back to our old ways. But this time with even greater impunity. The death of Al-afaaa would guarantee us a place in paradise. But there was something else we needed to attend to. It was a cloudless night, and the moon was full. The three of us linked hands and swore that once we had killed Al-afaaa we would be revenged upon the traitor Al-arba-ayn.

Once the wheels were set in motion the pace was feverish. We studied the plan of Al-afaaa's house until we could find our way blindfolded. We also learnt techniques, previously we believed we were experts at killing, but we had a lot to learn from the Hashisheen. Particularly in the art of remaining undiscovered, keeping to the shadows, moving silently, staying anonymous. A face in the crowd, easily forgotten, nothing unremarkable. We learnt how to kill silently, what were the most vulnerable parts of an intended victim.

After about a fortnight we were ready, or thought we were. The old gentleman led us into Hassan's chamber for what was to be our last briefing. Hassan was not there, but the old gentleman was fully capable of delivering his words. Once again we sat there sipping sherbet, but this time we were introduced to the meaning of hashish. Of the three of us only Al-waqif was familiar with its effects, both Al-akhDar and myself thought it the preserve of degenerates, but we were wrong. When used correctly hashish became a conduit for Gabriel, through it he could enter us and guide our hands, and through it we could draw on the strengths of an angel of darkness.

As we sat drinking sherbet and smoking hashish we found that we were never to use the name Gabriel again. A name we could use would be revealed in due course. This was to hide Gabriel's presence from the enemy, he would rather be seen as an errant demon than reveal his true nature. Secrecy was all important, as only in secrecy could the enemy be properly opposed. We also learnt that Gabriel had chosen me to be the chief assassin. The others were to follow my lead, walking where I walked as the shadows would be revealed only to me. More importantly, I had to deal the death blow, for Al-afaaa could only be killed by my hand.

The old gentleman left us. We were given food similar to that which had first greeted us when we first arrived from the dungeons. We were given more hashish, and even permitted to drink some wine. We were to make free use of Hasan's chambers, and sleep in supreme comfort for the next day was when we would strike.

It was a beautiful day, but we slept late, we had drunk a little too much wine and needed to take it easy. We had plenty of time, we weren't going to attempt the assassination until it was dark. Ever since we had been told of the nature of our task we were full of excited anticipation, unable to sleep well, but now the day had arrived we all felt an unearthly calmness. A fatalistic acceptance of what was going to happen. Even though we were at the centre of the evening's events we all felt as if we had no control over what was about to happen.

So it was, that as night fell we three found ourselves standing outside the house of Al-afaaa, each clutching a dagger. There were two sentinels guarding the entrance. Silently as in a dream I pushed my dagger up under the ribcage and into the heart of the nearest guard. He died instantly before he was scarcely able to register my presence. Al-waqif disposed of the other in a similar fashion. Then we were inside, running silently down the main corridor, to the main chamber, where Al-afaaa would be entertaining his guests. Twice we encountered guards, and each time we disposed of them as easily as before.

As we entered the main chamber we could see Al-afaaa sitting in front of us, but to our right enjoying Al-afaaa's hospitality sat the traitor Al-arba-ayn. Providence had delivered both victims, and both oaths could be fulfilled that night. Snarling Al-waqif and I both fell upon him. Only Al-akhDar remembered our mission and ran for Al-afaaa dagger drawn. I looked deep into Al-arba-ayn's eyes as I delivered the fatal blow. It was too late, the cry of 'Assassins,' was ringing out throughout the building, and we were surrounded. Al-waqif and I tried to fight our way to Al-afaaa, but there were too many of them. I saw Al-akhDar's dagger shatter against Al-afaaa's chest, then I received a fatal blow and sank lifeless to the floor.

Chapter 13

Watching The Detectives

'She's filing her nails while they're dragging the lake.'
Elvis Costello

'Wake up you smelly git wake up!' Someone was shaking me, and shouting. 'Wake up smelly!' It was a scouser. My ribs burst into flame. I struggled awake, opening my eyes to see Dodge grinning down at me. 'So you're awake then? Where the fuck have you been? There's been all sorts looking for you. I've just got back from the 'ozzie.' This was way too much information to take all in one go. I sat up rubbing my eyes, looking around, trying to work out where I was.

There was lots of grass, dandelions and rubbish. Someone had dumped me in my own back yard, possibly the person with the perfect set of teeth, perhaps not, but I had no idea how I had got there. I told Dodge to go back in, make me a cup of tea. 'How long have you been out here? You're lucky I came out, wanted a piss. Didn't feel like walking all the way to the bathroom.' I couldn't believe what I was hearing. I thought I was lazy, but I wouldn't dream of doing anything like that. Especially not when you're a guest in someone else's house. I suddenly felt very sick. How long had Dodge been using my back garden as a toilet? Had I been lying in scouse piss? I felt like having it out with him then and there, but my ribs hurt and I needed to sit down.

When we got in I could hear the telly blaring away. From the kitchen, I could just make out the picture on a small portable set in the lounge. Dodge had been watching a video. There were scores of evil aliens being blasted to oblivion by some muscle-bound twat; it could have been anything really. 'This is a fucking brilliant film,' he said. 'I've seen it five times already.' I had already seen enough, I walked into the lounge and turned the set off. Dodge must have got the portable out of the hall cupboard. I'd almost forgotten about it, it must have been there for at least a year. I walked back into the kitchen and put the kettle on.

'Not bad for twenty quid is it?' asked Dodge as we sat nursing cups of tea at the kitchen table. Tea was all there was, my packet of chocolate digestives seemed to have disappeared. I was too tired to argue, I felt myself agreeing with Dodge before I realised I didn't have a clue what he was talking about?'

'What's not bad for twenty quid?'

'The telly.'

'Who told you it cost twenty quid? I can't remember how much it cost, but it was more than twenty quid.'

'No it's *my* telly. *I* paid twenty quid for it.' I couldn't believe the repulsive way things were starting to go. I ran back into the hall, and checked the cupboard; the telly had gone, along with a pair of boots, a kite and an old longbow someone had given me in lieu of a tenner. I'd never even used it, all it needed was a string, but I hadn't got round to it. I stormed into the lounge, It was my telly sure enough. It had the scratch on the on/off switch, from when I'd tried to turn the telly off with a tequila bottle.

I ran back into the lounge, demanding to know where the telly had come from. 'It was that weird mate of yours. The one with the wild staring eyes. That moondog bloke. Came round here earlier on, had the telly under his arm. Said he was looking for you, heard you needed a telly. He just wanted enough to get a couple of grammes of Billy.' That sounded about right, Clay had done that sort of thing before, stolen from cupboards. He could have taken the stuff at any time over the past six months. It was just like him to forget who he had stolen from as well. I wish I'd been in when he called round. I'd teach him to take the piss like that.

It was all too much for me to take in, my ribs ached and I felt feverish. I could sense the vultures circling overhead, now was not the time for petty revenge, now it was time to run. It was just a load of shitty stuff that I would have to leave behind anyway. I took my last two paracetamol and lifted up my shirt. My ribs were really tender, and in a couple of places the shirt was stuck fast. I had to really tug before it would come free in a blaze of fire, setting off the bleeding again. 'Jesus Christ,' whistled Dodge, 'That looks bloody nasty. Looks like I'm gonna have to take you up the 'ozzie as well.'

'No,' I groaned. 'I haven't got time for that. Anyway, they know me at that hospital. I wouldn't get out of there alive if those bastards got their way. No, we're just going to have to do something about it here.' Dodge went a shade paler than usual, which with him being ginger, was quite unnerving, if he went any paler he would turn pale blue. It was obvious he was not at all happy with the situation, he wasn't looking forward to what I was about to ask him. 'Listen mate, you did first aid didn't you, when you were on the Mersey ferries?'

'Fuck off!' he yelled. That needs stitches. I can't do that again, not after last time.' I thought he was about to cry.

'But you have done it before?' I asked eagerly, I hadn't expected Dodge to have had any proper experience. 'Well?' I continued. I wasn't going to let him clam up now. I needed an answer.

'Alright,' he spluttered. 'I have done stitches before, but not on a human. I had to do it to the ship's cat.'

'And?'

'Well, you have to remember it was a very sick animal to start off with.' Dodge's voice started to tremble. He splurted out, 'I tried my best I really did,' then ran into the lounge crying.

It had been a really shitty day. My partner walks off with the most beautiful woman imaginable. I get attacked by something horrible out of some Lovecraftian nightmare. I have to kill someone with an illegally modified, illegally held, illegal firearm. I get run over. I have a blackout, I wake up in a puddle of piss. Some bloody speed freak rips off the hall cupboard, and now there's a huge scouser in floods of tears over some long dead moggy, when I desperately need some medical attention. Jesus, did I just say that or did I just think it? The paracetamol had done nothing to dent the fever, and I was feeling delirious. In any event Dodge returned from the lounge with the last of my tequila and a needle and thread. There then followed the worst half hour of my entire life. I almost passed out when he poured the precious tequila over my ribs. Then I endured Dodge's handiwork. If his fishing is as bad as his needlework, then the whole whelk industry will go into stark decline the second he puts foot on the boat. To try to take my mind off the pain Dodge chattered away inanely as he applied the sutures. A lot of it was his usual crappy jokes, but he did say a few things that made me sit up and pay attention.

'I've just been up the 'ozzie to see that partner of yours. I wouldn't normally like, seeing as I don't give a shit about him. But your secretary called round looking for you. God, she's a right cracker isn't she? I'd like to hammer on her shit-locker I can tell you.' This was too much, I may have my suspicions about Veryanne, but I wasn't going to let him talk like that about her. I told him to shut up. For a while he continued stitching me up in silence. When he continued his tone had softened slightly. 'Seeing as how you weren't around, I volunteered to accompany her to the 'ozzie, all gentlemanly like. She needed a bit of comforting, and I can be dead sensitive when I want to be. Your partner was in a right state, he'd just had surgery, was all a bit doo-lally from the anaesthetic. Talked a right load of old bollocks he did.'

Finally a bit of good news, something to salvage from this shitty day. It was a comfortable image, my partner sat raving in a hospital bed, recovering from painful surgery, at least I hope it was painful. I begged Dodge to tell me what had happened to my partner, but more than anything I needed to know if he was in any pain. Dodge mistook my schadenfreude for concern and softened his tone further still. When he resumed, it was like Thatcher telling someone their cat had died. 'Something bit him. They don't know what exactly. That bird thinks it was some sort of big lizard like a komodo dragon or something like that.' He paused and whistled. 'Jesus, the sort of things some bastards keep as pets, then when they get too big they just flush them down the bog, like crocodiles in the sewers and that.' I didn't like what he was implying, that if you flushed something down the bog it ended up in my office. He was getting off the point and I needed to know my partner's condition. 'Well,' said Dodge, 'The bloody thing almost took his thumb off. He was in surgery for an hour while they tried to sew it back on. Because he'd been drinking they daren't put him out, they had to do it under local. He put up one hell of a fuss apparently.'

Wonderful news. If Dodge hadn't been sewing me up I would have burst out laughing. But there was more. 'He wasn't making much sense when I spoke to him, but he fucking hates you. Seems to think you were behind it all, I told him you didn't have no lizards. I've not seen one all the time I've been here. He says it wasn't a lizard, says it was some sort of monster. I told him straight that it was bollocks, but that you didn't have no monsters either.' Dodge looked up pleased with himself, I thanked him for his support, not anyone would be prepared to say that I didn't have any monsters or komodo dragons. 'The pigs were there as well, asked all sorts of questions. They told me to phone them if I saw you. I've got their card somewhere.' Dodge put down the needle and thread, reached into his back pocket and pulled out a business card. I looked at it, the name sounded familiar, but I couldn't put a face to it. 'It's alright,' said Dodge, 'I'm no grass, and that secretary of yours is coming over in a bit.'

I didn't like the sound of that, a classic pincer movement. The pigs on one side, and Veryanne and whatever shady organisation she represented on the other. They would hold me down while The Cheat fed on my soul. No, despite my partner's painful predicament it was I who had picked up the shitty end of the stick, not him. And I felt terrible, achy, shivery with a set of ribs that felt as if they'd been dipped in hot fat. I just wanted to climb into bed and go to sleep, but if I did that I would be dead. No, I had to deal with all this terrible shit right now. But I wasn't going anywhere before I'd finished my cup of tea and smoked a spliff. I asked Dodge if he had said anything to the police about Weston-Super-Mare and the life of a whelk fisherman. Of course he hadn't, he was a scouser through and through. He would sooner eat his small intestine than talk to the pigs.

I'd forgotten just how good the mystery dope was. As I stubbed out the roach I felt a lot better. My ribs were still throbbing horribly, but I felt less feverish and was starting to think clearly. I knew what I had to do, and I was up for it, a nice leisurely drive in the country was just what I needed. I would know what to do once we got there. I went into the bedroom and packed a small overnight bag. Dodge was already packed. In fact he had never really unpacked, as if he was in a constant state of readiness, just waiting for the moment he had to move on. Even so, he didn't exactly travel light, and looked like some bizarre animated shop display, with bags and suitcases hanging off every available point. He insisted on bringing the telly, which he tucked under his arm. He was waddling towards the front door like a designer yeti when the bell rang.

The sound of a doorbell is one of the most disturbing sounds I know, particularly when you're on the run. I couldn't mistake the two shadows outlined in the frosted glass; it was my two chums Tweedledee and Tweedledum, and I remembered where I had heard the name on the business card before. Silently Dodge turned around, the bags swaying and creaking. The pigs were starting to peer through the frosted glass, trying to make out any movement. We would have to go out the back, but it would be a longer walk to the car, and Dodge was already puffing and panting under the weight of all his material possessions. He would have to leave something behind.

As we got into the kitchen the front doorbell became more insistent. I looked out of the kitchen window and saw Veryanne coming up the drive. We were fucked. I'd spent too long drinking tea and getting stoned. I still had my gun though; they weren't taking me without a fight. 'Bathroom,' I whispered to Dodge as we both huddled together under the kitchen table, 'We can get out there.' Dodge was only able to take one bag with him, and he took a few desperate minutes trying to work out what to leave behind, but we managed to crawl into the bathroom undiscovered. I locked the door behind us.

'Great,' groaned Dodge. 'Here we are locked in the bog. They'll never think of looking for us here. It's too late to go out the backdoor now, one of the pigs will have gone round the back and told that cracking secretary of yours that you're a wanted man. We should have gone off with her when we had the chance.'

'Don't be stupid.' I whispered. 'She's a pig too, been working under cover all the time.' For the second time that day Dodge looked as if he was going to cry. I was tempted to tell him the truth, but I couldn't risk him turning against me. The truth was so weird, that if I hadn't seen it myself, then I would want me locked away for my own safety. No, Dodge had no qualms aiding and abetting criminals. Madmen were another case entirely. He shook his head in disbelief. 'What a waste. A cracking bird like that. I'd never have believed it.' He paused as if in deep thought, before one last comment. 'I'd still shag it though.'

There was no time to talk about such things, we had to get out of there. I pointed out that the bathroom window opened out into a little concreted area. We could get onto next door's roof from there, slide down the other side into an alley. The far end of the alley was close to the railway station, we could get a train to Bristol or something. I still had most of the cash from the business account. That was another little surprise awaiting my partner when he got out of hospital.

There was a bit of a drop from the window to the ground below, but I wasn't too bothered, Dodge was going first. As I opened the window the phone started ringing downstairs. 'Never answer a phone,' whispered Dodge. 'That's just what those bastards want you to do.' Dodge was taking far too long trying to get out of the window, and I decided that I had been looking at his arse framed in the pane for way too long. I decided to give him a shove. With a little squeal and a loud ripping noise he plummeted to the ground. I quickly followed, making sure that he didn't have time to get out of the way. Scousers make wonderful cushions, they're so well padded, and I fell gracefully onto his stomach. There was a loud 'Oof,' as I landed, then nothing. We sat silently waiting to hear if we had been discovered.

Dodge sat rubbing his leg and groaning, calling me a bastard, and telling me that he would be revenged once we got on the boat. That all seemed so far away, but we were outside, and so far we had not been spotted. I gave Dodge a leg-up onto next door's roof, and we silently made our way round to the far side of the roof. I looked down, Tweedledum was still standing at the front door, whilst Tweedledee had gone round the back and was chatting to Veryanne with his tongue hanging out. Veryanne looked up, caught my gaze and smiled. It was the same smile that she left me with prior to the visit from The Cheat, but it wasn't the smile that unnerved me, it was her eyes, the pupils were slitted, like a cat. I felt a shiver run down my spine. However, it didn't look like she was intending to betray us to the pigs, and went back to her conversation with Tweedledee.

I'd seen enough, we had to get out of there. Dodge and I pushed and struggled our way round to the other side of the roof. From there we could easily slide down into the alleyway. Before I had a chance to think, Dodge shoved me hard, and I hit the tarmac with a heavy thud. I knew what to expect though, and rolled to one side, just in time to avoid a large scouser. We had made it, but there was no time to congratulate ourselves. We both got up and ran down the alley towards the station. This was no time for the green cross code and I shot across Commercial Road, only to be hit by a shiny black Porsche.

Chapter 14

Not To Touch The Earth

'Nothing you can do but run, run, run.'
The Doors

'You just ran right out in front of me! What the hell do you think you're playing at? Oh I say, are you alright?'

I opened my eyes and got up off the street. I was being addressed by a pimply young man with curly blond hair wearing white slacks and a striped blazer. He had a gratingly squeaky posh accent. Dodge was standing behind him looking concerned, and a small crowd was starting to gather. If I ran now someone was bound to start chasing. I wouldn't get very far. As I stood up my ribs roared into life once more. It was even worse this time, it felt like a couple were broken. I stared helplessly at Dodge, but he just looked back. I was going to have to do something.

'You've broken one of my ribs you bastard. I could sue you for that. You'll have to take me to the hospital,' I spluttered, leaning against the car, and getting into the empty passenger seat. Dodge saw what I was doing and got into the back seat. The pimply youth stood dumbfounded, and started spluttering. The crowd started to disperse, they weren't going to see any blood, but at least they'd have something to talk about when they got home. The youth got back into the car, and vehicles behind started beeping, they'd been held up long enough.

'Look this really isn't on,' he pleaded as he sat down. 'I've got to be somewhere. There's a mobile phone on the back seat. Why don't you let me phone you an ambulance?'
'A mobile phone?' screamed Dodge. 'I've never seen one of those before. Gizza look.' With that he pulled out a huge lump of plastic bedecked with antennas and large coloured switches. 'How's it work then?' he asked, but he didn't wait for a reply before he started poking and prodding experimentally. The phone started giving out distressed electronic beeps. The pimply youth looked horrified. 'Ey mate, I'm sorry. Is that

supposed to come off like that?'

The beeping of horns was becoming increasingly agitated. The pimply youth looked extremely uncomfortable. We needed to get away before Tweedledee and Tweedledum worked out what was going on. The last thing we needed to be doing was hanging around waiting for an ambulance. The last place I wanted to be was the hospital. There was no way on Earth that I was going to put myself at the mercy of those bastards. Thankfully, Dodge's amateur sabotage had put paid to the question of phoning an ambulance, and the angry motorists gave weight to my line of argument. 'Look mate,' I said. 'You knocked me down. My mate in the passenger seat saw the whole thing. I need to go to the hospital. If you don't want a massive law suit on your hands I suggest you start driving, now.' I had assumed that this wasn't the first time he had problems with his driving. He was only about nineteen, a privileged kid with a rich daddy. He reeked of inbreeding and soft living. Giving a kid like that a car with as much torque as a Porsche, was an accident waiting to happen.

That did the trick, he started up the Porsche and set off. I told him to turn right at the end of the road, going past the pig station before hitting the Millbrook Road. It was a tricky few minutes, the lights at the end of Commercial Road were red, and so were all the others as we crawled slowly past the pig station. I didn't relax until we were tearing up Millbrook Road heading west.

Once we had gone past the railway station and I could see that no pigs were following us, I jammed the Browning under his nose. 'Change of plan,' I growled. 'This is a fucking hi-jack. You make one false move and I'll spread your brains all over the windscreen.' He gulped. I looked in the vanity mirror Dodge was looking concerned. Things were all getting a bit too heavy for him. Hostage taking and hi-jacking were not in the same league as selling a bit of ooky gear and dope. The driver was sweating, and continued spluttering eventually he managed to say one coherent sentence.
'I'll have you know my father's a high court judge.'
'And mine used to drive for The Krays. Now get on to the motorway and head for Bournemouth. I'm deadly serious. I've already killed two people today, one more won't make any difference.' After that there was silence. I glanced in the mirror, even Dodge looked shocked.

It wasn't until we had turned off the motorway and were driving along the dual carriageway towards Salisbury that Dodge decided to try to smooth things over a bit. 'Ey mate. You need to relax. Things aren't too bad. If you do what he says you'll be fine. I'm telling you, if you think this is fucking horrible you want to see what he shagged the other night. I've seen better looking warthogs. Less warts 'n all.' This was all I needed, there was no way I wanted to be reminded of that grisly encounter, especially not in front of this spotty twat. But Dodge was in full swing, short of shooting him there was little I could do to stop him. 'And the real belter is, next day she did a runner, must have felt ashamed or summat like that.' At that even 'Spotty' started giggling. Strange I thought, it wasn't just police who used the Tweedledee Tweedledum partnering. We were doing the same thing; Dodge was positioning himself as Tweedledee, which meant I had to reassert the role of Tweedledum pretty quickly or lose control of things.

'Look,' I snarled, 'If it's horror stories you want, we can do one right now. Now shut up the pair of you. This is a kidnapping stroke hi-jacking. All you need to know is that you've been hi-jacked by mad bastards. Do as you're told and you won't get hurt. We're desperate men.'

'You'd have to be desperate to shag that.' quipped Dodge. I decided to ignore that, and continued in my role of menacing terrorist.

'When we get to Salisbury I want you to bear left, then take a right towards the racecourse, that way we avoid going past the pig station. Savvy?'

Spotty nodded, and did as he was bid. There was silence in the car until we got to the other side of Wilton, then Dodge leant forward and whispered in my ear. 'Look Zips, I'm not too happy about the way things are going. I'm supposed to be keeping a low profile, that's why I came to stay. If this all goes pear-shaped could you say that I had nothing to do with it, that I'm like a hostage too.'

'Sure,' I whispered. 'If you want, to make it more convincing I can give you a gunshot wound.' At that the silly grin disappeared from Dodge's face. I continued, putting on a mock reassuring tone. 'Nothing heavy of course. I wouldn't shoot any of your vital organs or anything like that, but the pigs may need a lot of convincing, like a bullet in the arm or leg. Or a bullet in the bollocks.'

'Er, no mate.' Replied Dodge sitting back. 'Let's just leave things the way they are for now.'

As we were driving through Warminster 'Spotty,' piped up again. 'You know earlier, when I said I had to meet people I was telling the truth.' He glanced at his Rolex. 'I should have been there an hour ago. They'll be getting worried. Can't we just stop off so I can give them a phone, let them know I'm alright?'

'Don't be bloody ridiculous.' I snapped. 'They're really going to be reassured when you tell them you've been kidnapped by The Kristian Van Der Lubbe Fire Bombing Society, because that's what's just happened. Do you think this all happened by chance, we've been watching you for weeks.' At this 'Spotty' fell silent once more, he didn't start talking again until we were clear of Warminster.

'If you don't mind me saying, it's a bit of a strange thing to hi-jack, a Porsche. Aren't you supposed to hi-jack aeroplanes and cruise liners and things like that?' I smiled back benignly.

'You don't think we just start off with aeroplanes. We've got to work our way up to it. Before today we hi-jacked a bicycle, two motor scooters and a Mini Clubman Estate.'

'Spotty' didn't expect that answer. He sat there silently. I could tell he was frantically trying to put some safe interpretation on what was happening. When we got to Frome he turned to me and smiled. 'I've got it.' he grinned. 'You really had me fooled for a while. You must be some of 'Chunky' Carruthers' pals.'

I wanted to smash the pistol in his face and scream how stupid he was. How on Earth could he possibly believe Dodge and I would associate with someone called 'Chunky' Carruthers. I'd read about the Stockholm syndrome, how kidnappers were supposed to bond with their hostages, but it wasn't happening here. Spotty's whiny tone and plummy accent were really starting to twat me off. Dodge was really starting to piss me off as well, I was only half-joking when I spoke about a bullet in the bollocks. I don't know why he had to start talking about my bedroom nightmares like that. I felt like telling Spotty to pull the car to the side of the road then carrying out a summary roadside execution, just like in one of those films set in depression era America. Then I'd relieve Dodge of one of his gonads. There were just a few flaws to this way of thinking. This wasn't depression era America, and the roads were bloody busy. And I was in enough trouble already. It would be hard to claim self-defence against The Cheat's junky pals when I'd just shot some rich little sod for having a squeaky voice and driving a Porsche.

More importantly 'Chunky' Carruthers offered a way out. If we could convince Spotty that this whole hi-jacking thing was some bizarre prank masterminded by some other rich gormless git, then we could get away with it. I wouldn't have to kill Spotty which was a shame in so many ways, and I wouldn't have to shoot Dodge in the goolies, which again was a great shame. No, tempting though it may seem, violence was not the answer. The answer was 'Chunky' Carruthers.

Spotty was studying me intently, a mixture of apprehension and excitement. Would I pistol whip him, or even worse? Or would I invite him on one of 'Chunky' Carruthers' famous romps in the country? I needed to ensure he believed the latter, so I gave him my best 'I will pay you the money I owe you,' smile. 'I was wondering when you'd figure it all out. All of this was 'Chunky's' idea.' I playfully jabbed him in the ribs. 'Had you going for a bit there though.'

'I knew it,' screamed Spotty. 'This sort of thing's got 'Chunky's' fingerprints all over it. Did you hear about the time he filled 'Sweaty' Saunders' swimming pool with marmite? It took them weeks to clear up that mess.' With that he collapsed into a fit of laughter. 'Hoop, Hoop,' he went, it was unlike any sort of laughter I had heard before, and extremely annoying. I was beginning to regret my decision not to use violence. When Spotty stopped laughing, he looked back at me with a flicker of suspicion. 'Just one thing though. How do you and Chunky know each other?' It was a good question, but frankly one which Spotty should have asked earlier. I was at a loss to explain. It looked like the 'Chunky' Carruthers plan wasn't working, and I would have to go back to plan B, violence. I was just getting ready to pull my pistol out again when Dodge piped in.
'We're bookmakers. Old 'Chunky' likes the gee-gees. He always uses us when he wants to put a big bet on. Knows we can get him the best odds.'
'Well I suppose that explains it then,' squeaked Spotty. 'Chunky's got no end of vices. Oodles of cash, little common sense. If you're his bookmakers you must be doing very well out of him.'
'Why do you think we carried out this prank?' I said joining in. 'We wouldn't do this sort of thing for just anyone you know.' This seemed to satisfy Spotty. All doubts were blown away, and he accepted us just as if we were a couple of old Etonians.'
'So,' he simpered, 'Where are we going? Is it a party?'
'Yeah,' answered Dodge. 'It's a party, on a boat with loads of booze and whelks.'
'Whelks?'
Dodge took this as an opportunity to launch into a piece of narrative about the life of a whelk fisherman. It was something I had heard time and again over the past few days and I switched off. For once I welcomed

Dodge's rambling prose. It effectively meant we could stop telling lies about 'Chunky' Carruthers, but more importantly it gave me a chance to think.

Green's words were coming back to haunt me. He had told me to get somewhere more 'secure,' and that to do that I was to 'follow my instincts.' Being stuck in the middle of the ocean aboard a poxy tramp steamer with Spotty and Dodge and a bunch of assorted arse bandits didn't strike me as being that secure. I had read *The Rime Of The Ancient Mariner,* and I didn't like the way it ended. I could just visualise The Cheat floating out to me on some horrible ghost ship whilst the engines failed, and everyone else was pissed out of their heads. It was an image I could see all too clearly, and it was one I didn't like at all.

'Head towards Glastonbury,' I told Spotty as we pulled into Shepton Mallet. I was deciding to follow my instincts. 'We're not going whelk fishing until tomorrow.' I continued. 'There's somewhere else we've got to be tonight.' This fuelled another round of frenetic questions from Spotty, interspaced with conjecture, and numerous anecdotes about 'Chunky' Carruthers. I wasn't able to answer because I didn't know yet, so I tried to appear enigmatic. One thing he said made sense though, booze. Both Spotty and Dodge seemed to want to start drinking, and drinking heavily. It suited me, when the hammer came down I didn't want to have to worry about either of them. If they were both paralytic, then all the better. We stopped off at one of the local supermarkets to stock up. I told Spotty that 'Chunky' may well be watching us, and we wouldn't want him to find out that Spotty had twigged what was going on, so we all went shopping together. Spotty paid by credit card, and I kept my hand on the pistol the whole time.

Half an hour later we were driving up a small country lane with enough hard liquor to sink a battleship. I had taken over the driving, Spotty and Dodge were drinking Pimms together, although more seemed to be going over the seats than was being poured down their throats. It wasn't all down to my driving either. The roads were terrible, pot holes all over the place. I was following Green's advice, taking turnings on a whim. Dodge and Spotty were becoming more and more frustrated, eager to get somewhere they could start some serious drinking. I felt like a parent in charge of two angry children demanding to know 'Are we there yet?'

Finally I found it, about two miles along a small mud track. There were two houses, the closest one was occupied, but the one in the distance looked, and felt empty, and what's more important, it felt right. There was a battered old Ford Cortina outside the first house. A tall hatchet faced man with sandy hair, wearing faded denims was unloading something covered in tarpaulins from the boot. As I drove past he looked right at me. There was an incredibly strange sensation of recognition, even though I was sure I had never seen him before he looked familiar. I even gave him a little wave, and he waved back before returning to his tarpaulins.

The house in the distance was empty, and it was unlocked. We walked in and sat down. It was clean, tidy and simply furnished, but there was no indication that anyone lived there. There was no post, and all the drawers were empty. But I knew it was right, this was somewhere extremely secure. Not in a physical sense, but esoterically it was a fortress. Spotty brought the shopping in and Dodge made a fire. I went outside to have a good look around, spot the vantage points and so forth. I felt an incredible sense of belonging. This time The Cheat would face me on my terms. I shut the gate and went back inside. The dusty name plaque rattled against the gate as I shut it. I could just make out the faded lettering. It said 'Lamassar.'

Chapter 15

The End

*'The killer awoke before dawn, he put his boots on. He took a face from the
ancient gallery and he walked on down the hall.'*
The Doors

Spotty and Dodge were already halfway through their second bottle of Pimms. Dodge wasn't the type to be content with fruity posh drinks and was already talking about starting on the flaming sambucas. That was something I didn't want to get involved with, I needed to keep a reasonably clear head. I went into the kitchen, made myself a cheese sandwich and a cup of tea. I went back into the lounge eating silently whilst they exchanged interminable anecdotes about drinking, each story more outrageous than the last as they tried to vie for the title of biggest drinker. I ate quickly, and when I finished I rolled a spliff. After a few puffs I passed it to Dodge, made my apologies, left them enough for a few smokes, then took the rest upstairs. I was taunted and jeered for not being man enough for the sambuca challenge, but they were too tied up in their drinking games to be overly concerned about me.

I could hear them both roaring with drunken laughter as I sat on the edge of the bed, rolling myself another spliff. That suited me fine, if they carried on like that they would both be comatose, and out of the way before anything serious happened. I lit up the joint and took a good draw on it, breathing the smoke deep into my lungs. I was hoping it would help me sleep, because I needed some rest really badly, my body was close to collapse, and I needed all my strength for what was going to follow.

Lying in bed, listening to the drunken riot going on below, I thought it strange how alcohol could unite two such disparate souls as Spotty and Dodge. Admittedly they were united in a hideous spastic stupor, but they were united nonetheless. I had more serious things to worry about. It had been a truly horrendous day. I had been run over twice. I'd been attacked by junkies and some ghastly supernatural freak. I'd lost two hours, been plagued by weird dreams from the Arabian Nights. I had killed, kidnapped and high-jacked. My secretary was in league with the devil, and I was being pursued by something out of the pyramids. The only good things that had happened were my partner being bitten, (I allowed myself to smile as I luxuriated in images of him squirming under the physician's knife,) and finding this refuge, a safe haven from the police, The Cheat and Veryanne's friends.

The main thing that worried me was the feeling that it was all bollocks. Thinking objectively about what happened I had to admit it all sounded like mad bollocks. I couldn't help thinking that all this weird shit happened after I went to that terrible party with the LSD. I had heard that people had acid flashbacks months and even years after they'd taken that filthy drug. What if that was happening to me, that everything could be explained by some chemical imbalance in my brain. It was not a comforting thought, because if it was true then I was going to be spending the rest of my life in a padded cell, drooling and screaming obscenities. I closed my eyes and I settled down for a troubled sleep full of nightmarish images.

I woke up abruptly at about three in the morning with an acute sense of urgency. No fuzzy, blurred, 'coming up from the layers,' experience for me, I blinked and I was wide awake and alert. It was a cloudless night, I could make out the shadow of Glastonbury Tor, and Venus was blazing brightly behind casting a faint stella shadow. It should have been obscured by bright moonlight but the moon was dying, almost completely hidden behind its dark side. The shadow fell into the garden below, and seemed to be pointing to something. The sense of urgency became overwhelming, this was no time to sit staring at the stars, there was work to be done. I pulled my boots on, checked the Browning and walked down the hall.

It was a beautiful sharp clear fresh evening. The stars seemed a lot closer than they did in Southampton, no light pollution. I stepped out and took a couple of deep breaths. It was fresh and crisp, not a smell I would normally associate with the country, but there was not even a hint of cowshit. This air smelled even nicer than the air back home. Even though it was really black, I could see quite clearly, the absence of moonlight seemed an advantage. I felt more comfortable in the darkness, it was easier to hide. All of Clay's priapic rantings about moon-goddesses had made me distrustful of the moon.

I walked over to the patch of ground where the shadow fell. There was a small cluster of mushrooms growing, like a fairy circle. As I stepped into the circle Venus came out from behind The Tor, and bathed me in her brilliance. One mushroom in particular stood out, and I had a sudden compulsion to stoop down and pick it. Before I knew it, I was chewing and swallowing. Somehow I knew exactly what it was once it hit my mouth, and I knew that this was no innocent fairy ring, but something altogether more sinister.

This was the epicentre, the source of this house's particular strength. I could feel it spreading out throughout the garden and into the house. I had to follow them, check the boundaries and at the same time get the lie of the land, see just how different things were after dark. And things were different, the starlight had given everything an unearthly glow. I paced out the garden, and became aware of the dimensions. I sought out the cardinal points. I became familiar with all the shadows, all the little hiding places. I soon realised that The Cheat could only get into the garden at one point. Once in, my immediate task was to guide The Cheat to the 'fairy ring,' once he was there I could kill him. I walked back to the circle and placed the phallus in the centre, then I went back into the kitchen to get a knife.

About half an hour later, sitting on the garden fence, smoking a spliff, I noticed the wind change. To be more correct, I smelled it change. It was that same foul stink that had been tormenting me for the past few days, faint, and far off, but unmistakable nevertheless. I stamped the spliff out, checked my weapons and slunk into the shadows, waiting as the smell grew stronger and stronger. Eventually I saw him also steeped in shadow, jaw hanging low like a wolf, something feral, unnatural, and wholly malevolent. It was slouching, sometimes on all fours, sometimes upright. Every so often it would sink its nostrils deep into the soil sniffing. It continued this way until it reached the garden gate, when it stood on its hind legs and howled. Yesterday it would have sent a shiver running down my spine, but not now. Now it made me grip the knife harder with a sense of grim fatalism.

He hesitated before coming in. Seeing his faltering footsteps gave me the incentive I needed. Up to now he had come loping along with purpose, it was strange and ghastly but it was confident. I had never seen this creature look the least bit uncertain, my instincts were right. I stepped out of the shadow, the knife flashed in the starlight and its ear fell on the ground. I darted into the back garden, into the shadow as The Cheat screeched with pain.

I looked back to see him clutching his ear and roaring. He was still standing on his hind legs, and looked enormous, well over seven feet tall, eyes glowing orange like a lizard's. A huge twisted claw clutched at the place where his ear had been, gouts of foul smelling black ichor came squelching out of the wound. He looked around, desperately trying to see me, but I was too well hidden. His huge nostrils twitched as he tried to catch my scent, but it was all in vain. He stood silent for a moment, uncertain, not sure what to do. Then he resumed his snuffling, slouching walk and started moving slowly towards me.

This was the sort of thing they never told you about when they warned you of the dangers of taking drugs. The government had got it all wrong. If the kids knew that taking heroin could lead to you being possessed by a bloodsucking, murderously creepy, foul breathed, Stygian bastard demon they might think twice before chasing the dragon. 'Don't chase the dragon or the bastard might chase you.' That's got a better ring to it than 'Heroin: Thatcher really screws you up.' LSD fares little better in drugs cautionary tales. One encounter with acid had turned me into a killer who keeps seeing monsters. 'Take LSD and you'll end up looking like this sick fuck-up.' Now that's a message the kids could take to their hearts.

As The Cheat drew level I stepped out, running the knife against his forehead, striking just as he put his nose to the ground. Instantly he was up and running, chasing me, as I ran to the patch of earth where the mushrooms grew. I carried on running disappearing into the shadow of the oak tree. Again The Cheat screamed in anger and desperation, looking this way and that, unable to find me. But something else had caught his attention as he found himself drawn to the ivory phallus at the centre of the fairy ring. Except that it wasn't a fairy ring, with nice jolly Father Christmassy red and white fly agaric, bedecked with happy gnomes and pixies smoking pipes and drinking beer. Neither was it the more innocuous hippy favourite psilocybin or magic mushroom. This was a poisonous variety of basidiomycetous toadstool called Amanita virosa. Better known as destroying angel.

As The Cheat stepped into the circle I stepped out of the shadows grasping the Browning with both hands. I pointed the barrel at his forehead and took a deep breath. The Cheat gave one final scream as I emptied the clip into his face, and that one did send a shiver down my spine.

Part 2

Detective No More

Chapter 1

I've Got You Under My Skin

'So deep in my heart you're almost a part of me.'
Frank Sinatra

On the wall next to the light switch there was a sign. It said, 'No Smoking,' so I didn't smoke. I just lay on my bed and stared at the ceiling. I was lucky to have such a good ceiling, not like some of the other poor bastards. Their ceilings were downright diabolical, total crap. But not mine, mine was the crème de la crème of ceilings. There was a little crack at one end that crossed over to the other side. It wasn't a straight crack by any means; it twisted and turned all over the place. Has your ceiling got a crack like that? Yeah, thought as much. Now you can see why it's such a brilliant ceiling.

Sometimes there was a river gushing across the ceiling. I could see boats and harbours, jetties and beaches. The river would flow on, through cities, towns and villages. Some of the places looked familiar. The river would keep going, through hills, valleys, fields, forests and jungles. The river swept across countries and continents until it reached the sea. It would flow into the sea yet still remain a river. Its current stronger than any ocean's tides. On and on it would flow until it reached dry land, then it would start all over again. I used to like the river, but then there was The Snake.

I used to think The Snake was really cool, he was as tiny as a worm, but as big as the river. He could flow too, always changing, spots, stripes flecks and wiggles. He was green, blue, orange, yellow, red, pink and colourless. He was patterned and plain. Sometimes he would twist, turn and whirl around, turning the whole ceiling into a huge kaleidoscope of colour. At first I used to like this, but now I can see it for the cheap parlour trick it really is.

The Snake did have a really good singing voice, just like Frank Sinatra. He would run through Frank's numbers like a Las Vegas impresario, and much as I despised him I had to admit he was good. Sometimes I would sing along, but then Eddie would come in with a big stick, telling me to, 'Shut the fuck up.' So I shut the fuck up. I could see Eddie's point, The Snake was a much better singer than me, best to let him sing unaccompanied.

Telling me to shut the fuck up and hitting me with a stick weren't the only things that Eddie did, although he did do those things quite a lot. He used to come and get me in the mornings, and take me to the others. A couple of times The Snake tagged along as well, but he didn't usually bother me when other people were around. I sat next to Sid. Sid was a grinning idiot, chewing gum and staring vacantly at the telly. There was no way I wanted to talk to him, so I watched the telly, it was nearly as good as the river, but not quite. Once the river came on the telly, I tried telling them that the river on the telly was the one from my ceiling. None of the bastards listened though, they just grinned stupidly. But not Eddie, Eddie hit me with a stick, and told me to, 'Shut the fuck up!'

The Snake liked *Hector's House*. We used to watch it together when the television wasn't on. He used to love all that crap about Ki-Ki the frog, Zsa-Zsa the cat and loveable old Hector. I hated it. I knew it for what it was, some twisted Anglo/French foray into psychiatric warfare, a sick attempt to bolster up the entente cordiale by making all the kids act like cats and dogs and frogs. And it nearly worked too. Then they got scared and took it off the air. That's why you can only see it when the telly's turned off. The Snake knew all of this, that's why he liked it. Whenever I tried to turn away the bastard would play it on the backs of my eyelids. I'd show him though, there was no way I was going to start acting like a dog or a cat or a frog. I might be mad, but I wasn't stupid. Anyway that's why they don't show *Hector's House* any more, even though they still show other stuff, like *Clangers* and *Herbs* and *Wombles*.

I've always thought of myself as a womble, that's what I told the pigs. I said I wasn't a thief, I was a womble. I'd just been caught with a rucksack of lead that I'd taken from the roof of my squat. I was on my way to the scrappies to cash it in so I could get myself some Billy. When they arrested me they took my knife, it was a good knife, too, and I needed it. I'd been stabbed the night before by Luddites, worshippers of the god Ludd, because I owed them a pile. I told them that Ludd didn't mind, because I knew him. I used to share a flat with him in Brixton. He wore really loud shirts and used to cheat at backgammon. I knew he was cheating, but could never catch him, that's what comes of being a god I suppose. I never told him I knew he was Ludd, otherwise that would be the end of me.

Anyway, after that I left Bristol and went to live in York. I got away from Ludd, but I was forgetting this biker that I owed two hundred quid. He laid some deals on me, and I just did them, straight up the nose. I ran into him down the pub one Friday night, and the guy wouldn't listen to reason. I lost two teeth man.

It's because I'm a dog that I get picked on. Anyway it won't be long before the spacemen come. I've been practicing my spirit walking in the woods, and I'm ready for them. Now I can grow to a height of eight feet tall, and talk to the tree spirits, and romp naked with the dryads.

I have to listen to that sort of bollocks every day. That's all Chris does, talk bollocks, day in day out. Still, it proves that what I've been saying about Hector's House is true. I don't know why I have to spend every day talking to these mad bastards. I can't remember the last time I went outside. I once asked Eddie if I could have a bit of fresh air, but he hit me with a stick, and told me to, 'Shut the fuck up!'

I glanced at my watch, it was ten past three. Brilliant, we would get a cup of tea and a piece of cake in exactly five minutes. At half past five we would have dinner, then at half past ten we went to bed. Rising at seven sharp, breakfast at eight and lunch at quarter past twelve. The rest of the time was filled in with telly, singing ceilings and shit like that. Anyway that's why you needed a watch. It was the only way you knew what the time was. Time has a habit of creeping up on you, and before you know it you've missed your dinner. Those bastards would never tell you, and there was no reprieve for the hungry man. Mealtimes never varied, they were cast in stone, but what we had for our meals, that varied, that varied a lot.

To the outside observer it looked as though there was no discernable pattern to what constituted our meals. It all depended on what the chef could get cheap. But that's what they want you to think. I must admit that it had me fooled at first, and I've still got a long way to go. After studying the menus at length, it became obvious they were all tied up with the lunar calendar. In order to crack it I had to work out all the variations caused by Venus' and Mars' relationship with both lunar and solar calendars. When I asked Eddie for an ephemeris he hit me with a stick and told me to, 'Shut the fuck up!' Now that's not like Eddie. Such uncharacteristic behaviour was all the proof I needed. Yesterday we had lemon cake and the day before that we had chocolate cake which meant we were due fruitcake. If I was right this would make it a run of three, and with teatime sorted out I could turn my attention to the main meal. When the tea lady served up the shortbread with a self-satisfying smirk I felt like screaming. She was grinning like a Russian grandmaster watching her opponent squirming in checkmate. But then I remembered that there were choc chips in the chocolate cake we'd had two days ago, that would affect everything. I would have to do loads more calculations now. The tea lady grinned triumphantly, she knew what she'd done.

Other than Chris, the only other person to talk to was Sid the grinning idiot. He wasn't at all interested in rivers, snakes or the rationale behind what makes up our meals. Whenever I mentioned it he said I was, 'talking bollocks.' He was more interested in what they show on the telly. We had our own special channel, telly for the criminally insane. The programme was specifically designed to remind you how horrible life outside was. It was the sort of programme that they could never show outside, it was just too depressing. If they tried to show this programme to anyone who wasn't dosed up to the nines on largactyl, the fall out would be catastrophic; random outbursts of violence by a society truly disgusted with itself. Even with a brain chock full of happy pills I had to fight back the urge to ram the set up Chris' arse. Kill two birds with one stone.

Sid liked it though, told me it was a modern day analogy of Milton's *Paradise Lost*, and that only the criminally insane understood it. I didn't believe that though, if Milton could see it he'd rip his eyes out if he wasn't already blind. The programme consisted of one group of barely hominid troglodytes trying to out-disgust another similar group. The programme should be called 'Extreme Gross Out.' These people confessed to all manner of disgusting behaviour, like the extremely obese who spent their days devouring waste lard. Other obese women spent their time being impregnated by a never-ending stream of junkies and alcoholics. Sad, stupid women asking why their husbands liked going out with other men and getting into fights. The audience wasn't much better, a bunch of tattooed pierced morons who looked like they had just stepped off the set of *Quest For Fire*. They insisted on imparting their wisdom which seemed to be, 'Grab hold of what you can and never let go.' No, they could never show this programme outside of mental institutions, its whole purpose was to reinforce just how disgusting the world outside was, and to tell us we were better off locked up. And it worked too, this place seemed like Noel Coward's holiday home in comparison.

I did agree with Sid in one respect the host was definitely based on the character of Satan, but they'd got that all wrong. In *Paradise Lost* Satan was given the heroic noble qualities of an Arthurian knight. Milton did this deliberately, to show that traditional heroism was not what was needed from a true hero, but love, kindness and self-sacrifice. That's why he wrote *Paradise Regained* starring Jesus. The programme makers seemed to have missed that. Admittedly the host was suitably malign, and self-obsessed, but she didn't have any heroic qualities whatsoever. She spent most of her time bleating about how her childhood was terrible, and how she had been suicidal, but managed to win through and come back to host this disgusting programme. This was the best argument for disbanding The Samaritans that I've ever heard. When not bleating on about herself she tries pop psychology, gleaned from the problem pages of the gutter press, on her 'guests,' and tells them to make a quilt. Quilt is the word. It doesn't matter what your problem is, how disgusted you are with yourself and the world around you, it can all be cured by making a quilt, and listening to a load of sanctimonious drivel. If they tried showing *Trisha* to anyone who wasn't heavily sedated there would be a riot.

Sid liked it though, and keeping Sid happy was one of the primary functions of the staff. It wasn't because they liked him, it was because he could get unbelievably violent, and need to be restrained. No, they were happy when he was grinning like an idiot and staring at *Trisha*. Not like me, I much preferred Sid when he was howling like a wolf and lashing out at the staff with broken chair and table legs. Eddie had a special electric zapper that he used to restrain Sid. I used to love watching the sparks fly off him as his eyes lit up like a Christmas tree. Apparently they used to have to restrain me a lot when I first came in, but not anymore. Now, other than the odd whack with a stick, and being told to shut the fuck up, the staff had very little to do with me. For me restraining was a spectator sport, and it was a darn sight more entertaining than *Trisha*.

Sid lost it at dinner time. I was quite pleased, I'd just worked out how many peas were on my plate, and I was trying to tell Sid what an achievement that was, but Sid wasn't interested. Sid was more concerned about the chicken. He said the animal was depressed when they killed it, and he wasn't going to eat something that had been depressed. Everyone had the right to eat happy animals, like the bacon we'd had for breakfast, that came from a happy pig, but not this shit. He accused Eddie of trying to kill us with chicken hormones. It had already been tried out on volunteers in

Viet Nam, and now they're trying it on us. Eddie tried reasoning with Sid, he told him to 'Shut the fuck up!' I tried telling Sid that we had to have chicken today, hormonal or otherwise, we'd had shortbread, so we had to have chicken. If the American army had given it to volunteers, it had to be safe. But Sid wasn't having any of it. He punched Eddie hard on the nose, it was really funny when all the blood started squirting out and I started laughing. Then it got even better, a load of Eddie's mates turned up and started beating the crap out of Sid with heavy bars. In the end they dragged his still twitching body off to the mortuary. Apparently Sid had choked on the chicken, so you can't be too careful. In all the excitement I forgot to take my pills, so I put them in my pocket for later.

Chapter 2

The Revolution Will Not Be Televised

'The Revolution will put you in the driving seat.'
Gil Scott-Heron

I awoke with a sense of resolution, of completion, but not of peace. No, resolution meant moving on. I had a sense of grim determination and purpose. I had been here long enough, it was time for me to go. It wasn't as easy as that though. I wasn't staying in a charming little B&B in the Cotswolds, I was in some form of secure accommodation. I couldn't just walk out, but I wasn't going to start digging any tunnels either. I hadn't got time for that. Much as I had enjoyed seeing someone being beaten to death, I was also a bit concerned about what had happened to Sid. I wasn't concerned emotionally, Sid had it coming and every time I thought of it I couldn't help laughing. No, I was more concerned on a personal level. If they're quite happy to club someone to death in front of everyone, then what's to stop them picking on me? I was going to have to be very careful, especially now that the happy pills were wearing off and I was starting to think clearly.

My main regret was not solving the mealtime enigma, it had been my holy grail for the past few years, and it was always hard to let an obsession go. I imagine stalkers feel pretty much the same way, but them's the breaks when you're ridding yourself of negative behaviour. I was also concerned about The Snake, recently he had taken to visiting me less and less, he had more pressing concerns. He no longer saw me as a threat, just a curiosity. I last saw him about a week ago, which means he'll probably come around again in about a fortnight. I'll have to be long gone by then, I may be able to fool the guards into thinking I'm still taking my medicine, but I won't be able to fool The Snake; he is the medicine. At the moment The Snake was far, far away. Even when he wasn't snuffling around my room I could tell when he was creeping around the grounds of the hospital.

I needed to make sure I acted normally, and if anything be ultra-passive. The guards had shown their ugly side last night and would be quick to jump on any dissent. I needed to make sure that I didn't stick out; I had to blend into the background while I thought about what I had to do next. I just had to keep my head down and shuffle though the day's routine, keeping my eyes open. What I had to avoid was losing it big with Chris over breakfast and shoving my cereal bowl up his arse, tempting though it may be. No, that was the Sid approach to crisis management, and we all know what happened to Sid.

Breakfast was a terribly dreary experience, but I managed to eat my sugar puffs without any problem. I made sure I kept the same vacant expression, following the lead of those poor unfortunates already dosed up. My main advantage over the others was how I was viewed by the guards. I had given up the struggle a long time ago. Apart from asking stupid questions I was totally compliant, and consequently they didn't watch me as attentively as they watched some of the others. This meant that it was relatively easy to palm my medication. I wasn't the only one who was keeping their head down. The events of last night had had an impact, and some of the more outspoken residents were similarly muted.

Something important happened at breakfast though. It concerned Chris. Previously I had viewed Chris as a sad and lonely individual. One whose annoying and disturbing outbursts could only be alleviated by the forcible insertion of various items of breakfast cutlery and crockery deep into the anal cavity. But I was wrong, he was much more than that, he was a link to the past. The more I studied him, the more I realised that there was something about him that reminded me of another time, a time before I was locked up. The memory was distant and hazy, and I could remember nothing other than a vague sense of déjà vu, but there was a memory there nonetheless. When I broke out I would have to take Chris with me. Then I would be able to crack open his head, revealing his secrets at my leisure. If nothing else I would be able to fully explore the breakfast crockery cure. It was something the staff here clearly had not tried, and it deserved a trial if nothing else.

Later on during *Trisha* I managed to get Chris' attention. I had to wait a bit, the first part of the show was about a nineteen year old girl who wanted to become a porn star. Surprisingly a lot of the audience did not agree with her career choice, and tried to persuade her to consider a raft of other career choices. This upset Chris, all the time she had been on screen he had been feasting his eyes upon her nubile young body, looking forward to the day when he would be able to see all of it. But now it looked as if that were being taken away, he cried out in distress. Ever willing to show his skills in man management Eddie hit him with a stick and told him to, 'Shut the fuck up!' After that Chris was a lot more subdued. He hardly murmured when an eighty-five year old alcoholic demanded to know why he no longer had any contact with his grandchildren. This was my opportunity to bring Chris on board.

I decided to treat him with concern, ask after his wellbeing, that approach always worked with Chris. Almost everyone was sick of his incessant ramblings, and consequently no-one ever showed him any concern. None of the patients anyway, Eddie had his own unique way of demonstrating concern which we had all experienced. Chris was understandably quite surprised by my questioning, but responded by telling me the plot of a porn film he was making up, starring himself and the girl who had just been on the telly. I listened attentively, but I wasn't listening to what he was saying, I was listening out for the gaps, the slight, almost discernable pauses as Chris stopped to take a breath. If he didn't have to breathe there would be no stopping him.

'Bit heavy, last night,' I whispered. Chris nodded dumbly; even he was not stupid enough to start talking out loud about the guard's activities. 'You know what it means don't you?' I continued, again Chris nodded dumbly. Then his expression changed, and he looked puzzled.
'No, I don't,' he whispered.
'Don't what?'
'I don't know what it means.'
'Then I'll tell you.' This was what I wanted to hear. Willing or not, I had to take Chris with me when I busted out. I would rather he was willing, and the best way to do that was to play on his amphetamine-fuelled paranoia. I leaned closer, conspiratorially. 'What it means,' I hissed, 'Is that they've decided that none of us are ever getting out of here.' Chris looked surprised, he opened his mouth to try to speak, but I wasn't going to let him. 'Think about it,' I continued, 'They beat the bastard to death right in front of everyone. It's not like they took him out of the way somewhere to administer a beating. They weren't at all worried about witnesses, so that means we're going nowhere. Look around you, look how subdued everyone is. Have you noticed how none of the guards have changed? It's the same lot that killed Sid. No one is being punished for what happened last night.'
'But Sid's a bastard. He choked on his chicken.'
'He choked on his chicken alright, but I didn't see anyone giving him the Heimlich manoeuvre. I'm telling you if we don't get out of here fast

we're all dead.' I paused while Chris digested this information. I could visibly detect the anxiety growing deeper and deeper within him. 'The only reason they're not killing us all at the same time is because they want us to eat the evidence.'

'What?' Chris spluttered. Murder seemed common place here, but cannibalism? That was just another little horror society was waiting to throw at us. I seized my advantage. Now was the time to make it more personal.

'Do the maths. Yesterday we had happy bacon for breakfast. At tea we had shortcake, then a depressed chicken. I'm telling you those sausages we had for breakfast today were definitely suspect. They tasted like they'd come from some psychotic razorback, or psychotic longpig.' Chris turned white, it was not the first time I had expounded my theories about the meals to Chris, and he was one of the few people who took them seriously. For a long time Chris didn't say anything. It was good to see him like this, too terrified to talk. He was a lot less annoying when he was terrified. When he finally spoke it was just one word.

'Fuck.'

'We're all fucked. The only difference between me and you is that you're going to be fucked with a dick three foot long.'

'Wh… wh… what'd'ya mean?'

'You're next. I overheard Eddie talking to one of the other guards about it. Reckons you get on everyone's tits.'

'Wh… wh… which guard?'

'That big ugly bastard, the one with all the roadkill tattoos. And at breakfast I saw the chef looking you up and down, and stroking that big knife of his.'

'I've never liked the way that chef strokes his knife, it gives me the creeps.'

'Well, now you know why.'

It was quite easy getting Chris to agree to come along after that. The only problem was, I'd overdone things a little, appealed too directly to his persecution complex. Chris was wound up tight like a spring, he could go off without warning. I had to ensure the spring stayed tight by reminding him of what had happened last night. Any weird behaviour on his part and they wouldn't hesitate, and we'd all be able to see another beating whilst having our meals. I told Chris to go back to his cell, keep his head down, and change his trousers. I'd come to him when it was time.

With Chris out of the way there was only one other thing I had to do, and that was get some tissue out of the bogs. After that I was just killing time, waiting until we were sent back to our rooms. I had to be careful to avoid provocation, the last thing I wanted to do was follow Sid's example when my head was just starting to clear. In order to take my mind off things, I allowed myself to indulge in meal predicting. After all, if things went according to plan it was going to be my last chance to do so for a long time.

Security cover drops right down once it gets dark. After all most if not all of us are so drugged up you could leave us to sleep in a field overnight, and we'd still all be there when you come back in the morning. Our rooms just had one lock. It was essentially a very large Yale lock. The guards only tended to use their keys to open up in the morning. When they wanted to lock us up they just let our doors swing shut. I had just stuffed a load of tissue into the cavity where the lock clicks. Eddie had just swung the door shut with an accompanying click. I was lying on my bed staring at the ceiling, I wanted to wait at least half an hour before I tried the door. I was twisting in the bed like a toddler waiting for his birthday party to start. Until I tried the door I wouldn't know if my plan was working. If I'd put enough tissue it the door it would open easily. If I hadn't then Eddie would spot it in the morning, and I would end up as that night's entertainment.

When I tried the door it opened easily, there was hardly any noise, just an almost indiscernible click. I crept back to my bunk and arranged the blankets to make it look as if someone was still there. Then I walked back to the door and slipped out into the corridor shutting the door behind me. It was gloomy and dull; the main lights had all been turned off, leaving the crepuscular jaundiced glow of the secondary lighting. I made no noise as I slunk along the corridor towards the kitchen. I gave silent thanks to the god of lax security when I discovered the door was unlocked. Inside it was pitch black. I shut the door behind me and turned the lights on. They illuminated the kitchen like a set of floodlights, and it took a few moments for my eyes to adjust. It didn't take me long to find what I was looking for. A good sharp serrated knife, suitable for skinning and gutting fish. It was the sort of knife I felt compelled to show to Eddie, he appreciated good steel.

I turned the light off, shut the door and went back into the corridor. I could hear noises coming from the day room, someone, probably one of the guards, was watching the telly. As I got closer the noises became louder and more distinct. I peered around the door to find Eddie totally engrossed in the television. There was so much grunting and moaning that at first I thought

Eddie was watching *Trisha*, but no, Eddie was watching something far more tasteful and cerebral than that. It was an outdoor scene, set in breathtakingly beautiful countryside. It was mid spring and the bluebells and daffodils lit up a piece of English woodland. A young willowy blonde woman was being fucked up the arse by a pig. At first I thought it was a Large White, but on closer inspection I realised it was a Chester White. It was an easy mistake to make, it was only when I listened to the grunting that I recognised the distinctive grunt of the Chester White.

The grunting was not confined to the telly though; Eddie was making his own farmyard noises as he showed his appreciation of the video by masturbating furiously. He was oblivious of anything else as I crept across the carpet towards him. As I stood behind him I could hear him whispering, 'Squeak piggy squeak.' As he grunted and wanked like a thing possessed. I looked down at Eddie's bell end. A tiny pearl of semen was just beginning to form at the tip. Eddie was just about to shoot his load. I didn't want Eddie's last experience to be remotely pleasurable so I stuck the knife into his throat. That stopped the wanking. Eddie made a ghastly hissing noise as his throat split in two, his arms flailed for a minute then he was still. Eddie may not have shot his load, but the second he stopped moving his sphincter relaxed and he shat himself.

That really took the shine off things, and totally bollocksed up my plans. I was hoping to change out of hospital pyjamas and get dressed in Eddie's uniform, but his shirt was covered in blood and I didn't want to think about his trousers. The stench was overpowering, as if all the festering corruption that had dwelt inside him decided to break free at the point of death. The only things I could salvage were his boots, a jacket, and a cap that were hanging on the door. I dragged his stinking carcass over to the corner of the room, behind some easy chairs. I didn't want anyone finding him too soon, although his stink had already made it outside, and I could hear muted groans and grumbles coming from the rooms as it worked its way down the corridor.

I had to work fast, inside the jacket I found Eddie's keys. I knew them all, and I quickly padded down the corridor to the medicine cabinet. What I found in there took my breath away. I was standing in the nerve centre of the whole hospital. There were thousands of drugs, all neatly labelled and categorised, uppers, downers, howlers and screamers. Some of them had huge warning labels on them. Those were the first ones I put in the little drugs carrying case, that was conveniently also in the cupboard. I took out all the insulin first, but I kept the hypodermics. I then loaded the bag full to brimming. If nothing else they would fetch a fortune on the streets, and I was going to need money. Eddie's wallet contained about seventy quid, and that wasn't going to get me very far.

For a minute though I just had to breathe in the wonder of it all. Not everyone appreciates the significance of the drugs cabinet and of he who holds the cabinet key. I had at my disposal enough drugs to knock out a medium-sized town, or send them crazy. I was tempted to hang around just to spike everyone's tea, then watch them all kill each other. I didn't have time though, Eddie's stink would attract another guard's attention long before teatime. And anyway The Snake would know if I started handing out drugs like that. He'd fill a paddy wagon up with his goons and send them in, wielding chainsaws and flamethrowers and shit. It did give me other options should anything else go wrong. I could always crank the loonies up with angel dust and turn them loose. That would give the guards something to do.

I took a couple of dexamphetamine. I was still a bit fuzzy, and needed something to liven me up a bit, it was going to be a long night. I couldn't think why they needed stuff like that here, I'd never seen any evidence of its use, everyone was sedated. But it was just what I needed, help flush the crap out of the system, speed things up a bit. There was always the added bonus of amphetamine psychosis, which could be an advantage in a situation like this.

On the way to Chris' room I walked past a door marked 'Files.' I decided to stop off, maybe I could find some answers there. I didn't even know what I was locked up for. I couldn't remember life before the hospital. But I wasn't alone in that, very few had memories of the outside apart from what they'd seen on television programmes. Chris thought he had been locked up for stealing lead, though it's more likely it was because he said he was a womble. Even so people shouldn't be sent to a place like this just for saying they're a womble. I found my file pretty easily, almost as if I had been lead there. For a moment I suspected a trap, but dismissed it as amphetamine psychosis, nothing more. Then something else caught my attention. There was a small metal safe under the desk. One of Eddie's keys fitted it, and to my delight I found £100 cash and a loaded revolver. There was also a further twenty rounds. I put them all in my jacket pocket and left the room.

As I crept down the corridor towards Chris' room I could feel the drugs starting to kick in. By the time I stood outside the door I was going through a terrific rush. I'd underestimated the speed's potency. I should have only taken one pill, because now I was totally wired, and looking for trouble. Even though I knew my number one priority was to escape, part of me wanted to stay behind for a shootout. Come out all guns blazing, Butch Cassidy and the Sundance Kid style. Fortunately I didn't encounter anyone on the way to Chris' room, because if I had, then all thoughts of stealth would be gone.

Chris was fast asleep, I opened the door silently and tiptoed over to him. Then I shook him awake violently. 'Wake up, wake up. Take these, it's time to go.' Chris came around groaning.

'What? Who?'

'Time to wake up and fuck off. Take these.' I stuck a couple of dexies in his hand. 'Go on take them now. You'll need them.' Chris rubbed his eyes, blinking like a mole that had just surfaced. Then his nose wrinkled up in disgust.

'Phwoar! What's that fucking smell? Have you shit yourself?'

'We're all shitting ourselves. But you and I have got more reason than most. If they find Eddie's body and we're still here, they're going to throw you to the dogs. Literally, those big fuckers you hear barking in the night. Now take your medicine and let's get out of here.'

'What is it?'

'Don't worry about that. Just take it. Trust me, I'm not a doctor.' Chris was used to following instructions when it came to taking medication, and swallowed the pills without any more arguments.

We decided to go out the back door instead of the main entrance. Chances were that it would be less heavily guarded. I had loaded up some of the hypodermics, two with largactyl, and one with one of the drugs covered with warning signs. We marched along, with Chris in front. I pulled the cap down tight over my eyes and wrapped the jacket around me. There were three guards in the office. Hopefully Chris would shield me long enough before they realised I wasn't Eddie. I passed one of the fentanyl syringes to Chris and told him to be ready to use it.

The first guard challenged us as we walked through the door. 'What are you playing at? You know there's no patients allowed in here.' I handed him a clipboard, one that I'd picked up in the office, there was a plain piece of paper attached to it.

'This one's being transferred.' I replied. 'We've only just been told. It's strictly hush hush. We've got to get him out without any of the others realising. It's all down here.' As the guard leant over to read the clipboard, Chris struck home. The needle went straight into the vein, and the guard slumped on the table. Again it was a case of a weakness being a strength. Only an intravenous drug user could hit the vein first time like that. The rest of us didn't have a prayer.'

I cradled his body, keeping him upright as I called one of the other guards over to countersign the docket. It was the vicious bastard with the roadkill tattoos. No fentanyl for him. As he leant over I stabbed him in the neck with the other syringe, the drug with warnings all over it. The result was spectacular. He didn't slump forward insensibly, he went into some type of fit, his arms and legs were thrashing about all over the place, and he was making a really nauseating gurgling noise. The last guard jumped up horrified, but it was too late, I was already pointing the revolver at him. He put his hands up.

'Well done.' I said to him. 'Now, this is a breakout. If you help us, you'll get a nice sleep like him.' I pointed to the guard Chris had whacked with the fentanyl. He was snoring, and smiling like a baby. Or, you could try out some violent spasmodic convulsions like your mate. If nothing else he should lose a bit of weight, and he'll be well cared for in here.' I didn't need to say anything else, he knew too well the fate meted out to this hospital's patients. He gave me 'Roadkill Tattoos,' car keys, and the seven digit number I needed to get out of the car park without setting off the alarm. Chris gave him a chemical cosh and we left the guards, two sleeping soundly, one twitching violently. Half an hour later we were tearing down the motorway heading south.

Chapter 3

Twin Cadillac Valentine

'Somebody open the cage, 'cause the monkey's busted loose.'
Screaming Blue Messiahs

Chris had really peaked on the motorway. We were both pretty euphoric after breaking out. I wasn't too sure where I was going, but I was determined to get as far away from that place as possible. We weren't going to get anywhere that fast, even though I had had my foot flat on the accelerator ever since we had hit the motorway. I was driving a really shitty Mini Clubman with a top speed of ninety. It really stank inside a dank mixture of woodbines, engine grease, poor personal hygiene and dead animals. We had to throw out a couple of flat hedgehogs when we got in.

It made me think about Scottish hedgehogs, there had been something on the telly about it just before I'd gone to bed. Apparently there's a hedgehog cull on a Hebridean isle. Since they were introduced, in an attempt to keep down the local slug population, they've gone crazy and threatened to take over the island. Wreaking havoc with the fragile eco-system, and threatening farmer's livelihoods. People are being paid to kill hedgehogs at a cost in excess of two grand per hedgehog. Some hippy was talking about what a waste of money it all was. I had to agree with him. They've got the sums all wrong. They shouldn't be paying people to kill hedgehogs, people should be paying them. In the right hands a hedgehog cull could be a real money-spinner. Offer hedgehog-blasting holidays with strippers for stag nights. People like 'Roadkill Tattoo' would queue up for that. I'd even go myself if I wasn't so concerned with evading the police.

'Thanks for the speed,' jabbered Chris. I was hoping that's what you'd given me, it's my ally.' Since we'd got on the road I had been concentrating on driving. It was strangely unfamiliar, I hadn't driven in God knows how long, and it took longer to adjust than I had thought. It wasn't until we reached the motorway that I'd given much thought to what Chris was saying.

'What the fuck are you talking about?'

'Allies man. *The teachings of Don Juan* man.'

'Wasn't he some randy bastard?' That figured, I could see Chris being into the writings of a notorious fornicator. But I was wrong, he was a Native American shaman who conversed with spirits by taking a heady brew of hallucinogenic drugs. If he got on with one of the spirits, it became his ally. Chris believed he had contacted the nature spirit dwelling within pharmaceutical grade amphetamine. The fact that there were probably no natural ingredients whatsoever in the compound, could not counter this belief, of which he spoke with proselytising zeal. I had real problems with it though.

'So, what does your ally do? Is he some little bloke sitting on a toadstool dishing out advice? Has he any suggestions about where I should be heading for?'

'No man, he's like a spirit guide, he shows me around, lets me know what's happening. Mais Je ne pas Français.'

'Comment?'

'Je ne pas Français. Je ne pas parlais Français.'

'Je parlais un peu.'

'Un petit peu.'

'Oui, parce que nous parlant Français maintenant?'

'Comment?'

'Parce que... Sod it. Why the fuck are we talking in French?'

'I do it all the time, just in case we get caught. It'll confuse the police. I used to do in the hospital to confuse the guards. They were trying to convince me I was French, so I used to have to talk French just to make them go away. That way they think they're succeeding man. It's not like anyone said anything about France or anything, they were way too subtle for that. Like when I got there I asked for a bag to put my shoes in so they wouldn't run out. They gave me this old potato sack. It was miles too big. I had to keep the telly in it. It was the same at the last place, only there it was Hungarian. You see, sac is the French word for bag. If I was French and I wanted a bag I'd ask for a sack. See, that's how they were doing it. The only thing is, it doesn't work the other way round. The French word for sack isn't bag.'

I could feel myself getting dragged into the conversation. He was way off course. The guy was mad, you'd have to be mad to think all that shit about foreign languages when it was so obvious they were using lunar cycles and mealtimes. I still needed to know the conclusion though, where this manic train of thought was heading. I had to ask. 'What is the French word for sack?'

'Nobody knows man, and there was no way of finding out. They didn't allow access to foreign dictionaries or language courses because that's the key. If we had known the French for all the objects in the hospital we would have been out of there. I sent off for a cassette, to try to learn Mandarin. It was in the paper. I thought it would be really cool, to be able to talk to oranges, just like Dr. Doolittle. But they wouldn't let me have it. Said it was in my own best interests. I was warned off. They said if I didn't stop they'd try out some genetic experiments on me, like they did with you.'

'What?'

'Yeah. When they first let you out of that experimental ward we thought you'd have three heads or something like that. There was some pretty weird shit going on. But tonight you came into my room with some speed and we escaped. It's just like Shakespeare.'

'What the fuck are you talking about? What genetic experiments?'

'Don't you know? Jesus, it was like Doctor Moreau's island up there, except that it wasn't an island. We weren't allowed up there, but we could hear what was going on, and there were stories and that.' Every pause, every delay made me want to grab him by the throat, but I had to let Chris tell things in his own infuriating way.

'One guy said he saw a really big frog coming out there. Only it wasn't a frog, it was some poor bastard who'd been shot up with frog hormones. They might have done that to you, for all you know. Anyway, it sounded just like a zoo, what with all the screeching and roaring. And all the jumping about, it sounded like you'd got a trampoline up there. Oh yeah, and there was that really square music they kept playing all the time, Frank Sinatra. Then, gradually, as they kept bringing out frogs, and alligator men, and duck people, and one guy with three arses, it started to get quieter. After a while they closed it down, and brought you down to live with the rest of us. You were the only one left see. All the rest either died or escaped or were turned into frogs. You were a really violent sod, always getting into fights. Especially with Eddie, that's why he hated you so much. And that's why Sid always left you alone. They just kept upping your medicine until you smiled like the rest of us. But that was years ago.'

I didn't pay much attention to what Chris said after that, I was too tied up in my own thoughts. I didn't like the sound of what Chris had told me. It sounded real enough, but I didn't have any memory of it at all. Chris wasn't exactly the most reliable of witnesses though, and it could all be the product of his warped and twisted imagination. I had a horrible feeling that most of what he said was true. The sooner I could read those files the better. And once my head was clear, I needed to take a full inventory of my body parts. How does a guy with three arses use the toilet?

Just south of Birmingham we had to stop for petrol. We'd both just taken another couple of dexies, just to banish the largactyl, and were gibbering like monkeys. I was starting to feel a bit weirded out, and the prospect of mingling with a crowd of strangers wasn't appealing. I didn't just have myself to worry about, Chris was a complete liability. At any moment I was scared he was going to start jabbering about moon-goddesses and Ludd. Because if that happened, I wasn't fully prepared for the ugly scene that would inevitably follow. I warned Chris to keep his trap shut and act normal.

There's something depressing about service stations, something about their transitory status makes them a bit like doctor's waiting rooms. Nobody wants to be there, they all want to be where they're going. And that's all anyone can think about, the rest of the journey. How much more driving they have to do, and a presentation box of shortbread doesn't make it any sweeter. Well, I suppose it was better than trying to act normal, which is what we were doing.

After years in our little institution, the bright light and sirens of the amusement arcade were intimidating. Chris was particularly freaked out, sensing that they could take his soul. We scurried quickly to the stainless steel shiny, lemon scented toilets. I have always liked urinating to be a silent affair, and remained tight-lipped throughout, but Chris wouldn't stop talking. Both during the urination itself, and the final drip removing process. Chris spent an unusually long time flapping his semi-flaccid penis from side to side. I suddenly realised I was staring at Chris waving his knob around in a public toilet. I started to get the fear. What if someone came in? I didn't want to be arrested for cottaging. But just as this thought went through my head, he put his willy away, and started washing his hands. I looked at myself in the mirror, I was starting to sweat, and my eyes were bloodshot. I splashed a bit of water over my face, but I don't think it did any good.

We decided to avoid the cafeteria, and get a few things from the shop. Just the bare essentials, I really wanted some clothing, our hospital pyjamas were a bit too conspicuous for my liking. All I could get were a couple of T shirts. One had a beefeater on it, and the other had 'I (big red heart) London.' We also needed some cigarettes, a breakfast bowl and something to eat, a packet of crisps and a mars bar each, and a really big bottle of pop. I was queuing up at the checkout, and had just got to the front of the queue when I became aware of a low moaning whine coming from the magazine rack.

Chris was staring at a copy of *Dirty Girls*, face contorted hideously, mouth drooling. People were starting to stare, the girl behind the cash register looked twitchy, something between fear and disgust. She was wondering whether to call security. I needed to take control of the situation, and at the same time reassure people. Put their minds at rest; let them know that we were not a couple of escaped lunatics, (which we were.) 'Chris!' I barked, 'Come over here, and bring that with you.' Chris bounded over like an eager puppy. I felt like a parent buying their small child a few sweets. I looked at the girl behind the register, she was looking back with disgust. I had to say something normal, something to explain our bizarre behaviour. 'You need to be commended for your magnificent selection of pornography,' I smiled. 'My associate and I have been in Saudi Arabia. He is a very passionate man. The only female company he has had, has been a Littlewoods catalogue. And now he has this we can throw the damned thing away. Thank you so very much.' I put my hand out to shake hers, but she just handed me my change and avoided any further eye contact.

Back in the car we changed into the T-shirts. I opted for the one with the beefeater, because I thought it had marginally better taste than the other one. Chris seemed pleased with his, it was almost as if he had only just got the joke. It did make us look a bit more normal though, and the bright colours distracted attention from the trousers. We did look like a couple of prats, either a couple of real hicks who had never been to the city before, or a couple of foreign tourists. Chris was happy to stay in the car while I filled up with petrol, he was looking forward to the opportunity of examining *Dirty Girls*, in more detail.

I drove the car up to the petrol pump, my hands were sweaty and slipped on the steering-wheel. I could feel my heart pumping savagely against my chest, as the dexies continued to rampage through my body. I wound the window down and took a couple of deep breaths. Unlike the shop there was no-one else around, the place was deserted save for the cashier, staring at me from inside his cubicle. I felt like I was being examined closely, like something on a specimen slide. I needed to get things into perspective, I was only buying petrol, it wasn't like I was planning to rob the place or anything. All I needed to do was act straight, and not to look remotely intoxicated. We didn't want to be pulled for drunk driving. The only problem was that I had an intoxicating cocktail of narcotics surging through my body, and it had been so long since I was straight, that I had forgotten what it was like.

I got out of the car, and went to pick up the petrol nozzle. I froze, all the petrol had changed, no more two and four star, but unleaded and lead replacement. For a moment I panicked, not knowing what to do, what was the bloody difference anyway? Fortunately there was a little sticker just above the fuel cap. I put in lead replacement. I couldn't believe that it came to over thirty quid. I replaced the hose, and walked over to the booth, concentrating on walking in a straight line. I had to pay the cashier through a little hole in a Perspex window. I wasn't able to work it properly, and could feel the cashier eyeing me suspiciously. I paid in cash, and walked slowly back to the car. Once inside I looked back at the cashier, he was on the phone. That could only mean he was on the phone to the police, and it was too late to go back and shoot him. The best thing to do was act as if I hadn't noticed. I started the engine up and drove slowly off the forecourt. As soon as we hit the motorway I put my foot down.

'We're fucked!' I yelled. 'Those bastards are on to us. We need to get off the motorway as soon as possible.' We were fucked, the motorway seemed to go on for miles and miles with no indication of any turnoff. It was like a rat run. All the pigs had to do was seal off one end, and send a few jam sarnies down to flush us out. I wasn't going to go quietly; I'd rather be shot down dead in the street than go back to the hospital.

'How are we fucked man?' asked Chris from between the pages of *Dirty Girls* 'Didn't you see the cashier as we left? He was on the phone man, the fucking phone. It can only be the pigs. Jesus I thought we'd have a bit more time than this before the shit hits the fan.'

'He might not have been talking to the pigs, he might have been talking to his dad about their cat or something.'

'At four in the morning?'

'Well yeah, if the cat was ill he might have to call out the vet or something. It can be really distressing having to cope with a sick animal.'

'Sod the fucking cat. He was talking to the pigs.'

'Look man, you need to get your facts straight. It's a bit stupid getting all freaked out about the pigs just because someone's cat's feeling ill.'

'I hope you're right that's all. I hope his cat is dead, because that means the pigs aren't onto us.'

'Dead! I just thought it was ill, I didn't realise it was dead. That's really sad.'

'Look, there is no fucking cat...'

My words were cut off by the loud wail of a police siren. I looked in the mirror, there were two blue lights on my tail. I had my foot down on the accelerator, and was screwing the Clubman for all it was worth. We were going way too fast for the engine and the car was juddering and shaking all over the place, but we couldn't get above ninety-five. I looked back in the mirror, the blue lights were getting closer. I could make out two separate lights, one on the nearside lane, and one on the outside. I was creeping past a red Metro in the middle lane, and one of the blue lights was right up my arse. I swerved back into the middle lane causing the Metro to brake. He beeped his horn angrily, I could only just hear it above the sound of the sirens. I waved apologetically, and shouted, 'Car chase,' but I don't think he heard me.

By now the police car on the outside lane had drawn level, the other one was staying back. I looked over at the pig who was driving. Unusually he was the only person in the car, I thought pigs always travelled in pairs. Then I could feel the hair standing up on the back of my neck, and a disgusting taste filled my mouth. The car behind was driving right up close, the Metro had fallen back completely now. The pig in the outside lane was staring right at me. His face was a contorted mask of hatred, of an intensity I had never seen before. And there was something wrong with his eyes, the pupils weren't circular, they were slits, like a cat's.

'She gets too hungry to wait for dinner at eight.' Frank's voice suddenly erupted from the speakers. 'She likes the theatre, but never stays late.' That was all the proof I needed, these weren't ordinary pigs. They were snake-eyes. I slammed my foot hard onto the brakes. The car that was level shot forward. There was a tremendous crash as the other one rammed up the back. At this point I lost control, and the car skidded over to the hard shoulder, locked together with the pursuing pig car. Just before we drew to a halt I pulled the pistol out and fired in the general direction of the pig. I felt something jerk my hand as the pistol went off. I had shot the pig right between the eyes, and the driving seat was a mass of blood.

'Oh my God,' screamed Chris. 'You've completely killed him. Let me out! Let me out!' He was terrified. He had gone completely white, and was looking at me as if I were the devil himself. His door sprung open, and he leapt out, scrambling up the embankment, still clutching his copy of *Dirty Girls*. I wanted to call out to him, let him know that everything was alright, that I wasn't really killing pigs but demons. I didn't have any time though, the other jam sarnie was starting to reverse back, and I didn't think it was for a quiet word.

I was dead in the water, the car had packed in completely. The police car stopped about a hundred yards ahead, and the pig got out. Just in time I realised he was carrying a machine-gun, I ducked down as a hail of bullets burst through the windscreen. My door was jammed shut, so I had to climb out through the passenger side. I could see bullets flashing in front of me, and something burned my ear lobe, but I got the door open, and rolled out onto the grass. As I fell I pointed the pistol in the general direction of the gunfire, again I felt my hand jerk as the pistol went off. Then everything went quiet. There was a sudden roar of acceleration as the Metro shot past, and off into the distance, then everything went quiet again.

The pig was lying dead in the middle of the road. He had also been hit between the eyes. I was tempted to take his machine-gun, but it was far too bulky. I tried calling for Chris, to let him know that everything was cool, both pigs were dead, but he had disappeared into the night. The clubman was a complete write-off, I had no choice. I took the car keys out of the dead pig's pocket, then continued on my way in a jam sarnie.

Chapter 4

Caught By The Fuzz

'We'll make you wish you'd stayed at home tonight.'
Supergrass

I was feeling pretty good which I found puzzling. By rights I should be panicking, I had just killed two pigs, and was making my escape in a stolen pig car. I had left a scene of terrible carnage on the motorway, and freaked out the driver of a red Metro. On the face of it, I was the sort of fugitive the police spared no expense in running to ground. At any moment I expected to hear the sound of a police helicopter swooping down. I didn't take the first exit, or the second, fearing that the pigs would expect that, and be setting up roadblocks.

The rest of the motorway journey passed without further incident. I was driving along some rural B-road in Gloucestershire somewhere. The sun had started rising about an hour ago, and despite a few whimsical twists and turns, I had pretty much kept it on my left shoulder. I still couldn't get over how good I was feeling. I now had a bit of distance on the night's events, and I was able to think without the adrenalin fuelled sense of urgency. I first started feeling good when I shot the pigs. After that, it all felt pretty wonderful. The more I thought about it, the more I realised that there was a distinct, and separate, rush of endorphins for each killing. And to a lesser extent stabbing Eddie. Even though at that time, I was so out of my head I wouldn't have realised, had it not been for the other more intense killings.

I was slowly drifting South, wondering what all of this meant, when I came across a battered, old, rusty, pale blue Triumph Herald parked at the side of the road, next to some woodland. As I drew up alongside, a tall lanky figure, hunched up in faded denims came out of the woods. Under his arm he was carrying something wrapped in a tarpaulin. We made eye contact at the same time. He didn't like the look of the jam sarnie that was for sure, and tried hiding the tarpaulin behind his back. I got out of the car, my right hand deep in my jacket pocket, still holding onto the pistol.

'This is the police.' I yelled, trying to sound authoritative. 'What are you hiding behind your back?' He stood stock still, not uttering a word. I looked back; his sandy hair and hatchet-face framed a pair of sharp, blue, quick-moving eyes. He was studying me intently, weighing up what was going on. I remembered my beefeater T-shirt and hospital pyjamas.

'You're a funny looking copper.' He replied quietly.

'I'm plain clothes,' I said pulling the pistol out, 'Now what are you hiding?'

'You're no fucking copper,' he yelled, ignoring the pistol and running over to the jam sarnie. 'But this is a proper pig car. How the fuck did you get hold of this?' I wasn't in the mood for twenty questions, I was affronted, he had ignored my gun, and I desperately needed to re-establish my authority.

'I got hold of it by killing the two pigs who were chasing me.' He looked me up and down, trying to determine whether I was telling the truth.

'Really? That's sweet. I hate the fucking pigs. They all want shooting. Well done.' He held his hand out to me, the gun was starting to feel awkward, but I wasn't ready to start trusting anyone yet. He let his arm fall back to his side. 'So,' he continued, 'What are you going to do now?'

That was a question I couldn't really answer. I knew I had to ditch the jam sarnie, and get a change of clothes, but other than that I had no plan. My plan was to get out of the hospital, then get far away. I had done both, and now I was uncertain what to do next. He could sense my hesitancy, so he continued. 'Shall I tell you what I think?' he asked. He took my silence as a cue to continue. 'If what you say is true, then you're desperate to dump that pig wagon. You come along here, see the Triumph, and decide to swap cars. It would have worked, too, if you'd been here half an hour ago. I'd even left the keys in it. You could have driven off no bother, leaving me with this.' He slapped the jam sarnie. 'Only thing is, I'm here now, so you've got to deal with me.'

He was right, this was something I hadn't bargained for. It's so much harder killing someone once you've struck up a conversation with them. If I'd shot him when he first came out of the woods I could be away by now, slipping back into anonymity, just another bozo in a crappy car. But now I had things to sort out. He kept talking, all in the same slow, reasonable tone. 'If I was you I would have shot me by now, but you're not me. I know this area, and these roads like the back of my hand. I could travel for miles without seeing anyone. I don't think you could. I think you're lost.'

'Alright then maybe I am lost. But why should I trust you?'

'I'm not asking you to trust me. You've got a gun for fuck's sake. It's just I want to be out of here.' He unwrapped the tarpaulin, and showed me the biggest lump of dope that I had ever seen. 'If the pigs turn up now we're both fucked, maybe you more than me. But I'm still looking at five years. So if you're not going to shoot me I'd like to be off.'

He stood there grinning, arms outstretched, one still clutching the block of resin. There was something reassuringly genuine about his ugly criminal countenance that I forgot all about shooting him. Anyway, if I shot him there would be another corpse to deal with. If I left it by the pig car they could tie it to the Triumph Herald, and I didn't want to be driving around with a stiff, what with everything else going on. 'Alright,' I said. 'It's a deal, but you're driving.' I kept the gun trained on him as I retrieved the drug box from the jam sarnie. Then we walked over to the Herald together. Got in and drove off. The keys were still in the ignition.

The interior was as tatty as the outside, and it was a bit of a step down from a police pursuit vehicle, but compared to the Clubman it was a limousine. For a start there were no dead animals floating about the back seat, and it didn't stink. It was very untidy, the back seat was chock-a-block with all sorts of bits and pieces, some covered in tarpaulin. There were cardboard boxes and screws and bolts, and old fag packets and CDs and sweets, and all manner of weird shit. My companion chatted away amiably, he told me he was called Steve. Offered me a place to crash, back at his house, which wasn't too far away, but it would probably take us about three hours to get there, because of the roads we would have to take.

There was something very familiar about the whole situation, as I sat down I had felt a very strong feeling of déjà vu. For the first time since we had left I felt nostalgic. The act of car hi-jacking was threatening to awaken some long lost memory. I sat back comfortably while Steve told me all about himself, and in particular his deal. Steve had bought the block cheaply, in March when the market was glutted with cheap Moroccan. It had laid hidden all through spring, and almost until the end of summer. Glastonbury's cannabis levels peaked during the Pilton festival, but then most of the dealers decided to follow the festival trail, staying away until October. By the end of August all the slack was taken up, and Steve was going to knock it all out in eighths and sixteenths, at a considerable mark-up.

I started to warm to him, so I told him all about the hospital, and what had happened to Sid. I told him how the pigs tried to kill us, and how Chris ran off weeping into the night. I kept quiet about The Snake. I was starting to feel like a character from *The Great Escape*, and I didn't want to shatter the illusion of reaching Switzerland by jabbering about snakes and demonic possession. That was the sort of thing that wrecked shaky new friendships. I was however, very pleased to show him the contents of the drug box, and together we plotted what sort of mark-up a drug starved town would pay for pharmaceutical grade mind-benders.

We had been driving for about two hours when Steve had to join the main road. We had managed to bypass Bath and Bristol, and joined the main Wells/Bath, Wells/Bristol road just north of Chewton Mendip. The road swerved round to the right, and on the corner, parked on a little spot of grass by the turnoff for Radstock, sat a white pig van, with the driver's door wide open. Steve beeped his horn, waving at the door. 'Shut your door, you'll cause an accident.' He then turned to me. 'Isn't that typical? If you or me sat on a junction with our door open like that, chatting on the phone we'd get pulled for sure.' I didn't answer, I was too busy looking at the pig. His face had turned white when Steve had beeped his horn. Steve didn't strike me as the sort of person who terrified pigs with a single beep, so something else must have frightened him. As I watched he got back in the van and started following us.

'That's bloody typical 'n all,' said Steve. 'He's going to give me a telling off now. Well I'm not apologising. Bastards!' But as we watched our pursuer was joined by two other pigs on motorbikes, and a large transit van. There were some road works up ahead, with traffic lights, and the light was red. Just as we stopped the lights turned green again, Steve was just about to pull off when one of the motorcycle pigs drew alongside and told Steve to pull over. Steve suggested pulling over just past the traffic lights, there was a layby there. Moreover, stopping at the traffic lights was a really inconsiderate thing to do, but the pig was having none of it. He demanded Steve pull over right away, which he did. I put my hand back in the jacket, and was reassured that the pistol was still there.

Steve pulled over as best he could, but it wasn't easy. One of the motorbike pigs drew up next to me, pinning me into the car. He took his helmet off and glowered at me. He looked like a thug, the sort of person that would enjoy Eddie and 'Roadkill's company. The police van and transit both pulled up behind us, but no-one got out. The first pig continued talking to Steve. 'Can you tell us where you've been today?'

'Yes I can,' replied Steve.

'And?'

'And I can tell you where I've been today.'

The pig sighed with exasperation. Clearly he had come across people like Steve before, and didn't appreciate the verbal literalism. 'Could you please tell us where you have been?'

'Why?'

The pig was starting to lose his patience. 'I'll tell you why,' he shouted. 'An hour ago there was a bank robbery in Bristol, whoever robbed the bank made their escape in a blue Triumph Herald. They were last seen heading towards Wells. Now if you look behind you, you will see a transit van. Inside that van is an armed response unit and a dog-handler. If you don't tell me where you've been I'll hand this investigation over to them.'

'Alright, I've been to Gloucestershire. I had to pick up this bloke,' said Steve gesturing towards me. 'He's a bricklayer, and we need him on a site I'm working on in Castle Cary. He's Latvian, he doesn't speak any English, but he's a shit-hot brickie apparently.'

I grinned at the copper and gave him the thumbs up. I blurted out 'Manchester United,' trying to sound as enthusiastically East European as possible. He looked back suspiciously.

'Why do you think he's wearing that twatty beefeater T-shirt? Would any self-respecting Englishman wear such a stupid thing?'

The pig paused for a bit, mulling over what Steve had said. After a minute he continued. 'Have you any proof you've been in Gloucestershire?' Steve thought for a moment then pulled out a petrol receipt, luckily for us it had the date and time of the purchase, putting us well away from Bristol. The pig took the receipt and went over to his colleagues in the transit van. The other pig sat glaring at us. After about five minutes he came back, handed the receipt back to Steve and waved us on.

As we drove off I gave him the thumbs up once more and shouted, 'Manchester United.' We got past the traffic lights, and about as far as the sign that said that Chewton Mendip welcomed careful drivers, when the pigs pulled us over again. 'I'm getting really pissed off with this,' groaned Steve. He wound the window down and addressed the pig once more. 'What is it this time?' The pig stood his bike up and got off. He took his helmet off and gave Steve a rueful smile. I could hear the dogs going mental in the transit. It sounded like they hadn't eaten in a long while, and had just caught our scent.

'We've just been on the radio, and you match the description of one of the robbers,' he said pointing to Steve. 'It's your choice. Either we wait here for one of the witnesses to turn up, or failing that, I'll have to arrest you on suspicion of armed robbery.'

At that moment a rather portly pig sergeant in his late fifties came cycling towards us from the direction of Chewton Mendip. He leaned his pushbike against the transit, took off his helmet and bicycle clips, and walked over to us. 'Can I be of any help?' he asked the motorbike pig. 'I'm the local bobby, I just heard all the commotion on the radio, and thought I'd best pop over, lend a bit of local knowledge.' He pointed to us, 'Are those the bank robbers then?'

'I'm no bank robber,' snapped Steve, 'I just look like one.' He sighed deeply and continued. 'Look I've had this all my life. It's a standing joke that my face is permanently on display at Bath Nick. I've got a criminal face, I can't help that.' He pointed over to the other motorbike pig, the one who had remained silent until now. The one that looked like a thug. 'What about him?' asked Steve, 'He looks more of a bank robber than me. Why don't you ask him where he was earlier on today? I bet he matches loads of descriptions.'

'He's got a point there,' agreed the sergeant. 'He does look a nasty piece of work, but he's a police officer, and appearances can be deceptive.'

The first pig, the one who had pulled us over ignored this remark, and started busying himself by looking around the car, kicking the tyres, looking at the tread, examining the lights. He pulled out a clipboard with an official looking form on it, and started to fill it out. 'Your rear off-side tyre looks a bit worn,' he said. 'You're going to need to replace that soon. And the rear lights and number-plate are obscured by a layer of thick black mud. The highway code clearly states that lights and number-plates should be kept clean and visible at all times.' He didn't even look at Steve as he spoke to him, but continued to address the clipboard as he went on filling out his form. 'Have you got a driving licence, MOT certificate and insurance documents?' Steve reached into the glove compartment and pulled out an MOT certificate. He told the pig he'd left his licence and insurance documents at home. The pig continued writing, still talking in his detached official manner. 'Both your road tax and MOT run out at the end of next month.' He tore the form he was writing on from his clipboard. 'This is a notice to produce,' he said, handing the form to Steve. 'You have five days to produce your driving licence and ins…' He never completed his sentence, because at that moment another pale blue Triumph Herald came roaring past. It was identical to ours in almost every way, except it wasn't a pile of crap. The driver looked like he was related to Steve in some way.

Both pigs jumped onto their motorbikes and sped off in hot pursuit, closely followed by the van and transit, leaving us alone with the police sergeant. 'Well,' said the sergeant, 'That's that then. All's well that ends well. But you can see why they had to stop you.' Steve wasn't going to be placated that easily.

'It happens all the time. You saw the way they were looking at me. I hate to think what would have happened if you hadn't turned up. They were looking for someone to pin this on. And what about my mate? He's not been in this country very long. What's he supposed to think?'

'Manchester United.' I grinned at the sergeant.

The sergeant wasn't going to be drawn any further; he changed the subject, and started talking to me in a very loud voice. He told me about the dairy farm and cheese factory just around the corner. He waxed lyrical about Wells Cathedral, and Glastonbury Tor. He also mentioned Weston-Super-Mare and Cheddar Gorge. Then he hopped on his bike and pedalled off, muttering things like, 'Well I never.' And 'Wait 'till my grandchildren hear all about this.' As we drove past I called one final 'Manchester United,' before we lost sight of him, obscured by a hidden dip.

Any lingering doubts I had about trusting Steve vanished. I breathed a huge sigh of relief, but Steve wasn't at all happy. 'It's amazing isn't it?' he groaned. 'How quickly pigs turn into mechanics and then straight back into pigs again whenever it suits them.' I didn't say anything, I was totally taken aback by the whole experience, and couldn't believe how close it had all been. We drove through Wells without further incident, and headed off towards Glastonbury.

As soon as we saw the Tor Steve looked at me in triumph. 'I've got it!' he yelled. 'I knew I'd seen you before. It was years ago, when I was living the other side of Glastonbury. I had a lovely little cottage, miles from anywhere, perfect for stashing stuff. Then you turn up in the cottage over the road. All sorts of weird shit happened that night. I'll never forget what I saw. Next day the place was crawling with pigs. It really fucked up my business and I had to move. Still that proves it. Today's events were all fate. Wait till we get home, I've got something I think belongs to you.'

Chapter 5

Twenty-First Century Schizoid Man

'Death's seed, blind man's greed. Poet's starving children bleed. Nothing he's got he really needs. Twenty-first century schizoid man.' King Crimson

There's a really terrible slogan on a T-shirt, about being a mushroom, being kept in the dark and fed bullshit. That was me, I am the mushroom, not that I mind the dark, I've always found it rather comforting, I was never afraid of the dark as a child, I found the day oppressive. I was in the dark now; I had been in the dark for a long time, a long, long time. I had wakened with a terrific jolt, and for an instant, no, not for an instant not at all, not for a second did I think I was back at the centre. I avoided that cliché, it was pitch black, but I knew exactly where I was. I reached over and turned on the lamp, my file was lying next to me, an ugly thick impersonal thing in a grey folder. I picked it up and started reading; the first page was an admissions report into the hospital.

Confidential Report; subject SZIOVJFRM
This man was found unconscious at the scene of a multiple homicide, two slayings both men in their mid-twenties, one stabbing, and one shooting with what has emerged as a mercury tipped bullet. Neither weapon has been recovered, although subject SZIOVJFRM was covered in blood from both victims. Subject SZIOVJFRM remained unconscious for the next five days during which time we have run extensive tests. When he resumed consciousness, he said he knew nothing about the murders, and when pressed he claimed he was an Arab living in Twelfth Century Cairo. His descriptions were vivid, and at times he launched into Medieval Arabic. However, when a transcript of his interview was given to the Head of Arabic Studies at **** University, he said it was like no Arabic that he had encountered, but he would not dismiss it as fake. After three days subject SZIOVJFRM uttered the only lucid sentence of the duration. 'Don't try pinning no fucking rap on me,' he then lapsed into the comatose state which he has now been in for the last three months. Blood tests found that subject SZIOVJFRM had ingested a fatal dose of a toadstool Amanita virosa, more commonly known as destroying angel. This normally takes up to a year to

kill its victim, but subject SZIOVJFRM appears to be degenerating rapidly.

I dropped the file on the floor, so it was all for nothing, I was about to die anyway. I took a cigarette from the side of the bed, lit it, and took a long blast deep into my lungs. I felt scared, and confused, because for a moment I didn't know what scared was, I'd felt on edge during the flight, but not scared, but now, I was terrified. Still, I had to know how much time I had left, I leant over and picked up the file, and looked at the date of the last entry. I gasped. It was dated over twenty years after the first entry. I couldn't believe it, I flicked backwards and forwards, reading the dates over and over again, just to make sure, but there it was, and not only that, there were reams of paper spanning the intervening years. Why was I not dead? What was going on? I was desperate to find out. The next entry was dated three months after the first.

Subject SZIOVJFRM
Since his admission he has stayed in the comatose state which he was in when first admitted. His life signs, have been slowly wearing down, and I fully expected him to be dead within three months. However, three weeks ago his heart beat stabilised and, his other lifesigns started improving. Two days ago he woke up. Blood tests have been taken, and his DNA has been eroded so badly that he should not be able to sustain vital life functions; in short he should be dead. However, he appears to be getting stronger, and I anticipate he will be ready to sit up and eat a meal in the next few days.

I flicked through the next few pages, the next page I settled on was dated exactly one year after my original entry.

Subject SZIOVJFRM burst through his restraining harness again today. He has become increasingly violent and abusive, two porters were hospitalised, one will not be returning to work. Traditional chemical suppressants are having little or no effect whatsoever, and he appears convinced that there is some sort of conspiracy going on. I have decided to try the retro-genal suppressant which is as yet untested. The subject's delusional behaviour has to change otherwise I will be forced to keep him in a straightjacket permanently.

I lit another cigarette, and flicked the dead match across the room. This was starting to sound familiar, all the stuff Chris was going on about, all that stuff about genetic experimentation. I needed to know more. Just what was I? I picked up another document, a slim glossy brochure that had been slipped inside my file, it looked like the advertising spiel for the new drug they were giving me, and it was produced by Krait Pharmaceuticals. I felt the cold fingers of The Snake clutch my heart, yes he was still with me, he could still reach out and grab me, The Snake wouldn't be satisfied until I was his. There was no way that was going to happen. I had taken the first step by escaping, and the answer to his defeat was in the glossy brochure. I gave it my full attention. It didn't take long to read as most of the document was taken up with photographs, diagrams etc.

In short Benway 5 was an experimental drug designed to 'normalise' the genetic code. The brochure claimed it was intended to cure genetic defects such as spina bifida. Small molecules known as receptors would attach themselves to the DNA helix, these receptors would then encourage 'normal' DNA activity, by healing splits in the helix, and by overwriting those genes that were harmful. Early experiments on rats had been favourable, but Krait pharmaceuticals had yet to receive the go-ahead for human tests. It was all too risky, but then again no-one was going to lose any sleep over a suspected murderer with no living relatives.

So I was the first human guinea pig, that was what Chris was going on about, but the brochure was a con trick. I didn't believe a word, it all seemed too altruistic, and altruism was not in the Snake's character. World domination was, I knew it in my heart, and at the same time I recognised that I had a part to play in all of this. It was no accident that I was the first to be given the drug. I needed to know what the effects had been, how I was able to escape. What was so significant about now? I couldn't escape the fact that something hidden had been guiding me, it was no coincidence that I had run into the one person who would believe me, and who would be able to offer assistance. I'd tried talking to Steve about 'that night,' hoping it would help me remember, but it wouldn't be drawn. This was a man used to life's depravities, but 'that night' was locked away, he didn't want to talk about it. Keep the nightmare door shut, because if you try peeking inside the door will come crashing down. I just had to be grateful for the sanctuary and hope I could remember things when all the drugs were out of my system.

Three years further on I found a passage that illuminated a bit more;
Subject SZIOVJFRM has had a partial response to Benway 5, the receptors have attached themselves to the helix, however, they don't appear to have had any other effect. He is now on quadruple the normal amount of tranquillisers, which finally appear to be calming him down. Whenever he

is spoken to, however, it is clear that the conspiracy theory is still there, but blunted by the drugs. He no longer needs to be restrained and has finally joined the other patients. Unfortunately, he does not appear to be very popular, and has the enmity of some of the more influential residents. His memory, both short and long term is in a terrible state, but this is probably due to his medication. There is no way of checking this, as to reduce the medication would be too great a risk. He spends most of his time in a trance, and occasionally bursts into song. There are long periods where he is preoccupied with listening to the voices inside his head. This is the most interesting aspect of his delusional behaviour. There appear to be two separate and distinct voices. It will be interesting to see which voice gains overall control.

This was all bullshit, there were two voices, my own and The Snake's. The Snake was something that they had put inside me with this Benway 5 drug. The Snake wanted me badly. It wanted to possess me, and had spent the last ten years trying. I didn't know why though, All I knew was that I hated it. I finished my cigarette and went back downstairs.

I was amazed at the amount of television channels Steve had, I was 'zapping' from one channel to another on his satellite system, still nothing about me, my escape, or the confrontation last night on the motorway. Steve brought through a couple of cups of tea, and lit his first spliff of the day. 'I was like that,' he said, 'when we first got it, zapping all over the place, but it's amazing how quickly you get used to it. Now it doesn't seem any different from normal.' I nodded, mutely zapping from one channel to another, still nothing, then something jumped out from the screen, and I dropped the remote. A young journalist was standing outside a pub, somewhere in the country. I turned the volume up.

'Local people are still coming to terms with the fact that something so hideous could have happened in such a picturesque little village as this. The police are being tight lipped, but it looks identical to the slaughter at Little Havering early this week. This pub, like the one at Little Havering was chosen because it was so remote, a group entered the pub sometime last night, and killed everyone inside .There are no witnesses, and the exact details are still not known. However, police contacts have confirmed that there was a ritualistic aspect to these slayings. All the victims appear to have been drained of blood. Police have issued a special help line, and are urging all pub landlords, particularly those in remote rural areas to be on their guard. This is Adam Wright for Cable News International, back to the *studio.'*

I turned the set off. 'That's it,' I shouted. 'That's what the bastard's been up to whilst I've been inside, cheap tacky vampirism. I'm really disappointed with him, I'd have thought he could have tried something a bit different, a bit more original.'

'What are you on about?' said Steve, a bit taken aback by my sudden outburst.

'The Snake for Christ's sake, the being that's spent the last ten years trying to possess me. It's him that's behind all this. I can smell him coming off the telly. It's him I tell you.'

Steve took a long draw on the spliff and passed the rest to me, 'You can understand why most people would think that sounds crazy can't you? I mean to me it just looks as if a bunch of sickos have just decided to start killing for pleasure, and doubtless it can all be blamed on their childhood, and what videos they rent. It all sounds a million miles from some scientist fiddling about with your DNA.'

'But you believe me don't you? It all sounds such mad bollocks, I admit, but you believe me.'

'Yeah I do, but that's only because of what I've seen. I don't like to think about that night, but what you killed was definitely not human. That reminds me.' He got up and left the room, returning with a shoe box which he handed to me. Inside was an automatic pistol with a set of mercury tipped bullets. It looked familiar. 'After the pigs left, I went to have a look around, I found that. I didn't have to look very hard. It was just lying in the grass. I don't see how anyone could have missed it. It's all mad'

'When the World turns mad the only sanctuary is madness.' I replied. 'Sanity is overrated, it cannot explain this, and when faced by it, it dissolves into nothing. I have an idea. It's about time we put the ball back in The Snake's court. He's had things his way for too long.'

'Does your plan involve going out?'

'It involves setting a trap, those guys on the telly are slowly moving our way, they're playing hit and run. Can't you feel it, it's like the shadow of some huge bird of prey getting ready to swoop down. Only it doesn't feel like anything natural, something filthy and disgusting, something that should have been dead a long time ago, something that will be dead pretty soon. I can smell it, I've just got to find out where it will be next. I don't know how I'm going to find out, but I feel that I can find out. Does that make sense?'

'No.'

'It's the difference between knowing something, and sensing

something. I actually know very little indeed, but I'm starting to sense quite a lot. Ever since I stopped taking my medication I've been acting solely on instinct. Instinct has led me here, now it's telling me to go after this, I've got to ride this all the way, it's the only way of knowing… of knowing… of knowing whether or not I'm right or totally barking mad.'

'What if you're both?'

'Another possibility, but I can handle being barking mad if I'm right, it gives my madness a purpose, an excuse, but if I'm wrong, well I just don't want to talk about that. The first thing I've got to do is work out where they're going to strike next.'

'How will you do that?'

'I don't know I'm going to need some sort of device for tracking, not a machine, something suitable, something esoteric.'

'Esoteric?'

'Yeah, you know, new age, magic, that sort of thing, but I don't know what, I need to be somewhere that's got all that sort of stuff, I need to sniff around, feel what's right.'

'I know just the place.'

Chapter 6

There's A Rainbow Round My Shoulders

'And it fits me like a glove.'
Al Jolson

There was a bright, fresh feeling in the air as we drove down the country lanes towards Glastonbury. It was still very early in the morning, and a thin sheet of mist still clung to the dips and gullies in the road and surrounding fields. The green was like something from my childhood, something forgotten, I didn't realise how green and lush the countryside actually was. I took a long pull on yet another spliff and passed it back to Steve. The early morning high gave everything a dreamlike quality, and it was easy to believe that we were driving through a different country, one that was idyllic, one where Nymphs Fauns and Tree-Sprites frolicked and gambolled in the morning dew. Glastonbury Tor accentuated the illusion, its bizarre mound acting as a beacon, a direction finder. Even if Steve hadn't known the roads, we did not need road signs, because it was always there, either in front of us or just to the right, getting slowly bigger the closer we got.

This illusion of pastoral paradise was shattered when Steve leaned out of the window and hollered at the Massey Ferguson ambling on in front. 'Oi, pull over you git, there's other people wanting to use the road.' The tractor driver raised the finger at us without even glancing behind him. 'Cunt,' screamed Steve changing down into second gear. 'These fucking bastards think they own the fucking road, get the plastic bag out from under your seat.' I leant forward and pulled a tatty shopping bag with some foul smelling brown muck inside.

'Jesus, what the fuck is this?'

'Dogshit, I always carry a bag in case of emergencies, now in a minute I'm going to knock it down to first, and we'll bomb past. There will be a brief window of opportunity in which I want you to lean out and throw the shit through his window.'

I undid my seat belt and rolled the bag down slightly over my right hand. Keeping myself clean, but keeping the shit on the outside. As soon as

Steve shouted I threw it. It hit him squarely on the cheek and exploded on the inside of the cab.' Bingo,' screamed Steve and then began to sing as we roared off down the road, 'Oh I can't read and I can't write but I can drive a tractor.' I was grinning from ear to ear, I felt strange, I felt something that I couldn't quite place, then I realised what it was, happiness. I felt happy for the first time since I could not remember when. It wasn't just the sight of a man covered in shit either. It was the fresh air, the sheer green lushness of it all. There is something inherent in man that craves the countryside, the open air. I had spent the last twenty-odd years cooped up in some hellish laboratory, and now was the first time I actually felt free. It had just dawned on me that I was out, and I was staying out.

Glastonbury like so many other towns welcomes you, but unlike anywhere else it claims to be the ancient Avalon. It also claims a load of other things, this is where Joseph of Arimathea was supposed to have landed with the Holy Grail. It's also claimed that this is the place where Arthur and his knights are sleeping, also where Merlin apparently climbed to the top of a tree and disappeared, eluding death, putting him in the same league as Jesus and Elijah. The welcoming sign however limits it to the Ancient Avalon claim. You have to check out the tourist information to hear all the other claims. Glastonbury is, however, a very weird place, all its claims have acted as a beacon for all the weird and wonderful people in the UK, and some from further afield. Pilton festival has acted as a catalyst, as all the hippies, beatniks, peaceniks, looked around after the festival and decided to stay put. Amongst all of this there is the traditional stuff associated with village life. It's like *The Archers* has been crossed with *The Hair Bear Bunch*, and this is the unnatural offspring. Let's face it, no-one in their right mind would want to set a soap opera in Glastonbury. There is a down side, what with all this new-age romanticism and the re-emergence of paganism there are fears that Satan has entered this once idyllic town.

I don't think so; most of the new-age thought buzzing around is so much bollocks that Satan would lose all his street cred if he associated himself with it. But it's not all bollocks, in amongst it all was something useful, something worth having, and that was why we were there. Glastonbury is essentially one long road with Glastonbury Tor bearing down from the top. The shops are eclectic, grocers, newsagents, the ironically Welsh-sounding bakers, the Dixieland Jazz Cafe, but along with all of this are antique shops, new-age shops, subversive writing shops, feminist writing shops, new perspective male writing shops, crystal shops, incense shops and Germanic Icon, (fuck knows what that sells.) All sorts of shops. 90% of it I'm sure was pure bollocks. Still, they would sell what I wanted even if I did not know what I wanted yet.

Steve dropped me off at the bottom of town. He at least knew what he was doing. He was knocking out eighths and pharmaceutical grade moon blasters down at The Beautiful Meadow. At the same time, I was going to act out some form of psychotic whimsy, and come back with the tools I needed to stop The Snake in his tracks. . We were going to meet up later on at The Marksman's Arms, and compare notes. It was with a sense of wild desperation that I burst into one of the New-Age bookstores.

There was very little of any real practical use. Ideally I was looking for a slim pamphlet called. 'How to predict the passage of demonic bloodsuckers collectively known as The Snake, and what to do when you catch them.' The place was fucking useless, they didn't have anything remotely like that. What they did have were a load of flock covered spell books aimed at over-sexed teenage girls. Unless I was trying to seduce the hunk at The Dixieland, they were no help at all. The only things that looked like they would be of any use were forbidding tomes, inches thick. The sort of thing that would take months to read, and I needed to know tonight.

And self-help books' they had one hell of a lot of those. Quite a few looked like serious attempts to cure severely damaging physical and psychiatric conditions. When all this had blown over I could do with checking some of them out. Others were truly bizarre, and offered a wealth of reasons why people were pissed off. Maybe it was because they hadn't awakened the inner Child/Goddess/Horned God within them, or maybe it was because they loved too much, or too little. Standing there surrounded by it all I experienced an epiphany. I would write my own self-help book, guaranteed to work, called, 'You Need A Slap.' Is the reason I can't keep a girlfriend/boyfriend because I haven't considered tantric sex? No, it's because you need a slap. Why don't I love myself? You need a slap. Do I need to awaken my inner child? No, you need a slap, and so does your inner child. I could go on a roadshow/book signing, signing books and giving slaps. 'This is a loving slap,' I would say, 'designed to dislodge your nose from your arsehole, and persuade you to look at something else for a change.' That's why my therapy would work where all the others have failed. They all encourage people to examine the arsehole in more detail. Even if my therapy didn't work, I would have lots of fun touring the country slapping people, so it was a winner either way.

The girl behind the counter didn't see things quite like that. And she threatened to call the police before I had the chance to fully explain the reasoning behind such radical thinking. But in that respect I was not alone. Galileo had suffered similar attacks when he had postulated his new way of thinking. It was pretty much the same story in every bookshop I went into, and I was beginning to wish that I'd kept my ideas secret. Sad and dejected I slumped into the Dixieland for a cup of coffee and a piece of cake.

Sitting there listening to some tunes that were 'way out there man,' I started to feel human again. On the whole, apart from the odd bookstore assistant on their lunchbreak, everyone was very friendly, and I didn't have the urge to kill anyone, which was a pleasant change. After I finished my cake I closed my eyes for a moment, just to let myself take in the music for a while, then I smelled it. I had been used to my nose telling me of The Snake's whereabouts, but this smell wasn't foul and acrid. It was rather pleasant, but it was no less important, and it was coming from the back of the café.

I went out of the back door and found myself in a courtyard, paved with polished flint speckled with crystals and minerals. There in front of me was the source of my olfactory arousal, It was called Astral Baby and it wasn't like any of the other shops. It was reassuringly dimly lit, and contained a wealth of oils, incenses, powders and resins. I cavorted around the shop sniffing and snorting as I went along. The girl behind the counter didn't seem at all bothered. After about half an hour I was convinced I had all that I could possibly need. I also got an incense burner and some little charcoal disks.

On the way to *The Marksman's Arms* I stopped off at a camping shop and bought a gas ring to burn the charcoal. I was on my way out of the shop when I saw a really savage hunting knife. It was a beauty, razor sharp edge, serrated on the top, perfect for slipping up under the ribcage and into the heart. I didn't really need it, I still had the kitchen knife I'd used to slit Eddie's throat. For a minute I agonised then gave into temptation. After all, I needed to pamper myself, give myself a treat. I also felt that I should try to blend in, or more correctly blend out, I stopped off at one of the hippy shops and bought some new clothes, more in keeping with the general populace. I bought a stripy multicoloured jumper, a pair of rainbow Doc Martens and some harlequin trousers, now I wouldn't stand out from the Treebeards, the Peregrine Tooks and the Larkflowers bustling about. After that I was fully equipped but totally skint. I hoped Steve had had a profitable morning, otherwise we would both be on the lime cordials.

I had no cause to fear, Steve had had an incredibly profitable morning. He had sold everything that he had taken with him, about three ounces of blow which he sold at £20 an eighth, and about fifty pills which he sold for a tenner each. He sold them under the generic name of ecstasy, but we weren't really sure what they were. It did mean that we were able to eat lunch. They didn't sell pasties, so I had a piece of French bread and a bowl of chilli. Over my second pint Steve showed me something else he had been able to procure, another fifty rounds for the Browning. A couple of old thermometers were all we needed to bring them up to speed.

After two pints we left. Steve was being hassled by assorted colourful characters, admittedly not as colourful as me, who had just woken up to the fact that once more Glastonbury was being flooded with drugs. A lot of them were quite insistent, claiming they were unable to wait until the following day. They tried to persuade Steve to return later that afternoon. I had to let them know that we had important things to do that day, and would not return until tomorrow. I needed to show my hunting knife to a couple of them before they would back off. Anyway, it took the shine off what had been an otherwise perfect day. We left The Marksman's at about two, and set to business.

Steve found some old thermometers under all the clutter in the back of the Herald. He was quite happy to go to work on the bullets while I categorised my purchases. I had to separate them into three distinct categories. There were those substances that were needed to predict where The Snake's cohorts were going to be. The second group were for deterring The Snake, making them step back, stopping them from passing. The final group would be effective in capturing The Snake. It took a lot longer than I had expected, some of the herbs had properties that covered more than one category. By the time we had finished, Steve was on his second cup of tea.

I had a cup of tea myself, even though time was pressing, I needed a few moments' tranquillity, to prepare myself for a highly intuitive exercise. We spent the rest of the afternoon out on the road lighting incense. Every time we came to a crossroads we would stop, set the censer up, and watch which way the smoke went. We had to double back on ourselves a few times, but by about eight in the evening we had pretty much worked out which isolated country pub was next on The Snake's list.

Chapter 7

9th & Hennepin

'And no-one brings anything small into a bar round here. They all start off with bad directions.'
Tom Waits

We arrived about nine. It was a small dingy hovel of a place, serving two houses and a farm. It wasn't even listed on the map. The moon was full and looked down malevolently at this squalid little piece of countryside. Wisps of cloud hung over a guano encrusted sign like troubled souls. Originally the sign bore the inscription Poacher's Arms, but someone had crossed out the m and added an e. Now it read Poacher's Arse.

An ancient red dog lay in the entrance, a long string of drool hanging from its jowls, like a senile Cerberus guarding a festering Hades. It snored, twitched its back leg and farted. Overhead a crow squawked and the dog awoke with a start, standing up and looking around for enemies. Its rheumy stare fixed on Steve and me. It stared myopically from one to the other, its lip started to curl up in a half-hearted growl which ended in a disgusting canine wheezing fit. Then it gave up, and sank into the doorframe and went back to sleep. The stink grew worse as we got closer, a mixture of cow shit, month old sweat, and entrails. At first we thought it was coming from the dog, but as we drew closer we realised the stink was coming from inside the pub. We stepped over the dog and walked in.

A fat, greasy man slouched behind the bar. His face was red from years of rough cider drinking, with a nose that would make W. C. Fields weep. A massive carbuncle with huge tufts of black hair shooting out of each nostril. Four strands of black straggly hair were smeared over his otherwise bald head. He was wearing an old string vest, smattered with cider stains, some of them seemed even older than the vest itself. His right hand was cradling a pint whilst his left was scratching his belly button.

Two others were sitting at the bar; one was a thin weasel-faced man in his mid-fifties. He was sitting to the left of the barman, old cloth cap pulled down tight, wearing an old donkey jacket. To the barman's right sat a grinning ginger youth, obviously the result of excessive inbreeding, wearing a tattered *X Files* T-shirt. Both were cradling pints of cider. It was dark and dank inside, with no decoration on the walls. The only light was an anaemic yellow bulb, complete with fly, flickering over the barman's head. A dying fire coughed up its last few glimmers in the hearth.

'Al-be-on then,' growled the barman in tones that suggested a deep rooted mistrust of strangers.

'Fine thanks,' replied Steve merrily. 'Two pints of rough please, and have one for yourself.' At this unexpected show of generosity the barman's demeanour changed. He grinned back showing a mass of twisted yellow teeth. He muttered his thanks almost obsequiously, probably counting on another from this benevolent stranger.

'That'll be nine pounds please,' he simpered. Steve gave him a tenner and told him to keep the change. We received a few more oily thanks, then went to sit over in the corner, furthest away from the front door.

The weasel-faced man studied us intently as we went to sit down. He, too, shared the landlord's revulsion towards strangers, but he hadn't been sweetened with a free pint of rough. He muttered something to the gormless youth. I suddenly realised he had a shotgun broken across his knee. 'That's right,' he called out, seeing I'd spotted it. 'It's a shotgun. I use it to shoot crows and rabbits and vermin.' He put an extra emphasis on 'vermin.' Steve and I smiled back, raising our pints in a conciliatory manner, but Weasel-face wasn't going to let us off that easily. 'We don't get many visitors round here... although we sometimes get the police in... They come in, in pairs like you. They buy Amos a pint, like you, the really generous ones let him keep the change. Then they go and sit in that corner over there. Just like you.'

'We're not police,' said Steve. 'All we want's a quiet drink, away from the hustle and bustle. Heard the cider was good, and it is.' He looked over at the barman for his approval, the barman nodded back. Weasel-face snapped the shotgun together and pointed it at us. I peered down the barrels, it was a fairly wide gauge, and at such short range, he could probably get the pair of us. I was clutching the Browning in my denim jacket, but it was a little tight, and would take more than a minute to get out. Anyway, this was all wrong, we weren't there to pick a fight with the locals, we were supposed to be a welcoming party for The Snake.

'His cider's shit!' he screamed. 'Now what the fuck are you doing here?

Look around. Can't you see all the blood fur and feathers? Does this look like some fancy tourist's pub? Now put your warrant cards on the table or I'll shoot.'

'Look we're not police,' pleaded Steve. 'We came here because we knew there wouldn't be any police. We're not exactly friends with the pigs ourselves. I can prove it.' He slowly reached into his jacket pocket and pulled out a sheaf of folded up paper. He handed them to Weasel-face.

'What's this then?' asked Weasel-face.

'Look at them,' Steve said, 'You're holding the plans for the National Bank on Glastonbury High Street. It cost me an arm and a leg to get those.' At the mention of the word 'bank,' Weasel-face's eyes lit up, but he kept his eyes on us. He passed the papers to the barman who studied them thoroughly.'

'Look right enough to me,' he said. Weasel face relaxed, broke the shotgun, and went to sit down.

'Now then,' he sneered scornfully, 'I won't ask what you want these for. But I will be keeping hold of them. You can get them back tomorrow, after you've told me all about your plans.'

There wasn't much else we could do but agree, and Weasel-face pretty much left us alone after that. Every now and again he would shout 'Tossers,' or 'Big time criminals,' and the barman and idiot youth would howl with laughter. But he didn't threaten us with a shotgun any more.

'That's two people have pointed guns at me in as many days,' whispered Steve. 'Do I need a fucking bath or something?'

'Not as much as he does,' I replied. 'Don't worry about him, if my instincts and those substances are right you'll watch him get his tonight. Well done for getting him off our backs. Where'd you get those plans from?'

'I've had 'em ages. Some junky got a job as a labourer when they were building a new cashpoint area. He lasted two days before they sacked him, he nicked the plans before he went. He was selling them down the pub for a tenner. I thought they'd be a useful future investment, and I was right too, didn't think it would be like this though.'

Every bone in my body told me this was the right place. I had the same creeping feeling I used to get in the hospital just before The Snake would make an appearance. He was getting closer, or part of him was anyway, just the tip of his finger. He was sitting over the country like some hideous bloated spider. All those reports of bloody murders in remote pubs across the country suggested a pattern. A pattern which was snaking its way across

Cumbria, North Yorkshire, Lancashire, Staffordshire, Gloucestershire, and now Somerset. Weasel-face thought he was in control of things, but he wasn't, we were. We were the fishermen waiting with hooks, nets and harpoons for the fish that would soon come knocking on the door. Weasel-face was the bait.

After about half an hour we could hear a vehicle approaching, too loud for a car, but not as noisy as a truck. The barman listened attentively, more trade. I could see the little cash registers light up in his eyes. When it drew up outside he grinned and started rubbing his hands together. Weasel-face swung round to look at the door, the shotgun still broken across his knee. 'Wonder who this is then?' he sneered, 'Perhaps it's some of your criminal friends.' He paused, trying to give his words extra gravitas. When he resumed, the tone was more menacing. 'Or perhaps they're mine,' he growled.

Even through the foul stink that totally engulfed the place, I could smell The Snake's approach. I didn't think he was wanting to make friends. As she stood in the door the three locals let out an audible gasp. A raven haired biker's dream, creamy white skin with glossy red lips, dressed in leather mini skirt and bra. Black stockings and a clearly visible black suspender belt completed the look. Weasel face's jaw nearly dropped to the floor. She arched her arms above her head and purred, 'What's a girl got to do to get a drink around here?'

No-one had a chance to answer because at that moment a slim twenty-something man dressed in a simple leather jacket and jeans strode in. He was smiling all over his face. 'Just give her a glass,' he ordered, without even looking at the barman. 'We'll help ourselves.' Behind him stood an older man, saturnine, enigmatic, somewhere in his mid-thirties. He was wearing a black suit and a long black trench coat. Their whole manner was far too confident and self-assured for the situation. For a second I thought that maybe they were the police, and we were going to get done for planning a bank job after all. But then I smelled the familiar reptilian stench, and I saw The Snake dancing in the older man's eyes. I glanced over at Steve, and saw that he was sensing something as well. All eyes were now on the barman. How would he react to this challenge to his authority?

The young man stepped forward and looked deep into the barman's eyes. 'How about it then?' he murmured. The barman wrung his hands, taken aback by the young man's overpowering confidence, and by his yearnings for the young man's companion.

'I…um…' he spluttered. 'No, bugger it. This is my bastard pub, and no bastard drinks anything in 'ere unless they bastard well buys it off me.' His mercantile instincts finally getting the better of his lustful urges.

I pulled the Browning high powerL9A1 9mm automatic out of my pocket and tucked it into my belt. I stuck a ready-made spliff in my mouth, and sparked it up. I breathed the black smoke deep into my lungs, and felt it comforting, but at the same time it brought everything sharply into focus, and made me realise what I was up against. If what I believed was true, these three had been going around the country slaughtering with impunity. No-one had been able to stop them before now, what made me think I was up to the job.

There was a bit of an impasse at the bar. The barman and the young man were staring at each other, waiting to see which one of them would make a move first. Weasel-face was starting to stroke his shotgun. The older visitor was standing back impassively, taking everything in. The idiot youth was looking to Weasel-face to show him what to do next. The girl slowly walked over to Weasel-face and stroked his cheek. Other hand on her hip, legs apart, pouting provocatively. 'I'm sure you can help me,' she sighed. Weasel-face nearly fell off his stool. When he regained his composure he grinned at the idiot youth and winked.

'Well that all depends on what you can do for me,' he chuckled, turning back to the girl. 'What about a little kiss?'

'Of course,' she smiled licking her lips. Then she leant over and thrust Weasel-face's nose between her cleavage.'

'Whoaaa,' roared the idiot youth pounding his glass on the bar. He stopped sharp when Weasel-face suddenly snapped back onto the bar a look of sheer terror on his face blood spurting out of his neck. For a moment I felt like I was back in the hospital, watching some poor git having their throat cut, but this time I didn't have a head full of largactyl to sooth away the rough edges.

The girl stood back, cut-throat razor glinting in the lamplight. Weasel-face twitched spasmodically as the blood spurted out of him in a wide trajectory. The girl stood underneath the jet, her mouth wide open, drinking some of it in, but letting a lot more run all over her. 'You can lick this off me later,' she smiled, looking back at her friends.

'I need a long drink first,' said the young man reaching behind the bar and pulling out a pint glass. At this the barman suddenly burst into action, and moving much faster than his bulk would suggest, he leant over Weasel-face, grabbed his shotgun and pulled it to, jamming it under the young man's nose. 'Go on then,' smiled the young man. 'Pull the trigger, you won't get another chance.' The barman duly obliged, letting the shotgun off into his face. For a moment the young man's face was obscured by gunsmoke.

For a moment I thought all our efforts would be in vain. The barman looked like he was going to do my job for me, and I really needed to capture a Snakehead alive. When the smoke cleared however, the young man was still standing there with his head very much intact. The shot was stuck to his face, like an alcoholic who had just woken up after falling asleep on a pile of ball bearings. He rubbed his face and the shot fell onto the bar, leaving tiny red marks that instantly started to fade away. 'Ow,' he moaned indignantly. 'That stings, I'm going to have to take my time over you.' The barman started to tremble, the shotgun now an embarrassment. For the second time that night I saw raw terror in another man's eyes.

The barman wasn't the only troubled soul in the bar tonight. I didn't like the way things were going. I thought we were dealing with demonically possessed bloodsuckers. Unnatural, inhuman, but vulnerable nevertheless to small arms fire. These looked horribly like vampires. I tried to remember what vampires were afraid of, and the list came readily to mind. Garlic, Holy water, stake through the heart, a crucifix; I had none of those. And no matter how hard I racked my brain I couldn't think of any occasion when a vampire was killed by a mercury tipped bullet, or a really cool hunting knife. I felt horribly out of my depth.

At the bar the vampires had helped themselves to glasses, and were collecting pints of blood. The barman's expression hadn't changed since the young vampire told him off. He was still holding the shotgun, but it was dangling uselessly from his arm, an impotent reminder of what he was facing. The idiot youth was grinning no longer, but sat at the bar holding his pint of cider in front of him, like it was some sort of talisman that could ward off evil. Weasel-face was the main course, his body still twitching as the last sanguinary remnants spurted out, but the eyes empty and vacant. I took another deep pull on the spliff, trying to find comfort in the black smoke, before handing it back to Steve.

Weasel-face gave one last little sigh, then fell down dead. It was then that I noticed the lurker in the threshold. Some ephemeral shadow that was lost in the windows and hiding in the curtains. None of the others noticed it hiding in the stairway, the vampires were too busy feeding, and the rest were transfixed with horror. It swept down on Weasel-face's corpse and took something, but on the way past it whispered its name in my ear.

'Ah Pook is here,' I mumbled. Uttering the words gave me strength, and I knew that I was dealing with something far more potent than garlic or a stake through the heart. I said his name again, feeling myself grow stronger with each syllable. It was then that the vampires noticed us, and Steve handed the spliff back to me.

'What did you say?' demanded the young vampire.

'Ah Pook is here!' I shouted, and the room grew darker. I stood up, pulling back my denim jacket to reveal the pistol sticking out of my waistband. They started laughing, I finished the spliff and stamped it out on the floor. 'Ah Pook is here,' I whispered staring back unflinching. The shadow was now fully upon me, I felt like Wild Bill Hickock, but still the vampires laughed. The Browning high powerL9A1 9mm automatic jumped into my hand like a living thing and exploded into the young vampire's face. Time shifted into slow motion, and I watched the bullet shoot out of the barrel. I could even make out the blob of solder, and the little scratches where the bullet had been held in the vice. I watched his expression slowly change to one of surprise. The mercury gave a little plop as it hit his forehead. His head slowly bloomed into a huge red rose, which floated through the air before finally blossoming on the wall behind him. I was taken aback by the incredible beauty of it all. For a minute he stood there, still looking surprised, then there was a slurping noise as the back of his skull broke off and sloughed onto the floor. A few seconds later the rest of his lifeless body followed suit. Now it was my turn to laugh. Still keeping hold of the gunfighter persona I blew the smoke from the pistol and asked the barman for a shot of red eye.

Time seemed to stand still, the four survivors crowded round the bar looked back in dumb horror. Then I felt the rush. Killing Eddie and the two pigs had prepared me for it, but their death rushes were nothing compared to the intensity that hit me when I blew this head off. There was a monumental rush of endorphins, I felt more alive than I had ever done before. I wanted to kill again and again, create rivers of blood that would put the vampire's efforts to shame. I could hear a kestrel flapping its wings ten miles away. I felt like Shiva, and I wanted to share this feeling with the others.

This feeling of exultation was short lived, there was a tremendous roar and my ear burst into flame. Blood was pouring from the side of my face. The barman had broken the shotgun and was desperately trying to fit another couple of shells. Either he was shooting at every perceived threat in a mad panic, or he was trying to curry favour with the two remaining vampires. I blew a hole in his chest, and he slumped forward over the bar. I felt another rush as Ah Pook captured his soul, but it was nothing special. It was a bit like smoking some crappy home grown straight after the finest skunkweed/Nepalese temple ball cocktail. It just made me feel hungry for more.

I pointed the Browning at the two remaining vampires. Steve ran over to the fire and threw in a cocktail of herbs and incenses. A think pungent smoke filled the room, instead of going up the chimney it floated around the door, effectively sealing off the exit. The girl looked at her mentor for help, but he just stared back helplessly. Then she looked back at me and smiled, the Browning started twitching again, and I felt Ah Pook's rage. 'Well,' smiled the girl. 'I guess that makes you my master now. You won't believe what I used to do for him.' She gestured to the other vampire still standing silently in the background. She licked her index finger then ran it over her breast, then her naval, before sneaking over her crotch. I suddenly realised she was trying to seduce me; it was almost the same cheesy routine she'd tried on Weasel-face. She couldn't have picked a worse moment, the Browning was twitching like a thing possessed, and any second I was scared I'd start to come tumbling down off the rush. It wasn't like she was all I had. I had the other vampire for later, and as far as I could tell, he was the only one in contact with The Snake.

I smiled back at her, she really was extremely beautiful, and mouth wateringly sexy. Everyone was looking at me, wondering what I was going to do. Fleetingly I felt like a character in a glossy magazine so beloved by teenage boys. I couldn't resist her charms any longer. I pointed to her companion. 'All the avenues of pleasure that you took him down, will be as nothing compared to what you will do for me,' I murmured dreamily. She smiled, licked her lips, gave a little nod then came to me.

When the mercury hit the back of her skull there was a distinct splash, not a plop like before. Visually, it was a lot more impressive at such close range. The top of her head came clean off, and landed on her friend, but the body kept on coming, at least five steps before she fell down dead. On a psycho-pharmaceutical level it was a bit disappointing though. I didn't get the huge rush that I'd got before, because I was already there, but it did stabilise things out quite nicely and got rid of the twitches.

The remaining vampire looked impassively at us, his enigmatic smile was gone, but he still didn't look very concerned. Maybe it was all an act, or perhaps he knew something that we did not. 'So,' he shrugged, 'What are we going to do now? Do you want to make a deal?' I wasn't up for negotiation, dark forces were whispering in my ear, and despite my feelings of euphoria, I was only too aware of the icy fingers wrapped around my heart. Any suggestion of a deal would turn those forces against me, so I shot his right knee cap off. Now he looked concerned, and as he fell to the ground I broke a barstool over the back of his head. He gave one sharp cry of pain, then fell silent. Steve went out to the car leaving me alone with four corpses, one unconscious vampire, and an idiot.

He was still quaking with fear, and by rights I should have killed him, after all he was the only witness. I smiled at him and he smiled back. 'You were really cool then mister.' He whimpered. 'I'd be dead now if it wasn't for you. What are those things?'
'They're aliens,' said Steve coming through the door with a coil of rope and some duct tape. 'You know how these bastards work. You don't know how close you were to getting an anal probe. You may still, if you don't do what's right.'

Steve's words fell on fertile ground. Our friend was receptive to any amount of bullshit. Steve told him we were the Men In Black, but we were wearing denim jackets and stripy jumpers as a disguise. Ginger thought that was really clever, even though he hadn't been fooled. We took Ginger into our confidence, made him an honorary MIB, and took his wallet. That way we would be able to contact him when the time was right. As a precaution Steve took everyone's wallet and emptied the cash register. Weasel face had over £2000 hidden in his shoe. We bound and gagged the sleeping vamp, and Ginger helped us carry him out to the car. There was a shiny black Land Rover parked outside. We had found the keys earlier, when we had been rifling the vampire' bodies, Steve gave them to Ginger as a reward. Then we told him to go home and sort out an alibi. We knew his address, and would return with the mother of all anal probes if he said anything to the police about us. Then we disappeared into the night with a hogtied Snake-eyed vampire under a tarpaulin on the back seat.

Chapter 8

You Can't Kill Me

'I'll be seeing you again. I'll be seeing you again. I'll be seeing you again. Again and again and again.'
Gong

I was in unbelievably good spirits as we blasted down narrow country lanes with our quarry tied up in the back. On reflection it was probably a good idea sparing Ginger's life, and giving him their car. The pigs would have been following those particular tyre tracks across the country. If we'd left it behind, they wouldn't be looking for it any more. This way they'd spend all their time and resources searching for it. It was only a matter of time before they found Ginger, then they wouldn't know what the fuck they were looking for. Steve had done a real number on him, and when they had sifted their way through all of his half-arsed bullshit they would be looking for Will Smith and Tommy Lee Jones. It always helps to spread disinformation.

My ruminations were disturbed by a muffled groan from the back seat. 'You awake then you tosser?' I shouted. 'Who do you support...? I bet it's Arsenal... Arsenal are shit!'

'Yeah,' piped in Steve, 'Arsenal are shit! D'ya hear that you fucking Gooner. Arsenal are shit. Any more noises from you, and I'll twist your fucking leg clean off. Come on the Rovers!'

'I didn't know you supported Bristol Rovers,' I enquired.

'Yeah I do. Why? It's not a problem is it?'

'No, not at all, it's just that they're shit aren't they?' Steve braked hard, putting the Herald into a skid, and we zig-zagged across the road, finally stopping on the other side. Then he turned to me.

'Bristol Rovers aren't shit. We're a small club, with a loyal fan base. My dad supported Bristol Rovers and his dad before him. Just because we don't have a lot of money like the millionaires in the premiership doesn't mean we're shit.' This was the most passionate and angry I'd seen Steve since we'd met. In the few days we'd been together we'd done a lot. Best not to jeopardise our partnership over a football team I knew very little about. I decided to take a more diplomatic approach.

'Sorry, it's just that when people think of Bristol they automatically think of Bristol City, because they're a bigger club.'

'Fuck off! I hate those bastards for what they've done to my city.'

'What's that?'

'Tits that's what. Bristol City titties, nice pair of bristols. every time Bristol's mentioned people think of tits. If City never existed Bristol would mean something else.'

'Like what? I can't think of anything that rhymes with Bristol Rovers.'

'Supernovas,' retorted Steve quick as a flash, it was obvious this wasn't the first time he'd thought about such a weighty issue. 'Don't you think it would be better if the only time you heard bristols was when you tuned into the sky at night to hear Patrick Moore going on about a magnificent Bristol in the crab nebula. That way Bristol would be associated with astronomy and learning and shit and not tits. Anyway who do you support?'

'Southampton of course. They may not be the best, but at least they're in the top flight.'

'God, you have been away a long time,' said Steve starting the Herald back up again.

It was then that the triumphal mood vanished, and a black cloud of despair came back as I realised how bad things had got. I turned my thoughts back to the vampire on the back seat. I wanted to keep him in the dark for as long as possible. Admittedly he was helpless, but The Snake wasn't, and I wanted to keep our whereabouts a mystery. I didn't want the interrogation to be interrupted by a gang of Snakehead reinforcements. If he thought he'd been kidnapped by a bunch of un-dead hunting football hooligans, so much the better.

When we got back we dumped our captive unceremoniously in the coal bunker just next to the kitchen. After the evening's events I was ravenously hungry, and my ear needed some medical attention. It was the same ear that had been hit previously, by the Snakehead pig when I was haring down the motorway. Despite the narcotic effect of the death rushes it was throbbing mercilessly, and I was concerned I might get an infection. This anxiety was doubled when I thought about the filthy state of the Poacher's Arms.

Fortunately Steve had a reasonably good first aid kit, with some clean, unused bandages. The bleeding had stopped, and I just needed a quick, painful spray of antiseptic, and a couple of loops of the bandage. That done we prepared ourselves for the next part of the evening with a couple of bacon sandwiches, and a good, strong cup of tea. We washed it all down with a couple of celebratory brandy chasers.

It was filthy and damp in the coal bunker, which was good, because we weren't choked with coal dust. The vampire was still wrapped up in the tarpaulin, lying on a pile of nutty slack. There was a dark crimson stain where his kneecap had been blown off. Steve and I brought in a couple of chairs from the kitchen so we would be comfortable. There was another muffled groan of pain as we grabbed one end of the tarpaulin and pulled, depositing our captive on Steve's winter fuel. The vampire was still making muffled noises; clearly the tape over his mouth was giving him considerable discomfort. The time for secrecy and subterfuges was now over, we had got him back without incident. We were in the middle of nowhere, he could scream and shout as much as he wanted, no-one would hear him. I reached over and yanked the tape from his mouth. He gave a brief gasp of pain, then started breathing heavily, coughing a bit when he inhaled a little bit of coal dust. His status as an immortal member of the un-dead was starting to fade, Dracula never suffocated on coal dust.

Eventually he regained his composure, still wincing with the pain he shouted back defiantly. 'Arsenal aren't shit, they're one of the top teams in Europe. Where are fucking Southampton? You're only jealous because your team can't match that.' I smacked him hard in the mouth, I wasn't going to listen to that mad bollocks. I despised Arsenal almost as much as I hated Portsmouth. Still it had confirmed a sneaking suspicion, that Arsenal were the team of choice for the denizens of hell.

The interrogation didn't go as well as I had hoped. Clearly he was frightened of us, and what we were going to do to him, but he was far more terrified of the consequences of betraying The Snake. We could only punish him in this world, The Snake was capable of following him beyond the grave. After a while the novelty of twisting his knee and causing him to scream in pain started to wear off. I became impatient, I wanted to blow his head off, the death rush was starting to fade and I was desirous of a top up. Some people take to torture like ducks to water, but not me, I found it irritating, something that had to be done before I could go back to what I was really starting to enjoy, killing.

After a couple of fruitless hours I decided to try another approach. Remembering what had been written in my hospital files I decided to go out into the garden and start looking for some destroying angel. It didn't take long at all, almost as if they had been planted there for me all along. I took the mushrooms into the kitchen and mashed them up in a small bowl. Then I sieved the paste through a tea strainer, added a spot of boiling water, then sucked the liquid up into a syringe. Ignoring all of the safety considerations, I tied a brief cord around his arm to make a tourniquet. Once the veins started to puff up I slipped the needle in and pressed the end of the syringe, it all went remarkably smoothly.

At first nothing happened, and I was just starting to resign myself to an evening of tiresome leg pulling when the rush hit me. It was like watching a piece of film at an incredibly fast pace. There was so much information I just couldn't take it all in, not just stuff about myself, but The Snake's plans as well. Even during my states of largactyl fuelled tranquillity, I had not been as confused as that. I could feel myself starting to pass out. I pulled the Browning high powerL9A1 9mm automatic from my belt and stuck the end in his mouth. I just managed to pull the trigger before being thrown into a beautiful dreamless sleep.

When I awoke I was no longer in the coal cellar, but neither was I in my bedroom. Steve had dragged me into the lounge, and left me to spend the rest of the night on the carpet. I lay there blinking, trying to come to terms with where I was, and what had happened, when I heard the front door open. I leaped to my feet, grabbing hold of the Browning. But it was only Steve, and he wasn't very happy. He had been driving all night, getting rid of the body, going a nice long way away, to an extremely remote spot only he and a few others knew about. And what had I been doing? I had been sleeping, but just before I had fallen into a comatose state from which he could not wake me, I had splattered a vampire's brains all over his nice clean? coal cellar. It was a tale of misery and loyalty, but I managed to persuade him to make us both a cup of tea before he shuffled off to bed.

I was wide awake, and in really good spirits, even though things were a lot worse than I had realised. I ran myself a bath, I felt like I had been reborn, which in a sense I had. Ideally I wanted to luxuriate in exotic scents and oils, in recognition of my status, but a brief search of Steve's bathroom cabinet revealed no such items, and I had to do with fairy liquid and carbolic soap. At the end I felt a lot cleaner in a lemony fresh kind of way, but I also felt like I'd dissolved four layers of skin. I put my new clothes back on, went downstairs, made myself another cup of tea, and thought about what I was going to do.

I could pretty much remember everything, all except the bit between blowing The Cheat away, and waking up in a high security bedlam which remained a bit fuzzy and indistinct, and probably always will. I couldn't just remember this life either but all the others as well, all the way back to Cairo. I could remember swearing an oath to Hassan I Sabbah, and numerous lifetimes in between. They all shared a common feature, botched up assassinations. I felt incredibly inept, having spent just under a thousand years successfully fucking up one killing after another. It also explained why I had been going through all this weird shit, and told me what I had to do next.

The Snake had killed me twenty-seven times, and I'd not killed him once; I only had to kill him once, and that was it. Is twenty-seven a magic number? Three times three times three, still it doesn't mean anything, if it did I'd have killed him last time. Anyway he can't kill me now, 'cause I'm too lucky just like Lord Cardigan. At The Charge of The Light Brigade, he lead his men right up to the Russian guns before returning home without a scratch. When he was a young man Clive of India put a pistol to his forehead, pulled the trigger and nothing happened. Years later when he had achieved all he set out to accomplish, he repeated the exercise, and this time he blew his brains out. Clive of India and Lord Cardigan had one thing in common, it was not their time to die, they were lucky. And when it's not your time to die, nothing can kill you. So nothing can kill me, not with Ah Pook riding shotgun 'cause it's not my time to die.

Because I didn't kill the Snake he kept going on and on, shuffling off the buffalo, like Hamburger Mary, but without the hamburgers, getting better and stronger all the time, 'till he got in the smack. Then he tried to sell the smack, but the smack dealers didn't want cutting out, so he went all Osiris on them. He tried to go Osiris on me too, but Ah Pook got there first, so he couldn't go Osiris on me, but he could lock me up, trying to go Hamburger Mary on me, but he couldn't, because Ah Pook got there first. Now he's in the pills, and he's everywhere. When I raided the drugs cabinet I took a lot of those pills with me. It was so fucking ironic, I thought I was fighting the good fight. But while I was killing Snakehead coppers and vampires, Steve was banging out new ones down the pub at a tenner a go. It was going to take a long time to put it all right. Part of me, the part that got the death rush, was looking forward to it, a blurred fantasy of driveby shootings and pub bombings. This also highlighted another aspect of the woefully inadequate drugs education programme in this country. If the kids knew that the true consequences of taking ecstasy would be demonic possession followed by assassination, they wouldn't be so quick to swallow a pill sold by a stranger.

The other, more sensible part of me was dismayed. The Snake was already far too strong, and was starting to gain a foothold within the population. I was only one person, the amount of blood that needed to be shed was breathtaking. In order to fulfil my oath, I was going to need to get rid of the Browning high power L9A1 9mm automatic, and start using nuclear weapons. Steve might know where I could get hold of some plutonium.

I had just finished my second cup of tea when there was a knock at the door, effectively derailing my train of thought. I picked up my pistol and threw the door open. Standing there was some hairy freak, a hippy that time had forgot, grey hair, flared jeans and rainbow sweater. His face was brown and wrinkled from years of living outside. A battered pince nez hung precariously on his nose, which was partially obscured by his hair which hung over his face. The untamed beard with evidence of old lunches made him look less like a human, and more like some other earlier hominid. When he saw me, despite registering the pistol, he burst into a huge grin.

'Hello Zippy,' he chuckled. 'Long time no see. Aren't you going to invite me in?'

Chapter 9

The Battle Of Evermore

'I hear war is asunder down in the valley below. I'm waiting for the Angels of Avalon, waiting for the eastern glow.'
Led Zeppelin

I kept pointing my gun at the hairy freak. This was exactly the sort of stunt The Snake would pull. I looked over his shoulder, trying to spot anyone else hiding in the bushes. At least it wasn't the pigs; they wouldn't try to smoke me out with a hippy, that's not the pig's style. I shouted up to Steve, but the only response was a loud snore. The hippy smiled and held his arms outstretched in a gesture of friendship and reconciliation. He smelled pretty disgusting, but he didn't smell like The Snake. 'Come now,' he reasoned. 'You don't need to point that thing at me, we're on the same side. Look at me. Have I changed that much since we last met? Don't you remember sitting in my office drinking absinthe and talking about cryogenics?'

The years had not been kind to me, the years of institutionalised abuse had etched themselves on my face. But compared to Green I was still a spring chicken. There was very little left of the successful lawyer. The man facing me looked like he had suffered a severe mental breakdown. He had scant regard for personal hygiene. His eyes had a wild desperate glare, and he kept looking back towards the gate as if fearful of being followed. It was Green though, and it was an amazing coincidence him turning up the moment I got my memory back. I put the pistol back in my pocket and invited him in.

I called upstairs again to Steve, and this time got a response. I waited until the volley of random swearwords had abated. Once Steve was speaking in coherent sentences I managed to persuade him to come downstairs. I went into the kitchen and put the kettle on. Green was sitting in one of the kitchen chairs smoking one of my Disque Bleu. I asked him how he liked his tea. He liked it chamomile, but he would have to make do with PG Tips, so he had it extra milky with two sugars. I made it just how he liked it, and it looked disgusting, I'd let mine brew a little longer until

Steve got downstairs.

'So,' said Green when we were all sitting down together sipping tea. 'I suppose you want some kind of explanation?'

'I want to know why you're here now,' I replied. 'I'm sorry if I've not been that hospitable, but last time we met you handed me a huge sack of shit. I hope you haven't brought another sack with you, because I've still not finished with the last one.'

'I have got something for you,' he replied. 'And I hope you find it useful. But I'll get to that later. Don't you want to know what I've been doing all this time?' To be honest I didn't give a shit about what Green had been up to. I bet it was a lot more enjoyable than what I'd been doing. But I feigned interest anyway. Today seemed to be a day for revelations, and I was sure that Green would tell us something of use by the end of it.

'I didn't hang around for long after you left,' he began. 'A friend of mine on the force told me about what happened to your partner, and the dead bodies in your office. It was only a matter of time before they'd want to talk to me, so I sold up and went. Anyway, it was not the police that bothered me so much as that charming secretary of yours, and her friends. What was her name again?'

'Veryanne?' I had almost forgotten about her, but the mention of her name caused my heart to flutter, and made me feel terribly lost and alone.

'Yes, Veryanne, that was it. Beautiful girl. Anyway I wanted to steer well clear of her circle. So I got on a plane and jetted off to a new life. It was really easy, I owned very little. The house and office were rented, so was the office furniture. I'd never liked a lot of clutter, I only packed one bag then I was off.

'I had money of course. I had salted plenty of that all over the place. I was a free man, I could do what I wanted. Of course the police still wanted to talk to me, but they didn't have anything that would warrant an arrest or deportation. So I moved to the South of France, to live that film star life I'd always promised myself. But after a while I started to tire of the endless rounds of parties…'

After everything that had happened I couldn't believe we were sitting in the kitchen, sipping tea, listening to such self-indulgent bollocks. My heart bled, it must have been terrible for the poor git, I had had it easy in my twisted world of psychedelic beatings. I felt like cutting my losses and shooting the bastard right there. I looked over at Steve, and he glared back, like he was reading my mind. He'd only just cleaned up after one killing, and wouldn't thank me if I put him through that again. So that put paid to that. I was going to have to sit through all of it, without interruptions, and without hob nobs.

'After a while I became listless, bored, homesick. I felt as if I were wasting my life, that there was something I still had to do to make sense of everything. The heat had died down; your case was stone cold. There was no reason why I couldn't come home. Start living the life of an Englishman again, no longer an émigré. As a boy I was always enchanted by Mallory's *Morte d'Arthur*. I set out in search of that chivalric innocence that had so captivated me as a child.'

I had a hideous flashback, many years ago, on a drizzly Saturday afternoon one forgotten Pilton festival, I had staggered into the theatre tent to get out of the rain. I had only just left 'Jethro's famous hot knife and tequila' tent and was looking forward to a bit of comedy. I was receptive, all twisted and giggly, the sort of person that would even find Jim Davidson funny, that's how screwed up I was. Despite having such a low entertainment threshold I was to be bitterly disappointed. Some skinny hippy chick, wearing something that looked like she'd made it herself, stumbled onto the stage. Speaking in a warbling wail, verging on mild hysteria and telling of way too much substance abuse, she welcomed us all to Glastonbury. At this point I should have walked out straight away, but a mixture of inertia and the rain outside kept me glued to my seat. Part of me still hoped it would all turn out right, that this was just a piece of ghastly self-mockery that would turn back on itself, turning the whole Pilton experience into one huge joke. Of course that didn't happen, she started reading some goddamn awful poem she'd written about one of Arthur's knights. Some git called Shade, who had to go on some flower-scented quest to save an elfin maiden. And it went on and on, all delivered in this near hysterical wail, each syllable given special import, as if this story we were hearing was as important as the Nordic sagas of old, written by king's command. For about ten minutes the crowd sat stunned into silence. Maybe this was alternative comedy, surely something funny had to happen soon. If only she'd stuck to ten minutes she would have been alright. But after ten minutes it seemed that the crowd's collective patience snapped, and everyone started screaming abuse. She ran off crying, straight into the arms of some ginger fuzzy freak, dressed as a Red Indian, who looked daggers at the audience. The next act rolled a joint on stage, and received a standing ovation.

I could see where all of this was going, and I was not in the mood for some morally uplifting tale about how a rich selfish man found redemption through a spiritual acceptance of the Arthurian legend. 'What sort of school did you go to?' I queried. 'It's just that nobody at my comprehensive was remotely interested in Mallory, let alone being 'enchanted' by the bastard. We were all reading books by James Herbert. I got the cane for reading *The Fog* during a Geography exam.'

'Yeah!' chimed in Steve, thankful for an opening in the conversation. 'That bit with the lesbians was fucking brilliant, I lost count of the number of times I read that.'

'Exactly. That's the sort of stuff that 'enchants' teenage boys. Is there any graphic description of lesbian sex in *Morte d'Arthur?* Because that's what makes a good book.'

Green was rather taken aback by this loutish excursion into literary criticism. He had forgotten who he was talking to, and needed bringing back down to Earth. He wasn't sitting with a bunch of independently wealthy professorial hippies. We weren't interested in social niceties. Steve had only had a couple of hours' sleep, and was feeling understandably cranky. I was looking for an excuse to kill someone. I told Green to cut to the chase; neither of us were in the mood for any more long drawn out stories.

After that Green became a lot more succinct. He had moved to Glastonbury, and become active in various local history societies. Always he was in search of any link to Arthur. He made pilgrimages to Wales, and to Tintagel in Cornwall, Arthur's supposed birthplace. He read every book he could find on Arthur no matter how obscure. In many cases the more obscure titles he found more useful. Mimicking John Steinbeck he named his house 'Joyous Garde,' in memory of Lancelot's garden. Eventually he became more closely involved with the shadowy figures on the fringes of Arthurian research, people who claimed they had found the whereabouts of the Holy Grail.

Finally he came across one paranoid old archaeologist who was in fear of his life, a man who claimed he was being stalked by The Glastonbury Gargoyle. This forbidding figure appeared as a dark angel, a malevolent sentinel who warned off those that got too close. It wasn't the Grail itself that was a problem, for that could only be found by the pure of heart, and could never be used for any malign purpose. It was what lay hidden with the Grail that was of more serious import. Before the archaeologist died he confided in Green, and it wasn't long before Green also received a visit from The Gargoyle.

'In order to fully appreciate the significance of what The Gargoyle told me,' continued Green, 'You need to understand just how old these islands are. The 'Grooved Ware People', who inhabited these islands thousands of years ago, and who built Stonehenge and Dunharrow were the true founders of civilisation and science. They're even mentioned in Jewish scripture. The prophet Enoch describes a journey to Dunharrow where he learns ancient wisdom. Eventually the 'Grooved Ware People', fearful that a comet would strike these islands fled to Sumeria, and took their secrets with them. But they left their treasures behind.'

At this revelation Steve's eyes lit up. He was always on the lookout for material possessions, and the lure of ancient treasure was too much to resist. 'What's it all worth?' he asked. 'We're going to need a new source of income once the drug money starts to wear off. If that Gargoyle's giving you grief, you've come to the right place. You should have seen the heavy fuckers we had to deal with last night, for very little cash reward.'

'No I don't want you to deal with The Gargoyle,' Green groaned. 'It wasn't the first time I'd met him, although he didn't call himself The Gargoyle then. The Gargoyle told me to come and see you. I've got to give you the whereabouts of the sacred site. You'll know what to do once you get there. And may God have mercy on all our souls.'

He took a deep breath before continuing. 'All this time you've been running backwards and forwards, between Southampton and Glastonbury, Alpha and Omega, The Beginning and The End. The 'Grooved Ware People' knew the significance of Southampton. All the ley lines that travel through Glastonbury and Stonehenge gather north of the city, near to Winchester. Southampton is Albion's centre of gravity. If you could lift Albion up out of the ocean, it could be balanced on Southampton. Why do you think that so much of it is still forested, despite local property prices? The sacred and the profane both know of its significance, and the profane have done their best to upset this balance. Have you ever wondered why somewhere as beautiful as Southampton lies so close to Portsmouth? It's the powers of darkness trying to upset the balance.' Steve and I both nodded enthusiastically, Green had been talking a lot of weird shit, but that part at least made perfect sense. With its rotting skyline, bands of roving shit gorillas and assorted fish fuckers, a place as foul and disgusting as Portsmouth could only be the work of the devil.

'And this is why I am here now,' Green continued. 'If Southampton is the beginning, then Glastonbury is the end. Hidden by the mists of The Tor lies a gateway to the most significant treasure on the planet. I am cursed to lead you there. Once I have done this I will be left alone.' Saying that he got up and walked out into the garden. Steve and I got up and followed him out.

It was a misty cold day, the sun was hidden behind a huge black cloud and the moon was still clearly visible despite the daylight. 'Almost a thousand years ago,' intoned Green, clutching both mine and Steve's hand. 'We three stood in a garden like this one, and swore an oath under the moonlight. That was an oath we kept, but in so doing, we forgot our primary oath. Let us swear again, that this time you will not fail. Now is the time of The Snake's death. By whatever means possible.' We all swore, but despite the déjà vu, I couldn't help thinking that all the work was going to be down to me.

Chapter 10

White Rabbit

'Men on the chessboard get up and tell you where to go, and you've just had some kind of mushroom and your mind is moving slow.' Jefferson Airplane

Glastonbury is festooned with hundreds of tiny lanes going all over the place. In fact, it's not just Glastonbury, but the whole of Somerset, you can plot some pretty interesting journeys if you put your mind to it. A lot of the lanes are paved, although some of it dates back to the war, with tufts of grass spouting out of the middle of the track, where the wheels don't go. Some of them are nothing more than dirt tracks, just wide enough to squeeze a Triumph Herald down. There are so many that even Steve didn't know all of them. Green seemed to know the way though, giving directions with almost messianic certainty. All turns and bends were clearly identified long before we came to them. At first Steve drove with the confidence of a man who knows his own patch, the chief rabbit in the rabbit warren. Of late he had become a lot more subdued, as Green pointed out places Steve had never seen before. We spent the last ten minutes in silence as we drove deeper into medieval greenery. It was a strange feeling, almost like going back home, and I was just starting to nod off when Green told Steve to stop the car.

I stood in the shade of a yew tree watching the Herald disappear into the distance. Their part was over, and now it was down to me to finish off what I'd started hundreds of years ago. I wasn't too sure exactly what lay ahead, I didn't really take what Green had said too seriously. Most of it sounded like a load of hippy bollocks, sacred treasures and groovy bear people, but it might just be able to let me bring things to a head with The Snake, finish things once and for all. I wasn't dismissing everything Green had said; The Snake's ivory phallus dated from supposed Arthurian times, and there was a possibility I might meet the sick bastard who'd carved it in the first place, King of the Groovy Bears. Then there was Ah Pook, I now realised that he had been there for a long time, before, he was just a feeling, an instinct, a train of thought, but now he was manifesting himself in my consciousness in all his glory. Things had just become a lot more complicated, my priorities had shifted.

I had a decision to make, I had to give Ah Pook a name. Names are very important, if you knew someone's real name it gave you power. The drugs I'd been given in the asylum had had a long term effect, my psychic link with The Snake was still there, he may not know where I was or what I was thinking, but the odd stray notion or feeling could still bleed through, that's why I needed to choose a name. It's a trinity, the real name, Gabriel, the given name Ah Pook, and now a chosen name. Names were puzzles, the more names that could be placed along the way, the harder it would be for The Snake to fathom what was actually going on. And I had made my choice, I decided to call him Harvey, after the invisible rabbit from the film of the same name. This was as much for my own benefit as anything else, with all the crazy shit that was going down it helped if I could blame it all on some psychopathic six foot three and a half inch bunny, it helped me focus, and gave me a bit of distance.

It was a deeply beautiful morning, the early mist was starting to fade, but the dew still glistened on the branches. Ahead of me stood a vista of Silver Birch leading to a small chapel. The sun's warm rays poked through the clouds, and the birds were singing in the trees.

I had reverted to type. As soon as Green had given us his revelations I went into Glastonbury to buy a white shirt, red socks, purple tie, beige slacks, black brogues, trilby and a blue trenchcoat with really deep pockets. I bent down, picked a buttercup and placed it in my buttonhole to finish off the effect. The final showdown was coming up, and I needed to reassert my identity, it had been chemically caged for too long, and now it was time to let it out. I felt like I was standing on the abyss, whatever I did next wouldn't only affect me, but it would have a profound impact on the planet itself. I gave my pistol and knife one final last check, put a spliff in my mouth, and set off down the vista.

Even though the sun was shining brightly there was still plenty of shade under the tree canopy, and I found myself naturally gravitating towards the shadow. I didn't see any point in announcing my arrival until it was absolutely necessary. I felt comfortable skulking in the shadows, pistol in hand. I had a clear line on all directions, if anyone tried creeping up on me, I could blow a hole in them before they could draw breath. Not that I expected any trouble, not until I entered the chapel anyway, but it always helps to play the boy scout, and be prepared.

The chapel was ancient, old stonework stained with verdigris, there were tiny stained glass windows far too high to look through, and too tiny for any real effective illumination. There was a heavy oak door with a huge brass doorknob barring the way. I felt like giving up, going back home and getting stoned. The door was far too strong to break down, and the stonework was similarly formidable. I wished that I'd brought a sledgehammer or a crowbar, but when I tried the doorknob the door opened easily. It swung open smoothly without a sound, showing that despite its age, it had been well looked after. There was a noticeable smell of oil as I walked through the door.

When I looked up I had to take a deep breath in astonishment. I was expecting a dingy, badly lit little chamber, but I couldn't have been more wrong. It was enormous, composed entirely of polished white marble. I felt a little like Doctor Who entering the TARDIS. This place seemed substantially bigger on the inside, and unless it was all some clever illusion with smoke and mirrors, this was a seat of significant power.

I felt as if I had gone back in time, beyond the medieval years, and into some kind of Greco/Roman classical period. I felt like I was standing in The Coliseum, or The Acropolis, when it had first been built. I had to stand quietly blinking, as my eyes adjusted to the brilliance of it all. I was standing in a huge circular room, the air was heavy with the smell of incense; the walls were covered in rich tapestries and various religious paraphernalia. I immediately thought of Steve, he would have loved to ransack this place, and could amass a fortune in gold and jewels in a few brief moments.

I sat down on one of the carved wooden benches, and started to get my bearings. I felt very small and insignificant, like an ant. I was sitting at the end of a series of pews that stretched out towards an altar some way in the distance. There was a small antechamber just behind the pulpit, some form of inner sanctum. As I looked forwards I saw a diminutive figure dressed in white coming out of the door.

'Begone creature of filth and horror, there is nothing for you here,' yelled the figure, speaking with divine authority. I hadn't expected to be welcomed into the inner sanctum with open arms, but his tone took me back a bit. He may well be beloved of God, but his manners were appalling. I felt like shooting him in the guts then and there, teach him a few lessons in etiquette. 'I said begone you creature of filth and misery. There is nothing for you here. Leave now or face my wrath.' He scurried towards me bellowing.

'Do I know you?' I asked, still mildly upset by such a hostile reception.

'I know what you are,' was the response. 'And you have no place here.'

He was closer now, and I could get a better look at him. He was taller than I thought; he only looked small next to the grandeur of the altar. He was wearing long white robes which seemed to capture all the light in the room, constantly shimmering and flickering, impossible to look at for any length of time. He was clutching a gnarled ancient staff. His beard and hair were snowy white as well; he was certainly very old, but walked with energy and vigour. This was no aging dotard, but a fit and powerful individual. He looked down at me with the majestic and self-assured demeanour that is only to be found amongst the righteous. Sitting there clutching the pistol with which I had killed so many people, I felt as if I had just crawled out from under a stone.

At the same time I wasn't just going to sit there and let him insult me like that. Talk about prejudiced, this guy needed a visit from The Equal Opportunities Commission. I had good reasons for what I have done, and I would like to see what he would have done in my situation. Anyway, I may have just escaped from a secure mental hospital, but at least I didn't look like I was going to an audition for *Lord Of The Rings*. I wanted to say something witty and scathing. Something so caustic that Oscar Wilde would stand up and applaud. 'Fuck off Gandalf!' I sneered.

'So, with your words you reveal the filth that lies within,' he replied, his voice showing once more his own sense of righteousness.

'All right then,' I answered. 'What about fuck off Yogi, king of the groovy bears?' I pointed the Browning high powerL9A1 9mm automatic straight at him. I couldn't kill him, not yet anyway, but I could still squeeze a homemade mercury-tipped special straight into his bollocks. I wonder how aloof he would seem after that.

'Your tool of Satan will not work in this hallowed place. Now for the last time. Begone! Or face the wrath of God!'

Yogi had completely lost the plot. My Browning high powerL9A1 9mm automatic, though responsible for many deaths is not a tool of Satan. It's what the SAS use, they're a bunch of brave lads, desperate men, prepared to take risks, but I don't think even they had completely thrown their lot in with Satan. Also, I was a bit pissed off by Yogi's flippant use of the phrase 'Wrath of God'. Just because you have experienced God's love doesn't make you an expert on his wrath. I, however, knew from personal experience what the wrath of God actually meant.

Before I was able to let loose a bollock shot, Yogi struck his staff on the floor. There was a blinding flash, and a rush of purple smoke. When it had cleared, I found myself standing face to face with what looked like one of Arthur's knights. He was dressed in dazzling white armour. He was carrying a shield adorned with a golden lion. His sword was hanging from his side, the scabbard decorated with precious jewels, what looked like diamonds, emeralds and rubies. Again I thought of Steve. He pulled the sword from its sheath, and its majestic brilliance put the rest of him to shame. I couldn't help but gasp in wonder. He looked at me with a mixture of pity and love. He was not just a knight, but a paladin, in the truest sense of the word. He appeared a lot more reasonable than Yogi, and I wanted to prostrate myself at his feet, and beg for mercy and forgiveness. I would have done, had it not been for Harvey.

The bullet entered his helmet just above the bridge of the nose, the armour wasn't strong enough to stop it piercing his helmet, but it was strong enough to stop it continuing out the other side. There was a look of total astonishment on his face, then he fell forward, stone dead. I barely had enough time to blow the smoke from the barrel before another knight appeared. And then another.

I started to get into the routine of it, knight would appear, I'd blow a hole in his head then another would take his place. It was like a turkey shoot, as the whole of Arthur's court queued up to get slaughtered. The only tricky bit was when I had to reload, but by stepping backwards, and pulling out a fresh clip, I was able to keep killing without too much difficulty. The rush was quite respectable as well, nothing as intense as a vampire or a Snakehead of course, but a lot better than some ordinary Joe, like a pub landlord, or a security guard.

When it was all over twenty knights lay dead on the floor. Yogi stood looking horrified. Obviously this wasn't the outcome that he had anticipated. He looked like he was going to cry. Mistakenly I assumed he was a spent force, and made my way towards the altar. I wanted to check out the inner sanctum, look at what was on offer. Yogi wasn't as spent a force as I had thought, he pointed his staff at me, and a lightning bolt shot out of the end. It would have hit me square in the chest had Harvey not deflected the blow.

I felt a slight tingling sensation, followed by mild nausea. Then there was an unbelievably foul stink, a mixture of raw sewage and rotting flesh, I could feel myself starting to gag. I turned back towards Yogi just as he fired another thunderbolt. This time the stench was far worse, and I nearly threw up. I fired three shots and the staff exploded, splinters flying everywhere, one of them caught me on the cheek, just missing my wounded ear.

This time Yogi was a spent force. He sunk to his knees and started to sob, I almost felt sorry for him. 'You see,' I muttered, trying to appear magnanimous in victory. 'You've not watched anywhere near enough cartoons. The rabbit always beats the bear like he always beats Elmer Fudd. There was no need for any of this. If we could have talked this could all have been avoided.' I gestured towards the chivalric corpses. 'You Tories have had things your way for far too long, don't you know there's been a dramatic swing to the left. You need to get your facts straight before you start throwing stink bombs at people, and setting knights on them.'

'We're not on the same side. I know you well, and however many weasel words that fall from your mouth, you will never be able to hide your true nature. It is of no matter. You may be able to enter the chapel, but you will not be able to penetrate the inner sanctum. When you walk behind the altar you will face your death, spawn of Satan'

'The Devil doesn't want my soul,' I replied. 'He'd choke on it.'

I wasn't in the mood for any more of Yogi's apocalyptic rhetoric, and returned to the altar. There was another heavy wooden door, similar to the one that barred the door to the chapel, and like the other door this one swung open easily. Feeling like Prometheus I pushed the door open and strode inside. There was another tingling sensation accompanied by nausea and a foul stink. But this time it was too much, my stomach started to heave, and I left my breakfast all over the polished marble floor.

When the muscle spasms ceased I looked up, to find myself in a small room, surrounded by levers, dials, and walls bedecked with thousands of tiles, each with its own symbol. It was as if all the alphabets, hieroglyphs and other symbols known to man had been jumbled up together, and then some archaic, pre-human symbols had been added just to make the numbers up. The levers looked as if they required some sort of coded sequence. But it was a code that put the Nazi's enigma machine to shame, and I knew that if I sat there until the end of time I would never be able to solve it.

'There's been a coup.' I called to Yogi 'Up there it's all very civilised. Your chap's out of favour, and mine has the influence now. You're very good at wearing your saintliness on your sleeve. I see things a bit differently, you've got to go with the flow. You lot have ballsed up, now it's our turn to give it a bash. I know you're not too happy about the way things have turned out, but Que Sera Sera. Now you're going to help me.'

Chapter 11

Walking Spanish

'He got himself a homemade special. You know his glass is full of sand, and it feels just like a jay bird the way it fits into his hand.'
Tom Waits

Returning somewhere after a long absence is always an incredibly surreal experience. A mixture of the familiar and the new. Nothing tells you things have changed as much as new roads, new routes, and new roundabouts. So it was as I came in on the western approach, past Millbrook.

The change was more profound than just new roads; buildings had changed, and so had people. Southampton was becoming gentrified, a huge influx of students had pushed house prices and rent through the roof. Huge swathes of Bevois Valley were now student only. Even the football team had gone up-market. The old Dell had been knocked down to be replaced by a state of the art stadium at St. Marys. The Madhouse was no more, even the Carpenters was a pale shadow of its old self, surrounded by derelict shops and offices, still just about managing to stay open.

Nothing epitomises the rush to gentrification more than the waterside developments. The yachting fraternity has in effect taken over the soul of Southampton. Ocean village is one vast marina complete with tapas bars and luxury flats. The jewel in the crown is the boat show. Every September corporate Southampton indulges itself in a multi-million pound yachtfest, with little if any benefit going to the ordinary people, except for a few no-hopers who manage to get a bit of seasonal work catering to the filthy rich, at minimum wage naturally.

In September the filthy rich, celebrities and aspiring middle classes swarm on Southampton like a plague of martini-drinking-coke-snorting-yellow-wellied locusts.

The roads are clogged with huge four-wheel drives, which have never seen as much as a dirt track, and they are all, without exception driven badly. I should know because I was driving one, a huge red arsemobile, some Landrover/Suzuki/Cherokee bollocks, I couldn't even be bothered to find out what. And I was driving like a twat. At first I was just trying to act naturally, but by the time I'd been stuck in traffic in Salisbury, I started to get into the role a bit too literally. It's just too easy ploughing motorbikes into hedges when you're driving an arsemobile at 110 mph along a duel carriageway, especially when you're towing a luxury speedboat. I had calmed down by the time I had reached the motorway, (and my third motorbike and second Mini Cooper,) because I did not want to get caught before I got to Southampton. I had business there, both personal and professional, and it wasn't as if the owner was complaining, he was lying in the boot with his throat cut.

I didn't mean to kill him, I just wanted a lift, but I was in a really weird mood after my encounter with Yogi. He had cracked eventually, but it was an arduous journey. I don't particularly enjoy torture, there's no rush, and there is precious little enjoyment to be had in torturing the guilty. There's none whatsoever to be had in torturing the pious. Besides it's hard to claim the moral high ground when you're wiring electrodes to their testicles. So I wasn't even going to go there. Whatever he suffers down here he will be rewarded ten-fold in heaven, and he was tough enough to take it. Similarly he had nothing to fear from Satan, he could not be tempted. Ever. He'd been made the sentinel of this place for a reason, so torture was out. I'd already loaded up a hypodermic, if it worked with vampires it should work with him. A dose of destroying angel would give me a direct conduit into the cerebellum. The threat was all that was needed, he didn't fancy spending the rest of his tenure on Earth being just like me, shouting at giant rabbits. It was the only time I ever had the satisfaction of seeing fear on his face.

His face suddenly turned ashen, years suddenly weighed upon him and a tear came to his eye. Then he told me, how to use the equipment, and the codes. The demolition codes, once entered, would set the planet off on a path that would bring on Armageddon. Yogi's job was to protect it from the forces of darkness, and to wait until the appointed time before he heralded the end of the Earth. Not now, now the planet's safety was in the hands of a paranoid psychopath with a death wish. For once the world could sleep soundly. I was excited to fever pitch, I had a huge erection, I wanted to do it, set it all off right now. That would piss everyone off, Michael and Satan, but not Harvey. No, he had been preparing silently in the darkness, Michael was not going to win over the Earth with peace and love, Harvey was going to storm the gates of Hell with truly dark angels, that had always dwelt in the darkness, that had never gone over to the lightbringer.

Hell will finally know just how terrible the wrath of God can be. I was Harvey's instrument upon this Earth. I was to do it. It was so fucking beautiful. I would destroy the planet, making myself the greatest, most bloodiest murderer of all time. At the same time destroying The Snake utterly, and completing my mission, meaning I was to be allowed in to heaven, albeit one of the rundown parts, whilst lesser killers, mere amateurs like Hitler and Genghis Khan roasted in Hell. Yeah, that's right Gandhi, I made it and I'm going to fuck up your paradise, the neighbour from Hell, firmly ensconced in Heaven, fucking up the peace and quiet with death metal. And doesn't that piss you off more than anything. I was shaking with excitement, ready for the rush of a lifetime. Laughing I danced to the controls, and without hesitation began to input the codes.

Barely had my fingertips touched the crystals when I felt Harvey's cold hand tighten his icy grip on my heart. 'Redemption,' he whispered in my ear. 'The Snake has to have the chance of redemption, or I can't swing it upstairs.'

Redemption; I hated the fucking word and all it stood for, and so I suspect did Harvey. We both wanted to set the wheels in motion, both looking forward to the showdown, both relishing the pre-emptive strikes that were all in readiness, but no. Destroying the World to be rid of The Snake was all right in theory, but only if The Snake knew that is what I was doing. And he didn't. So, I couldn't blow up the World until The Snake knows about it and has the opportunity to sacrifice himself to save the World and get Redemption. Wishy-washy liberal bleeding heart bollocks. The guilty have had plenty of second chances, and still Michael gives them more, and his solution sounds a bit too home-grown for credibility. No second chances, fire up the electric chair, 'We're frying tonight.'

I knew the way to go, but was not too sure where I was going, so I left Yogi to his own devices, he was a spent force now anyway, and all his knights were dead. I slipped back into the real world. Ten minutes later I was sitting on the back of a bus heading towards Bridgwater. I was at a bit of a loss, I suppose it was because I'd just got a plan, something I had been doing without for so long, and the sense of focus was a bit unsettling. My mind kept wandering, fantasising about Armageddon, like the husband stuck at the office yearning to go back home to his beautiful sexy wife that he'd just left that morning, unable to concentrate on the job in hand, too preoccupied with the promise of future bliss. Yogi's pyrotechnics had left their mark as well, I couldn't get the stench of righteousness out of my nostrils, and judging by the other passengers on the bus they could smell it too.

I suddenly jumped up and ran to the front of the bus. The driver was only too happy to let me off, he'd been eyeing me with a mixture of apprehension and disgust ever since I'd got on. I stood in the slight drizzle, breathing in the signs and sounds of a town that was at peace with itself. Right in front of me was a large family / yachties pub, close to the water's edge, car park overflowing with opulence, cars bought for their image rather than any practical considerations, arsemobiles a-plenty, and one with a powerboat on a trailer, that was the one for me. Bridgwater wouldn't be at peace with itself for a long time after I'd finished.

I shuffled into the bar like a cloud of anthrax, the barman could scarcely conceal his disgust when he looked at me.
'What do you want?'
'Pint of Stella please sir.' I replied, trying to look my most humble.
His expression softened, I was still disgusting scum, but I was disgusting scum that knew my place. A man overblown with his own pomposity, landlord of the biggest pub in town, a pillar of the community. Little did he know he was talking to a murderer, and not just any murderer, someone who was going to kill one of his best customers. A murder that would smear a repulsive connotation all over his bar. People would soon feel uncomfortable drinking there, unable to shake the knowledge of what had happened, fearful it would happen to them. In two years' time he would be bankrupt, a successful family business for generations destroyed by just one visit from me. It wasn't just people and vampires I killed. I grinned at my prophecy.

He poured my pint , and snarled, ' We don't normally allow your sort in here, but if you sit down and behave yourself you can stay.'
'That's very kind of you sir, you won't even know I'm here.' Little did he realise how true that statement was to be.

I took my pint and went over to sit in the corner in the shadows. No one bothered me, at first I attracted a few anxious glances from worried parents, but as I made no eye contact or displayed any interest in their children, they soon forgot I was there. I had bigger fish to fry anyway, but first I needed to concentrate on being inconspicuous, to blend into the shadows, and do nothing whatsoever to attract anyone's attention. I was getting really good at this, and it wasn't long before I could start to look around, and to focus on my intended victim. A very loud young man was sitting with a group of admirers. He was in the middle of a long rambling anecdote, that I didn't think was going anywhere, but I could see the rapt attention on the faces of his listeners. Christ, there can't be much in the way of entertainment around there, that may explain why so many people locally seemed to walk with their heads permanently bent to one side, constantly straining their necks in a vain attempt to hear something to liven up their otherwise dull existences.

Unfortunately for me, this guy really loved the sound of his own voice, one dull overblown story led to another until the landlord finally called time. It was the end of the lunchtime session. I followed him out, now nothing but a shadow flickering in the doorway. He waved cheerily to his friends and family before turning to the arsemobile. Up to this point I had only meant to stun him, knock him out, and lock him in the boot, but things did not go as planned. For a start, I was really wound up about having to listen to all the shit he had been spouting, and secondly I had spent so much energy focusing on not being seen that I forgot that this was not an assassination, but an abduction. Before I really knew what was happening I had already slit his throat. His lifeless body twitched a couple of times. I slipped my hand into his jacket pocket, took the keys and his wallet, undid the boot, and then slid the corpse into the boot. No one appeared to have noticed, so I got in the driver's seat and pulled away, ready to show off my power-boating skills at the boat show.

So that's how I got myself into this situation. Now the hardest part of the whole operation was about to begin. I had to pass myself off as some rich over-privileged git who was used to getting everything his own way. I needed to check into his hotel room, establish a base, then get some sleep, I was knackered. I was taken aback, by the splendour and décor when I opened the door, there was an underlying wealth and opulence. If I was out of place in some yachties pub in Bridgwater, then I was distinctly out of place here. I swallowed hard and put my hand in my pocket feeling the comforting, familiar feeling of the Browning. I was almost overwhelmed by the lift it gave me. That was always an option, if all goes badly stick to what you know best and shoot the place up. It was not my day to die.

Chapter 12

Hang On St Christopher

'Get him all jagged up on whiskey, lemme turn the bad dog loose.'
Tom Waites

For a few seconds I day-dreamed, relishing the wonderful images of slaughter that the Browning's touch had given me. Fortified, I strolled over to the counter, a middle-aged businessman in a blue pinstripe got quickly out of my way, before making a bee-line for the exit. He glanced back nervously before running out of the door. My hand was back in my pocket ready to shoot him in the back, no fucker gets away from me. I just stopped myself in time, and continued over to the hotel reception. The clerk had his head down, he was writing something into his ledger. He looked up at me then went back to his writing.

I swallowed hard, then put on my best plummy git accent.

'Excuse me my good man!' He reacted like someone had just fired a starting pistol in his ear. He jumped back, almost falling off his chair.

'I'm really sorry sir, I didn't notice you there. I'm sure you weren't there when I looked up just now.'

I tried to smile back reassuringly, although that's not really my thing. 'Don't worry, it happens all the time.' He smiled back, reassured. Things were not going as planned, I was supposed to be some obnoxious rich git, my main role in life was to make life miserable for people like him, not to reassure them. I reverted back to the plummy accent, and tried to look down my nose at him. 'I have a reservation,' I crooned, passing him the documentation, 'and I expect you to hand me my keys without further delay.' I paused, deliberately, just long enough for him to register my annoyance. 'People have been sacked for far less, believe me. You do not want to have me as an enemy. My name is Tarquin Carruthers. My friends call me 'Chunky,' but you call me Sir.' He looked troubled, flushed, then tried to compose himself. I was starting to feel sorry for the poor bastard, my grievance was not with him, just some poor sod trying to earn a living as best he could. But no matter, it could not be helped, I had to play my part. He was starting to sweat, tiny beads of perspiration were forming on the bridge of his nose. He shuffled uncomfortably, instinctively he knew something was not quite right. He felt chilled, he knew I was not wholesome.

'Of course Sir, I'm terribly sorry, here's your keys, and if there's anything I can do to make your stay more pleasurable please don't hesitate to...'

I snatched the keys from his hand without making eye contact. 'Just have my bags sent up, if you're capable of doing such a simple thing.' I could feel the relief emanating from him as I turned my back. I swung round and fixed him with my death glare. He almost collapsed, his mouth started twitching, searching for words that could not come. 'One more thing, no-one is to touch my car, or the boat, I'll do that myself. I'm holding you responsible. Do you understand?' He nodded dumbly, incapable of speech.

I'd made my point. He was scared shitless. Not the usual fear of some rich obnoxious guest, but a true primeval fear. Something most people had forgotten about. Well this was my chance to jog a few memories. The prodigal had returned. I turned my back on him and sauntered towards the lift whistling a merry tune, things were going well, I almost felt happy.

When I got upstairs I lay down on the king-sized bed and closed my eyes, I needed a bit of rest before the night's escapades. I lay in a semi-dream state, imagining what was going to happen that night. Southampton was where it all had begun, and where it was about to end. Certain individuals needed to be tracked down, and my nose was as strong as ever. I had got the scent, and this time I would not fail, all of it was going to come to a final, glorious, bloody conclusion.

About forty minutes later I turned on the sports news, I had been out of circulation for a while, and needed to concentrate on something other than killing, football was a good distraction. Arsenal were doing too bloody well for my liking, still, if this didn't all end in Armageddon, then perhaps I could concentrate on taking out a few of their key players. I ordered steak and chips from room service, I felt like dining alone. It wasn't as simple as it should have been, I had to impress upon the clerk that I wanted my steak well done, not some poncy cordon bleu definition of well done, but really well done, not a trace of pink, and certainly nothing remotely bloody. I spilled blood, I didn't want to consume any. I ended the conversation screaming. 'I don't care what your policy is, I want a cocktail with my meal, the mini-bar just won't cut it. I want Canadian Club whisky, with vermouth, orange bitters and fresh grapes. Talk to the desk clerk, he'll sort it.' The hotel manager brought my meal up, full of self-importance and bluster. He left a lot quicker than he entered, and without a tip.

Five minutes later, there was a knock on the door. I ignored it and continued eating. The food was really good, and I needed to indulge myself. Or, more specifically, that part of myself that had been neglected of late, hitherto food was fuel, I had existed on a diet of toast, cereal and takeaways, it was good to eat something that was well prepared, and to be fair, the steak was as I'd ordered it, not a trace of pink. He also brought up Chunky's bags. I tipped them out on the bed, a collection of vastly oversized tweeds, no use whatsoever, but there was one thing that caught my eye; hidden in one of the side pockets I found a Samurai throwing star honed to razor sharpness, so Chunky wasn't as innocent as it would seem. I tucked it away into my trenchcoat pocket.

The knocking just would not go away. I continued to ignore it, and eventually I could hear keys opening the door. This was something I could not ignore, I pulled out the Browning high powerL9A1 9mm automatic, complete with mercury tipped bullets, and levelled it at the door. Slowly, the desk clerk sweating heavily peered around the door. We made eye-contact, he froze, in the doorway. His jaw dropped, there was a look of extreme panic in his eyes. 'Sir, Sir,' he babbled.
'Come in, and close the door behind you'
For a moment he stood wide-eyed and aghast, unsure of what to do. 'I don't want to kill you, but I will. Come in and shut the door.' I cocked the pistol, and aimed it at his head, from this range no-one could miss. He complied, shut the door behind him, and stood there staring at me, sweating profusely. 'Sit down, over there.' He obeyed, sheer terror dictating his every move.
'I had to tell you sir.'
'What?'
'The police.'
'What about the fucking police?'
'They're looking for you, they've gone to examine your car. I tried to stop them, they'll be up in a minute.'
I put the gun away, I didn't need it. This was just typical. I had wanted to have a bath, and I'd not even started my dessert. There must be loads of murderers at large, why did the pigs have to hone in on me so bloody quickly? What about Jack the Ripper? He murdered loads, and no-one caught him. I bet he was able to have a bath in peace. This also meant the credit card was no good, once the pigs realised it belonged to the corpse in

the boot of the arsemobile it would be cancelled. I had about twenty quid left in cash, with no transport, no leads. It was all turning to shit. The desk clerk leaned forward hesitantly, 'There is one other thing sir.'

'This is not really the right time to ask for a tip, I've put my gun away, you should be happy with that.'

'No, a young lady was looking for you, she asked me to give you this.' He reached into his jacket pocket and pulled out a small card, the same size as a credit card. Pure quality, vellum with perfect copper-plate writing, it looked like it was printed in gold leaf. It was an invitation, made out to Elwood P. Dowd, for some address in Highfield, where the big houses are, near Safeways. Elwood P. Dowd, that was clever of The Snake, letting me know he knew about Harvey, that he'd cracked the first name.

'Sorry, it's just that she was quite a looker, not the sort who... um... er..'

'You don't need to say anything else. Do the pigs know about this?'

'No, I wouldn't, I mean,' he shuffled nervously, still visibly uncomfortable.'

'Go back to the desk, say nothing about this to anyone. Don't worry about the pigs, I'll keep you out of it. Don't worry about the apocalypse. I'll put in a good word.'

He almost bolted out of the door. I put on my trench coat, and took a quick inventory; loaded Browning, with fifty spare rounds, all mercury tipped, a hunting knife with a razor-sharp edge, samurai throwing star, lump of resin, packet of rizla, and full packet of Disque-Bleu. I stuck one in my mouth, lit it, and slunk out of the hotel. I passed a couple of pigs on the stairs, but I grasped hold of the shadows, still, one of them stopped and sniffed. His companion asked him what was wrong, he thought that he had seen something. He definitely could smell something, something unclean, something unnatural, something French. 'Don't be fucking stupid' was the reply, then they were gone, and so was I.

There was no bus. I remembered a guy I used to work with called Mark, back in the old days, back in the days of Solent Investigation. Worked in the office above, always late, used to storm in blazing, throwing down a copy of Hampshire bus timetable screaming,' Biggest work of fiction in the English language.' Only it wasn't, it was Solent Blue Line or Citibus. Blowtorched fagburnt illegible type, behind Perspex. The only thing that made sense was scribbled black felt tip, next to a weathered flyer for Horselover Fats. 'Boz is a fucking twat.' Right on brother, tell it how it is.

So I had to walk, and it was pissing down. My gayness and gilt all besmirched with painful marching in the rainy streets. I arrived at some mock –Tudor mansion looking like a sack of shit, and smelling a lot worse. I checked the address on the invitation, this was certainly the place, but God alone knew what they wanted to invite me for. I checked the Browning was loaded, ran my thumb over the edge of the knife until the blood came, stuck a spliff in my mouth, then marched up the drive. I felt like I was walking into the pages of Hello magazine, all the time Harvey was whispering, 'Bloodbath, bloodbath,' in my ear.

Chapter 13

Gimme Shelter

'War children. It's just a shot away.'
The Rolling Stones

I trounced up the drive, to the oversized, ostentatious porch and rang the doorbell. It was one of those curious affairs where you had to pull a chain, but still rang an electric doorbell. The ding dong seemed out of place, as did everything else, especially me. The door was opened by a tall, dark saturnine vampire, with smouldering good looks. He looked down at me with utter contempt, a sorry little shit-bag like me wasn't even good enough to feed to the rats.

'What the fuck do you want?' he growled. I peered back at him to see another vampire filling out the door-frame. This one was massive, easily six foot six, and an enormous muscular build. An individual that would inspire fear wherever he went, but he was the beta-vampire. The good-looking one who opened the door was most definitely in charge. I put my hand in my coat pocket to get the invitation, and felt the cold embrace of the Browning.

'Go on then,' hissed Harvey. 'Show him what you want, blow his fucking head off.'

Fighting back the urge to spit flame I took the invite out, and handed it over in a gesture of abject humility. I still might kill him, but I didn't want him to think that I was anything other than a pathetic piece of washed up street detritus, not until it was too late anyway.

There was a slight hint of recognition and surprise when he looked at the invitation, but he was careful not to give anything away, it was a bare flicker, and I only noticed it because I was staring at the jugular whilst fingering my hunting knife.

'Where did you get this?' His tone was as aggressive as before, but now there was a slight lilt of uncertainty. This was something that should not be happening, something like me turning up to his nice posh party with one of his nice posh invites. The very idea was sacrilegious.

'To be quite honest, I'm not too sure where it came from, someone delivered it to my hotel room.'

'Hotel room,' he almost spewed out the words in one huge belly laugh. 'Now I know you're lying. You've not got a hotel room. You'd be lucky to get some shitty bed-sit. Now piss off before the real owner of this invitation comes along, because he's going to show you how to die.'

That was it, I tightened my grip on the Browning. I was just about to drill him through the forehead when a voice floated out on the breeze.

'Actually, I gave it to him.'

I looked over his shoulder to see *her* drifting gently down the stairwell. My heart jumped, my mouth went dry, my forehead started to burn and the sweat glands all over my body suddenly came to life. I was reduced to some sweaty, spotty, stuttering teenager, and she was a goddess who floated on air. She hadn't changed a bit in all the years that had passed since I last saw her. If anything she was even more alluring, more desirable. My jaw dropped wide, and for a moment I was robbed of speech. The good looking alpha vampire noticed, and burst into torrents of mocking laughter.

'You don't think she will be at all interested in an insect like you.'

I became immensely self-conscious, of course she wouldn't be remotely interested in me. She who looked like Aphrodite had been made flesh whilst I looked every inch the slack jawed yokel who had just been shit-gliding. I still had my hand on the Browning though, and I still had Harvey. I may have lost the power of speech, but actions speak louder than words.

'I gave it to him because I wanted him to come. In fact all of this is for his benefit.' The words came trilling like soft music. They set me aflame, I started to swell up with incredible pleasure. I couldn't stop smiling, I let the Browning drop back into my pocket and grinned at the two vampires, who looked back with a mixture of astonishment and suspicion.

'Why would you want to invite him?'

She looked back at him with sublime derision and whispered, 'I don't have to tell you anything. Remember who I am, and what I can give you, now get out of his way and let him in.' They both parted, and I walked in feeling like royalty.

It was only once I had entered that I started to take my bearings. It was a truly massive house, an enormous hallway leading off to various reception rooms with a majestic staircase leading to balconies from which all the bedrooms lead off. The air was thick with heavy incense, and lavish erotic paintings hung from the wall, Enochian symbols were everywhere, some I was able to make out. I couldn't place the music, it seemed vaguely Arabesque, but then became Oriental, there were hints of Celtic melodies, and at times I could make out the Pipes of Pan. We were not alone, apart from the two vampires at the door I could sense another three, but these were way down the list in terms of ranking. There were about fifteen others there, all very young, early twenties at most, mostly women, and all exceedingly beautiful.

It was some form of initiation ceremony, membership of the local vampiric community, with sexual abandon thrown in. Apart from the two at the door, people were wearing hardly anything. I could hear the sounds of lovemaking coming from some of the downstairs rooms. The doors were wide open, and people were coming and going as they saw fit. It was orgiastic, but the main event had not yet begun, these were some pre-ceremonial couplings. I looked at Veryanne and she smiled back, and I could see the Snake glistening in her eyes. It was only at this point that I realised that Harvey had disappeared.

Harvey went the minute Veryanne appeared, the minute I heard her voice. I wasn't sorry to see him go, he always brought a certain amount of rage and hatred with him, along with a twisted yearning for carrot juice. Had he been there I would have been caught in a terrible dilemma. I was totally captivated by Veryanne's beauty and at the same time driven by a desire to rip the Snake's lungs out. This time I was able to look at her with open-mouthed wonder, I even felt quite warm towards The Snake, like the old days when he used to sing Frank Sinatra numbers whilst I sat in my cell, goofed out on largactyl, dribbling and giggling. The Snake had set out to seduce me with Veryanne, and it was easy, because without Harvey I wanted to be seduced. I wasn't stupid though, I knew she didn't want me because of who I was, she wanted me because of what I was. Still, it was curious Harvey just giving up like that, not really his style.

Veryanne said nothing just took my hand in hers and began to lead me up the staircase toward one of the bedrooms. I followed willingly, almost somnambulantly, two minutes later we were alone in the master bedroom together. She took me over to the magnificent four poster, and we sat down together. She held my face in her hands and stared deeply into my eyes. Her breath played softly against my breath, and its subtle perfume was almost hypnotic. I was acutely aware of my own stench, and began to squirm self-consciously. She ran her hands through my hair reassuringly, and whispered, 'There, there calm down, everything's going to be alright now.'

'But how did you know…'

'I've known exactly where you were ever since you came back to Southampton. It's my city, I can feel the pulses, know who and what are here and there. You know what I mean, you can do something similar yourself, although not on the same scale.'

It was true, Harvey's legacy allowed me to reach out through my surrounding area and catalogue all the souls, living and undead in my immediate vicinity, but I couldn't do anything as huge as a city. I could only just work out who else was in the house, and that was pushing it to the limit. 'We've been interested in you for a very long time,' she paused, and looked up at me coquettishly, 'And I've been interested in you even longer, ever since we first met, long before I ever became involved with Al-afaaa . I said nothing, tried to remain as non-committal as I could, which was not much, considering I was almost drooling. I still didn't know how much she knew, was she aware it was me who'd originally tried to assassinate Al-afaaa all those years ago?

She continued, 'Still, you left me in the clutches of that beastly partner of yours.' When she said 'beastly', she wrinkled her nose in such a way that I wanted to grab hold of her. I could have stayed looking at her for eternity. 'It was when you killed The Cheat that Al-afaaa became interested in you, no-one should have been able to do that, he was possessed by the spirits of ancient Harpes. Do you have any idea how much it costs to get hold of that kind of muscle?' She lowered her eyes again, and spoke softly, almost in a whisper, 'The kind of hired muscle that can withstand a nuclear warhead.'

She leant back smiling, waiting for her words to have their full impact before continuing. 'Still, that was no match for you was it? And then to keep us all in suspense you went into a coma for six months. It was then Al-afaaa tried to get you to join us, but you wouldn't would you? That was the real puzzle, because no-one was ever able to resist him before.' She stopped again, but this time with an aura of finality, as if that was it, she wasn't going to say anything else. Typical, just at the point that I was actually interested in what she was saying, not just in her. I leant forward expectantly.

'Go on,' I pleaded.

'It was like trying to put a video cassette into a video player when there's already another video cassette in there.' She threw her head back and rolled her eyes. When she looked back at me I knew I was no longer in conversation with Veryanne but was having a one to one with The Snake. He ran her hands through her hair and smiled coyly. He continued talking in her voice, with her mannerisms, but we both knew who we were talking to. 'It's like this, Come over to me and you can have it all, this house, all those nubile young women downstairs. This body,' he ran her hands seductively down her body, ' She even wants you, I guess she always did. Come on, you can't imagine what pleasure can be like when you're fucking her and you can experience what it's like for her at the same time. Flick around different bodies, be the head of a collective. I'll make you my right hand man, second only to me.'

So this was it, my moment of temptation, my forty days in the wilderness. I wasn't like Jesus though, I was sick of all of it. I just wanted peace, but The Snake was offering me something that I hadn't dared dream of before. I jumped at the offer.

'Alright then, on one condition, leave Veryanne, let her come to me of her own free will.'

'Gladly,' Veryanne shivered slightly, then smiled back at me with her own eyes. She licked her lips, then sunk her exquisite teeth into my neck.

Chapter 14

Mac the Knife

'Five'll get you ten that Mac, he's back in town.'
Louis Armstrong

This was it. My moment of temptation, my forty nights in the wilderness, my twenty years in the nut-house, and I gave in without a second thought. No more pain, no more monomania. It would mean being damned, but I would have her. I knew she wanted me for the wrong reason, but I was wanted, desired, I sank deep into her embrace. Making the changeover to vampirism was not all sex and pleasure though, it would also mean a lot less killing. Now I kill for the hit, go for it like the junky I was, but being a vampire would mean drinking blood as well. I'd pig out if I went on at the rate I'm going now. What if you're in a killing frenzy, do you have stop and drink the blood after every killing, or can you kill everyone and then sit down and drink all the blood? I suppose being a vampire meant a lot less killing, or a lifetime of morbid vampiric obesity. No, more shooting them in the head, then warming up a pasty in the microwave. No more pasties, still that was something I could easily give up. I sank back blissfully into her caress.

She suddenly went stiff, let out an ear-piercing scream, and threw me to one side, a long stream of bloody vomit went spewing out of her mouth, and splashed against the wall. She began to convulse waiting for another spasm. This one shot from out of her throat with a stench of burning flesh, long red welts appeared along her stomach. They grew redder and redder, until they, too, burst open, splashing their contents all over the floor. There was an audible hiss as it came into contact with the carpet. 'No!' I screamed, they must not take my darling way from me. I had tasted paradise, only to have it snatched away. My face felt like it was about to explode. Icy shivers shot up and down. I fell flat onto the floor and landed on my knees. Her eyes widened with fear, and she started to hold her hands out to me, just as her jaw dropped off. Then her features began to dissolve like on some tacky Australian horror film. With a loud crack her spine suddenly split, both halves started turning into goo. I covered my head with my hands, and began to cry.

I sat there sobbing for a couple of minutes, trying to come to terms with what had happened, when repulsively and unbidden the hit started to come on. It was slow for the first minute, I just started feeling slightly disorientated, instead of feeling totally bereft. It hovered for a couple of seconds then accelerated to full blown head-rush. I stumbled to the floor, gasping for breath. It was glorious, I had actually forgotten how deeply pleasurable killing Snakeheads was. I sat caught between two worlds, one desperately wanting to acknowledge the loss, the other being shot with total euphoric bloodfury. I could hear Harvey chuckling in my ear. 'What's up Doc?' He'd never been away, there was no way I could ever betray him, the same way that Veryanne could not betray The Snake. It was just as she had put it, I had already got my cassette plugged in, received my programming. Harvey had played a master stroke that was all. The moment I heard him chuckling, saw him standing there nibbling a carrot, all traces of grief vanished, to be replaced with that most constant of companions, rage. I remembered, the handsome vampire and friend were just at the bottom of the stairs, they would know what just happened, probably been listening in the whole time.

The door flew open with a loud clattering and they both stood silhouetted in the doorway. Their sense of disgust was even more apparent now. With a cry of animalistic fury the Snakehead launched himself at me. He did the full Nosferatu change as well, leathery skin, sharp fangs, elongated skull, bat-like eyes and ears, the works. The mercury made a delightful little splash as it burst against the front of his skull, and the back splattered all over the ceiling. His shrunken corpse splattered to the floor like treacle. This time the rush took my breath away I stepped forward smiling at the beta-vampire who up until this moment still had not moved. He was no Snakehead, just a standard vampire, no-one else knew what was going on, and we were not likely to be disturbed. I put the pistol back in my pocket and pulled out the samurai throwing star. I took a step forward, and he stepped back automatically.

'Guess you're in charge now.' I murmured, 'Have you any idea what I am? Because I don't have a fucking clue.' He just turned tail and ran. I was completely disgusted. I had expected more of a fight than that. I threw the star, getting him in the back of the head, splitting the skull in two, killing him instantly and carrying on down the passage way.

I sat down and rolled a spliff, time to take Harvey into me, accept that this time he had won. I was totally buzzing, my forehead pounding. I needed to take stock of events. The Snake's biggest mistake was offering me a place at his right hand. That could never be, it wasn't in my nature to sit on the right of anyone or anything. I was a left-winger pure and simple, still it meant that, even though he knew about Harvey, The Snake was still some way from diving my true nature.

There were about twenty people left in the house, and only about three were vampires, and they weren't Snakeheads, the rest were either sick randy bastards, potential new vampiric recruits or victims. I really didn't give a fuck what they were, I wanted to kill them all. First thing to do was seal off all the exits, no-one must escape, they all needed to know just how fucking pissed off with them I was. All could do with one last lesson, they had toyed with evil, now they needed to reckon with the powers of darkness.

As I sat there thinking I was interrupted by a young acolyte, about twenty-five, sporty type, tall, muscular build, blond, he came pounding down the corridor, being chased by two beautiful priestesses. He nearly ran straight into me, and I shot him instinctively, and dodged to the right avoiding his falling corpse, just in time to get a good clear shot at the priestesses. I got the first one right between the eyes, the second one was just starting to turn away as I shot her through the back of her head. I sat back and listened, I could hear no change at all, same old party sounds, it was really loud. I got the feeling that the ceremony was already late starting, the party had gone on a lot longer than usual, and was starting to run wild. The three junior vampires were taking advantage of their master's absence. I had a choice, I could be lazy, just sit back and wait for them to come to me, like some giant spider taking it easy. Or I could go downstairs and start shooting. I was way too high to start taking it easy. I decided to check out the bedrooms.

Forehead pounding, eyes bulging I kicked open the first door with a hideous, spastic, slobbering stupor. It was rather anti-climatic, just a rather ordinary couple making love on the bed. I shot him through the forehead, and her through the mouth. Shut the door quietly and left them in peace. There were only two doors left before I had to go downstairs. And still the music played on and on. The second door was empty, tiny, full of boxes, and what looked like the sound system. I could hear laughing coming from the third bedroom. I kicked the door open. There were five of them, two girls and three boys. I started shooting without thinking, and shot both the girls and two of the boys before I ran out of bullets. The guy I hadn't killed was at the bottom of all the bodies, struggling to get up. I dropped the Browning back in my pocket and pulled out the knife. I lunged forward, and slit his throat just as he got to his feet. I sat back down on the corpses, things were going really well, and already I'd killed about half, although there were still three vampires left. They were all together, in the huge banqueting hall at the bottom of the stairs, the epicentre of everything. I couldn't just burst in on all ten and start shooting, I needed to create more of a surprise. I walked back into the storeroom, and decided to change the music. I was in luck, along with a load of stuff I'd never heard of before was a CD by Louis Armstrong. I flicked it on, re-loaded the Browning and went downstairs.

At the top of the stairs was a hole in the wall. It hadn't been there before, and at first I wondered what it was. It was from the samurai star, it had sliced through the vampire's skull, shot down the passageway, gone straight through the wall and sailed out into the night. Fuck knows where it would end up. I didn't think I'd thrown it that hard, and it made me pause. When I asked the big vampire if he knew what I was, I was being serious, I didn't have a clue, but I knew that Harvey had thrown my humanity away, and all I was left with was rage, incredible strength and caustic bodily fluids. Still Que Sera and all that.

I'd always wanted to be a bit of a crooner, and I didn't have a bad singing voice, that, and my love of forties dress and film noir, meant that had I not decided to become a raving psychopath, via the world of being a private detective, I could have bashed out a reasonable living at some end of the pier show in a tiny seaside resort like Frinton-On-Sea. Also, I thought if I managed to go in all singing and dancing, they wouldn't know what to do, I could get into position, before I started shooting. I got to the top of the stairs just as 'Mac the Knife,' came on. I put on my cheesiest grin, and started doing the soft-shoe shuffle down the stairs, joining in with Satchmo.

It was good, or was that bad news, at the bottom of the stairs the three vampires were seated, two male, and one female. They each had their own victim, and were greedily gorging blood. Of the others, two, both female, were in attendance, the other two male and female were watching, and mutually masturbating.

I looked like a sack of shit doing the soft-shoe shuffle, but I was really starting to get into it I wanted to put a good show on. I was half way down the stairs when we got to the line, *and he shows them pearly white*. I grinned demonically at the two male vampires and showed them the hunting knife. *Just a jack-knife has old Mac Heath.* They looked a little confused, they'd seen me earlier with Veryanne, knew I must be important, perhaps it was some sort of test. *When that shark bites with his teeth dear, scarlet billows start to spread.* I gestured meaningfully with my knife at their victims. The tallest, and most senior-looking smiled back, maybe this was something Veryanne had laid on for a laugh, some sad git trying to show off.

On the sidewalk, one Sunday morning don'tchaknow, lies a body just oozing life. I lurched drunkenly towards the two 'watchers.' They stared back stupefied, and I stabbed the geezer in the neck. The female vampire gave a little gasp as the blood started spraying across the room in one long burgundy crescent, but the senior vampire, started laughing, pushed the lifeless body from him, and stood under the red shower with his mouth open. I took heart. *There's a cement bag just dropping on down.* I plunged the knife deep into the top of the girl's head, she died instantly, unlike her partner who had just sunk to his knees, and was watching the blood spurt across the room horror-stricken. I started spinning, and kicking my legs furiously, really getting into the song.

The other two vampires sat back, their two attendants hiding behind them for protection. This was as far as I was allowed to go, they were planning on killing those two themselves anyway, but their attendants were important, not to be touched. I wasn't too bothered, I was really getting into the music, and exploring my love of dance. I had time to finish dancing before I made my next move. *Five'll get you ten old Mac, he's back in town.* I swung up high, and then down low, smiling down at the two seated vampires, whilst still acknowledging the most senior. They were all smiling now, even the two attendants were starting to smile weakly. I continued moving back and forwards, a bit more slowly now, as I was starting to get out of breath. The vampires all exuded confidence, they hadn't known how to take me at first, not too sure what sort of risk I posed, now they could tell I was pathetic and sadly mortal, no threat to them whatsoever. The song was starting to come to a close, *The night falls on the right babe, now that Mac he's back in town.* I threw both my arms in the air, and shot the head vampire through the eyes. There was another cheeky splash of mercury, and then all the smiles stopped.

I don't think I'll ever tire of the look on a vampire's face when it suddenly realises it's no longer immortal, an open-jawed almost gormless look, not the sort of thing you would normally associate with vampires. The CD moved onto the next track, Hello Dolly. I was getting bored with it all now, I shot both the remaining mid-transformation, it was all rather a disappointment after the good looking alpha vampire earlier, his Nosferatu moment was so much better, scarier almost, now I felt like they were just going through the motions. This feeling was made all the stronger when the two attendants fell to their knees, and started begging for their lives. Some chance, they throw their lot in with vampires, then when it all goes pear-shaped think they can just say sorry, and everything will be alright. That might work for Michael, but it didn't work for Harvey. Before I stabbed them, I explained this to them, and especially stressed the fact that they must realise just how pissed-off with them God really was.

I sat down and finished my spliff, you never can tell just how an evening will turn out, but I'd best be getting a move on, all the Snakeheads in Southampton will know exactly where I was, the police were probably on their way. I went into the kitchen and turned the gas on, it would be quite a while before the fire in the hall would catch it, should be quite a tasty explosion. Sure enough, I was in the middle of the Common when I heard it go up, all 'Halloween Orange and Chimney Red.' Tonight had been an interesting diversion, but I was forgetting why I had come to Southampton in the first place. With my mind filled with stabbings, shootings, bombs and explosions I ran off giggling into the night, it was the most fun I'd had in years.

Chapter 15

Hyperactive!

'But tonight I'm on the edge, better shut me in the fridge, cause I'm burning up.'
Thomas Dolby

'If you make just a squeak, I'll pull this knife clean across your throat.' I had the knife pressed up tight against his windpipe, it was just beginning to cut the skin, a faint pink line half an inch long was just starting to appear, but not quite deep enough to draw blood. He had gone quite stiff, cold and clammy, faint beads of sweat were beginning to form on his forehead, a highly repugnant odour was coming off him, a mixture of BO and stale beer. I felt slightly nauseous, still it couldn't be much worse than the stench that was coming off me. I was acutely aware of my own body odour, a sense that was intensified by being so physically close to someone else. Admittedly, having a knife to someone's throat was not exactly the same as being intimate, but you still wanted to create a good impression.

This was not how I had imagined this meeting, and it was a meeting I had imagined many times since I'd regained my memory, I'd always imagined saying something clever, but in absence of wit, a knife to the throat would have to do. Let's face it, my partner wasn't likely to open the conversation, he was being uncharacteristically silent. 'Well, this is a turn up for the books,' I continued, 'Who would have thought we would have turned out like this? Still, you seem to have done alright for yourself. Looks like the Private Detective business started paying for itself after all.' I pushed my mouth close to his ear, 'Anything to say for yourself? Tell you what, you can start with how you decided to rip me off.' My partner started to make a low gurgling noise, then he gave a violent spasm, and went limp. I let go, and he slumped onto the floor. The smell grew considerably worse as I realised he had shat himself. Still, it made a nice change, not smelling worse than the person you're with. I'd had one hell of a night, walked for miles in the pouring rain, reeking of death, and blood, and vomit, and sweat. So, I may have looked like a bag of shit, but at least I didn't smell of shit.

It was all very well whooping and howling off into the night like that, but I hadn't gone very far before I felt knackered, and had to slow right down, puffing and wheezing, at least I was going in the right direction, our old office. With hindsight I probably should have sorted all of this out earlier, but there I was acting on impulse. It took about an hour to get to St Mary's Lane, only to find everywhere boarded up, and being redeveloped, bright blue plastic signs announcing how there was going to be an exciting new development, encompassing a new shopping centre with flats for the criminally insane. I peered through our old front door and there was a torn piece of card wedged into the top window, in badly faded felt tip it gave a forwarding address in Millbrook. Millbrook! That was bloody miles away, back past where the boat show was, where the pigs were already looking for me. It was a long hard slog, back up to the common, and then along Winchester Road until eventually I got to the Millbrook roundabout once more. The whole place was crawling with pigs, but they were looking too hard, and it was relatively easy to slip past them. They were handing out flyers to passers-by, warning of a dangerous terrorist loose in Southampton, with an accompanying identi-kit photograph. Out of interest I picked up a discarded one from the roadside, and put it in my pocket.

Solent Investigation's new suite of offices was set in a garishly new industrial estate. All the lighting looked different, more modern, all very Milton Keynsian. It was a real mixture of the old and the new, all the fittings and features, sat well with the general ambiance of the estate, a technogarish mix of chrome and electric blue. Inside most of the furniture seemed to have been shipped wholesale from the previous location. He even had my old Athena poster of Humphrey Bogart, but it was framed with a phoney signature, and a cheesy little plaque, authenticating the validity of the aforementioned signature. That was typical of my partner, anything to save money, and appear upmarket, but at the same time appealing to the lowest common denominator. Let's face it, the clientele would have to be really thick to be taken in by that one. Humphrey Bogart was dead long before Athena produced that poster in the eighties. Still, knowing my partner, he was probably just as mean when it came to security. For all its flash post-modern chrome, I bet the alarm system was totally crap, and not at all difficult to disable. Not that there would be anything of any real value, my partner may be mean, but he wasn't stupid. However, there would be data, and that's what I was craving. A tired old plastic blue box, containing a couple of wires, I wasn't even certain whether it was even connected to anything, but I pulled the two wires out of the back, and nothing happened. It was then a simple matter to smash one of the windows with a handkerchief, again nothing happened. Clutching my hankie to my chest I undid the window and climbed in. Finding my partner's address was easy, only the second chest of drawers I came across, but what was the real pisser, it was a huge rambling mansion of a place, not far from Safeways, about five hundred yards from the vampire's mock Tudor orgiastic house of death, or where I had started from.

So it was that I got to my partner's address about five in the morning, puffing, panting, wheezing, soaked to the skin, feet blistered and bloody, but still feeling deliriously psychotic and happy. It was huge, four stories at least, put the vampire's pad to shame, and I felt totally dwarfed by the sheer majesty of it all, as I slunk up the drive. I walked up to the front door, and there, protruding out of the woodwork was the samurai throwing star. So the rush of superhuman strength had a purpose after all, I should have followed my instincts and followed the star's trajectory after all instead of wandering all over town in the pouring rain, dodging pigs. I tried pulling the star out of the door, but it was wedged in too tight, and the superhuman strength had long gone.

To my surprise, my partner was still up, no doubt he had stayed up all night to watch the emergency services dealing with the fire at the vampire's gaff. He had retired to the living-room, sitting back on the sofa with a large calvados and a spliff, some things never change. Something really dodgy was going on though, either Solent Investigation was doing a lot better than its garish Millbrook offices would suggest, or my partner was pulling a fast one somehow.

In many ways he hadn't changed, same piggy eyes and puffy cheeks, stomach a bit bigger, hair a bit less, but in all other respects, he had stayed the same. He was lying on the floor unconscious with a small stream of drivel leaking out of the corner of his mouth. I was very suddenly, and almost overwhelmed with a surge of nostalgia. This was the sight that had often greeted me when I arrived for work in the morning. I sat down and picked up my partner's spliff and relit it. My partner had left it slightly moist, but he was never any good at sharing, always had to do something to make it less enjoyable for the other one, even when he thought he didn't have to share. Even so, it wasn't that bad a smoke, very fresh Moroccan, and I thought there was even a hint of Harvey in there, but perhaps he was only there for me. Drawing deeply on it helped to clear my head, even though I was still physically knackered my head was still firing at over a hundred miles an hour. Death high is a lot like speed in that respect, you could only go for so long before you need to come down, and someone else's dope is always best for that.

My partner let out a long grunt, I turned my attention back to his slumbering mass, and saw him and his surroundings together in sharp relief. Seeing such opulence juxtaposed with such slovenliness was almost surreal. It looked like something from late night telly, fit only for the unemployed and the mentally ill. My partner, had tried to make an effort though, velvet dressing gown with Paisley pattern, quite a stylish garment, on anyone else that is, but on my partner it looked ridiculous. He really had a gift for making good look crap, no-one could look worse than that, except me of course. I made him look good, despite lying in his own spittle and shit he still exuded a certain élan which I didn't. Personal hygiene problems aside though; how did such a pathetic joke of a man come to be living in such a palace? Something stank, and it wasn't just me and my partner.

I went into the kitchen to get a bucket of water, quite a big bucket, a huge Victorian fire bucket, easily twice the size of the ones we use today, full of icy cold water. I had a bit of a job picking it up, but I managed to soak him completely from head to toe, all in one movement. I was expecting my partner to jump up screaming, but he didn't, he sat up screaming. 'Don't do that, it's not insured.' He didn't say anything else, because he was too busy blinking down the barrel of the Browning. Like a startled owl caught in the headlights of an approaching car he sat back mutely blinking. I could sense the intense mental effort that was going on as he tried to comprehend what was happening, and more importantly, what to do about it. I was in no great hurry, and sat back enjoying my partner's discomfort A slight flicker of awareness crept across his pasty face as he decided to revert to type, his 'Don't hit me I'm a haemophiliac' approach to combat. His lip began to tremble, and he squawked out pitifully, 'You're wasting your time mate, there's nothing worth nicking.'

'Bollocks, everything's worth nicking, even this bucket. It's Victorian, worth two hundred quid at least. I can't imagine what the really tasty stuff must be worth. Anyway, half of this is legally mine anyway.' A sudden look of dread flashed across his face.

'Oh my God, you're not Lionel are you?'

'Who the fuck is Lionel?'

'Suzy's brother.'

'Who the fuck is Suzy?'

'It's her house.' He stopped, and looked back with a peculiar expression which would have been anger, were he not being threatened with a pistol.

'Look, if you're not Lionel who the fuck are you?'

I took a few minutes to reply, taking in his spluttering impotent fury. Through the pre-dawn, crepuscular gloom that was making everything spectral I whispered, 'Don't you recognise me Pard-ner?' After what seemed like an eternity of mumbling, a light went on in his head. It was like watching tortoises mating, eventually something had to happen. He peered back at me through the gloom.

'But it can't be. You're supposed to be locked up in a coma somewhere. They said they'd let me know if there was any change. Anyway if you are my partner, why couldn't you have phoned, it's a hell of a lot more conventional than holding someone at both knife and gunpoint.' He paused and looked at me confused, frightened and angry. 'Zippy, is it really you?'

'Yeah it's me,' I murmured, 'Why would you have been told if I got out?' As I asked the question I started to feel myself getting angrier and angrier. 'What part do you play in all of this?' I could feel the white heat burning in my forehead, Harvey was chuckling in my ear. 'Just what does The Snake mean to you?' I really screamed it out, my partner sank back into the carpet, and I blew a hole in the ceiling, accidentally letting one shot go. My partner went completely white.

'Jesus Christ! Please don't shoot me. I don't know anything about any fucking snakes, I don't like reptiles. I thought I would have been told when you came round because I am your fucking business partner, a business which incidentally I have been running really well. You've got no family, I'm the nearest you've got to next of kin.' Now that was a real stomach churning thought. It calmed me right down. I took a deep breath and put the pistol back in my pocket. 'Thank you,' my partner gasped.

'Alright then, you tell me what happened from your point of view, because I don't really know how I came to be inside the nut house.'

'OK then. Do you mind if I sit down on a chair first?'

'Go on then, but don't try anything funny, I'm not the guy you used to know.'

'I can see that... look, I don't know why you've come in all guns blazing, but you've really not got any axe to grind with me. When I got out of hospital I tried going into work, only to find the pigs all over the shop. Crime scene, blue tape, blood, guts all over the place, but no body. Treated me like a bloody criminal, couldn't believe I wasn't in on it, fortunately I had an alibi, or they would have locked me up too. Pigs told me they were investigating two murders, the one in the office, and The Cheat's.' He stopped for a minute to see what effect The Cheat's name would have on me. I wasn't going to give him the satisfaction, and sat poker-faced and indistinct.

'Dirty little junky thief. What's he got to do with me and the nut house?'

'Well the pigs told me that you lost the plot and hijacked a car. They tracked you down to a house in Somerset somewhere. You were in a deep coma lying next to The Cheat's corpse, and covered in his blood. They said that if and when you came out of the coma you might be facing charges for murder. I told them straight that you were no killer, I would have been able to tell, I'm quite sensitive to these sort of things. Said it was a put up job, it must have been. I told them to go looking for that fucking scouser, the ginger git, the fat fucker.'

'Dodge?'

'Yeah him, turns out he disappeared about the same time you wind up comatose next to a corpse.'

'What about the money? You seem to have done alright for yourself, bloody big gaff like this, fancy new set of offices in Millbrook. Where's my bit?'

'What money? You took it all with you, I had about fifty quid, that's all. I'll tell you who's got the money, that fucking scouser, that's who.'

'You didn't only have fifty quid, you had the office, And I didn't take all the money, I paid all the bills. I left you the sole owner of a solvent business. A thriving business, I'd just solved a murder, private detectives don't do that sort of thing in real life, only in stories. You had, what's the name? Goodwill, that's it.' I started to feel myself getting angry again. 'You had fucking goodwill! They would have been lining up outside!' I screamed it out, and my partner blanched once more.

'Alright, alright we were solvent,' he spluttered, 'But we didn't have goodwill, ill-will's more like it. You hadn't solved any murders, but you were the prime suspect in two other murders, they wasn't exactly queuing up. I had to start right back at the bottom, nickel and dime stuff, debt collection work mostly, almost got beaten up a few times, then I got lucky. I managed to get a contract to dig up dirt on environmental road protestors. After that I was able to get to where the real money is.' Again he paused for effect. 'Industrial espionage, that's where it is. Companies pay a lot for that, and they can afford it too. You're not going to make any money chasing after murders, and thinking you're like some character out of some naff 1940s film noir.'

'You still ripped me off, my name is on the deeds, you needed my permission before you could take my name off.'

'I didn't take your name off, you're still a partner in this business, still entitled to your share of the profits. I've not ripped you off, you can go back to work tomorrow if you like, and start drawing a wage. There's plenty of work on.' He paused reflectively, as if unsure how to go on. 'Look,' he continued, 'I've done nothing wrong, you were the one that left me in the lurch. You know I could've just fucked off, sold the office furniture to the yuppies downstairs, and jetted off to Mexico City, done a Malcolm Lowry. I was tempted to, but I didn't, out of some misplaced sense of loyalty to the firm...' he paused again trying to collect his thoughts before continuing, '...and to you, my sense of loyalty to you. Look, I'll show you, some of our headed notepaper, with your name on it, there's some in the bureau over there.' He started to get up.

'Hang on a minute!' I bellowed, 'How do I know you've not got a gun stashed over there? I'm not stupid, I'm not that sorry git you used to work for anymore. I've changed. You tell me you're my friend, but I remember you of old, you'll be telling me you're a born again Christian next. I'll check out the bureau.' My partner sat back down again.

'Sure whatever you say, the notepaper's on the top shelf. But I don't know what you mean about old times, you could always rely on me.' Either my partner had developed a selective memory or he really thought I was stupid. I got up and walked over to the bureau, keeping my eye on him all the while.

'And another thing,' I quipped, almost as an afterthought, 'You couldn't do a Malcolm Lowry, he didn't just get pissed all the time he wrote books too.'

'I write books.' My partner hissed, looking like I'd really hurt his feelings. I ignored it and slid back the shutters on the bureau. It was beautiful, a real piece of art, about two hundred years old, solid mahogany, lots of little drawers, and a couple of larger ones for bigger documents. There was a green velvet covered writing space, with a brass inkwell and quill. All beautifully preserved, smelling of polish. It was the sort of bureau I could imagine Charles Dickens writing *Great Expectations* on. My partner always had good taste when it came to antiques. I opened the top drawer, and to my astonishment there was the headed notepaper. 'Solent Investigations,' it had the new address in Millbrook, and at the top in pale blue ink both mine and my partner's names. I was just about to apologise to my partner when I noticed something glinting in one of the other smaller drawers, I slid it back to find a tiny Derringer. It, too, was also very beautiful, and didn't seem at all out of place, it could have been part of the bureau, it looked about the same age, and had the same brass and velvet inlay. I pulled it out and pointed it at my partner.

'So, what's this then?'

'Shit, honestly man I'd forgotten all about that. It's an antique, it came with the bureau, it's just for show, it's not a proper gun.'

'So it's not loaded then?' I levelled it at the vacant spot between his eyes.

'I didn't say that.' My partner's expression suddenly changed, an almost steely determination came over him. 'Look I'm getting really sick of this, either shoot me or put the gun away, one or the other. I can't take this hot and cold. Shoot me now, I'm ready.' I almost did, what with Harvey chuckling in my ear, and my delight with the Derringer itself. The Browning was compact, but this was tiny, really enchanting, and I was itching to try it out. Still, I hadn't come to see my partner just to wreak a bloody revenge, I still might, but I wasn't sure whether or not to believe him, just yet. 'Look,' my partner ventured, I want to hear about you, we've got a lot of catching up to do, but I don't want to sit here like this, and you look like you could do with a bath.' I put the gun back in my pocket, a bath and a clean set of clothes sounded good, something to mask the stench of death. My partner reeked, and it was getting worse. We both needed a bath. I still didn't trust him though, he was always a mendacious little toady git, I couldn't leave him while I was having a bath. I felt sick, disgusted, and more depressed than I had felt for a long time, as the slow creeping horror suddenly dawned upon me, we would have to bathe together.

The next half hour was the worst of my entire life, by a long chalk. Worse than being interrogated by the pigs, worse than being locked up in a secure mental institution and being experimented on for twenty years. Some would describe two men bathing together as homoerotic. This particular bathe would never be described as such. Only the truly disturbed could find the sight of my partner's naked bulk scraping the shit off his kex as remotely erotic. As well as the pressing need for us to get clean there was also the security to be aware of, I couldn't afford to give him the chance to jump me. Every move had to be carried out in chorus, we had to duck our heads underwater at the same time, on the count of three. Having said that it was a lovely big bath with plenty of room for the pair of us. I got the distinct impression that my partner had spent a lot of time entertaining in the bath before. This sent a whole host of unwanted disturbing visions scurrying through my brain. Not that my partner was at all happy about the situation, he was extremely reluctant, and I had to hit him a couple of times before he finally agreed. He was tight-lipped and taciturn throughout, communicating in grunts. It was as if we had committed some form of sacrilege, what was the inner sanctum of my partner's erotic encounters had been besmirched, and would forever be tainted with the vile memories of our communal wash. He was also quite jumpy, not quite believing that all my years in secure institutions had left my heterosexuality intact. For my part, I thought that I had seen all the horrors that life had to offer, but nothing could have prepared me for that half hour of hell.

It was after all only half an hour, both of us washed as quickly as possible, it was an experience that neither of us wished to prolong. My partner's clothes were all too small for me, so I had to wear 'Lionel's,' which were almost a perfect fit. It turned out that the house was owned by an old lady who was off in a rest home in Devon slowly dying. My partner was engaged to her daughter Suzy, a sad old spinster who had spent the best years of her life nursing her sick mother. My partner had seen the financial rewards ever since Suzy had come into my partner's office begging his help in trying to contact her long lost brother Lionel, who was an explorer type, last heard of heading up the Amazon. It was the old lady's final wish to see her son before she died. Naturally this was something that my partner wanted to avoid at all costs. He didn't want to share Suzy's inheritance with anyone. He had tracked Lionel down to some seedy backstreet hole in Columbia, and was paying to keep him there. He didn't have the bottle to have him killed, so he was doing the next best thing, paying some Columbian lowlife to keep him in booze, dope and whores long enough, so that a) he wouldn't come home to claim his inheritance for a long time, and b) he would get into a bad situation and get killed without my partner getting his hands dirty.

My partner blurted all of this out as we were getting dressed, as if his enforced period of silence were somehow unnatural, and he had to talk ten to the dozen to make up for lost time. His tone was boastful, he was very pleased with the way he was handling things, and he thought that I would approve. I took it as an opportunity to remind him what a treacherous, duplicitous git he was, and that was why I could not trust him, which is why we had to bathe together. That shut him up for a bit.

So there we both sat, two lost souls who had bonded in the same way soldiers bonded in wartime, not because of any particular friendship, but because of the shared experience of something horrific and soul destroying. I felt a lot closer to my partner, but I still didn't trust him. We both sat in comparative luxury, drinking calvados and smoking my partner's best Nepalese, at seven 'o clock on a Saturday morning. As we both had been up all night it didn't seem too early. I started to open up, go right back to the beginning, telling him the sort of stuff I should have told him at the time. I was still buzzing though, and it all came out in one mad rush. Vampires, Hashisheen, Armageddon Codes, malevolent white rabbits, ancients cocks and dissolving sirens all merged together in one long garbled rant. My partner looked up and grinned.

'And after you told the pigs all this, they just let you go, felt you were safe to let back into the community?'

I didn't like this, my partner was getting far too cocky, starting to take the piss, and steal my story. I pulled the knife out and pointed it at him.

'I don't like your fucking tone, of course they didn't let me out I had to escape. That's another thing if I hadn't hane escaped I wouldn't have found out what I am. Now you may think it's all a load of bollocks, but there's two ways of looking at things. Let me say something a little less contentious, something we can both agree on. Whatever the truth is I'm an escaped mental patient with a history of violence. I don't think that is something you should lose sight of. My partner suddenly regained his previous demeanour, dropped his pretensions, and went back to being the nervous, mumbling wreck before we had bathed together.

'I'm sorry, I didn't mean to take the piss. So, you're a vampire hunter then?'

'I'm not a vampire hunter, vampires are collateral damage, I'm Hashisheen. Haven't you been listening to what I've been telling you?' I screamed back at him. My partner looked at me almost piteously, clearly he didn't believe any of it. I had to admit it all sounded completely insane, had I not lived it, I probably would not have believed it either.

'Do you remember that party you went to years ago? The one with the convoy, and the spiked punch? It seems to me that everything started to go strange after you took a whole bunch of unknown hallucinogens, maybe that's it.' My partner looked sincere, full of genuine concern for me, or maybe it was just his instinct for self-preservation. He was wrong though, he had to be, and I could prove it.

'Let me ask you this; can you describe me? Despite all that's happened tonight, all the vivid happenings that must be etched in your memory, could you pick me out of an identity parade? If you passed me in the street would you know it was me? Or is it that the only words you can use to describe me are vague, hazy and indistinct? The pigs are looking for me you know.' I reached into my coat pocket and handed my partner the flyer. 'That's supposed to be me. Take a good look. Is that me?'

My partner took out an old pair of reading glasses and perched them on the end of his nose. According to this you're a member of Al Qaida, you're armed, highly dangerous, and wanted for murder. On no account should you be approached.'

'Yeah, I know all that, but the picture. Does it look like me?' My partner screwed up his face like a man sucking a lemon, trying to concentrate, after a minute he gave me his answer.

'No you're right. It doesn't look anything like you. I'll tell you who it does look like, Jimmy Stewart. James Stewart, dead Hollywood legend is now an Al Qaida operative on the run.' There was a long pause, a deep sigh then he grumbled, 'Isn't that typical of the fucking pigs?'

Chapter 16

Sympathy For The Devil

'Let me introduce myself. I'm a man of wealth and taste.'
The Rolling Stones

There's a hell of a lot of pubs in Winchester, considering it's not a very big city. Someone told me that the only other place with as many pubs is York, which I have been told has a pub for every day of the year. Winchester's not got quite that many, but there's enough for a different pub every week of the year at least. I suppose it's because they both were once the capitals of England, now they could both be swallowed up by London and then some. Maybe the large amount of boozers is the way the former capitals had dealt with their respective falls from grace; it wasn't only people who reached for the bottle. I had a very pleasant stroll from the car park up by the railway station, musing such mildly pleasant bollocks. Not the mind-jarringly violent bollocks that I normally mused. I was so taken up by these thoughts, that almost before I knew it, I had arrived at my destination. I'd ended up in The Brewer's Barrel, not quite central, but very handy for the pig station. There was as jolly an old mixture of Art students, spaced out hippies, drunken bums, sad wankers and criminal lowlife, as you could hope to meet. If you were new in town, and had to score without any references, your best bet was The Barrel, or 'Bottom of the..' as it was more commonly known.

I'd only been there once before, after abusing ether, I was coping with the effects really well until I went in there. The minute I walked through the door everyone turned around to look at me, because I stank of ether. People at the far end of the bar, near the door to the beer garden twitched their noses. I didn't realise that it was because I stank of solvent abuse, I thought it was because they wanted a fight, and I was all ethered up and raring to go. Fortunately I was with someone sensible, someone who had not been abusing ether. The minute I started screaming 'Hippy wankers!' he pulled me straight back out again, then drove me home where we sat up for the rest of the night drinking tequila until collapsing into wretched drunken heaps. Those were happy carefree days, nothing to worry about but random violence.

And here I was again, so many years later, I wondered if they would recognise me, I wondered if I would recognise any of them. Apart of course from the person I was supposed to recognise, right where my partner said he would be, Chris, Clay, Moondog, The Snake's primary host, and the beginning of the end. I nearly wet myself. Once I had cut him loose, it was only a matter of time before Chris gravitated back to Southampton. Both consciously and unconsciously this was the place where he had to be. I'm sure Chris was blissfully unaware of what dwelt in his subconscious. Chris was just following some sort of hippy homing system, he was just going back to the place he knew well; the only place where he could genuinely claim to have friends. The Snake's reasons were altogether more mercenary. Southampton was his power base, the epicentre of all his operations. He needed Chris there, because he was fast becoming a liability. Chris was the one, the person whose death would have snuffed out The Snake at one fell stroke. Ironically had I not been too preoccupied with getting away I could have finished everything off on the night of our escape from the asylum.

Killing Chris was no longer an option, I was positive that The Snake had sorted out another bolt-hole by now, probably wanted me to kill Chris, let him go off to his new primary host. I bet it was someone a lot classier than Chris. Still, Chris had served his purpose, it was alright living in a shit-hole if you never went home. That was all over now, time to move up-market, somewhere undetectable. The Snake may no longer have any use for Chris, but I definitely did have, all I had to do was get him out of 'The Barrel,' and back to Glastonbury without killing him, and Armageddon should be able to go ahead as planned. It wasn't going to be as easy as it sounded.

My partner had been uncharacteristically compliant. I got £300 cash, which was all my partner had on him, he also gave me his car and the information, on condition we call it quits. I knew he would have what I wanted, my partner always liked keeping tabs on people, no one from the old days could avoid coming back to Southampton without my partner's team of snoopers finding out about it and passing it back up the line. My partner was only too glad to get rid of me, I was tempted to shoot him, but decided against it for old time's sake, and because of what happened last time I killed him. He could keep the business, it wasn't really practical for me to try to take a legitimate job again, not after all the killing. What my partner had said about goodwill was correct, £300, a perfectly acceptable red Skoda Felicia was a good deal. More importantly he had given me the information I needed, and he wasn't going to go running to the pigs, I knew that. Either he had been affected by the speech I had given about my shuffling anonymity, or he didn't want anyone else to find out about the whole bath thing, which I assured him would be number one on a list of things to tell the arresting officers. Either way I didn't care, just so long as he kept his trap shut.

It was a pleasant drive, marred by only one ugly incident. I had not even reached The Avenue when I saw some people crossing the road on the zebra crossing ahead. Naturally I didn't want any hassle, preferring to leave Southampton quietly, get away from the heat, drive friendly. They were still some way off, I took my foot off the accelerator, that would give them plenty of time to stop without me having to brake. I was pleasantly stoned and mellow, and didn't feel like running anyone over. I'd been killing vampires, and really needed to give it a rest for a while, it was just too addictive. I needed to keep focused on why I had gone for a weekend break. Alas, 'twas not meant to be, two of the group had reached the other side but the third was standing in the middle of the road. I would have to brake. I took a good look at them for the first time. They were a group of teenagers about fifteen to sixteen, two girls and a boy. The girls had both crossed to the other side, one fat, wearing black crop top, gut pouring over mini skirt, with torn fishnet stockings, dark greasy hair, heavily made up. The other was a long thin streak of piss, mousy blonde, blank expressionless face, wearing a fluorescent pink shell suit. Both were smoking and giggling, looking in cow-eyed admiration at the boy. He was tall, skinny with pale sandy hair, jeans, an Arsenal top, and a stupid twatty chav Burberry baseball cap. His face was completely covered with yellow suppurating acne. He was grinning towards the girls. By now we were close enough to see each other's eyes, and still I hadn't braked. His eyes were full of adolescent arrogance, and defiance. He was going to show how important he was. He was going to make a car stop, admittedly it was only a poxy Skoda, but it would stop and he should be able to shag one of the girls, if not both, later on. It wasn't the Arsenal shirt that did it, or even the Burberry cap, it was the personal nature of it all, the fact that he decided to come out to pick a fight with me. I couldn't let that go. I put my foot back on the accelerator and headed straight for him. Instead of frowning back I gave a wide welcoming grin, and all the time getting closer and closer. Arrogant defiance turned into confusion, the penny finally dropped, just at the last second he leapt out of the way, into the welcoming arms of his lady friends. The Skoda mounted the pavement like a howling banshee. There were some screams, thuds, and reassuring cracks. I zoomed off towards the Avenue, leaving three dead bodies behind me, with a lovely warm comforting feeling in my stomach. It was just as well it was a red car.

Walking into The Barrel was like stepping back in time. It didn't seem to have changed at all. Still the same mixture of undesirables, still the same depressive fat bastard barman, who was wearing the same shirt, shabbier, with a button missing, I only hope it had been washed at some point since I last saw it, but I doubted it. He was slightly greyer, and fatter, but otherwise no different. I looked around the bar for Chris, with the practised step of a man who walks into pubs to buy things they don't sell behind the bar, and walks out without buying a drink. I could feel The Snake's presence, scuttling around at the back of the bar, he knew I was here, but he was content to watch, observe, see what I intended to do. Last time he made the first move he got his fingers badly burned. I scoured the shadowy recesses where illegal transactions were being made, attracting some filthy looks in return. Eventually I saw him sat in the corner, in the exact spot I had seen him for the very first time, all those years ago. He looked up, and smiled in recognition before beckoning me over. It was just Chris and me, The Snake was definitely in the background, with a sense of cold dispassionate interest, detached, like that of a scientist. After all he was more interested in what I was going to do next, than he was concerned about Chris. I waved back, smiling, Chris' grin became wider and wider, the waving more and more frantic. 'Oh wow...! I really don't believe it, it is you, but how?'

'Oh I'm just passing through' I smiled back clutching both his hands in mine, and warmly shaking them. This was really genuine, I hated The Snake, but I didn't really have any axe to grind with Chris. He was a hapless victim, harmless in his own right, and fairly amusing, too. My partner and I had spent many a long night laughing at the bollocks that came pouring out of his mouth.

The more I thought about it the more obvious it seemed, all the signs of unwitting possession by an unearthly demonic entity were there. I felt really stupid, and unprofessional, because that's the first thing you should be looking out for in the private detective game. Yeah, but I got there in the end, and looking at Chris' beaming eyes I could see the end of all things reflected in his eyes. I just wanted to grab hold of him, and get him out of the pub, and into the car, then hightail it all the way back to the enchanted chapel. At gunpoint if necessary, what did I mean by that, it's always necessary. Nowadays you can't leave a pub without shooting at least one other person, or can you? I got a bit carried away with the thought of it all, and I had to bring myself back to earth with a jolt. The car was parked some way away, and I wasn't prepared for a gun battle so close to the pig station. I was supposed to be keeping a low profile, even Harvey had shut up, he didn't want me losing control right now. There was nothing else for it, I would have to use guile, and tact, at the very least persuade Chris to walk to the car park. 'I've just pulled off a really good deal in Southampton, and I thought I'd stop off here to celebrate.' The mention of drugs caused Chris to sit up, interested, perhaps very interested, it all depended on what the drugs were. 'What do you want to drink?' I continued, deliberately changing the subject, and forcing him to answer instead of ask a question. He asked for a pint of snakebite, (again, yet another clue!) made with special brew and scrumpy. Chris was not a man to do things by halves.

There was a bit of a queue at the bar, and the miserable fat git took forever to pour a pint, but after about ten minutes I went back to the alcove with a pint of snakebite and a cocktail for me, kirsch, apricot brandy, orange juice and soda. Ideally I would have asked them to frost the rim of the glass with egg white and castor sugar, and decorate it with cocktail cherries and a slice of orange, but that wasn't going to happen. I was lucky to get a clean glass. By the time I got back Chris was sweating heavily. He grunted his thanks before taking a sip, then leaned back, trying to act nonchalantly'

'So... You're dealing then?' He leant forward smiling, either he'd forgotten about our motorway chase, (which was likely,) or his desire for illegal substances over-rode all notions of personal safety, (which was even more likely.)

'Yup.' I took a long swig of the drink, I wasn't giving anything away, let him dangle on the hook a little loner, and hope The Snake would stay sitting back watching. I lit a Disque Bleu, and offered Chris one. He took it and accepted a burning match, smiled, and continued his half assed interrogation.

'So... What are you dealing?' He paused, then his eyes lit up, 'Any Billy?' Amphetamine was Chris' raison d'etre. That and pornography were what made his life worth living.

'I have got some lovely sulphate in the car, I was wanting to take some back for the girls.' Again Chris' eyes opened wide.

'Chris,' I continued. 'Really lovely friendly nature-loving girls.' I hesitated a moment, allowing the information to sink in. 'Moon-goddesses, young, beautiful, sensual girls.' He sat with his eyes wide open, eagerly awaiting every juicy word on the subject of girls.

'Yeah, how d'you meet them?'

'They were at an ecologically friendly neo-pagan love festival I went to in someone's back garden.'

'Back garden?'

'Yeah, in Shepton Mallet.'

'Isn't that just down the road from Glastonbury?'

'Yeah, that's where I'm based now, it's really sweet. You'd love it. What are you doing now? Where are you staying?' Chris' eyes sparkled with black intensity, he was thinking of moon-goddesses, he sat quietly for a while relishing his own private little fantasy before continuing the conversation.

'I'm with the brothers.'

'Black guys?'

'No, religious dudes. Some sort of monks. I was hitching, they just turned up, brought me back to their pad, which is just around the corner. They're really nice people, I'm living there for free, and they're feeding me. Nice grub, like monk food, like wholemeal bread, lots of fresh fruit and veg, and mead, like really strong mead. I'm living there, but I've hooked back up with the scene, it's really good.'

'Have they got a name these religious guys?'

'Yeah, Brother Arnold, and Brother Cyril and...'

'Not their individual names, like an order or something, some sort of saint or something.' At this Chris became quite excited, and a whole lot more animated than usual. He started rocking backwards and forwards in his seat.

'Yeah they got that, that's what they got, an order with a saint.' He sat back looking pleased with himself.

'So what are they called?' I was starting to regret this line of questioning. I'd forgotten, that despite all the amusing neo-visionary bullshit, Chris was a useless twat. This conversation had the potential to go round and round in circles. Unfortunately, it was something I really needed to know. Who were these monks? Were they going to be a problem? Were they working for The Snake, or someone else? I wouldn't put it past bloody Yogi to have mates down here, trying to heal the world with love, and putting the kibosh on all my schemes. I was brought out of my train of paranoid thought by Chris' pathetic attempt to answer the question.

'Er, um... I'm not exactly sure exactly what they're called, but it is definitely an order, with robes and that. It's just round the corner if you want to have a look.' That was something I definitely didn't want to do, I didn't know what I could be walking into, and you could bet that whatever it was, it wouldn't be friendly.

'Are any of them in here?

'Shit no man, they're monks, they're not allowed to be amongst women.' I looked around at the stringy old hippy tarts before replying.

'They should be all right in here then.' Chris looked offended. 'I mean they're not exactly moon-goddesses are they?' Chris' look vanished to be replaced with one of slow simmering lust. We had just returned back to his favourite topic, not women, but goddesses. The Snake may have been rampaging his way around loads of different hosts, having a wonderful sexy time, but by my reckoning Chris hadn't had it for years, probably as long as me. 'You'd love the girls in Glastonbury, real nature lovers, really passionate, really into films, want to make, um, er, what's the word...? Green movies.' Chris nearly fell off his chair.

'Green movies?' He almost screamed the words out. Green movies were blue movies outside in the countryside, I'd only ever heard Chris use the phrase before. I still wasn't too sure whether anyone other than Chris would recognise the term, but Chris most certainly recognised it.

One of Chris' serious obsessions was appearing in a naturist's sex video. Many years ago, in a fit of drunken bonhomie I had promised to have a word with Bazzer on his behalf. I never got the chance, in a rush of amphetamine crazed euphoria Chris burst into the mucky book shop and accosted him, screaming 'Are you Bazzer? I'm Clay, I want to make green movies.' Bazzer took me to task about it later on that day in The Carpenter's. He was furious, turned out his boss was in to talk about Bazzer's poor sales performance. When Chris burst in the boss thought Bazzer was running an amateur porn business on the side, it did not go down well. 'I almost got cut, it wasn't at all funny, tell that cunt he's got no fucking chance, better still portfolio 'im.' What 'portfolioing' meant was getting a set of photos of Chris in the nude with, 'Flaccid shots, half-up shots, and full on bronco; various assorted shots of the tackle. Then we bring 'em down the pub and flash 'em about, it'll be a real laugh.' So that was it, Chris would be humiliated, I wasn't too sure it was a very good idea, I didn't think Chris could be humiliated, the whole concept was too sophisticated for him. He would probably get off on people laughing at his naked photos. The only problem was getting the portfolio together, Chris would only be photographed by 'a horny female photographer,' that was the stumbling block, none of the women we asked were that sad and desperate. Even the one woman we knew who had actually had sex with him, (a right dirty cow who was rumoured to have had sex with donkeys) refused point blank, then went outside to throw up. So the opportunity of being filmed having sex in the country was something he couldn't possibly turn down. I carried on feigning innocence.

'Yeah green movies, I'm not too sure what they mean by that, but they're looking for the right bloke, got to be into nature and that.' At these words Chris literally began to salivate. He started making a rapid jabbering noise, too excited to get any words out for five minutes.

'That's me man, I can do green movies, I'm really into nature, I can show them the hurdles I've been weaving.'

'I do believe you're right, apart from the hurdles, they won't fit in the car. Drink up, I'll take you to them, they'll love you.' Chris downed the remaining snakebite in one.

'Yeah, I've just got to let the brothers know. It won't take long.' Sod that, I thought, I didn't want any brothers in on this.

'I can't see religious people, they do my head in. You'll be back in a couple of days, best not to let them know you're about to commit cardinal sins, they'll be ever so jealous.' I looked Chris full in the eyes, but my words were not having the impact they should have, he appeared strangely resolute. I had to play my trump card, I pulled out a tiny bag of the finest sulphate Steve could get his hands on, diamond pink, not enough to get high on, but enough for a taster. 'Have this for now, I've got a lot more in the car.' Chris snatched the bag out of my grasp and shot off to the toilets. I slugged back my drink and followed straight on behind him. I didn't want to let him out of my sight, and I badly needed a piss.

I couldn't see Chris in the bogs but I could hear him. There were two toilet cubicles, one was empty, the other had the engaged sign showing, but it sounded like it was being occupied by a vacuum cleaner with emphysema, a horrible orgy of squelching and wheezing. I went over to the rusty steel urinal. No sooner had I started to piss when I felt a hand on my shoulder, and a warrant card being shoved under my nose, and the bellicose barking of an undercover pig. 'Empty your pockets. You must be a fucking moron thinking you can get away with openly dealing. How much more have you got?' I couldn't believe that, after all I had been up to in the past couple of days, to be pulled over for a lousy three quid's worth of whiz, someone was having a laugh. I put my hand in my coat pocket as if to oblige, whilst trying to pull my best scared shitless expression. The hunting knife just leapt into my hand, I pulled it out in one easy fluid motion, into the pig's stomach, up under the ribcage and straight into his heart. He made a really comical gurgling noise, and I had to put my other hand over his mouth. I was trying really hard not to laugh, when it came to farty noises I was just like an overgrown schoolboy, they always cracked me up. He only took a few seconds to die, and I waited until I could feel the death hit before I let go of him.

Fortunately his legs were still fairly stiff, and I was able to prop him up against the wall as if he was still having a piss. As I did so I got a good look at his face, and to my surprise recognised him, he was the bastard pig that kicked the shit out of me all those years ago, talk about tying up loose ends. However, it probably meant that the other pig, the 'nice' one was nearby. Chris was still slobbering away in the cubicle, and apart from the corpse there was no-one else around. I decided to take a quick look outside, and sure enough, there standing guard was Tweedledee. He barely had time to register my presence, before I slashed the knife across his throat. I caught him and bundled him through the toilet doors, just managing to dump the stiff in the vacant cubicle in time. A split second later the other door flew open, and there stood Chris blinking in the moonlight with a wide grin on his face.

'Oh wow man! This shit is the business. I'm spinning with my ally.'

'Good,' I replied. 'Now let's get to the car and get some more up our noses, this place is giving me the fear.'

The journey to the car was filled with paranoia and dreadful heart stopping pauses and false leads. On my own it would have been a breeze, I could have hugged the shadows, slunk back silently and unseen, past all the posters of Jimmy Stewart. But Chris was a walking advertisement for drug fuelled bad craziness. He was really speeding out of control, eyes bulging out of his head like ping-pong balls, an inability to communicate without shouting, every single word accompanied with a gallon of saliva, a complete unawareness of anybody's personal space, plus a tendency to stop dead still, make weird animalistic noises and contort his face into bestial grimaces. I was starting to regret giving him the speed. I was more of a problem than Chris, I was covered in blood which although not that noticeable in the gloom, became sickeningly obvious every time I walked underneath a lamp-post. Where Chris looked like a harmless colourful eccentric, I looked like what I was; a blood spattered pig killer. I didn't want to risk going past the pig station, so we had to walk up the high street, and cut across to the station once we got to the council headquarters.

To my astonishment Chris didn't kick up a fuss about not taking the most direct route to the speed, he was content to go the long way round. This was because it gave him the opportunity to show off and lust after the young students just arriving for the beginning of 'Fresher's Week'. To young naïve girls away from home for the first time Chris appeared a harmless free spirit, not the incurable acid casualty he really was. Up until now I was quite convinced that all my exploits would be hard to reconstruct, having passed through Southampton like a ghost in the night. I had visions of this journey being re-enacted on crime watch with no shortage of student witnesses testifying, interspersed with testimonials from grieving widows, and senior pigs about what fine pigs Tweedledee and Tweedledum were. Hopefully it wouldn't come to that, I'd bring about Armageddon first. Failing that they would probably only really remember Chris, I would just be some shadowy accomplice.

Amazingly we made it to the car without further incident. Just as I was opening the passenger door to let Chris in, he began to convulse, and his howls which hitherto had only seemed an affectation, became more urgent and genuine. He stared at me with The Snake's eyes and hissed, 'Let's stop all the playacting, tell me what you really want.' This was the moment I had been dreading, I knew he was going to make an appearance at some point during the evening, I just hoped that it would be later rather than sooner. I gave him my best smile and opened the door, gesturing to the seat.

'What have you got to lose? We both know you don't need this body any more, why not get in. There's something I want to show you. We can talk on the way. Aren't you the teensiest bit curious?'

Fifteen minutes later we were hurtling out of Winchester on the Stockbridge Road. The Snake was reclining in Chris' body serene, confident and masterful. I on the other hand was a sweaty heaving mess, I'd been here countless times before, so close to The Snake's annihilation, only to fail, yet another disgusting death, another botched assassination, having to put plans on hold until the next reincarnation. And this time the stakes were so much higher, The Snake had spread, insinuated himself into the general population, he was no longer an individual with all an individual's frailties, he was beginning to develop a hive mentality. By the time I was reincarnated, and ready to take up the sword once more it would be too late, no going back, The Snake would have infected everyone. I nervously looked over, waiting for him to make the first move. He was relishing my discomfort, and leant over to whisper in my ear. 'You must be terribly lonely.'

I kept my eyes fixed on the road. I was coming to Stockbridge, and was wary of being pulled over, either by The Snake's drones or by the police, or maybe both. Unlike The Snake I was an individual, I couldn't afford to lose this body. The Snake continued in his slow, relaxed, unhurried tone, 'I mean, it must be really terrible knowing you're the only one who can't join a club, have fun and games, let your hair down… the only one locked out of the world.' I breathed a sigh of relief as we passed through Stockbridge without incident, but the journey was far from over, I still had to go through Salisbury. I wasn't going to allow myself to be drawn in, I didn't want to lay my cards on the table just yet.

' Maybe I like being lonely… There's so much I know about you, I know where you came from, how old you are, what deals you've made, how widespread you are… Pretty much the whole tamale. What do you know about me? Have you guessed who I am?' I was banking on my anonymity, my trump card, all The Snake could possibly know was my current incarnation's identity, and what I could do, not what I had become. 'I'm not going to tell you where we're going, because it's a secret, but I might answer some of your other questions.' I glanced over to see the effect of my words, but he sat back poker faced. Did he know who I was? The Snake sucked on his teeth and smiled.

'Alright Mr. Dowd, Who's Harvey?' When The Snake asked the question I felt an enormous sense of relief. He was still stuck at the first puzzle. I could spin it out, talk about the film, that should kill a bit of time.

'You've seen the film, he's a six foot three and a half inch white rabbit.'

'That's just how he appears, it's not what he is.'

'You've seen the film, you know what he is, he's a nature spirit, a pooka.'

'He's Ah Pook?'

And that's how The Snake solved the second puzzle. It was my own fault, I thought I could have just kept talking about the film, forgetting it was a line from the film that had made me think of calling Ah Pook Harvey in the first place. I could see the look of joy in The Snake's eyes. He stayed silent for a while processing all the information. When he spoke again I almost jumped out of my seat.

'So who's Ah Pook?'

'Come on now, you should know that, he's Mayan. And I'll tell you something about the Mayans that might interest you. They're the only civilisation, other than the Sumerians, the groovy bears, to have come up with a written language from scratch. All the other writings throughout the world can trace their origins back to either the Sumerians or the Mayans.'

' Alright then, Ah Pook is the Mayan god of destruction, but what about you? are you Hassan I Sabbah?' Jesus, that was fucking close, The Snake was on a roll, I had to try to put him off the track. I tried to look impassive, but when I spoke there was a slight quiver of uncertainty in my voice.

'What does it matter who I am? I'm just a tool. Anyway Hassan I Sabbah wasn't Mayan, you're a couple of continents out.' The Snake could sense he was on the right track. He studied me intensely, it was very uncomfortable, I couldn't stare back as we were coming to Salisbury, and I had to keep my eyes on the road. It was chucking out time at the pubs, and I kept checking the mirror for flashing blue lights. Suddenly in a rush of new found confidence The Snake continued, still studying me intently.

'That was a lot closer than you're letting on, you're Hashisheen.' I braked hard as a rusty blue Volkswagen pulled out in front of me. I swore under my breath, I could sense The Snake's delight at my discomfort, he had me on the ropes, I would have to tell him where we were going, and I wasn't ready for that just yet. 'Yes, you're definitely Hashisheen, I should have known, it's just been so long since I had any dealings with them. So, if you're not Hassan I Sabbah then you're someone close to him. You're the old man of the mountains.' The Volkswagen turned off down a side street, I breathed a sigh of relief as we shot past the pig station, which incidentally is almost directly opposite a pub ironically called The Hogshead. Every time I go past I wonder if it is deliberate, or one of those funny little coincidences.

'You know a lot of people think that Hassan I Sabbah was the old man of the mountains, but you and I know the truth. I'm sorry to disappoint you but I'm not Rashid al din Sinan, but you're really close, you deserve to know the truth.' I then told him my original name, and didn't stop there I told him of all the other incarnations in between. In total there were about twenty-six. It was strange, a lot of them I was only remembering at that moment, it was if the floodgates of memory had opened, and once again The Snake was acting as my therapist. We reminisced over the past centuries like two old friends. I could tell The Snake was getting something out of it too. That must be the terrible thing about immortality, there isn't anyone that you can really share it with, and to think he called me lonely.

We had shot past the turnings for Longleat Safari Park and Frome before The Snake changed the subject, back to where we were going. He may know who I was but he still hadn't worked out Ah Pook's true identity, and finding out where we were going might help, I didn't want to tell him yet, but I had no choice. We still had to get through Shepton Mallet before we could disappear into the Glastonbury Lanes. Shepton Mallet could be dangerously unpredictable on a Saturday night. Hopefully I could keep him placid for a little while longer, I didn't want him to know the truth until we were right on top of it. 'I'm taking you somewhere you could not get to without me, a place of great power and sanctity, perhaps the most powerful place on Earth.' I was trying to sound mysterious, but The Snake could sense bullshit.

'Cut the crap now, you've almost told me all I wish to know. If you don't start making sense I'll say it's time to shuffle off the buffalo. Jumping out of the car at this speed would be fatal.' I took my foot off the accelerator and slowed down.

'Alright, I'll cut to the chase. I told you we're going to Glastonbury, well that's true. And you know of all the legends surrounding it. You know there's no smoke without fire. Underneath Glastonbury Tor there's an enchanted chapel. It fits in with all the legends, Joseph of Arimathea and all the Arthurian stuff, I'm sure you can check it out, you must have people on the internet and that, you could flash a command easy as pie. Inside the chapel is the key to the end of it all, the device to trigger Armageddon. Ah Pook wants to cut a deal. We're talking about power sharing here. Think about it, you'll pretty much be able to continue as before, but you'll have me off your back.'

The Snake said nothing, but continued to study me intently. I'd slowed down to about forty, and we were still about five miles the wrong side of Shepton Mallet, and the last couple of miles had taken an eternity. I was really starting to sweat, it was running down my cheek, my guts were all churned up, and my mouth was bone dry. In the end I broke the silence. 'Look, if you throw Chris out of the car now you'll be missing out on the greatest coup ever. You've read Revelations. Doesn't your side lose? If you control the Armageddon device, you can make sure it never happens. You'll win on a technicality. Won't that earn you a lot of brownie points?' The Snake took his time replying, and when he did he had resumed his combative tone.

'What makes you think it'll happen anyway? I can't remember what it's like to be an individual. I'm spreading more and more each day. It won't be long before everyone has joined me... Everyone that is except you. Then there won't be any need for God, because I'll be God. There will be life everlasting, everyone will be happy.'

'I've seen your version of everlasting life, all The Cheat's victims, and those exsanguinated by your vampire hosts didn't look too happy to me.'

'We're all entitled to a bit of childish indiscretion, I dabbled a bit in vampirism, it was a bit of fun that's all. Once everyone has joined the party, there'll be no need for vampires. Anyway, who are you to sit in judgement on me? I've seen you in action. Remember? I have never seen such a ruthless cold-blooded killer, and I've been around for centuries. At least vampires kill for sustenance, you kill for kicks.'

'You say that like it's a bad thing. You don't know what a rush it is.'

The Snake paused to collect his thoughts, when he resumed his tone was messianic. 'When all have joined me, all will come into the fold, all will be forgiven. There will be love, love, love in big sloppy buckets. What can you offer?' The words came into my mouth unbidden.

'I offer nothing, I am not a politician.'

The roads were uncharacteristically quiet as I drove through Shepton Mallet. I didn't like it, I was beginning to feel as if I were being herded. 'This is all very familiar,' said The Snake. 'I remember the last time we went this way. You probably won't remember me. I was looking through your friend Dodge's eyes at the time.'

'Rubbish.' I replied.

'Come now,' murmured The Snake. 'The poor fool, he didn't even know I was there, but you did. Isn't that why you killed him?' I didn't like the sound of that. Dodge had been a mate, admittedly a pretty shitty mate, but a mate nonetheless, and I didn't like the idea of killing mates. The problem was that I couldn't remember, and The Snake could always be playing mind games.

Just as I came to the turn off for Glastonbury, and the last few remaining miles I saw a flashing blue light in the rear view mirror. As I moved out of sight, I accelerated hard, hoping to get to the next junction before he got to the end of the road. It was futile, he was getting closer, and I was driving flat out. This wasn't going to end at all well. 'Look,' I said, 'without me you can't enter the Chapel, you won't be able to find it, it's too ethereal for you. Get the pigs to turn back, we don't need anybody else, we're cool aren't we?'

'Why do you think they're working for me? It's not like you've been doing anything to attract police attention?' The pigs were right on top of me now, I had to pull over on the off chance that they weren't really after me, but were attending an emergency call somewhere else. I sat there willing them to drive past, but they pulled up behind me. I looked over to The Snake, but he wasn't giving anything away. I threw the door open and rolled out into the roadway. I managed to loose a couple of shots before I hit the ground. I could feel Ah Pook jerking my wrist as I fired. The instant rush told me I didn't need to check the bodies, and that they were both Snakeheads. I got back behind the wheel and drove off.

'You know just for once I'd like to be able to drive somewhere without having to shoot a pig. Now where was I? I know, we were talking about why we're going to the Chapel, what I really want. I'm going to offer you something no-one else can. I'm offering you salvation. Don't think I want it mind, but you can forget vamping about and take on the role of Jesus. Or there is the other better option.' The Snake would have burst out laughing if I'd not wiped the cocky look off his face with my swift despatch of his two operatives. Instead he sat there looking bemused, not knowing whether to believe me or not. Now was the time for the truth. 'You know who I am, but not what I am, who I work for. All you need to know is what I plan to do, the preferred option, there's only one way you can stop me. Love, love, love in big sloppy buckets.' I'd finally got The Snake's curiosity engaged. I told him all about Gabriel. I told him about Armageddon. We both knew it wasn't due for another couple of hundred years. Neither side was ready, there would be a terrible stink. Lucifer wasn't ready to conquer the world, and Michael wasn't ready to save it with love, the whole thing would go off half-cock, or would it? We were ready, the dark angels, those who had stayed loyal when the light bringer lead the rebellion. The Earth would not be saved with love, Hell would face an onslaught so bloody and ferocious, that only God could imagine it. Lucifer would pay for rebelling, and he would pay in spades. I pulled into a tiny alleyway that doesn't appear on any map, drove a couple of hundred yards, and almost as many dimensions before pulling on the handbrake. 'We're here,' I said, turning off the engine.

Chapter 17

The Earth Dies Screaming

'People lie, eyes closed, no longer dreaming, the earth dies screaming.'
UB40

In the moonlight the Chapel looked especially magical, the tiny minarets twinkled. There was a feeling of intense serenity, a nightingale was singing high in an ancient oak tree that would have been a sapling when Alexander the Great ruled. The sky was crystal clear, and the stars looked a lot closer than normal. It all looked like an illustration from a children's book, I half expected Toad of Toad Hall to come walking around the corner. Even The Snake let out a silent gasp of astonishment, as if he were experiencing some long forgotten emotion, centuries old. The Skoda looked strangely incongruous, and I felt totally out of place. Now that we had got this far I wanted to get it over and done with. 'Come on,' I said getting out of the car, 'Now's your big chance, get ready to save the world.'

The whole place was pretty much as I had left it, Yogi was sitting on the floor, the twelve Knights were all laid out in a circle in front of the altar. And there hidden behind the altar were the switches I'd been longing to touch ever since I first set foot in there. 'Yoo Hoo!' I called out to Yogi, 'I'm back, and you'll never guess who I brought with me. If you think I'm bad just wait until you cop a load of him.' Yogi eyed me balefully, he knew he was beaten. Then he looked in horror at The Snake.

'You can't bring this foul creature in here, it's the greatest sacrilege of them all.' The Snake glared back, hackles rising. Instinctively hating, it was like watching two vicious dogs meeting for the first time, each one hell-bent on killing the other.

'You foolish old dotard, you will watch as all your work is destroyed and I am crowned ruler of the world.' The Snake had lost none of his arrogance and megalomania. I was hoping he would have been a bit taken aback by everything, but if anything he was more aggressive than usual. They both appeared to have forgotten about me, lost in their mutual hatred.

'Now then, none of that. That's no way to talk to each other. How about a pot of tea and a few hob nobs?' Neither of them moved, but continued glaring at each other. I sauntered over to the altar. 'You're both forgetting something,' I called out. 'I have the demolition codes. You're both going to watch Armageddon. It's time to kick ass.' Finally I had their attention. I smiled benignly, 'Thank you,' I continued, 'The whole point of me being here is to kill you.' I pointed at The Snake who nodded politely back. 'And I have had some limited success, I think you'll agree.' Again The Snake nodded. 'However, you're no longer an individual, in terms of killing hosts I've barely scratched the surface. It would take too long, much longer than I've got. So it looks like you've won.'

'So let's cut a deal. I've been given carte blanche. All I have to do is kill you, by whatever means necessary. If you want to stop me you must suck all your tentacles back in, become an individual, become this individual. Think about it, it will be the greatest possible irony. You'll do what only Jesus has done before you, you'll have to be granted salvation. That'll piss a lot of people off. All you have to do is become an individual, and let me kill you. I promise you it will be quick, I'm no torturer.' The Snake eyed me with chilling disdain, 'You're bluffing,' he snarled.

Result! I jumped back up on top of the altar and began keying the codes in. This time Gabriel did not stop me. I was so happy, I could already hear the screams of the dying. 'No!' screamed Yogi, but I kept going, I was almost half way there. Then 'Alright,' shouted The Snake, and Gabriel made me pause. I turned around, The Snake was walking towards me with slow measured footsteps. Tiny sparks of light were sweeping through the Chapel, flowing into him, as he absorbed soul after soul. All over the World hosts were shrivelling up and dying. 'No cheating now!' I called, I'll be able to tell if you're not all there, and your sacrifice will be in vain.'

The Snake continued the steady pace until he reached the base of the altar. He threw his head back and waited. Still the tiny flickers of light that were souls continued to coalesce inside him, he started glowing faintly. His eyes shone with power and majesty, he seemed so pure and magnificent it was almost a shame to kill him. We both stood waiting for the last soul to make its way in. His smile was tranquil and sublime. I felt small, pathetic, insignificant, yet at the same time I was trembling with excitement. Just killing one Snakehead was incredible, and there must have been hundreds inside Chris' powerful throbbing form. My mouth went dry, just trying to imagine how strong the hit would be made me feel dizzy.

Eventually the last soul made its way inside Chris. I reverently pulled out the Browning high powerL9A1 9mm automatic with the last of the mercury-tipped shells and took careful aim at Chris' forehead. I lowered the pistol, it didn't seem right just shooting him like that, this was not an assassination, or an opportunistic killing, this was something else. This was altogether more special, it was a sacrifice, ordained by God, I just couldn't blow his head off, not without saying a few words first. Maybe Yogi would have been more appropriate. Let's face it I don't know much about the Love of God, I deal mainly with the Wrath side of things. I looked over to where Yogi was standing and beckoned him over.

'Fool,' screamed The Snake, 'Did you really think it would be that easy?' He moved with incredible speed, and he seemed to have grown a couple of feet. His right fist smashed the gun out of my grasp nearly breaking my wrist in the process. The left fist gave me an uppercut under the jaw that literally took me off my feet. I went hurtling into the brickwork, and he came leaping after me, grinning dementedly. I had a really peculiar feeling from my childhood that I suddenly remembered was sheer terror. I dodged out of the way of a flailing boot just a little too late and it caught me a glancing blow across the ribs. It was like trying to fight some huge malevolent robot, my breath was coming in short gasps as I pulled the knife out dragging myself to my feet. There was a cut over my right eye and blood was dripping across my field of vision. Half-blinded I blinked at the huge bestial shape bearing down on me, feeling like a field mouse about to be devoured by a cobra. I held the knife out in front of me like some sort of magical talisman. 'Come on then,' laughed The Snake, 'Show me what you're made of. Bring it on.'

I threw the knife at the spot between his eyes, it was a good shot, right on target, but again he moved like lightning, dashing the knife out of the way. The Snake smirked like a particularly obnoxious schoolboy. 'That was stupid wasn't it? Now you've thrown away your last weapon. You may be no torturer, but I definitely am. I'm going to enjoy this.' He started moving closer, licking his lips. I backed away but there was nowhere left to go. My guts were churning over and over, and I thought I was going to shit myself, but I just let out a huge cannonade of wind. The Snake's nose wrinkled in disgust. I looked around frantically trying to find anything that I could use as a weapon. I put my hands in my pocket and pulled out a packet of Disque Bleu. Desperately I threw them at him, followed by a lighter. Then my fingers touched the Derringer I had taken from my partner. Such a pathetic weapon to use against such a creature. I fired both barrels at point blank range.

The Snake recoiled from the shot staggering back towards Yogi. He had taken both bullets in the right shoulder. It was only a flesh wound, but it gave me time. I ran back over to the altar to retrieve my pistol. This time there would be no hesitation, no sentiment, I would deal with The Snake the same way I'd dealt with those two pigs earlier. Rapid firing, mercury-tipped dum dums. Powerful as he was, even The Snake couldn't survive that. As I bent over to pick the pistol up I heard The Snake calling to Yogi, 'Forgive my sins O Lord, and take this worthless life to save your wonderful world.' I turned round to see Yogi raising a huge bejewelled sword high above his head. Before I could take aim he brought the sword crashing down on The Snake decapitating him with one deft movement, crying 'May Excalibur purify your soul.'

I couldn't believe it, I'd lost it all. That night I had walked into the Chapel about to summon Armageddon. Not being able to destroy the world had been a bitter disappointment. Destroying The Snake was my consolation prize, and just as the cup was to my lips Yogi had torn it away. Still I could still blow his head off. He may be brandishing Excalibur, but it didn't have mercury tips. I aimed right between his eyes. But as my finger started to pull on the trigger, Gabriel's talons clutched my heart once more and I sank to my knees. 'Game Over,' he hissed in my ear.

The Chapel suddenly filled with light, a huge stream of light cascading down from Heaven. Slowly all the trapped souls started rising out of Chris' body, and began to swim towards the light. Finally The Snake's soul rose out, shining with newfound sanctity. The heavenly choir began to sing. It was an intensely beautiful sound. Heaven rejoiced with the redemption of such a huge sinner. An overwhelming sensation of peace and harmony flooded throughout the Chapel and out into the rest of the world. For a fleeting moment everyone in the world was touched with a sense of divine peace and universal brotherhood. God smiled on the World new-born in its innocence, saved by the sacrifice of the damned. This was almost as great a victory as Jesus had wrought, hatred was destroyed by Love. I wanted to throw up.

Merlin, (I could call him Yogi no longer) walked towards me wielding Excalibur and smiling beatifically. Stardust shone in his eyes, despite his grey hairs he looked surprisingly young. Commandingly he held his arms wide stretched. Glowing spheres of light shot out of his arms and landed on the bodies of the dead knights. One by one they arose Lazarus-like, shining perfectly in their white armour. Merlin looked me in the eye and his expression changed, grew a great deal sterner, I was really going to cop it. You don't treat your tormenter with love. I closed my eyes and waited for the thunderbolt. Merlin screamed imperiously 'Piece of filth and vermin, you have completed your task. Now begone!' There was an almighty flash of light then I passed out.

I awoke shivering, to a cold drizzle in the half light of the early morning. When I tried to sit up I realised my left wrist was broken. A few yards away the Skoda lay on its side, the front badly smashed up like it had just been hit by a wrecking ball. My head was killing me, throbbing intensely. My trousers were soaking wet and I still needed a piss really badly. I looked down at my knees, they were soaked in blood. Lying just next to me Chris' lifeless corpse stared up at me with dead eyes. His throat had been cut, and my knife was lying next to him, the blade stained crimson. In the distance just above the sound of the dawn chorus a pig siren was getting closer. I could feel the heat closing in.